THE
PROJECTIONIST

First published 2022
Rymour Books
45 Needless Road,
PERTH
PH20LE

© Kirsti Wishart 2022
ISBN 978-1-7398466-0-2

A CIP record for this book is
available from the British Library
BIC Classification FA

Library of Congress CIP Data
Wishart, Kirsti
The Projectionist
Library of Congress Classification PN3311=3503

Book and cover design by Ian Spring

Printed and bound by
Imprint Digital
Seychelles Farm
Upton Pyne
Exeter

THE PROJECTIONIST

KIRSTI WISHART

ACKNOWLEDGEMENTS

Huge thanks are due to Sam Boyce who guided me through the first draft of *The Projectionist* as part of the Scottish Book Trust mentoring scheme. Without her, this book would never have seen the light of day. Thanks to Writers' Bloc for providing early encouragement and to Helen Jackson, R A Martens and Laura Vivanco for being such excellent, generous readers. Thanks also, of course, to Ian for designing and publishing it.

Thanks too to my parents for giving me time and space to write and to Siobain, as always, for her love and support.

This one's for all the grand old cinemas that inspired it: the Dominion, the Odeon on Clerk Street, the Filmhouse, the Cameo and the New Picture House, St Andrews. Long may their front of house lights shine.

KIRSTI WISHART 2022

# PROLOGUE:
THE LIGHT DIMS

It's the last thing he thinks before he jumps.

Not of Mags his wife or Harry his son. Not of the sea below, cold enough to stop his heart. Standing there at the end of the pier, beneath the lights of the Big Wheel, Alec Lawson remembers only the night Orson Welles came to visit.

A big man in that projectionist's booth, his handshake firm, telling of someone skilled in close-up magic. And that voice, hypnotic enough to make a man do anything.

'I can't tell you how pleased I am you've agreed to meet me, Mr Lawson. I hope I'm not disturbing you, I understand how protective you must be of your workplace…'

'Alec, call me Alec.'

Though he's there, teetering on the edge, Alec smiles. Imagine the cheek of it. Interrupting Orson Welles.

Welles's mouth had flickered. 'And you can call me Orson. Alec, I have a favour to ask and I know a man of your reputation can be trusted. I need you to hide a film and I need you to hide it well. Tell no one, not even me, *especially* not me, where it's hidden.'

He lifted his black cane and tapped Alec's breastbone once, twice with its silver top, the head of a devilish man with a grin wicked enough to match his own.

'Will you help me? Will you give me your word?' Orson offered his hand and Alec took it and, even after the years of pain his promise caused him, he wouldn't have it any other way.

But something bothers him. He can't be sure if his memory of what he saw on opening the door to his guest is real or not. The gleam of well-polished shoes, a slant of shadow, the bottom half of a figure in light. This is the curse of the projectionist. Your memories are not your own, reality and myth blurred to the point where all you're left with is lies and fragments.

Alec is tired, bone-tired, and it's bliss to fall into the dark, the wide embrace of Seacrest bay not enough to hold him, his splash drowned out by cries of delight as slot machines waterfall coins. And the Big Wheel turns, lifting its passengers up to wonderful heights before beginning a gentle, slow descent.

CHAPTER ONE

For our grand entrance the only way to travel was by sea, flying as the seagull flies, skimming over water, zooming like a tracking shot until we eased back, rose up, and there it was. The arms of the bay were open in greeting, the evening sunlight turning the cliffs of Seacrest golden. Rising higher, riding air currents until we found the best vantage point and drank it all in, the exciting span of it. Tilted right towards the pier, high enough to peer into the windows of the topmost carriage of the Big Wheel, saw children point and wave before we ducked down, glided past amusement arcades, burger stalls, coin-operated telescopes.

Raced through the pier's entrance, entered a maze of hilly streets, dodged trams, made ourselves giddy, perspective lost. It was as if we'd entered the set of a German expressionist film, what our eyes told us making no sense but we had to keep them wide open. This was a town *drunk* on cinema. Where there should have been supermarkets and off-licenses, banks and building societies, there were cinemas. Signs glowed, rippled in neon or bulbs, brought to mind images of Piccadilly Circus in the 1950s, Times Square, Las Vegas, Blackpool; the Electric, the Alhambra, the Regal, ABC, Empire, Palace, Imperial then we moved too fast, they blurred into one and we rose clear of rooftops. Took it easy, soaring, admired the brightly-painted terraces running along the top of the bay, before noticing the residents, our sense of time and place slipping.

The people of Seacrest realised years ago that to celebrate the idols of the silver screen properly they would have to look the part. Tourists were easy to spot by their drabness, their ease in jeans and sweatshirts, whereas the true Seacrest souls blended in perfectly with their stage set surroundings in their stylish Forties suits, long flapper dresses and Fifties leisurewear.

Where better to perch than the sign that ran along the uppermost tier of cliff-top houses, letters three metres high proclaiming 'WELCOME TO SEACREST!' a plasterboard seagull stretching its wings out above it. Steadying ourselves, we looked right towards Seacrest Studios where the same seagull decorated the roofs of the wide flat buildings. But this gull had faded and although the studios were once responsible for a steady stream of quota quickies, B-movies and Britsploitation flicks, the lack of movement between lots indicated those days had passed.

We scanned from the studios to the disused lido surrounded by high wire fencing to keep out vandals and skateboarders to the crumbling grandeur of the Fulmar Hotel and the stretch of the promenade where a handful of walkers were buffeted by sea winds. Realised this town could do with a lick of paint, a spring in its step. Noticed how precarious we were, the 'W' flapping in the wind, the leaning 'CREST' trying to separate itself from the 'SEA'. No queues waited for tickets in the cinema foyers, desperation in the cries of barkers outside clubs and bars trying to attract the attention of visitors.

Despite the cinemas, the costumes, the love of films, Seacrest was not so very different from any other seaside town running down the tail end of the summer season. Humming the Smiths' 'Every Day Is Like Sunday' we decided it was getting too chilly for comfort and the Alhambra sign with its golden script attracted our attention. Through the wide windows behind it were two figures sitting on either side of a desk, deep in conversation. Tipping forward we enjoyed a brief, delicious moment of falling then were caught up and carried towards a spell of discreet voyeurism.

Straight away we could tell one of the two women was not from around here: short hair, dark and curly, jeans and jumper, serious black-framed glasses, her lankiness obvious even when sitting down, a lack of ease in her skin. Whereas the other woman was so at ease we blushed to look. As gaudy as a stick of hot pink rock.

Bloody seagulls, Dr Jo Ashe thought, catching the beady black eye of one that had landed on the final 'A' of Alhambra. She bet that one had woken her up at half five that morning, smirking away. Could seagulls smirk? Dear God, she'd been beside the seaside too long but the way those gulls looked at her sometimes... as if relaying back information, fitted with Callum Boyd security cameras.

Bugger, now Kim was looking at her in that pissed off way that meant she'd been talking for the past few minutes and Jo had not a clue what about. Where had they got to? Festival Parade, ticket sales, caterers, accommodation for journalists, impending arrival of the fraudster Cameron Fletcher.

'Some more coffee, Jo, you're beginning to flag. Glazed look, mouth open like a half-wit. Few more seconds and you'll be dribbling and I won't have dribbling in my office. Not from boredom at least.'

Kim raised a sardonic eyebrow and Jo was struck by her resemblance to Barbara Stanwyck. The same amused weariness of a world not clever or sexy enough to keep up. Jo had always fancied Stanwyck, ever since seeing an Elvis film at an impressionable age. Did that mean she fancied Kim?

'Oh, ah, yes please. Great. Some coffee that would be... great. Yes.' She really must find herself a girlfriend if it had come to this, fancying her boss. Well, not her boss exactly but...

Kim leant across the desk to pick up her mug while Jo studiously avoided staring at her cleavage. Kim Taylor was one of the finest examples of what could be achieved by following the town's retro-dress code. If Jo ever walked into Kim's office to find her in an M&S trouser suit she'd know the end of the world was at hand.

In her late forties, hair a glossy, golden blonde, lips so red it always brought to mind Dali's Mae West couch, she looked like a woman on the cover of a Fifties pulp novel, 'With a Dangerous Past and a Hell-hot Future!'. When Jo had been introduced to her as the new official Seacrest historian at a Consortium meeting Kim had slowly looked her up and down. After agonising seconds she removed her black cigarette holder from between her teeth and nodded approvingly: 'Stick with me, kid, and you'll do just fine', in her ground-glass and velvet voice. 'I'm as big a piece of this town's history as you'll ever need. Now stop staring and fetch me a martini.'

'We've done well this afternoon when you've managed to stay awake. The 85th Seacrest Festival… '

Kim paused at the percolator to look towards the wall of her office decorated with pictures of the glory days, the Mitchums and Grants, Burtons and Taylors. Jo noticed her smile fade, how worn-out she looked.

'I don't mind admitting, there have been times when I didn't think we'd make it this far,' she said wearily and Jo felt a moment of panic as she always did when she saw how the town's decline had affected friends. Then Kim rallied quickly, with something close to anger. 'With our guest star this Festival's going to be the best one yet.'

The Fletcher effect, Jo groaned inwardly. Right, hold your tongue, she decided, tried to share Kim's excitement. She would study the wall opposite to shut herself up. Posters and postcards, photographs and old premiere tickets, an open scrap-book detailing Kim's past, her cinematic obsessions, as fascinating and colourful as a Paolozzi collage. Most of the cinema owners had done the same and Jo had sometimes learnt more from the walls of their offices than in interviews and here… hmm. Kim did seem to identify strongly with femme fatales who resorted to violence when crossed.

'Here you are.'

Jo jumped, tried not to look guilty as she took her cup of coffee.

'You won't believe the amount of interest we've had, journalists who wouldn't dream of returning my calls months ago now *begging* for tickets. They're billing it as the biggest comeback since Lazarus.'

'Look, I know you don't want to hear this but remember those people are *journalists*. One of the reasons they're so excited about Fletcher is because they smell a hoax. I know I keep on going on about this but I don't want… '

'*Jo.*'

Kim's voice was as sharp as the rap of a gavel.

'I appreciate your concerns, your many, *many* concerns, but at this precise moment in time I couldn't give a flying monkey's fart as to whether it's a hoax or not… '

'But… '

Kim closed her eyes and raised an imperious hand. 'No buts. I'm willing to make allowances in your case because, well, worrying is what you *do*, it's what drinking was to poor Ollie Reed. But what you have to realise is that while you've been digging in the archives this town has been *dying*.'

Jo's nerves turned to anger. She was sick of being made to feel guilty at not having grown up here on a diet of popcorn with a living room kitted out with fold-down seats.

'Of course I know how difficult it's been,' she retorted, 'but I don't think bringing a con-artist in is going to help!'

'Listen to the figures,' Kim replied, irritated. 'Hotel bookings up 175%, three quarters of our events sold out. Fletcher is a *coup*, the biggest event this place has seen since Judy Garland sang in the foyer of the Empire. So please, stop worrying and *enjoy* it.'

The second Kim stopped, the Alhambra sign switched on, sending the seagull up into the darkening sky as the room pulsed with red and yellow light. That's put *me* in my place, Jo thought, even the bloody *advertising* conspiring against her. She knew to be cautious of apparently random occurrences in Seacrest. Delve a little deeper and you'd often find a stage crew lurking in the shadows.

'Wouldn't I be right in thinking anyway,' Kim's voice had softened in a way that was far from reassuring, 'that were it not for the Archive, you wouldn't be here? I understand why you're upset about it, your theories disproved, but *surely* under that dry academic exterior you're excited?'

'You know very well I had other reasons for coming here, that I was *invited*. OK, so I was intrigued by what Luke was doing but that was only one reason.'

They both knew the main one and silently Jo dared Kim to mention her name. 'And for the record my theories *haven't* been disproved. We still don't know if it's *the* Cameron Fletcher and we still don't know if 'he'' – shit, Jo hated herself for doing the finger quote thing – 'ever existed in the first place.'

'OK, OK,' Kim waved her hands in submission, aware she ran the risk of hearing such words as 'post-modern' and 'ludic'. 'I take on board what you're saying… '

'But it makes bugger all difference.'

'Exactly. And that concludes our business for today. I'll call you in the week to discuss the Parade, come up with a few more float ideas. I've had another primary school on the phone panicking about *Lord of the Rings* copyright. That and the Health and Safety risks of bloody hobbits' feet.'

Showing her out Kim surprised Jo by giving her a brief hug,

something she rarely did. 'Physical contact between friends? What do you think I am? A *Christian*?' Admittedly a mannequin with intimacy issues could have achieved something warmer, but still.

'Everything is going to be fine, believe me. Finally we get the chance to show off properly and you're going to be at the centre of it. Now go and mark another footnote or whatever it is you academics do when you're not drinking coffee.'

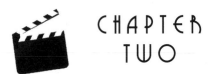

CHAPTER TWO

We'd left the streets of Seacrest, travelled hundreds of miles south to its polar opposite in style. The bedroom of a drab maisonette in a non-descript cul-de-sac in a suburban Yorkshire town. Even in such uninspiring surroundings, however, the Seacrest spirit was at play. Here an unremarkable man called Arthur Dott was getting into character.

Admittedly, it didn't look much. Instead of the alchemical process of an actor's transformation – for Arthur was a trained actor, a promising career having dwindled to the likes of 'Decrepit Gent in the Woolpack'– it looked like an old man having an afternoon nap, passing the time until *Countdown*. But in the twitching of Arthur's facial muscles, his hands, we could tell a change was coming. He was getting into character, creating the man he would play in a few weeks. He was thinking that since he received his invitation to Seacrest, Cameron Fletcher had rediscovered an enthusiasm for life missing for years.

Being dead had suited him, freed him from the constant attention of his fans. He'd filled filing cabinets with their letters asking when his next piece of writing would appear, if any of his scripts were being filmed, if he'd be willing to let them direct one, asking for an autograph, a small piece of a great man. The announcement of his death stemmed the flow yet not as much as might be expected. It seemed his fans believed him capable of evading Death himself, charming the Grim Reaper into a drink before hammering him at chess. When photographs of his funeral were released there were still those who wrote to congratulate him on such an elaborate practical joke but really, enough was enough. When was he going to start writing again?

At first the coffin was comfortable. The afterlife afforded him the perfect opportunity for change. He sloughed off the identity of Fletcher, sold off his books and papers. He'd always envied actors their opportunities for trying out new personalities. He still wrote, had things published under pseudonyms, changing his style whenever doubts were raised over the true identity of Taylor Stannard or Eliot Green. As the years passed though, he began to feel there was something missing. He had cast himself adrift. Being dead was becoming a bore and he began to realise how much he'd enjoyed being Fletcher. Seeing his name out there, being listened to, inspiring others to be as creatively reckless and surprising as his writings.

And then Luke Howard appeared.

At this point Arthur sat up. Although he appeared awake his eyes were as unfocused as a sleepwalker's. He looked different somehow from the man we met a few minutes ago. The way his shoulders were held, how he got up and walked from the bed to the small desk and chair with an ease we wouldn't have expected. In front of him were a box of cigars and a neat stack of notes, clippings and photos. From the top he lifted a scrapbook labelled 'Seacrest'. He started to leaf through it, wearing a smile that was not his own.

With three weeks to go before his first visit to that remarkable town, Fletcher flicked through his scrapbook until he reached an article from the *Seacrest Gazette* from seven years ago. The year a strange and enigmatic young man arrived from nowhere and gave the town hope. He read:

Although, regrettably, Cameron wasn't able to visit Seacrest during his life-time, he often wrote about how a number of postcards sent by an uncle there on holiday inspired his early interest in films. He described it in one of his earliest articles as 'the perfect place for moviegoers – here they take worship of the flickering lights thrown out by the projector as seriously as it deserves to be, building wonderful temples to celebrate this love. It is *the* place for all those who love to watch and if you count yourself in that number you should make your pilgrimage there.' I think you'll agree that it is fitting Seacrest is the new home of the archive of the great man, a living memorial to his work. I am proud to act as its curator.

In the accompanying photograph, there was Luke standing with arms folded in front of the open doors of the van he had driven into the town, a van full of books and photographs, one of those filing cabinets, reels of film and scribbled over scripts. Dressed in black, looking like a young, skinnier Anthony Perkins. An inset photo showed some of the proof, a number of books laid out on a table that caused Fletcher's heart to twinge: *Red Harvest*, *Nightmare Alley*, *Kiss Me Deadly* opened at the flyleaf to show the stamp of Fletcher's personal library, the drawing of a cinema screen framed by curtains and 'ACF. Entertainment' in curled script across it. Next to those Cameron Fletcher's death certificate. Every time he saw it, Cameron shivered. Haunted by his own ghost.

The final paragraph was a quote from Dr Jo Ashe, a lecturer in Film Studies at Manchester Metropolitan University, proponent of the theory that Cameron Fletcher was a fake, a forgery: 'If the artefacts Mr Howard has brought to Seacrest are authentic this has to be counted as one of the most important discoveries in recent film history. Please bear in mind, however, there is still plenty of evidence to suggest 'Cameron Fletcher' was the creation of a group of highly creative individuals, a very convincing prank. I'm sure Mr Howard is genuine in his belief these were once Fletcher's belongings but I think it best for all to keep an open mind.'

Arthur's shoulders had broadened. He appeared to have gained more weight, more presence. Although he gave up smoking twenty years ago, he stretched for the cigar box, pulled out one of Cuba's finest. He lit it with a battered Zippo lighter that had arrived with the rest of his new past, Cameron's past, three months ago.

After he'd taken a few puffs, relishing the rich, dark taste, he tapped the unlit end on the picture of Luke. Instead of his own Leeds accent he spoke in an American drawl, like a man possessed. 'I'm very much looking forward to meeting you Mr Howard,' and he laughed wheezily 'but even more excited about being introduced to *you*, Dr Ashe. Proving my existence to you will be *most* entertaining.'

 # CHAPTER THREE

We were back at where we came in and wouldn't it have been nice to let poor, uncertain Jo know that she was right to argue Fletcher was a fabrication, a fake? Perhaps, but we were only there to watch so we left her in ignorance as she pushed through the art-deco doors of the Alhambra, trying to convince herself that Kim was right to see Fletcher as the saviour of Seacrest.

Why was she so bothered about this? The greatest film critic the world had ever seen coming back to life and choosing Seacrest as his place of resurrection. Did it matter whether he was real or not? Jo was the one who chose to leave a nice, ordinary city where she taught nice, ordinary students for a place where children ran away to join insurance companies rather than stay and become extras or make-up artists. Dressing up was in this place's DNA, Fletcher a fitting figurehead. Only a boring fool would question that.

But I *am* that boring fool, she admitted to herself. A sign of her misery was instead of fully appreciating her favourite time of day, when night was approaching and the High Street, Sunset Strip, came to life, Jo kept her gaze down. If she had been in a better mood her head would have been full of Seacrest trivia: the bus stop where Marilyn Monroe once stood for a publicity shot, the café where Douglas Sirk spilt his strawberry milkshake on Nicholas Ray. That night she stayed wilfully blind, failed to appreciate the buzz Kim was talking about, the work being done to repair frontages, strings of bunting appearing between lamp-posts.

And the fact she didn't have the sheen of the locals made it easy for the person following her progress by security camera to keep her in shot.

The Wizard of Oz, that was Jo's problem. First trip to the cinema, she'd been taken out sobbing after Dorothy drew back that curtain and discovered there was nothing magical about the Wizard, just a scared old man keeping a city afraid. She couldn't understand why they were so ready to forgive him. Her first glimpse of the truth that movies were lies and there was always some mad soul behind the screen deciding what we see. By pretending to be real, she felt Fletcher falsified that truth, was the equivalent to a work of fiction passing itself off as a documentary. Plus she was convinced whoever had set this thing up hadn't considered the consequences it could have for Seacrest, the people who lived there. Like Luke for example.

The warning clang of a tram sent her jumping across the tracks, avoiding a death kitsch even by Seacrest standards, and she realised how far she'd walked, right through the town and half-way along the promenade. It was a still night, the air starting to have the bite of autumn, and she stopped by the sea wall, lulled by the sound of the waves. The beach empty aside from a solitary dog walker. *That* was the reason the Consortium leapt at Fletcher's visit. A chance to attract young blood who would create a new future for Seacrest instead of those content to wallow in Seacrest's particular brand of magical nostalgia.

'People like me,' she murmured, looking over to the lights of the pier brightening against the darkening sky, remembering her first visit. Seven years old, summer holiday with Mum and Dad and it was like Christmas and birthdays and Bonfire Night rolled into one. She'd never been anywhere so exciting, the lights and noise, and the thought of people actually *living* here… incredible.

And eight years later, she saw her. Shona Boyd, Queen of the

Festival, and knew she didn't have any other choice. That Jo Ashe would have to make this place her home.

Thoughts of Shona forced her away from the view. It had been two years since the note on her pillow telling her she'd gone. Best to forget it, keep focused.

She'd been meaning to do this for weeks, ever since that letter and the first photograph arrived. It was time to check on Luke, to find out how he was coping with the prospect of a dead man coming to town.

She passed the white sweeps and curves of the lido accompanied by the melancholy drone of two skateboarders surfing the smooth concrete. A site marked for 'renovation' by the Consortium although everyone knew they meant demolition. Perhaps knocking the place down wouldn't be such a bad thing though, sitting there as dead space. Jo caught herself, thought, God, listen to me! That was exactly the sort of nonsense Callum would come out with. Surely there was a place for relics in this world?

It was a relief when she reached the gates, a wrought iron seagull stretching its wings across the top of 'SEACREST STUDIOS'. She showed her pass to Dougie, the uniformed guard stationed in the wooden booth beside them, and got a brief, unsmiling nod in response. Progress, a nod! Another twenty years and she might earn a smile.

There it was, one of the best sounds in the world. The click and whirr of the gates opening, stepping inside, across the boundary as delicious as trespassing. The buildings as large and bland as supermarket warehouses but inside were deserts, ocean liners, cities, strange planets, exotic countries, the Pyramids.

Down the Studio streets, walking across large white numbers marking out the lots, Jo could hear the echo of voices from people unseen. See, there *was* still life down here. Callum ranting on about how they could be better utilised, that the Consortium should sell them off, make a profit, always a profit –

There was little doubt that Jo would think even less fondly of Callum Boyd had she known she was being tracked by him via security cameras dotted about the corners of the studio buildings. Owner of the Phoenix, the most powerful cinema boss in Seacrest, Callum liked to know what was going on before anyone else and found out in a room with a wall filled with television screens showing different corners of Seacrest, a fly's eye view. He might not yet be king of all he surveyed but he was working on that. Sitting forward in his black leather chair, he whispered to Dr Ashe. 'Off you go, visit your autistic friend. See how he feels about a ghost coming to town' and smiled.

After nearly being crushed by a mechanical elephant backing into Lot 44, Jo made it to Lot 45. She always hated this bit, right before seeing him. She knew it was daft but there was something about the boy that scared her. It was probably because he was a true believer, like a Charismatic Christian or a Star Trek conventioneer. She hesitated. She could head back, visit The Moviegoer instead, not have to deal with this crap. She pulled herself together, pointless trekking all that way for nothing.

Pressing the button next to the wide green door always felt like an act of faith what with no red flashing light, no buzzer sounding. After a while she peered at the security camera above the door, mouthing, 'Come on Luke, stop arsing about!' Another minute and she'd turned to go when there was a sharp click behind her. A small door within the larger door swung inwards.

She couldn't be sure if she was relieved or not to see him standing there. At least he didn't look the way he usually did when she turned up, like a sullen kid about to be told off for not cleaning his room. Was the fact he looked *scared* any improvement? He peered over her shoulder, making sure there was no one in the shadows between 44 and 46.

'Hi, sorry, had to make sure… ' He faltered and Jo felt pity, him a lost boy. 'I've heated the office up for you,' and he disappeared into the darkness behind.

CHAPTER FOUR

When she'd first met Luke it had taken Jo a while to work out who he reminded her of. Shona always argued it was a young Morrissey, that aloofness bordering on arrogance. Jo thought more of El Greco, those agonised saints with high cheekbones and dark eyes enjoying their pained devotion a little *too* much. Then one night watching *The Cabinet of Dr Caligari* on DVD, cuddled up with Shona on the couch, Cesare, the murderous somnambulist, made his appearance and they'd both screamed out 'Luke!'

Stepping over the threshold of the Archive felt like entering a library or church. Briefly she studied the two large cork pin-boards hanging either side of the entrance to the Archive's exhibits and when we see them we understand others came here as an act of pilgrimage. Visitors leaving mementos that gave a sense of how they felt about Fletcher or the movies, both boards covered in cinema tickets, photographs, film programmes, autographs, letters of appreciation expressing heart-felt thanks to Fletcher, postcards showing Godzilla, Paul Newman, *The Bitter Tears of Petra Kant*, Lassie. A Mother Shipton's Cave for movie-lovers.

Jo took those boards as a personal affront, thought 'This is what I'm up against' every time she saw them. Not just Luke, one nutty eccentric, but thousands who had helped create a monster. Within months of Luke's arrival the Archive had tripled as bits of Fletcher's so-called life flooded in. And there Jo was, a cranky academic determined to spoil the fun, take Santa away from the kids. Even she couldn't resist the lure of Fletcher though, tempted instead to forget Luke, to spend an hour wandering along rows of glass vitrines and cabinets. She snapped out of it, headed down a narrow corridor to Fletcher's – see how easy it was for even Jo to slip? – *Luke's* office.

It was typical of Luke's perversity that he kept the Archive's crowning glory out of sight to the general public, a 'Restricted Access' sign on the dark wooden door that opened gently as Jo approached. She paused to remind herself Luke was in there, no one else. Entering the office always caused a few seconds of doubt though before reason returned. The fear of walking in to be confronted by a man who didn't exist.

In the 1980s a glossy brochure appeared entitled *Cameron Fletcher, At Work and Leisure: Pictures from a New York Apartment*. Naturally the man himself was absent but the photos conveyed the sense of a room recently vacated – the open pages of a magazine left abandoned on the couch, fuzzy sections of window panes blurred by smoke. Fletcher was known as a connoisseur of fine cigars and in Lot 45 there was always the aroma of rich tobacco. And Luke didn't smoke.

As soon as he had been granted permission to house the Archive, Luke had gone to work recreating the office: the battered couch with blue and white stripes and cigar burns, the green leather arm-chair, a glass cabinet filled with single malts, book-cases crammed with paperbacks and movie magazines. A desk covered with novelty paperweights, a black Remington at its centre looking out onto a New York street scene. In front of Jo was the view, provided by a backdrop painted so successfully it took a few seconds to work out why the taxis and pedestrians were static. An ancient record player with Steve Reich playing. Even a fire flickering in the grate, a flame gas effect so realistic it had Jo looking for a log to chuck on it every time.

So cosy in there, it was easy to forget you were in a draughty warehouse. The recreation of a place that existed only in the imagination of others yet felt absolutely authentic. Jo felt faint with the urge to give in to the lies it told. To admit defeat and accept Cameron Fletcher once lived and breathed out plumes of cigar smoke, clouding the air about him.

Luke sat in a director's chair in front of the desk and watched her do what she did every time she visited. Examine the details, trying to find the glitch that would give the game away. Proof there was something not right about the place, that it was too uncanny to be true.

'You know who did this, don't you?' she asked, picking up a snow-globe featuring a Minnie and Mickey, shaking it until they disappeared in a blizzard of glittering snow.

'Disney, wasn't it?'

She tutted. '*No*, not this, all *this*, everything around you. D'you know who's responsible? Who's *actually* responsible?'

Luke left his chair for the drinks cabinet, took out two crystal tumblers and a bottle of Ardbeg. 'I believe we've already have had this conversation. Or at least you explained and I listened. You were in tutorial mood. Thought it best not to interrupt.'

Cheeky bugger, Jo thought, making out *I'm* the one who needs to be humoured. She knew her explanation would fall on deaf ears but it might do her some good. Remind her of the truth of the matter and stop her peering into corners, checking she couldn't be proved wrong.

'Mitchell Jackson, film director, Lauren Stern, set designer. They're the ones who set you up. They heard about your plan to recreate the set they'd built for that brochure and decided to give you a helping hand. Ever wonder why it was so easy for you to find stuff *identical* to that photograph? I've done my research, can show you the file. Friends of Avi Fleischer, the director who made

The Magician's Daughter, subject of the first review Fletcher ever published and… '

'Actually, Jo, I got most of this on ebay. Apart from that.' Luke nodded towards the leather armchair Jo was sitting in, handed her a glass.

'Oh yes, I forgot, the mysterious benefactor who managed to track down *the* chair, graced by the buttocks of Fletcher himself.' Jo hated sounding so spiteful, took a gulp of whisky that set her throat burning. She hoped it would distract her from how *right* the chair felt. Burn marks on the arm-rest where Fletcher would tap his cigar when crafting a paragraph… genius.

Luke watched until she regained her composure, wiped alcohol-induced tears from her eyes, with the same wired stillness he had when watching a film. When he spoke there was a slight tremor to his voice.

'Any news? Any word from… you know. Him.'

He'd not touched his drink, the glass turning, turning in his hands and Jo scolded herself. Idiot, forgetting what a big deal this was for him, the pressure he was under. It wasn't as if Luke had loads of friends up here to reassure him everything would be all right when the man he'd pronounced dead turned up.

'Luke… sorry, no. I haven't had any word since the letter Fletcher' – Jo checked herself – 'or whoever sent. It's out of my hands pretty much. The Consortium, Kim and that lot are dealing with him. It. Whatever.'

Both knew who she meant by 'that lot' and Jo looked away from Luke's glare as he muttered 'Callum'. The suspicion that had flickered at the back of her mind ever since the envelope had come through her door flared. What if this was a set-up with Boyd behind it? The perfect way to get rid of the Archive and clear the way for the bulldozers. Callum was bad, but *that* bad? Really?

She took another sip, hoped it would take her back to her senses.

'I take it Fletcher hasn't been in touch with you directly?'

Luke shook his head, stared at the bottom of his glass before downing the drink. For most other people that would bring a flush to their cheeks, but if anything Luke appeared paler.

'He mentioned me though, didn't he.'

Not a question, a challenge.

'In the letter you got. He said he was looking forward to visiting the Archive and that means he's on my side. That he respects what I'm doing here.'

When he looked up the fear had gone, replaced by determination. More like the Luke of old, the one Jo had seen arguing his point in Consortium meetings, a thorn in the side of Callum and his cronies.

'Luke, really, I don't think you have anything to worry about. He... '

'Oh, I'm not worried. I'm ready. All these years I've been waiting. Even with the death certificate, I always suspected. Always knew. Cameron Fletcher could never die.'

Oooookaaaay, Jo worried, Luke was getting a *little* scary.

'Listen, we, *I* don't want to see you getting carried away. We don't know for definite who's going to turn up, I just want you to be careful, OK? We've had our differences but I do... I don't want you being disappointed or... hurt.'

Oh for God's sake, Jo was trying to help the guy and he was smiling as indulgently at her as if she'd been arguing that no, honestly, I *am* the reincarnation of Dietrich, give me a top hat and a monkey suit and I'll prove it.

'Right, fine, so you don't believe me. We'll see. Anyway, I've brought something for you. Meant to bring it out here weeks ago but...'

She rummaged in her laptop bag until she found the cardboard folder holding the photograph; the photograph that had caused her to slide down the wall of her hallway to the floor as soon as she'd opened it a month ago. Because when she saw that man smiling up at her she'd known it was impossible. She found it difficult to hold the photo's gaze and she was quick to pass it to Luke. It was worth it to see him beam like a love-struck teenager, holding it by its edges. Tender.

Previous photos of Fletcher had been as indistinct as those of the Loch Ness Monster, blurred shots of him turning the corner of a city street in the rain, sitting in the back row of a New York cinema, a hat pulled down over his eyes. If someone told you the man in these pictures was Pynchon or Salinger or Big Foot on holiday you'd take their word for it. With this portrait there could be no doubt. For a man who didn't exist, Cameron Fletcher was immediately recognisable. Jo hadn't realised until she'd sat there in her hallway, knees drawn up, photo propped against them, that she'd always had a clear picture of him. This was him exactly. She couldn't help thinking, 'We've done this. Magicked him alive.'

He was in his sixties, possibly older, the thick dark beard turning to grey, concealing his jowliness. The sort of old man solidity that made you think of fine dining, glasses of port, Falstaffian chuckling. Handsome in an Orson Welles sort of way, charisma conveyed as he was snapped mid-joke, leaning forward, laughing. Smoke from the cigar he was holding blurring the right side of his face. He was sitting in a director's chair, his back to a desk and a view identical to the one Luke was sitting in front of and suddenly Jo felt like she was in the Hall of Mirrors down on the pier, an infinite reflection, with no Rita Hayworth there to focus on and save you.

Dizzy, Jo started to wonder if Luke was behind it. Wouldn't that make a strange kind of sense? Dr Frankenstein letting loose his creation on the world? But look at him. He was practically stroking that photo. He couldn't be that devious... could he?

Naturally curious to see what all the fuss was about, we looked over Luke's shoulder and even we, in full possession of the facts, were impressed. Because although we *knew* this was Arthur Dott, were present during Arthur's preparations, it didn't prepare us for this; the complete transformation of a non-descript man. OK, there was something familiar about the eyes, their humour, but other than that the man before us was unrecognisable as the one we met in Arthur's bedroom. This man had the aura of fame about him. Secure he'd made his mark on the world and that there were thousands out there who adored him.

'Can I keep this?'

Although it was silent in the office Jo hardly caught Luke above the soft hiss of the gas fire.

'The photograph? Yes, sure, a negative came with it. We're going to print a supply of them, for the signings. Just think, less than a month until he'll be here, in the Phoenix… '

Jo stopped, told herself off. Why not open her mouth a little wider, fit a film canister in.

Luke's eyes slid from the photograph and he leant to one side, stretching out his long frame to drop the photo at the furthest corner of the desk. As if to make sure Fletcher wasn't contaminated by the mention of the hub of Boyd's Empire. This was the version of Luke Jo liked least, deathly pale, his eyes cold. Her own fault, letting slip Fletcher's first port of call wouldn't be here but at the lair of the man who wanted the Archive demolished.

'It's the twenty-eighth, by the way, the day he arrives. Don't know if you knew that or if… but, well, you do now. I'm sure if I speak to the Consortium they'll let you… '

'It's fine. You don't need to speak to *Them* on my behalf. When Fletcher gets here, you'll see. I have faith. Once he sees this place he'll know who's on his side.'

Was that a dig there? Jo prickled. In Luke's head if she wasn't entirely for him then of course she was one of Them.

'Right. Well, then. Thanks for the whisky.' She lifted herself from the comfort of the green chair. 'Best be off. I'm meeting Harry at The Moviegoer, you could come if you want.' Christ, she worried, what if he said yes? But she knew the answer would be no. She could see him already retreating back into his own world. He managed a smile, even stood up from his seat.

'It's always good to see you out here, Jo, thanks for coming. Sorry for being preoccupied but... '

'No, no, fair enough, there's a lot going on, must be a stressful for you.' He was already sitting down again, looking towards that bloody photo. 'I'll see myself out,' she muttered.

It was a relief to be back in the corridor, avoiding those pin-boards then into fresh air, trying not to shove her way through a crowd of prop handlers carrying plastic flamingos. Back in the real world, or as real as Seacrest allowed.

(She didn't notice cameras tilt in her direction, Callum watching her leave. Peering at the screen, zooming in on her face, seeing she was upset made Callum happy. Everything going to plan. He sat back, content, flicked a switch to turn the screens black, leaving him facing an audience of his own reflections, who grinned back in admiration.)

For the first time ever, the sound of the Studio gates opening to let her out was as sweet to Jo as when they let her in. She crossed the promenade to the sea railing, breathing in deeply, looked over to the pier. A low band of fog on the horizon, the famous Seacrest haar turning the lights of the Big Wheel hazy, and she thought of Harry. It would be a relief to catch up with him, have a drink and a laugh, not to worry about what she said, how it would be weighted.

She dug out her phone, tried to call him and failed, mobiles well-nigh useless here. The twenty-first century was welcome to visit but must do so on Seacrest's terms. Jo smiled, decided not to get a tram as the walk to the club would help clear her head. There Harry would be holding court, his company exhilarating, his confidence contagious.

We watched her go, disappearing into the encroaching mist, then pulled back. Slipped back through the gates of the studios, retracing our steps to Lot 45. Faded through the green doors, down the corridor to discover the answer to a question Jo had often asked herself, 'What does he *do* out there in the Archive by himself?' Because Luke was so opaque, whenever she tried to think of him alone she encountered only an absence. It was as if, like Cesare, with no one there he retreated into a box as motionless as a recharging automaton, became an exhibit.

She appeared to be right. Luke was sitting as she left him, his head still turned in the direction of the photograph. Instead of being entirely fixed, however, we saw his right knee, pistoning up and down, up and down. A tic Jo would recognise from Consortium meetings when he was forced to listen to speakers he disagreed with. We waited, a curious tension in the air, expected him to leap up, rake his arms across the desk, hurl his chair through the fake backdrop. Instead he got up, retrieved the photograph, his face as blank as an empty cinema screen.

Luke wasn't a smoker and it was dangerous to do so there. With his eyes fixed on Fletcher's though, he reached forward to open a box of Cohiba cigars, the brand he was smoking in the photograph. Luke pulled out a Zippo lighter from a desk drawer before crossing to sit in the green leather chair.

Next to it was a table decorated with tin toys. Luke propped the portrait there as he lit the cigar. Others would relish the taste but it was difficult to tell the pleasure Luke got from it, his face doing something odd, turning into something like an animated mask. Slowly we realised why; he was attempting to mirror Fletcher, to match his easy charm, the relaxed bonhomie. The effect was unnerving, like watching a mannequin trying to sing.

FLASHBACK: A boy, Luke, identifiable by his dark eyes, his

strangely adult stare, stood hand in hand with a woman who must be his mum. Same eyes but hers were tired, red-rimmed. She was smart in a skirt and blouse, her black coat beginning to show its age. We understood instinctively this bothered her, that she would like nothing more than to replace it. However, any spare cash was spent on Luke.

They were standing in a cinema queue and we sensed Luke's excitement. For his mum this was a necessity, a short holiday from worries about rent and bills. She peered over the heads of those in front, impatient for the opening of the doors. This was their ritual, what they did to settle into a new town. Home changed every few months yet the cinemas were always familiar, always a comfort.

'D'you think there's a chance Mum? That we'll see him?'

'What son? Come on, shift up, we're going in. Check your pocket, make sure your popcorn money's there.'

'But will we? D'you think Dad'll be in this one? It's American isn't it and you said that's where he's from, where he went. There's lots of actors in it, he's *bound* to be in it.'

She pulled him close to make sure he didn't get carried away into another screen and to keep him quiet, stop others overhearing, smiling those knowing smiles. 'He might be, son, he might be. You keep an eye out and nudge if you see him.'

'What does he look like again, Mum? Tell me, I've forgotten.'

They both knew Luke hadn't forgotten, he just wanted to hear yet again about his movie star looks, the dark hair and eyes, how handsome he was. A description vague enough to fit any face he took a fancy to. His mum was already lost to him though, her eyes fixed on the ticket booth, desperate for the ease of the darkness beyond.

# CHAPTER FIVE

As Jo approached The Moviegoer the haar took full possession of the streets. She shivered, pulled her jacket tighter. Her fifth autumn and she still couldn't decide if she liked the mist or not, its vaseline-added-to-a-film-lens effect. Shona loved it of course, *everyone* else in Seacrest loved it. The blurring another layer of disguise, atmospheric conditions turning the place into a film noir set. And the way people dressed here. Turn a corner and there was someone in a top hat and frock-coat and your bearings were lost, not just in place but in time.

It was beautiful, yes, softening the garish edges but eerie too. Sound started acting strangely. Someone laughed a street away and it was too close for comfort. Jo slipped down Scarlet Street, an alleyway between two bars, Piccadilly and Nick and Nora's, her footsteps reverberating as loudly as a woman's high heels stalking away from the body of her husband even though she was only wearing Converse.

She stopped in front of an unremarkable door, grey and scuffed with a white box sign above it, black letters telling us this was The Moviegoer in a font Jo had identified as Gill Sans-Serif (how exhausting it must be to be Jo at times, constantly noticing things in a town *desperate* to be looked at). A door as welcoming as a dentist's waiting room. For those in the know, though, it was one of the sweetest sights in Seacrest.

Jo always paused before pushing it open, savouring the moment of transition, as pleasurable as the dimming of lights before a film starts. Then she was through and in at the top of a short flight of stairs and it felt like home.

A dive of a place, hacked into the cliffs, the bare rock walls softened by candlelight. The tables and chairs were so much flotsam and jetsam; giant cotton reels found by train tracks, oil drums cut in half, wicker chairs the work of some famous designer, old cinema love seats, deck chairs. It should have looked a state, more a salvage yard than sanctuary, but instead felt like a fantastic underground venue in Prague, Budapest, Berlin. The clientele helped. This was the place where those on the seedier fringes of glitz relaxed. Jo made her way to the bar, easing past male and female impersonators, fortune tellers, cabaret artists, experimental film directors, retired stuntmen and magicians' assistants.

Jo could tell you it had been this way for centuries with illicit stuff always going on in and around the site of The Moviegoer due to its proximity to the Tunnels. Smuggled goods, drinking clubs, criminals on the run. She attempted to catch the eye of a version of Marilyn Monroe, aka Karl the Barman, and tried not to think of the Tunnels. Naturally could think of little else, the secret warrens beneath her feet.

Twelve completed chapters of *Seacrest Cinema: Stories from Wonderland* by Dr Jo Ashe and the one about the Tunnels was the shortest, taken up with 'Here Be Monsters' rather than research. The smell down there, the damp. Junk left to rot and the weight of the town above you, hundreds of people sitting in the dark a few feet above your head...

'Jo! Lovely to see you! You all right? Look a bit peely-wally. Head still in a pile of old movie magazines?'

Karl's thick Glaswegian accent – Jo marvelled at how he *still* looked far more feminine than she did, even with his three-day stubble – was enough to ward off any Tunnel-induced claustrophobia.

'Yes, sorry, fine thanks. I'll have a G&T please and have you seen Harry about?'

'Yeah, he's around. Least he was... '

Karl looked towards the tables at the back next to the small empty stage that would later feature late-night entertainment, anything from Hungarian fire-eaters to 'Rita-Mae and Her Wandering Bongos'.

Jo recognised some of the pale young men as Harry's acolytes, members of his film society, The Diaboliks. What was it he called it again? Oh yes, his 'underground force for changing the face of cinematic narrative,' although Jo and others tended to think of them more as a bunch of geeks. All dressed in black, hair styled into either the Lynchian pompadour or the Jarmusch quiff. Jo fretted, Christ, if she had to spend time with them after Luke...

'Oh, I remember,' Karl told her, raised a suggestive eyebrow, 'he's down under. Said he had some Tunnel investigating to do. Tell you what, while you're waiting for him to surface, you can sign the petition. *Our* petition.'

He waved an elegant hand in the direction of a red clipboard holding a crumpled sheaf of pages before turning his attention to the demands of a rowdy crowd of Munchkins standing on each other's shoulders to get served.

Jo pulled the clipboard towards her and read through some sticky green stain, 'We, the undersigned, wish to register our opposition to the plans put forward by the Consortium to demolish the Seacrest Studios to make way for a mutiplex and 'shopping experience'. Save our Studios!' No Consortium double-speak here about 'redevelopment' and 'retailing opportunities'.

Who had been the first to sign it? 'HARRY LAWSON' of course, in red ball-point pen, underlined three times. Flicking through the pages, Jo was unsure if Consortium members were going to be shaking in their boots to discover 'Ernie Tux – Penguin Impersonator – Scarborough' or 'Lillian Cruickshank – Hand Artiste – Broughty Ferry' were opposed to their plans.

Reaching the blank boxes at the end, easing the pen out of its holder, Jo was suddenly nervous. What was wrong with her? Hesitating about putting down her full name, toying with J Ashe or Dr Pathetic. Yes, OK, Callum had supported her book, provided sponsorship, his name opening doors and archives. It didn't mean she had to follow his line, be his tame academic. For once, she didn't have to think, just write.

She did, eventually, a barely legible scrawl, taking a big gulp of G&T once she'd finished. Watched in mild disbelief as the incongruous bookcase at the right of the stage started to ease away from the wall. A door opening, as if the act of signing her name had caused something to rise up.

The back of her neck tingled even though she knew who was making an entrance. Harry Lawson, who had probably spent ages arranging the lighting so that only below his knees caught the light, the rest of him in shadow. We were waiting for a black cat to wind around his ankles when he stepped aside, allowing the bookcase to shut, and hit the beam of a spotlight that would grant anyone watching the benefit of the famous Lawson smile.

Except Harry wasn't smiling. He was deep in thought, frowning at a notebook before slipping it into a pocket of his huge green coat. He rubbed his messy beard then scratched his curly head. Half-man, half Hobbit. Underground Harry, still lost to the Tunnels and whatever it was he got up to down there.

'Harry!' Jo shouted, desperate for him to snap out of it, and he glanced up, shielding his eyes from the light. Saw her, waved and the old Harry was back.

'Dr Ashe, you old alkie! Get Karl to pour me a Guinness, will you?'

It was like a switch had been thrown. This was Harry the Fixer, the Main Man, the Diaboliks starting to grin, bashful in his presence. Watch him now, a mover and a shaker, slapping people on the back, shaking hands, squeezing cheeks. He knew everyone and everyone knew him and Jo thought fleetingly, 'There's no way I can match this, I'm so dull and boring and quiet.' Then he was in front of her. 'Where's that Guinness then?' and despite the fact that no one, not even *family*, could wind her up as much as Harry Lawson, it was great to give him a hug.

'Hey! You drunk already? Or has my irresistible manliness finally turned you?'

She pulled out of the hug, hit him on the arm. 'Charming as ever. Here's your pint, you oaf. Nice to see you that's all… just been down to the Archive to see Luke.'

'Oh right, yeah, Luke doesn't really go in for the whole physical contact thing, does he? Tried it on him a couple of times when drunk. Like hugging an irate clothes horse. How's he getting on then? Come on, let's get a table.'

It was always like this. You started to answer one question and Harry Lawson would interrupt with another, recognise someone he hadn't seen for ages and you were left talking to empty air before he was back again, remembering something funny that happened at the Kinotech and then he was off to get crisps.

'So yeah, Luke, how's he getting on?'

Harry re-focused after ripping open a packet of salt-and-vinegar, 'Tuck in', taking a handful and half the packet. 'Was down there for *ages*. Should get a vending machine installed.'

'What were you down there for anyway?' Jo asked, her researcher's instinct kicking in. Because Harry wasn't usually one for secrets. He had his plots and plans but, with his loose mouth, they usually made the front page of the *Seacrest Gazette* the morning after he'd thought of them. 'You were looking very thoughtful with your notebook. Not like you. Thinking.'

'Hoy, cheeky!'

They were sitting in an alcove, out of the buzz and hum of the rest of the pub, not in listening distance of the nearest pocket of Diaboliks. That didn't stop Harry looking over each shoulder before leaning in so close his soggy bristles tickled Jo's ear as he whispered, 'That's for me to know, nosey bugger'. He sat back, smug, before taking pity on her.

'OK, OK, no need to look as though I've ripped up your subscription to *Sight and Sound*. Can't say too much at the moment but I will need your help with it later on. It's about,' – another quick glance over his shoulder… 'the Dominion. There's something I need to find there. Something that's lost. I think I've finally got a map to get me there.'

'*What*? The *Dominion*? But that's… how?'

For all the warmth and noise of the bar Jo suddenly felt a chill, as if the mist had crept in. An entirely appropriate response when a ghost of Seacrest's past entered the conversation.

The Dominion, the grandest of cinemas, setting the standard every cinema in the country aspired to. Owners came to study it, gasp at its Vistascope sized screens, themed bars, swimming pool for staff. The best films, best employees, best UK Picture Palace five years running and when it burned down the awful heat was felt the world over. Jo had some photographs of the Dominion in its pomp pinned up in her flat and every time she looked at them she felt a deep nostalgia for a place gone years before she was born. She visited it in dreams.

'A map? You've got… plans? Showing where it is beneath the Phoenix?'

No answer from Harry apart from an increase in his smugness levels.

'How the *fuck* did you manage to get them? I've been asking

Kim if anyone in the Consortium has them for months, I'm *always* fobbed off, then you waltz in and… '

She stopped. Harry was becoming serious, his expression back to the one she'd glimpsed after he'd emerged from the Tunnels, and she realised. Idiot, of *course* Harry would have access to the plans, Kim making an exception for him. The legacy of Alec Lawson.

'Shit, sorry Harry – your dad. What happened to him in the fire, his hands… '

Harry waved away her apology, embarrassed by that tone that always came into folk's voices when they start talking about Alec. Poor wee Harry and his crippled dad.

'Yeah, well, Dad wasn't much use to me when he was alive, about time I got some benefit from his surname. Reckon Kim had a soft spot for him along with most of the women in this town. Christ knows why. Though the charm of the Lawson males is indeed still irresistible to many.' He twirled part of his beard-moustache in a way that had Jo choking on her drink.

'Hey, I can't help it if you're one of the few who's immune. But yes, to answer your spluttering, I have the plans. So expect to be accompanying me on a spot of pot-holing shortly.'

'What? Harry… I dunno, the Tunnels, I'm not mad keen… '

'Whit! Call yourself an academic? Where's your Freudian spirit, doctor? Don't worry I'll give you fair warning, get Luke to come along to hold your hand at the scary bits. Another G&T is it?'

'Yeah, thanks. No, hold on, have you told your mum about this? She'll be chuffed, you know, you finding out about… '

There was that switch again. Happy-go-lucky Harry vanishing, replaced by the frown that accompanied any talk of Alec.

'No, I've not told my mum. Why would I?'

'For God's sake, stop behaving like a *teenager*. Your mum misses you, I know she does, and you can't be comfortable sleeping down there in the Kinotech, washing yourself in the public toilets… '

It was too late, she was left shouting at the back of that ridiculous green coat as he headed to the bar, not giving his mum a second thought and why should Jo pick him up on it when he came back? She would just drink her drink, have a good time, enjoy the floor show, though 'enjoy' may be a stretch when faced with a Dietrich impersonator murdering 'From Paris to Berlin' in a flat German accent.

Later on and was it five gins she'd had? Jo realised it was pointless keeping track of drinks on nights like that one, especially when the tequila started flowing. Caught up in Harry's crowd, a friend to everyone if you're a friend of Harry, him with that glow about him and Jo was bathing in it, his charisma to spare, laughing and joking like the old days before the trouble with Shona and there was that feeling growing stronger, that Jo belonged, that it was her home and she was accepted.

And then Harry showed her the postcard.

They'd been talking about Luke, how she was worried about him behaving even more oddly than usual.

'Jo, honestly, you worry about *everyone*... believe me, I'm probably the closest friend he has, I love him, y'know? I reckon this could actually do him some good. Be the shock he needs. Bring him to his senses.'

'His *senses*? He's hardly got any bloody senses left and what if it tips him over? He's close to the edge as it is. What's going to happen when he finds out the man he's dedicated his whole life to is a fake?'

Harry downed his fourth tequila, slurped his slice of lime and pointed with the peel to the stage where Rita Hayworth and Doris Day were singing a duet.

'Fakery? In *Seacrest*? Fucksake Jo, look around you! This place doesn't know any better! You're talking as if Luke's some crazy exception when he's just going with the flow. Personally, I'm looking forward to meeting this Cameron chap. Shaking him by the hand, saying 'Welcome to the land of the living dead! You're going to fit right in.' Oh and that reminds me. This Fletcher guy has quite a pull.'

From an inside pocket he pulled out a crumpled postcard with a picture of King Kong at the top of the Empire State building swatting away fighter planes on the front. Handed it over to Jo who flipped it over, knowing with a lurch in her stomach not caused by the alcohol whose handwriting she'd find.

There it was. Spiky capitals ready to punch a hole in her heart as Harry said, 'Shona's coming back.'

'Hi there Harry! Here in New York, having a fantastic time but heard all about Cameron Fletcher rising from the grave! Will be back for the big event, hope you're OK, got yourself a girlfriend, see you soon, love, S'.

There was the anger back. It had never really gone away for Jo, was always bubbling under the surface. That time, five years ago, newly arrived in Seacrest and Shona dithering – not dithering, that woman was incapable of indecisiveness. She was messing her and Harry about, having her cake, eating it, taking seconds. That awful time of hating Harry, hating herself, because he was one of her few good friends there and she was causing him pain – no. It was Shona. Remember? Shona was the one causing everyone pain.

Sorted itself out eventually and they were adults about it, Harry gallant, everyone friends. But there were times when the three of them would be out and Jo would be at the bar, buying a round, look over to where they were sitting with their heads together, laughing, sharing some story from when they were kids, the jealousy would flare again and Jo would wish she'd never heard of this bloody town.

Staring at the words, difficult to read when drunk but Jo had enough sense to look at the postmark, the date. Even in the state she was in, she realised. It was a week too early. A week before Cameron Fletcher's letter. A week before anyone in Seacrest knew he was coming. Too much to think about properly and she handed the card back.

'You OK?' Harry asked, looking concerned, Jo thinking, bit bloody late, should have thought about the effect of that card before handing it over. 'You don't look so good. You can keep it if you want. The postcard.'

'Why would I want it? It's yours, she wrote it to you. You're the lucky one.' Jo cursed herself for sounding such a petulant cow. 'I'm fine, stop fussing. Another round of slammers then home.'

Forcing herself up, Jo nearly knocked over the table, staggered a bit, focused on Karl behind the bar. Tried not to think about Shona writing to Harry instead of her and instead focused on Shona being there, actually *being* there in a fortnight's time. Two years, two years without her, not knowing what was happening, if they were still together and when she decided to come back, who did she tell? Harry bloody bleeding Lawson.

'You're pissed off, aren't you?'

The small plate of lime slices Jo had carried over hit the table hard, sending green crescents sliding across the surface.

'No, Harry, I'm not. Not with you at least. I gave up trying to work out Shona years ago. I'm glad she's coming, hope it means we can... sort things out. Yes, I admit some word from her apart from the occasional rubbish, say-nothing email would have been nice seeing as how we were together for... what? Three years? Three *years*. But hey. Let's hope she finds Cameron Fletcher worth the trip.'

Harry nodded, about to say something and she stopped him, held out the salt shaker.

'Hurry, last orders in a minute, Karl's taking his wig off'.

They gulped down the golden liquid as the lights came up,

stripping the place of its seedy glamour, turning it into a motley collection of shabby props and drunken extras.

Somehow, battling gravity, they made it up the stairs and into the alley, clinging to each other. The mist thick around them, Harry offered to walk her home, 'You'll get lost in this, a right pea-souper!' before both got an attack of the giggles, had to rest against a passing wall.

Eventually Jo recovered enough to say, 'Don't be daft, I'm away up there' – she stuck a thumb in the direction of the cliffs – 'and you're away down there' – the thumb switching towards the pier. 'Miles away. Though you shouldn't be there at all, you should be back at home with your mum who loves you and… '

'Enough with the lectures!' Harry roared, pushing himself free from the wall. 'Jo,' and he was in front of her, hands on her shoulders, looking so serious she couldn't help but laugh. 'It's been a great night. I mean… really. Great.' Before she could protest he had her in a bear hug, arms trapped.

'Get off me, you big hairy ape!'

When he'd released her and they said their cheerios, it was nice to look back and see him making sure she had got half-way up the stone stairs leading to the Cliffview flats OK. She waved, shouted, 'It *was* a great night, wasn't it Harry!' then teetered away from view.

He chuckled, 'Poor daft Dr Ashe.'

Lighting a roll-up, his eyes were attracted to a light at the top of the Phoenix. Behind the cinema sign a black figure stood in the office window, the room behind dark, a small red dot at head height showing Callum Boyd was smoking too. Keeping watch. What was he doing now? Saluting, the cheeky prick. Harry lifted a finger in response, stomped towards the pier, powered by the anger Callum always induced.

Immaculate in his dinner suit, Callum watched until Harry was swallowed up by the mist. He breathed out smoke, winked at his own reflection.

'So like his father. Always raging away at slights. Well,' he took a long drag on his cigarette, enjoying its heat and bitterness. 'Wouldn't want to let you down, would I? If you want something to rage against I'm happy to oblige. Let's see if you're a braver man than your father ever was,' the grin of his reflection shining.

# CHAPTER SIX

It was time for us to leave Jo for a while, stumbling to her lonely bed with a hangover and a nasty shock to greet her in the morning. We would take a break from her anxiety about belonging to enjoy the company of someone who felt entirely at home in Seacrest.

That didn't stop him hating the place at times despite many regarding Harry Lawson as the living embodiment of the town. In part that was because he was the son of Alec Lawson but mainly because of Harry himself. He provided the reassurance that it *must* be a grand place to live because people like him, who could have moved on years ago, had chosen to stay.

There he was, down on the pier, slightly unsteady on his feet, a showman, larger than life in front of gaudy rides and attractions that were dark and quiet way in the hours past midnight. His natural environment.

Yeah, he was telling himself, still should have got out years ago, on to bigger and better things. Like Shona gallivanting off to New York. But then again… he couldn't imagine living anywhere else. Seacrest was in his blood and sometimes there was nowhere else he'd rather be. Like now, at the Ghost Train, skeletons and monsters, mummies and werewolves on the front, eyes glowing red. The helter-skelter down the end of the pier lit up like some mad lighthouse, the Penny Arcades, the Hall of Mirrors, the Fun House and to top it all, the Big Wheel.

You could stick your London Eye, he thought, this was where it was at. Standing below it, his head craned back as far as it would go, admiring the size of it. It was weird how, although he got older, it seemed as massive as it did when he was wee. As if it grew at the same rate. He remembered going there with his Mum and Dad, between the two of them, holding their hands. His Dad with his leather gloves on to protect the skin, the burn marks and even then Harry knew it was also to hide the sight from others. To stop them staring, wondering what had happened before realising who he was and then the whispering starting. 'Yes, that's right, Alec Lawson. Injured in that fire, terrible shame. Best projectionist there ever was, once.'

The names Harry got called at school. Getting into fights, still angry at the thought of that wee boy having to defend his Dad.

Down on the pier though, they were happy, Dad letting him hold his hand, gently. His Mum too scared to go on the Wheel, always just Harry and him up there and when the carriage stopped and they were hanging, as high as the seagulls, his Dad would get chatty. Pointing out the landmarks, the pride shining out of him, the love he had for the town. As if he owned the place. Harry would hate it when it started up again because as soon as they were back down it was back to normal. No more hand-holding. Alec silent, walking off ahead on his own. Maybe he was planning it then, Harry couldn't help thinking. The jump... fucksake. Harry shivered, started searching for his keys.

There were some who couldn't fathom why he lived down there, where his Dad was last seen. They didn't understand that by the time Alec left them, it was a relief. No more having to put up with the brooding at home, the silent treatment. Why would he let a dead Dad get between him and the place he loved? His home. The Kinotech.

On a pier full of marvels the Kinotech was the high point of kitsch. It was also the tattiest of the pier attractions, seemed to have landed from a different age altogether, its frontage paying homage to the travelling cinema shows that roamed the country before cinemas became settled in high streets. It promised the magic of a voodoo technology: 'MARVELLOUS MOVING PANORAMAS! WONDERS OF THE NATURAL WORLD – THE PYRAMIDS, THE TAJ MAHAL, HANGING GARDENS OF BABYLON! EXTRAORDINARY BEASTS, INCREDIBLE BEINGS! ALL TRANSMITTED DIRECT TO YOU THROUGH THE MIRACLE OF THE MAGIC LANTERN!'

Along the top appeared a sinister moustachioed figure, black mask covering his eyes, one hand tipping his top-hat, the other held out in greeting, welcoming guests with a psychotic glint, hoping to distract from the faded paint and seagull splatter.

After he'd located his keys, rattling away in the lock, his swearing increasing in vigour and baroque imagery, Harry eventually opened the side-door to the Kinotech. Although he didn't need to, could navigate the place in the dark, he switched the lights on. He liked to see the machines properly and once the fluorescent strips had batted into life we could understand why.

We were faced with a wonderland, a playground dedicated to delight, to the serious business of fun. A place people would travel thousands of miles to see, to pop their pennies into the working examples of old 'Penny-a-Peep' machines, mechanical moving postcards, zoopraxiscopes, zoetropes, mutoscopes before playing on the pin balls. The machines stood quiet but energy radiated from them, feeding off the charge of ghostly punters who had whiled away hours there, turning their change into pleasure. Rescued from skips and auctions by Harry who had got to work with those famous Lawson hands, given them much needed love and attention. As he headed towards his office Harry instinctively ran his hand over wood and brass. Pulled a lever here, pressed a button there because these were machines that *needed* to be touched, they'd rust away without it.

Who *wouldn't* want to live there? Wasn't Jo being boringly conventional suggesting he pack up and go back to his Mum's? But before we got carried away, we had a quick peek at Harry's living quarters off to the side; a camp bed stuck in a former janitor's cupboard next to a small, stained washbasin, a Calor gas stove on the floor and an unsettling reek similar to that of a teenage boy's bedroom. Perhaps Jo had a point.

Warped by damp the office door needed a good tug. Inside was big enough to feature a swivel chair, a desk, a safe and Harry who picked his way over the springs and cogs littering the floor before slumping heavily into the chair. He opened a desk drawer, pulled out a bottle of cheap supermarket blend labelled 'Whisky' and a coffee cup. Poured out a decent measure then toasted the on-looking pictures of Orson Welles, the walls *covered* with Welles.

It sort of just happened, you know? The Wellesian wallpaper. He'd stuck a few pictures up and folk brought him more and the next thing he knew... bloody *collage*. Some people saw a resemblance between him and old Orson although Jo always took great joy in telling him that was just because they were both fat with a beard... And yeah, he had to admit, looking around there weren't too many of Orson in his younger days. They were mostly less Mercury Theatre and more Optimus Prime, and those awful lager ads.

One photo though, Orson as Harry Lime, looking over his shoulder down in the sewers, waiting for the police to come get him, everyone said was the spit of him. Handsome devil. Even if he was playing some evil child murderer...

There was that rumour his Dad had met him once. Shaken his hand. Harry had always meant to ask him about that but then...och, there was no point getting maudlin when it was far too late to do anything about it.

Harry looked away from Orson's gaze, studied the bottom of his mug then switched his gaze to the Macbook in front of him. The one gleaming concession to modernity in the place, the hub of the Diabolik network, the command post where every week Harry sent out his dispatches to his global army of film fans, ranting and raving about anything that took his fancy: how CGI was wrecking fantasy, the under-rated genius of Owen Wilson, how to make your own moving diorama using a torch and a waste-paper bin.

He could always log on, check how many had signed up for next week's showing in the Tunnels… naw. He'd learnt the hard way drunken blogging was never a good idea. The apologies, the lawsuits. Anyway, he had other things to be getting on with.

He slipped the laptop into a desk drawer, rubbed his hands in anticipation, shifted bills, old copies of the *Seacrest Gazette*, tools and half-filled packets of sweets to the outer edges of the desk to clear some space. It was time to find his treasure!

He took the notebook from his coat, left it on the desk to crouch in front of the safe. In the delicate way he turned its dial we witnessed his Dad's legacy: fingers attuned to tension and give. There was a loud click, the door swinging open to reveal a takings box and a long blue cardboard cylinder stuck at a diagonal that he carefully removed, giving it a brief, triumphant shake before sitting back down at the desk.

He eased off the lid, a tricky job with oily fingernails bitten to the quick, a musty smell released. It must have been years since it was last opened up. Good old Kim. He'd thought she'd ask a few more questions, say she'd have to check with the Consortium but no. Leaning back behind her desk, nice navy dress, pinched in at all the right places, tapping this tube against her palm like a bloody truncheon.

'What *are* you up to Harry Lawson? No good no doubt… must be serious if you're prepared to see me. One of the evil Consortium.

You know, I really should report this to Callum… I'm sure he'd be interested in your interest in the late, great Dominion.'

Green eyes bright, red lips curved into a wicked smile. No more tap-tapping, the plans gripped tight in both hands.

He'd thought about laying on the old Lawson charm but this was Kim Taylor. She'd see through a ploy like that in seconds. It was best to go with the truth. The lady deserved it.

'It's about my Dad, Kim. I think those plans can help me find something of his. Something that was lost in the fire. I think he hid something in the Dominion and that's why he was running back in, that's why they found him where he was with his hands… anyway. That's why I want those plans. It's important, believe me. Wouldn't be asking otherwise.'

The change in her expression… it always amazed Harry, the effect Alec Lawson still had on people. It left him wondering what sort of man he'd been before the fire. If they knew what he'd been like afterwards he was sure you wouldn't see so much of that soft-focus glow. But it didn't take long for the hardness to return to Kim's cat-like eyes as she handed over the plans, kept a hold of the other end when Harry tried to take them away.

'Only, if you *are* going to blow the Phoenix up be sure and give me fair warning. Promise? Now stop grinning at me like some lunatic teddy-bear and get out. And Harry – ' he stopped his bounce towards the door and turned, grinning – 'if only you knew how like your Dad you are,' and his grin vanished.

At his desk, he teased them out, as delicate as ancient parchment, worried they'd crumble to dust on hitting the air. They didn't and he unrolled the thin paper, holding down each corner with pieces of junk until it was spread out before him.

'Fuuuuuuuck.'

Although the plans were faint Harry knew he was looking at a marvel. A lost world, the hole in the heart of Seacrest. He had always thought folk were exaggerating when they went on and on and on about how great the Dominion was, how things had never been the same without it… but *look* at it.

Better than that, we could take the tour.

The lines of the plan seemed to glow then expanded, filled the tiny office, walls growing up from the floor until we stood before the Dominion's impressive entrance with its Greek columns, plaster ferns, Sphinxes crouched at either side of the Dominion sign covered with tiny, glittering light-bulbs flashing in countless sequences. Everything was designed to make the visitor feel as though they were a star and that the red carpet covering the white steps had been rolled out for *them*.

We wandered through richly decorated corridors eerily empty, waded through thick carpets, under chandeliers and began to experience the curious sensation that this was a place that had never been meant to last. Peeking into Screen One from one of the Upper Circle doorways, we saw the size of those huge red curtains, the number of balconies, the waves of empty seats, we considered perhaps a blazing fate had been entirely fitting. Far better than the drawn-out decline of the derelict cinemas we passed by unnoticed on our city streets, a shadow of their former selves.

We were startled by a shuffling behind us, the sound of a door creaking open and closing. A pause and a low whirring. The lights in Screen One dimmed to black, the curtains slid apart to reveal a blank screen. A shutter opened, we looked to our right and saw a beam of light, dust motes caught and dancing. Instead of watching the numbers count down to the film, we backed into the corridor, paced until we were in front of the black door of a small room that we leant against, pressing our ear to its cool surface.

The whirring was louder, the noise of the projector hypnotic until there was a burst of zither music from Screen One and we knew who was in there, the name of the man who had loaded the projector and we were about to knock when we heard voices. Not from the screen but inside. The projectionist had a guest. His voice deep and resonant and we were on the brink of realising who when… the Dominion vanished and we were back, blinking, in the office with Harry.

His forefinger tapped a square right at the heart of the Dominion, in front of Screen One, labelled 'Chief Projectionist Booth'.

'Poor sod,' he murmured, sighed, then pulled from his coat pocket a large sheet of folded paper. He opened it with distaste, held the corners as if he ran the risk of contamination. Once it was opened up we could see why: plans for Callum Boyd's Phoenix.

Bloody typical Harry thought, that these had been harder to get than the Dominion's. Lots of Lawson charm and a week's wages paid to one of the Seacrest librarians had got him them. Had been a big help that she hated Callum but then anyone with half a brain did…look at the place. 'Like comparing the Taj Mahal to a Barrett bungalow', Harry muttered, placing the Dominion's plans over those of the Phoenix, creating a palimpsest.

Even taking into account Harry's natural antipathy towards Boyd's empire, on seeing the plans of the Phoenix showing through those of the Dominion, it was difficult to disagree. Instead of the eccentricity of the earlier cinema, the straight lines of the Phoenix lay down the law of customer control. The number of screens had increased but screen size was small, there was only one bar, exits had been widened, everything geared towards getting the customers in and out as quickly as possible and selling them things while they were there. Everything kept bland enough to induce a low-level boredom proven to lead to the buying of more fizzy drinks and popcorn. No gold-scalloped light fittings or plaster gods and goddesses in auditorium alcoves to distract from the watching of trailers and adverts. The Phoenix was a building designed purely as a money-making machine, soulless and brutally successful.

Harry scrutinised the basements of both cinemas. Down where his Dad had been rescued on the night the Dominion set the Seacrest sky ablaze. Running into a blazing building, found an hour later, choking on the smoke, his hands black, burned into unfeeling claws, restrained by firemen as he screamed at them, 'I need to get back! I need to get it, I promised him!'

Harry's hands prickled when he saw it. A tiny forgotten room in the depths of the Phoenix. He clenched his fist, hissed a 'Yessss!' and a 'Kerching!' came from the 'Perfecto!' machine next door.

Eh? Harry froze. Those machines didn't make noises by themselves… 'Shit!' Listening for movement, he pulled a *Seacrest Gazette* over the plans. Leapt from his chair, hefted up a spare lever from the floor.

Waving it in what he hoped was a threatening manner, he called, 'All right you fucker! Show yourselves, I'm armed and dangerous here!'

As he did so it occurred to him that if you *were* going to raid a place like the Kinotech, would you waste precious looting time on playing a game? It was no great surprise then when he edged past a Flash Gordon pinball machine to be confronted by a sheepish-looking Luke.

'You *idiot*, Luke! Scared me half to death, must be gone two in the morning, I could have ended up braining you what with my ninja skills and… '

They both looked to the lever he was waving above his head then lowered slowly.

'Anyway, you all right? You look knackered. Come through, have a sit down and a drink.'

Luke's smile transformed the Luke we had seen back at the Archive, his angles and edginess gone. Here in Harry's company he looked almost normal. Relaxed.

While Harry cleared a space on the office floor to open up a fold-out seat, his surprise guest explained, 'Saw the lights on, tried the door and it was open so thought you were up. Didn't think you'd mind, should have tried to phone or... Sorry, didn't think, but... I like this place. Helps me sort things out in my head. Calms me down. And the Archive at the moment...'

'OK, OK, I know you love me, now shush a minute and take a seat. You want a drink? I've got...ah...whisky or water. Or both.'

To Harry's surprise Luke nodded. Must be serious if he was taking a drink. Look at him, poor sod, hands in his hair, elbows and knees akimbo on a seat too wee for him. Harry kept forgetting what a stress it must be for him, the possibility of the Archive being taken from him. He must try and be a bit more like Jo, remember to be more sensitive, not upset him.

'Soooo... zombiefied Fletcher back from the dead and maybe wanting his stuff back? No wonder you're in a state.' Or Harry could just carry on taking the piss. Might confuse Luke otherwise.

Luke took the mug offered and gave Harry a Look.

'Thanks. Thanks a lot. I've told you before. I was given the Archive in good faith. As far as I was aware that death certificate was genuine. Just *try* and imagine how I felt when I heard he was alive and well and coming to town.'

His large dark eyes bored into Harry and while it took a lot to make him feel uncomfortable, Harry shifted in his chair. Luke downed the whisky and stared into space, looking like one of those kids who'd lost their parents on the pier, wandering about, on the brink of tears. Eventually he came to.

'I tell you, if anyone's been conned here, it's me. I've maintained the Archive, watched it grow, respected the memory of Cameron Fletcher. Bet I know who's behind this. Someone wanting rid of the Archive, finish off my reputation... '

Harry winced, couldn't be doing with much more of this self-pity shite.

'Luke, *listen* to yourself, whining on. Now, you know I hate Callum as much as you do and you could be right. But you can choose to see this as a positive thing – no, wait, listen – think about it. I can't believe you're not *excited* about this, *dreaming* about the moment you shake Cameron Fletcher by the hand… am I right? Eh? What's that then? A wee grin I see there? Knew it. You moaning on, seeing conspiracies everywhere but you're loving it really.'

'Yeah, OK, but what if he wants his stuff back, what if he wants… '

'Chrissake man, he's not even *here* yet! Trust me, it's going to be fine. Can feel it in my bones. And when has Harry Lawson ever lied to you?'

'Well, there was… '

'Right, shut it. Just… get over here and have a look at this. Will cheer you up.'

Sceptical, Luke moved around the desk, frowned at the papers on it. When he realised what he was looking at, Harry laughed at his widening eyes, jaw dropping like a kid at Christmas getting a glimpse of the presents under the tree.

'How – wait – how did you manage to get *these*? The Dominion…' shaking his head in disbelief. 'I thought Kim kept these under lock and key, how on earth did *you*… '

'Charm, my dear boy, charm. Now stop salivating, you'll make this ink run. You and I and Dr Ashe are going on a treasure hunt. To *here*… ' And he pointed to a tiny storeroom in the Dominion's basement. 'X marks the spot, Lukey boy, X marks the spot. Dad nearly died trying to rescue whatever's in there. And we're going to be the ones to dig it out.'

CHAPTER SEVEN

We left the boys being boys, planning their expedition. Remember at the start of the last chapter a nasty shock awaiting Dr Ashe was mentioned? Well...

Jo was dreaming.

Climbing the Empire State building, tiny planes buzzing, whining about her head, as irritating as midges. Someone was throwing green bananas at her and she looked up to see Shona leaning out of a window, laughing, aiming another fruit at her head before disappearing from view. A huge, hairy hand reached down from the top of the building and Jo knew it wasn't King Kong but Harry and Cameron Fletcher combined, a massive hand stretching to grab her head between thumb and forefinger, squeezing until the pressure became unbearable and jabbing, stabbing strings started to play...

'Christ almighty,' she groaned, right hand searching for her 'Psycho' alarm clock without success. It had been a present brought back by Shona from one of her disappearances. Two weeks away without explanation and what did Jo get in return? A big plastic knife evil alarm thing. Jo must have set it for a reason though, it was usually something soothing on Radio 3 that woke her up in the morning.

Admitting defeat she hoisted herself up as Hermann's score increased in volume. Resembling something last seen emerging from a Hammer Horror tomb, she lunged at the knife sitting atop the nearest bookcase and succeeded only in knocking it to the floor where it switched to the swirling theme from *Vertigo*. Discovering her brain has been replaced by some highly toxic fluid, bringing pain wherever it settled, the music provided some respite and she eased back down until images of spiralling designs made her feel sick.

Getting up, finding painkillers and water and freshly squeezed orange juice seemed the best option were it not for the whole getting vertical thing causing a problem. Murmuring 'Eeeeeaaaasy, eeeeeeaasy now,' moving with all the grace and speed of an arthritic 87-year-old, realising that bending over would *not* be a good idea, Jo's right big toe reduced her misery by hitting the button that silenced the Hitchcock soundtrack.

If she'd remembered to set it when wasted, when she knew she was going to be hung-over, it must have been for something important. Checking the time, 9:15am, a slow feeling of dread began to build. The meeting! A bloody Consortium meeting! Hence *Psycho*, representing Callum Boyd! A meeting at 10am!

'Jesus *Christ*!' Jo exclaimed whilst amazed the way blind panic proved as effective as Nurofen Plus. Realising she had forty-five minutes to get herself down to the Fulmar Hotel powered Jo through the physical distress of getting washed and dressed. Lurching through the hallway, passing by the door of her tiny office, she noticed the animated screen-saver of her computer; Dorothy and her three companions making their way along the yellow brick road. Which was weird as she was sure she switched it off before going out to see Luke. Dimly she remembered switching it on when she came back. Drunken internet surfing was never a good idea and she decided to check what damage might have been done.

Sitting in front of the screen, vaguely it came back to her. Finding something that had made her stop and stare before punching the air and drunkenly dancing off to bed. She hesitated then twitched her hand on the mouse and there it was. Headache and suffering forgotten, replaced by amazement.

She'd been looking through a file of old Fletcher articles, tracing the links, hoping that being drunk might help, offer her a different perspective. The postcard from Shona had triggered something with its New York connection. She'd stared at her notes on Avi Fleischer, a New York film director, the Jean Vigo of his time who'd died too young at 26. An electrical accident on the set of his first feature, *The Walker*, planned as a celebration of the joys of city life, a development of the themes of his award-winning short film *The Magician's Daughter*. The lengthy review of *Daughter* published in the *Village Voice*, Fletcher's first published work and remarkably similar to Fleischer's writings. But then Avi died two years later and his obituary appeared in the same publication written by Fletcher. Fleischer, Fletcher, Flim-flam, Fooey...

Then she'd remembered the website. One devoted to unsung character actors like James Robertson Justice, Alistair Sim, Bernard Lee: those who rarely made top billing but whose presence always guaranteed moments of filmic pleasure. The thought that she should pay it a return visit had been niggling away at her, ever since the arrival of Fletcher's photograph. Trawling through lists of forgotten actors, getting increasingly miserable as the alcohol began to wear off, about to give up when she found him.

Stared at his photograph as she stared at it now. Recognising the eyes, the humour of them, although different from Fletcher's. Touch of desperation in them, a plea for a part. Younger, fuller head of hair, no beard and... ordinary. She couldn't be *entirely* sure, there were those who would argue it wasn't, that there was only a resemblance, not the actual man. There would still be a lot of arguing and convincing for Jo to do but in the meantime she did exactly what she had done in the early hours of the morning. Gave a small salute and whispered, 'Why hello there, Mr Fletcher.'

She would have to fully consider it later, make further connections, hunt down the proof then think through the ramifications, what it meant for Seacrest if she was right, but there wasn't the time. Twenty-five minutes to the meeting, she would have to bookmark and go, trying not to brain herself on a passing bookshelf.

After the door slammed shut behind her, we stayed in her flat, had time before the screen saver kicked in to study the photo on screen with a curious mix of happiness and anxiety. Because Arthur Dott had the kind of face that always made an audience happy to see it and while we were glad Jo had taken a serious step forward in proving her theory this Fletcher was a fake, we were worried what she would do with this knowledge. Spoil Arthur's big moment? Steal away Seacrest's star? Before we got too concerned, however, we acknowledged the woman with the potential to undermine Fletcher's arrival had fallen upwards onto a tram to slump against a window, near unconscious.

Jo had always found the sound of the tram bell evocative, redolent of a gentler time of crinolines and clippies; that morning she wanted to rip the stupid prissy twee stupid bell from its holder, especially when a vigorous bout of ringing pulled her from her doze and she realised she'd missed her stop and would have to jog back to the hotel. Imitating one of the more active zombies from *Night of the Living Dead* she shuffled along to the wide white steps of the Fulmar, a pitiful sight, doubled-over, wheezing, trying desperately not to puke on the pavement.

Come on, Jo, she told herself, pull yourself together, straighten up! Admiring the sight of the hotel, its opulence, white and gold frontage, helped her to make it up the shallow steps without being put off by the thought of negotiating its heavy revolving doors, even the *word* 'revolving' making her heave.

Once inside the plush red foyer, the hotel worked its special balm. Her headache began to lift as she took in the greenery, the high-back red armchairs, wondering where exactly Stanley Kubrick sat and took notes a few months before filming *The Shining*. Owned and run by the formidable MacSween sisters, now in their eighties and famously dismissive of the town's unhealthy absorption in films. Hardly a Festival went by without some story in the *Gazette* telling of another famous film star cut down to size by Morag or Margaret – 'I couldn't care less about all this Godfather nonsense, *you* try cleaning white linen sheets of half a tub of Neapolitan. Mr Brando can moan all he likes but he won't be getting prised out of our revolving doors again. '

Ironic then that it was one of the places in town that most resembled a film set. Its Vistavision staircases, screwball comedy luggage trolleys, balconies and cocktail bar. Jo always meant to have a Special High Tea there sometime, never having seen a tiered cake stand in actual action before.

'Dr Ashe? Danish?'

An unnervingly pretty girl behind the reception desk was peering at her causing Jo to wonder, where *did* they get the staff from? All of them looked as though they should be starring in the next Gus Van Sant, driving middle-aged novelists to write *Death in Seacrest*. This one, some miraculous genetic cross between Greta Garbo and Scarlett Johanssen was looking at her as if she was some deranged Withnail impersonator.

'Ah, sorry... no, English.' Too late Jo realised her mistake, thankful it seemed as though the receptionist had training on how to deal with guests driven imbecilic by booze, smiling with sympathy as she pointed to the tray of pastries in front of her.

'Right, of course, Sorry! Danish! As in... pastry!'

Resisting the urge to slap her forehead and so fully display the wit and poise of a Jerry Lewis clone, Jo took her complimentary coffee and Danish, blushing with a ferocity rarely seen outside a 1950s girls' finishing school and escaped up the stairs to the

Fulmar's conference suite.

It took Jo's breath away every time, walking into the suite with the wide windows, the view of the Front and the blue, blue sea. The long mahogany table glowing under a chandelier that summed up Seacrest; ridiculously camp and yet utterly impressive.

As to the occupants… at first it was like entering a fancy dress party but after a while you felt it, the tingling in the air generated by power. Yes, there was the Seacrest Town Council but everyone knew the Consortium ran the place. Jo smiled and nodded towards the Council representatives, Richard Thomas and Harriet Kidd – Dick and Harry as they were referred to by the other Consortium members – waving hello in relief at seeing someone as sedately dressed as them. Poor souls, they looked like two civilians who'd wandered into an Oscar party.

It was at off-guard times like this one, when still mildly drunk, Jo caught the full force of Seacrest's weirdness, as if she'd been living in Disneyland for a few years then suddenly noticed how odd it was, queuing up with the walking mice and fairy princesses in the local shop. She gazed around, ticking off the cinema owners. Seacrest royalty, their passion for the films they loved evident in the way they dressed.

There was Charlie 'Chuck' Weston (formerly Jim Nelson from Bolton), owner of Silverado, tipping back his Stetson, thumbs hitched on his chaps, laughing so hard his spurs jangled as he shared a joke with Dr Vlad (Gordon Hargreaves of Grangemouth) manager of The Black Cat and a Peter Cushing look-alike. Vlad, an industrial chemist until a penchant for black velvet jackets and a Lon Chaney obsession saw him take a one-way train trip to Seacrest. And Molly Malone – real name a mystery, from Dublin perhaps? – owner of Pandora's Box specialising in 'queer delights', in her 1920s dinner suit, giving most of the men a lesson in how to look dapper and though Jo knew she shouldn't approve of butch

stereotypes she had to admit, Molly looked fantastic. She was sure
her and Shona shared more than a box of popcorn once and she
blushed when Molly caught her gaze and winked.

'Jo! Stop standing there looking like a mental patient. And
believe me, that's quite an achievement in this company. Here, I've
saved you a seat.'

Jo thanked God Kim was there to take her in hand, calling her
over from near the top of the table. As she edged past a Goth, a
gangster and a martial arts expert gossiping she noticed the buzz,
a noticeable difference from the tense silence preceding meetings
of the past few months. Of course, the Fletcher effect, and she
experienced a sudden tilting as if the floor had shifted beneath her
feet.

She knew or rather, believed, she'd discovered. Cameron
Fletcher's dirty little secret. She could ruin this, spoil the party with
a print-out, and a sheen of sweat spread across her hands, her face.

'Good God, Dr Ashe, you look fucking awful. Haven't seen eyes
so bloodshot since Peter O'Toole propositioned me after a three-
week bender.'

'Great. That's just… great. Thanks Kim, makes me feel a lot
better,' managed Jo as she slumped into the seat next to Kim. 'And
you look… ' finely coiffured hair, red-tailored suit, immaculate
make-up and those shining emerald eyes ' … stunning. Absolutely
stunning.'

Kim nodded, accepting the inevitable compliment. 'Drink your
coffee, dear, might make you look a little less lobotomised. Well,
isn't this exciting' – her dry tones leaving nothing without a thin
coating of irony – 'haven't seen the gang so pleased with itself
since the Confectionery Truce.'

Then abruptly the irony was gone, Kim's eyes taking on an extra
sheen.

'This, *this* is what I meant when we had our meeting the other day. You can *feel* it. What Cameron Fletcher has done for Seacrest. Look at them.

Jo did look, the sight exacerbating her nausea. There was no *way* she could tell them the truth. Faces previously seen frozen in despair as Callum reeled off statistics proving ever-decreasing visitor numbers were bright with optimism. Even Philippe Gilbert, owner of the Marienbad, who had an unnerving habit of appearing to be in profile no matter where you stared at him from, was wearing his beret at a jaunty angle.

As always, the chairman, Callum Boyd, was the last to arrive. How the atmosphere shifted when he did, those he passed quietening their chatter as if in the presence of a movie star.

He was immaculate in a dark grey suit, triangle of lilac in his top pocket, nodding a greeting, those icy blue eyes fixing on Jo's for a second... Shona's eyes. That look he had in some of the pictures shaking hands with famous male film-stars, looking straight into the camera, challenging the viewer 'Now... who would *you* rather sleep with?' Greeting Paul Newman or helping Bette Davis up a staircase he didn't have that incredulous look you see in photos of non-entities with celebrities. With Callum it was a meeting of equals. Those cheekbones sharpened by the years, the sheen of his swept-back black hair now a distinguished silver. A handsome devil.

Once he'd taken his place at the head of the table, a hush descended and Jo tried to forget the image of Arthur by scanning the printed agenda in front of her, expecting the usual: further discussion of Callum's plans for redevelopment then general Festival business. But, wait a minute... she turned the sheet of A4 over, making sure she wasn't missing something.

'Kim,' she whispered, as Callum opened the narrow box in front of him containing the Consortium gavel. 'There's nothing about the redevelopment, only 'Vote for Judging Panel for Float Displays' and 'Health and Safety Procedures for Roller Derby' nonsense. As if everything's been decided when nothing's been agreed or finalised yet. Just because the Festival's coming up we can't forget Callum's threatening to knock the studios down, wreck the pier...'

The gavel rapped. Callum smiled in her direction, Jo determined not to feel she'd been caught out by the headmaster. Kim only shrugged, switching her sharp eyes towards Callum. Jo checked to see if anyone else was outraged to discover they wouldn't be discussing the most substantial changes to Seacrest since the Great Dreaming when cinema owners had been encouraged to come to Seacrest to set up their pleasure palaces in the Fifties. No, everyone was hypnotised by Callum's glamour and then Jo noticed the empty chair mid-table. Luke's seat. Where was he?

'Ladies and gentlemen.'

Boyd rose from his chair and Jo had that tipping sensation again as the Consortium members all gazed up at him like they were attending some revivalist meeting. Jo felt Luke's absence keenly as he would be the one to galvanise the opposition, to point out how much they stood to lose if the studios were knocked down and 'improved'. When he got going he was a lightning rod, focusing the opposition's argument.

'I'm very glad practically all of you could make it,' Callum began, the tiniest of smirks aimed at Luke's empty chair. He'd *planned* this, fixed it somehow, Jo realised. She took a drink of water, tried to will herself not to feel so faint. Luke couldn't have chickened out from such an important meeting... could he?

'I'm especially pleased that for once there is *good* news to share.' There was soft laughter as Jo swallowed down bile.

'I'm sure I don't need to remind you,' Callum continued, 'but since the announcement that Cameron Fletcher will be visiting, interest in the Festival has rocketed. Hotels are fully booked, clubs and restaurants have had their opening hours extended thanks to the Council' – Dick and Harry glowed from the acknowledgement, failing to notice the wink Callum gave the rest of them – 'all of which means we're riding the crest of a wave.'

Callum waved away a smattering of applause from his more sycophantic followers with a perfectly calibrated 'It was nothing' air.

'Although I'd love to, I'm afraid I can't claim all the glory,' and Callum looked directly at Jo who turned red again, suddenly knowing what was coming. 'Most of the credit has to go to my daughter Shona.'

Bingo. Jo had guessed Shona *must* have been involved somewhere, what with the date on that postcard. Whatever was going to bring her back to Seacrest had to be remarkable and Harry, Jo or Shona's Dad for that matter, didn't fit the bill. Fletcher was the only name big enough.

'Yes, after months of careful detective work we were able to track down the real and very much *alive*' – dammit Luke, Jo cursed, silently, you should be here defending yourself! – 'Cameron Fletcher. Naturally we had to tread carefully, use our powers of persuasion, but once the name of Seacrest was mentioned his acceptance was assured.'

A round of applause filled the room drowning out Jo's 'Ha!' that caused Kim to aim a painful nudge at her ribs. Jo's arms were folded, refusing to join in, but the applause wouldn't stop, a few whoops and whistles added. Good Lord, she thought, they're hysterical, some wiping away tears. Jo absorbed this release of emotion, shivered.

She hadn't appreciated just how much they'd been *praying* for this. Some kind of hope. There was no *way* she could tell them what she thought was the truth with the flimsy evidence she had available and take Fletcher away from them. And not just because it would be mean and cruel but because she'd never make it out alive. Even

Kim was swept along by it. Kim! Clapping and cheering away like a giddy teenager at her first boy-band concert. Slowly, grudgingly, Jo's arms unlocked as the applause began to die and she began a light handclap until Callum's smile became too much to bear.

'Now, while you've made *extremely* clear this is fantastic news, I hope I won't spoil things too much by offering a note of caution,' Callum's expression switched smoothly from one of satisfaction to furrowed concern. The room followed his emotion, whispered anxiety replacing the joy of a few seconds ago.

'It is my firm belief that this Festival will be one of this town's greatest successes. But, fellow members, how do we maintain that momentum? How do we prevent a dismal slip back into the red? Over the past few years this town has seen occasions when, briefly, we thought the glory days were restored. But we slumped back onto our laurels and where did it get us? I'll tell you where. Twenty-five cinemas closed in the past ten years and, if we're lucky, only fifteen in the next five.'

An uneasy shuffling, nervous coughing with Callum letting the silence build.

'I know we've had our disagreements in the past regarding my earlier proposals for the regeneration of the town' – a quick glance again at Luke's chair – 'but it's my sincere hope that during the Festival celebrations you will realise we owe it to future residents to ensure the continued prosperity of Seacrest. I understand many of you prefer the comfort of the past. I admit my plans for the town are radical but that's because terrible problems require drastic solutions. Unless surgery takes place this patient will *die*.'

Shameless, Jo thought, Elmer Gantry would collapse in tears at such a display. She was tempted to start a slow handclap but picked up instead on murmurs of assent rippling around the table. Headache beating against her forehead she wished Luke would burst through the door and save them. But it was too late. Callum had got them. He would bring Fletcher here, work the town into a frenzy, give them a glimpse of the good old days then scare them shitless with the prospect of taking it all away. A master-stroke. Then someone exclaimed,

'I can't believe I'm hearing this!'

Jo's spirits lifted, someone prepared to take a stand, to halt the progress of the Boyd bulldozer! Who was brave enough to – and then she saw. Bugger.

Monsieur Max Reynard, owner of the New Electric specialising in silents and late night showings of odd lost fragments of films, rose slowly to his feet, the tips of his waxed handlebar moustache trembling with indignation. A lovely man but as French as a Forfar bridie, as mad as a Dundee cake.

'Will you idiots *listen* to what this tyrant is saying? What he's threatening?' Such was the force of his anger his usual attempt at a French accent was non-existent, more Govan than Gallic. 'He's offering you a fantasy, a dream land and you're all willing to knock down everything we've built up over the years! He's not interested in cinema, the *soul* of this place. It's all about the bottom dollar and if you're not making money you're dead. This talk of innovation, *progress*... I'd rather this town became a ruin, a *beautiful* ruin than somewhere with the life sucked out of it.'

Go on, Max! Jo clapped vigorously along with a pitiful pattering from others. Then her head reminded her of her precarious state and she stopped, enjoying a glance of pure venom from Callum before he turned his attention to M Reynard.

'Max. Max, I understand your concerns' – 'Bof!' – 'but you seem to think I'm waiting to give the signal to move the demolition squads in *today*. That couldn't be further from the truth. All I'm asking for is a clear sign of consensus. Don't you think we owe *that* to the soul of Seacrest? The world's press is going to be on our doorstep in a fortnight's time. Can we afford to waste that opportunity in bickering? Instead we should seize the opportunity to show a new face, one that's open to the future, prepared to meet the challenges of the twenty-first century. Prepared to *change*.' Callum opened his arms wide, offering himself up to the table, giving them a *vision*.

'Callum's right, Max.' Jo groaned to see who was speaking up. Miss Havisham herself. Sheena Paterson, owner of The Flashing Blade – speciality costume dramas, anything featuring Douglas Fairbanks Jnr and tediously long sword fights – dressed in her pale pink crinolines. And looking *tired*. She was usually so sprightly and who, in this day and age, ever looks sprightly?

'If we don't change, shake the place up, Seacrest is dead and our children, our grandchildren will hold us responsible. We've been stumbling along for years now, not living, *surviving*. Look at us, really *look* at us, Max. We're old and tired and we need to move on. I for one am sick of feeling like a museum piece. A freak.'

What did she expect dressed like bloody Little Bo Peep? Jo thought angrily but oh, what followed was awful, the bewilderment on Max's face, appealing to the room for support and finding nothing, only faces as worn as Sheena's. And what could Jo do, what choice did she have but to look away as he swayed back down, his knees weak from the realisation the future, *Callum*, had won. Jo was only there to watch, not to get involved. What good could *she* do, an outsider?

'Thank you Sheena. Couldn't have put it better myself,' said Callum and from the slight flush to his cheekbones, Jo could tell he sensed victory was near. 'I'm not suggesting any final decision be made today. I want each and every one of you to enjoy the Festival but also to think about how we can maintain Seacrest's place as the top destination for cinema lovers. Because isn't that what everyone here wants, what we *deserve*? At the close of the Festival I propose an Extraordinary General Meeting to cast our votes on whether my proposals for the renovation of Seacrest are carried forward. All those in favour please raise your hand… '

'Jo, *Jo*! For God's sake girl, wait! Don't go storming… '
It was too late. Kim was left standing at the top of the Fulmar staircase watching the revolving doors spin empty having cast a furious Jo out onto the Front. Kim rarely experienced doubt, but at that moment she had difficulty pin-pointing what frustrated her more. Jo behaving like a moody teenager or her own decision to give in so readily to Callum's proposal. Honestly though, when that man got going it was like trying to resist Satan himself. A Satan who bore a heart-breaking resemblance to Gregory Peck.

Rummaging in her red leather handbag for cigarettes she caught the scent of lavender. Without looking up she said sharply, 'All right Callum, you got what you wanted. No need to gloat. Hardly gentlemanly behaviour.'

'And I'm hardly a gentleman. Thought I'd come over and thank you for your vote. Nice to see the place finally coming to its senses. Pity your friend Dr Ashe had to rush off. Would have liked to offer her my commiseration but no doubt she's off sharing the news with her cohorts. Shame, isn't it, that Luke couldn't make it. He'd have livened things up a bit. Put up a fight.'

Kim snapped her silver cigarette case shut, the sound like a miniature guillotine blade hitting home. She'd seen him like this before in the aftermath of some big movie event. During it he'd be his usual cool, professional self but afterwards you'd catch a glimpse of this other Callum; less controlled, as flushed and exhilarated as an actor seconds after leaving the stage.

'I wouldn't be too smug yet.' Kim's teeth gritted around a cigarette dyed red to match her dress. 'You've won a battle not the war. Still plenty of time for people to change their minds. And if you carry on like this you might not like the way people jump.' Both dropped their gaze to the gold revolver-shaped lighter she held, pointed directly at Callum's chest. Raising his arms in mock surrender, he nodded towards a 'No Smoking' sign on the wall beside them, the trigger click, click, clicking in response. 'Dammit! Why's this bloody thing not working!'

With a grace perfected from years of studying Cary Grant, Callum reached into a jacket pocket and produced a box of matches decorated with the Phoenix logo, a bird rising from flames. 'Hate to see a woman in distress. Keep them. Something to light your way.' Their eyes locked as she took the matches, Kim wishing she could turn back time, had kept her hand down.

She found Jo at the sea railings opposite the Fulmar, glaring at the horizon as though willing an armada to appear. 'Don't jump,' touching her lightly on the shoulder. 'I'd have to dive in and save you and you've no *idea* the damage sea water could do to this dress.'

In the time it took Jo to turn and face her, she'd spent three matches in the sea breeze. Anyone else and she'd have walked, left them to sulk. But this was Jo and *someone* has to look after her. Especially as she looked about as cheery as Bette Davies being told they'd need another take of her carrying Joan.

'Of all the people in there, Kim, I thought you were the one I could rely on. Instead what happens? Callum asks you to jump and you're tripping over your high heels to oblige. With Luke not here someone had to speak up for the town, to… '

Kim's patience, never one of her strongest attributes, snapped. 'Wait one minute, *honey*. Who exactly are you angry with? OK, so you're hung-over, big deal, there was nothing to stop *you* kicking up a fuss. You're an academic, for Chrissake – a *visiting* one to boot, someone who could stir things up and not worry about the consequences.'

Jo stood, speechless, eyes red-rimmed and Kim briefly felt something close to shame. 'Jo, listen, I'm sorry. D'you hear that?

An apology from Kim Taylor, hold the *Gazette* front page! I'm just trying to get you to wake *up*. Do you honestly think Luke being here would have made *any* difference? Oh, he'd have made a show of it, given a fine speech and we'd have clapped and cheered and when the bulldozers moved in a few weeks later kidded ourselves on we'd put up a fight.'

She inhaled deeply, breathing out a plume of smoke that turned their view of the pier ghostly.

'Look around you. Take a good long hard look,' waved her cigarette at the tourists wandering by. Jo saw elderly couples, last here in their youth who still thrilled to the memory of having been within kissing distance of Ava Gardner. A few younger couples but not enough, wearing their 'I've Been To Seacrest!' t-shirts, the seagull's wings spread across their chests, clutching copies of *Weird Britain*, taking photos to upload on to websites featuring Portmeirion, crazy golf courses and derelict amusement arcades.

And there *He* was. The Film Buff. A ubiquitous presence in Seacrest, very occasionally female, identifiable by the uniform of black clothes and Harry Palmer glasses. This particular specimen was standing in front of the Fulmar, stroking his goatee in reverent absorption, a book in his other hand open at a set of photographs. Jo felt a surge of geek pride at knowing exactly which book it was: Gerald Winchester's *Champagne and Tea-cakes: Images of the Great British Hotel in Film*.

Kim's contempt quickly crushed that pride. 'This... *bunch* is who we rely on. In a few years half of them will be dead, the others putting their trip here down to a phase they were going through. Young folk who have the misfortune to *live* here can't wait to get out. Those who stay do so only because they know dressing up every morning as Monroe or Gable might not be accepted Out There.'

She stabbed her thumb in the direction of the cliffs, a gesture

Jo had noticed typical to other residents, one she found repeating herself when friends came to visit. It spoke of the division between the world of Seacrest and the drab world beyond. Them versus Us, reality versus fantasy, gangsters and cowboys against call centre operators and middle management.

Kim's voice softened. 'It's about time we gave real life a chance. We've been running away from it long enough.'

She dropped her cigarette which gave off a tiny, desolate shower of sparks before she ground it out under her heel. 'Otherwise we'll end up mad and poor. Picturesque perhaps, glamorous sure, but nothing more than a freak-show.'

When she looked up she wore an expression Jo had come to loathe during her time there, one of pity tinged with envy, 'You don't have to live here, Jo. You can leave any time you want. You're here as an audience member, to watch. For those of us *bound* here, tied up in celluloid, we don't have any other choice. Callum's right. It's about time Seacrest faced up to the twenty-first century. People can't survive on candyfloss and popcorn alone.'

Jo tried to reply, to say something to convince Kim otherwise. But either the smoke or the sea spray caught her throat and instead she turned to the comforting blank of the sea.

CHAPTER
EIGHT

Two hours later and Jo was still recovering from the trauma of the meeting. Once Kim had left she'd stayed clutching the railing until her hands turned purple then trudged into town. Drifting into gift-shops, the kitsch worsening her headache, she was desperate to prove Kim wrong, to find some sign that Seacrest could be rejuvenated without its heart being ripped out. Instead she found cafes occupied by the odd middle-aged couple who'd given up on conversation years ago, desolate foyers, ticket prices set ridiculously high in a useless attempt to cover overheads.

Even Bernies' failed to cheer her up; the best burger joint in the town, a riot of chrome and leatherette booths and burger buns, signed by stars fixed in Perspex boxes lining the walls. She'd go there if a chapter wasn't going well, have a cheeseburger with the face of Edward G Robinson scorched on the top and suddenly life would seem a whole lot better. It wasn't doing it for her that day, though, staring at a half-eaten burger and Edward G's frown. At least the painkillers were kicking in. She wondered idly how many you'd have to take before passing into a coma…

Absent-mindedly tracing 'C F' on her plate with a chip as a nib, ketchup as ink, a loud rap on the window by her head sent pain ricocheting about her skull. Bloody Harry beaming down at her and although she responded with a vigorous flicking of Vs he took this as an invitation to join her.

'All right Stacey!' he called to the fearsome waitress behind the counter who bore a striking resemblance to Diana Dors: The Adam Ant years although stonier-of-face. 'Triple Choc Sundae with cream for me with extra marshmallows and heavy on the sprinkles, tah. You gonna eat that?'

He squeezed himself into the seat opposite as Jo scowled then slid over the congealed burger to him. How the hell could he be so cheery after all that drink? Not natural. The man was a walking rum baba.

'Jesus Jo! You look like… '

'Yes, yes, I know, like something last seen leaving Las Vegas in a box. Your bloody fault. I've told you before when it gets to the point I start saying 'You know what would make this night perfect, bubblegum flavoured shooters!' that's your cue to get me a cab.'

'But it was tequila we were drinking. With lime. Practically a health drink. Anyway,' he continued through a mouthful of chips, 'glad I bumped into you. 'Member what I was saying last night about taking a wee trip down into the Tunnels? Well, Luke's been round at the Kinotech and we've decided… '

'So *that's* where he was! Tosser!' timed perfectly to coincide with Stacey slamming Harry's sundae down on the table. 'Sorry, it's him, was… '

'That's all right, love. With the tab this boy has, tosser's putting it mildly.'

'Hey! Bit uncalled for, Stace' Harry responded in hurt tones before scooping up a tottering heap of cream with a wafer.

'I don't believe you two, *you're* bad enough but Luke… ' Jo muttered. 'D'you know where I was this morning? Eh? Where Luke *should* have been? A Consortium meeting. One where Callum effectively cleared the way for his proposals. One of the most important meetings in Seacrest history and you and Luke were busy planning some bloody Scooby Doo adventure! I could weep.'

'Here, have a napkin. Dry your tears. Want a taste? I'll let you have my cherry.'

'Harry… oi! Cut it out!' as he tapped her head with his sundae spoon.

'Trying to knock in some sense. Listen, Luke's beyond all that nonsense, Consortium meetings, dealings with the council. What does he need to worry about them for when he's got God's own film critic on his side? Reckons when Fletcher sees the Archive, hears what Boyd's planning for Seacrest, the bad publicity will be enough to…you all right?' Jo was moaning, slumped face down on the table. 'What you gibbering about?'

Jo propped herself up on her chin, told him dully, 'There *is* no Cameron Fletcher. There's only Arthur Dott'. She sat back up, pausing as her body readjusted to being vertical. 'I found him on the internet. At least I *think* I did. Still have some work to do, research, get some more evidence somehow, but I reckon, the actor playing Fletcher, it's a set-up. Shona's involved in it somewhere, must have hired the guy. He was in *Emmerdale* years back. Dairy owner with a mad cow.'

Harry nearly choked on a chunk of chocolate brownie 'But that's fantastic! This is what you wanted, isn't it? Proof you're right, Fletcher doesn't exist!'

'Sssshhh… ! It's not as simple as that… oh. Thanks,' as Stacey placed a latte before her. 'On the house, dear. You need as much caffeine as possible when talking to this one.'

As she waited for a sugar cube to break through the thick layer of foam, Jo explained. 'You didn't see them at the meeting. The owners. Haven't seen anything like it in all my time here. The optimism, the self-belief… I can't start waltzing about telling them the one piece of good fortune to hit for decades depends on some background artiste. It'll tip them the other way, make them think the only salvation is to follow Callum. People are already suspicious of me because I don't dress in Edith Head, didn't make paper chains out of rolls of cinema tickets at primary school at Christmas. And if you don't stop smiling, Harry Lawson, I'm going to ram that spoon down your throat. Don't you *care*? It's *your* town we're talking about that's going to be turned into some giant multiplex. It'll be like that George Lucas film, the one no one likes, what's it called, named his production company or something after it… '

Harry seemed more concerned with scraping the bottom of his sundae glass. He sat back, patted his stomach, dabbed his beard daintily with a napkin. Then his eyes became serious, determined.

'Of course I'm bothered. If there's anyone entitled to hold a grievance against Callum, it's me. The things he said about Alec after the fire, blaming him for it. Going back to what we were talking about before you started getting all maudlin,' mischievous again, 'I reckon after we dig out what's in the Tunnels, Callum's in for a nasty shock. A shock big enough to put his plans on hold for a very long time. So… are you in? Or are you going to carry on moping about like someone in a Mike Leigh film? And it's *THX 118*, since you asked.'

'Oh… tah. Underground? I dunno. The words 'wild' and 'goose' immediately spring to mind.'

'OK, fine. You give me no other option but to push your research buttons. Remember the Dominion plans? Well, follow me underground and you'll end up *inside* that old cinema.'

Bugger. The Dominion. The best ever cinema in Seacrest lost in the foundations of Callum Boyd's empire. Jo sighed, knowing she was too weak to offer serious resistance, watched the sugar finally break the surface and sink. 'All right. You've talked me into it. Only because I'm still drunk.'

'Excellent!'

'So who gets to be Sam Gamgee then to your Frodo? Me or Luke?'

'Tsk, daft question, *Luke* of course. How else are we going to generate all that homoeroticism? The way you're looking, Gollum's definitely – ooyah!' Harry reached under the table to rub his shin. '11pm next Saturday at The Moviegoer.' Harry winced. 'And I'll be sure to pack my shinguards.'

 # CHAPTER NINE

During the nights that followed Jo visited the Tunnels many times in her dreams. She'd wake with a start, heart pounding after being chased by some creeping, tentacled thing whose leering face flickered between Harry and Callum's.

Jo knew every inch of the town, every cinema's archive, basement, cleaning cupboard. If insomnia struck, she'd lie with her eyes shut and take a tour. Stroll past the Palais, the Phoenix, the Black Cat, duck down an alley, turn a corner, cross a junction and she was opposite the Alhambra, Kiss and Tell movie magazine and poster shop on her right. Plonk her blindfolded anywhere in Seacrest and she'd be able to tell you from the sounds, the smells, where she was. Obsessive? Jo? But the Tunnels... they were her terror incognita. She'd been down there a couple of times but ever since that trip with the Diaboliks...

Harry had invited her to one of the Diabolik underground screenings not long after arriving. It had been a nice gesture, lovely actually, being granted honorary Diabolik status for one night. She'd met Harry and the rest of them at the back of the lido next to some huts storing pool cleaning equipment. Beside those, a raised slope of concrete with wide wooden yellow-painted doors set into it. Passing by you'd think it some sort of coal bunker, file it away as a useful hiding place in the event of hurricanes, nuclear weapons, alien attack. Those in the know would recognise the yellow as exactly the same shade as the seagull's beak on the Seacrest sign, thereby indicating a Tunnel entrance. Jo knew of five of them but Harry assured her there were plenty more. Find overlooked, borderline places and there they were portals to another world.

As they'd waited for everyone to turn up, Harry ticking off names on a sheet, Jo had begun to wonder if her joining was such a good idea. She had no idea where they were actually going, Harry the only one who had that information, arguing that the less they knew the less chance the police had of finding out and charging them with trespass. It wasn't so much his control freakery that was getting to her as the freakiness of some of the other Diaboliks.

Most were wearing masks. Some had opted for a loose-fitting black hangman's affair while others had aimed for a more tasteful look with blank white Venetian masks last seen in *Eyes Wide Shut*. This did little to calm her fears concerning the evening ahead. Dull, slow-moving orgies with Eurotrash anyone? Even the Zorro-types looked less jaunty, more *American Psycho*.

To take her mind off her concern she'd signed up to some weird Goth pot-holing sect, she started chatting with one of the be-masked types about an Elvis article she'd written. They were discussing *Viva Las Vegas* and she was trying to work out if they were one of the lido instructors she'd admired from afar, attempting to match the muffled voice to tannoy announcements instructing those with green rubber bands to leave the pool, when Harry shouted out 'Right! Diaboliks, time to move off!'

He and another Diabolik heaved open the doors. There it was and Jo knew she would have no choice but to join them. The smell. Over-riding the stench of chlorine was a perfume unique to the Tunnels. It was like… an old library doused in sea-water, a fishing-boat house stuffed to the rafters with newspapers, a harbour log-jammed with floating timber. But muskier, sexier. There was an underlying enticing chemical note and a sigh of recognition went up round the group when they caught it. Film. The unmistakable, tantalising aroma of celluloid.

'Come on you lot, stop dithering, cops will be on to us like bubblegum on the heel of a fat man!'

They trooped after Harry into the dark, beams of light from Valiant torches flailing initially, skin tingling from the slam of the doors behind them. There was no time for polite chit-chat now, the light of her torch quickly trained on the back of the person in front of her because the thought of becoming distracted and wandering off to find herself alone in the dark, prey to ridiculous thoughts of Minotaurs or underground mutant cannibals…

After what felt like hours of shuffling they stopped, the group bunched up at a doorway standing in a semi-circle around Harry, torch beneath his chin, grinning at them like something from the imagination of Roger Corman. The door he was standing in front of was disappointingly non-descript; sloppily painted white, the wood underneath showing through in patches. Jo wished all those idiots would take their masks off to let her see if they looked as angry as she felt.

Standing there in the foosty dark, trying not to think about the small thing with claws that was scuffling in the shadows, she wondered how many others found Harry's ring-leader act annoying. Realised in the breathless quiet surrounding him it was probably just her.

'Ladies and gentlemen, so glad you could join me. We've a real treat in store, truly one of the seven wonders of Seacrest.' As Jo was working out what the other six were he shoved the door open, disappeared inside, leaving the rest of the group stunned, trying to make sense of what they were seeing.

Palm leaves and tendrils around the edges of the door and a wave of heat, a glass-house humidity drew them forward. After they'd brushed against the greenery, discovering it was plastic but convincing nonetheless, they saw the pool and then the moon on the wall behind it. An underground, indoor moon, Harry beneath it, smiling, the place bathed in its blue and violet light and that was when Jo started feeling dizzy. The heat, the uncanniness, scrabbling around in her head for something real to fix on and she focused and thought until she knew where they were. The Pharos.

The hidden swimming pool of the Pharos. A sea front hotel once famed as a rival to the Fulmar, closed and near-derelict for years. She'd assumed the people she'd interviewed about it had turned the memory of a dodgy mural and a few pot plants into something fantastic. But no, they'd been telling her the God's honest truth because here it was.

Three walls decorated tropical forest style, Rosseauesque, flamingos, toucans, monkeys, a tiger and jaguar lurking in the undergrowth, their glowing eyes some trick of the paint and that feeling, exactly as one interviewee had described of walking into some secret place with an audience watching, waiting, holding its breath. Movement, just visible, out the corner of your eye. Turn and it was gone. Probably some effect of the pool, lapping softly, underwater lighting turning it the turquoise of Seacrest bay.

And the fourth wall, the one that faced them when they entered, that squeezed the breath out of you. Arching palm trees framing a beach of white sand, a wide bay reflecting the full moon embedded in a deep blue sky dotted with starlight, its glow perfectly cold and bright, a moon to make Méliês weep and... hold on... yes. *That* was why it felt so familiar to Jo. The bay in the mural mirrored the contours of Seacrest. The same but its opposite. A reflection. The shoreline switched, re-imagined as some exotic paradise.

Jo walked round the pool to trace her fingers across the painted waves, enjoying the texture of glitter, the tips of her fingers sparkling. Perspective manipulated to create the impression of breakers breaking, surf ebbing and flowing and like the painted birds and animals decorating the other walls, they froze when Jo faced them straight on. Turn to one side, pretend to ignore it and there it was. A pulse of waves matching the beat of the swimming pool.

She was muttering to herself – 'How do they *do* that?' – didn't notice Harry sidle up alongside until he murmured, 'Do what?'. Taking care not to startle her, spoil the magic.

'The waves, moving. Can you see it? *now*, there, look I'm sure but… '

Harry gave a low whistle and he was smiling at her, looking as though he was both impressed and wondering if she was taking the piss. 'Might have guessed you'd be one of the 'special' ones. Not everyone sees it. Got to be a particular type of messed up brain. You and Shona both.'

Before she had the chance to ask him how many other secret places he'd taken Shona to, he was off, chasing two Diaboliks away from the projector, leaving her with a stupid sense of pride. Shona and her sharing a trait like that? Surely it was meant to be that they stayed together!

Yeah right…

The projector sat on a small Hawaiian-style bar in the far corner to Jo's right. It said something that even this, with its pineapple ice dispensers and Easter Island-head bottle openers, didn't tip the place into kitsch. It still felt like the set of some unseen Cocteau film. Harry was behind it getting the reels fixed and Jo couldn't help but think about his Dad. Against the wall opposite was a screen on a stand, in front of that, five rows of white plastic chairs, the light turning them Bauhaus sleek.

Most of the Diaboliks were sitting down, discussing von Sternberg's lighting techniques or the politics of Kurt Russell or whatever geek nonsense took their fancy. Jo sat at the back feeling suddenly self-conscious without a mask. So when the person next to her, some gay highwayman in a black eye-mask done up in sequins and feathers, turned to ask, 'So, *Solaris*...Tarkovsky or Soderbergh?' it was a relief to hear the whirring start behind her. Harry announced, his voice booming and echoing off the tiles, 'Fellow Diaboliques! I give you... *The Cat People*!' and Jo thought 'You *bastard*.'

This far underground, with her having no clue how to get back to the surface, of *course* he'd picked a film with terror round the edges. The black-and-white Tourneur original, it was a film that should be ridiculous. A B-movie reworking of *Jekyll and Hyde*, a woman fated to turn into a panther when her emotions were strong. Instead it was beautifully done, understated in its hints and glimpses of something evil lurking. Wild caged beasts pacing at the zoo, Simone Simon breaking the audience's heart as she fights her fate. The poor woman crying on a sofa, gaining our sympathy before her nails turn to claws, ripping the cloth. And the swimming pool scene. The reason Jo knew Harry had chosen it and she cursed him as a sadist.

That scene, a darkened pool empty apart from a lone swimmer, Simone's rival for love. Light ripples on the water, against the tiled walls, but you're not thinking about how it's done, the skill of the lighting technicians. You're absorbing the fear, the horrible vulnerability, the woman treading water, her cries increasingly frantic, desperate as she becomes aware of the unseen beast prowling, circling, snarling distorted by the poolside echoes.

The intensity of the film and the audience about her, the heat, no escape from what they were watching, unable to turn her head away to remind herself of the safe surroundings of a cinema. Jo would look away from a darkened swimming pool on screen to see... a darkened swimming pool.

Jo lost it, that sense of boundary between fantasy and reality, and was hit by what felt like claustrophobia and vertigo combined. She felt dizzy, then faint and all she could do was sit there like an idiot with her head between her knees, hands over her eyes praying it would stop.

Harry was kind. Next thing she knew he was crouching next to her, hand on her shoulder, whispering, 'Jo, you OK?' When she came to, saw how concerned he was holding a glass of cool water, she could have kissed him. 'Yeah, fine,' was all she managed before another wave of panic hit as she desperately wanted open space and fresh air and realised how far away those things were.

'I can take you out, it's no problem, there are folk here who'll be able to take the others back,' Harry offered and that brought her back to her senses. The thought of being ushered out like some kid overwhelmed by their first visit to the cinema. 'No, honestly I'll be fine.' And she was, eventually. Harry pulled his chair next to hers, the bulk of him beside her good. A marker between the world on the screen and the world down there.

So yes… we can understand now why Dr Ashe was not at all thrilled to be standing outside The Moviegoer's door that Saturday night with the prospect of a return visit before her. After several squirts of Bach Rescue Remedy and a few deep breaths, calling on the spirit of Jodie Foster for strength, she was through and in, half blinded by the dazzling pleasures of 'Scarlet Ladies Night'.

Any other night Jo, dressed in a manner resembling a Girl Guide leader about to lead a troop up Ben Nevis, may have attracted amused glances. Tonight the clientele had other sights to keep them occupied though, ones that didn't appear to be sponsored by camping equipment suppliers.

Red glitterballs sent ruby sequins of light spinning around the rough stone, red light-bulbs turned corners of the bar into scenes from Scorsese at his most baroque. After squeezing past a cigarette girl he recognised from the Regal dressed as Scarlet O'Hara – 'Oops, sorry, my torch', 'Yeah, yeah, heard it all before, you're just pleased to see me' – Jo's attention was taken up by the Jane

Russell and Marilyn performing on the tiny stage.

They were singing a slower, sexier version of 'Two Little Girls from Little Rock', wearing the same red-sequined, figure-hugging dresses as appeared in *Gentlemen Prefer Blondes*. It wasn't only the clothes that matched, the charm and chutzpah was there too with the thinnest coating of irony preventing it becoming just another tribute act and turning it oddly poignant.

Not for the first time at a Seacrest cabaret Jo found herself wondering what gender she was looking at up there and if it really mattered? She was pretty sure one of them was Karl but in that dress with those curves… surely not. Nothing fake could wobble so convincingly. But what did it matter, really? If they *were* men then yes, it did make the impersonation even more impressive, a further level of fakery. Which reminded the audience what a construct Marilyn was, turning herself into a fantasy, losing her 'self' in the process. The person up there was probably more 'Marilyn' that Norma Jean ever was… or was Jo over-analysing things in an attempt to distance herself from the fact that she found whoever was up there attractive and if they were a man it meant…but that Jane Russell, the jaw-line, the shading round the chin, it can't –

'Hey, don't want to ruin your Saturday night or anything but once you've stopped gawping we need to get moving.'

'Harry, I wasn't *gawping*, I was observing a very interesting post-modern treatment of celebrity with… '

' …great tits and ass. Fine, whatever, but save your theories for later. Luke's acting even more of a nutcase than usual, need you to calm him down.'

'What? *Me* calm him down? How am I supposed… '

But Jo was talking to Harry's back as he strode towards a cushioned alcove where Luke sat bolt upright, weird half-smile on his pale face, shining. 'Jeeeeezus', Jo breathed. It looked like he'd been filmed in high definition, everyone else on video.

Possessed and luminous. What had he got to be so cheery about? she wondered. Carrying on with Harry when he should have been defending the town against Callum…

The full horror of that Consortium meeting returned to her along with her anger at Luke's absence, intensifying until by the time she'd reached their table she was furious, the surrounding red glow perfectly matching her mood.

'Jo! Great to see you! I was saying to Harry I hoped you would turn up, wasn't I, Harry? Wouldn't have been the same without you, always meaning to say how much I enjoy it when you come out to the Archive and we have one of our chats, and… '

No wonder Harry was keen to get going if *this* is what he'd had to put up with until she'd got here. The only thing more disturbing than Luke in expert mode was him being cheerful, gabbling away like Robin Williams on speed.

'What the hell d'you think you're playing at Luke? Huh? And don't look at me with those puppy dog eyes, you know *exactly* what I'm on about. The Consortium. Callum. Did you not see the report in the *Gazette*? Hasn't this big oaf told you?'

'Ah… Jo,' Harry broke in, 'maybe you could sit down, hon, eh? You're drawing a bit of attention and… '

'*Hon*'?' For one brief, glorious second a total silence seemed to descend as Jo discovered just how fantastically withering she could be. Even Harry shrunk back and seeing this, shocked by her new found power, Jo relented. Sat down, kept her voice low as a Michelle Pfeiffer carrying a miniature piano took to the stage.

'Luke… I'm sorry, I'm disappointed, that's all. Thought you'd more *sense*. I was there at the meeting, hung-over, useless when it was decided when the vote for the plans would take place. Everyone cheering Callum on and what made me sick to my stomach wasn't the tequila the night before but knowing that if you'd been there it would have been different. Because when you're on form you remind the owners of what Seacrest is all about. Because you're *them*. When they were younger, when all they cared about was films. Not just about business, about bums on seats. You remind them that the only important thing is showing the punters some *wonder*. Magic.'

Remarkably Jo's words seemed to have an effect. Luke's aura was dimming, fading with his smile. It was replaced by an expression she recognised from afternoons when they'd gone to see a matinee together; they'd leave the safety of the cinema, blinking in the cruel light of a Wednesday and she'd be shocked by his confusion. The real world rushing in, overwhelming him.

Bugger. Had she gone too far? Jo reproached herself as Luke cast his head down, fiddled with a box of matches. She looked away, back up the length of the club and that was when she saw it, cursed herself for not noticing it before. Luke's audience, the rubber-neckers, those who would slow down to get a better look at a pile-up, to peek through the ambulance doors. Looking over, pointing, whispering, laughing. Even *here*, in the previously safe surroundings of The Moviegoer.

Harry had got it wrong. It wasn't Luke's messianic glow drawing attention but the release of a feeling that had followed him for years. The sense there was something not quite right either with him or the story he'd come to town with, of Cameron Fletcher being dead and him the one charged with maintaining the great man's legacy. Now those suspicions were being proved right. Luke's life blown apart by – the irony of it – Cameron Fletcher himself.

Jo turned away disgusted to find herself confronted by a Luke back on full beam. Where had she seen that look before? Oh yes, documentaries about David Koresh. The Unabomber. Kamikaze pilots.

'Jo, believe me, I had every intention about going to the meeting, of making a stand. But after I'd spent time with Harry' – who was suddenly devoting a high degree of concentration to pulling apart a coaster – 'I realised Cameron Fletcher is so much *bigger* than the Consortium, than Callum Boyd. To go along to that meeting would have been like admitting defeat, telling them that they're *right* to think they're the ones who hold power in this town. I know this is going to sound daft, crazy even' – Jo laughed in a 'You? Luke Howard? Crazy? The very *idea*' sort of way – 'but I do believe when I meet Fletcher he'll understand and he'll *see*. Especially after we show him what we're going to dig up tonight, then… '

Harry snapped, 'Right, can it, eejit. Fucksake, instead of you shooting your mouth off about our wee', he checked no one was eavesdropping, whispered it, 'treasure hunt howsabout we get on with it. You ready Jo? Brought your crampons?'

'God, the things I'd rather be doing at this moment… plucking my eyebrows, filling in a self-assessment tax form, having major surgery under local anaesthetic… '

'Oh, stop your moaning. An evening of fun, adventure and mild claustrophobia awaits.'

Harry led them down a corridor towards the toilets where, half-way down, stood a non-descript yellow door Jo had never noticed before.

He stood, hand poised on the handle, as serious as Jo had ever seen him, serious enough for her mouth to dry, her heart to stutter and she wished she'd told someone where she was heading before she'd left her flat. 'There's something I want to make *absolutely* clear before we get started. Before we head down there and face… whatever it is that's down there I want it agreed…I'm Shaggy, you're Velma – hey! With those glasses and that polo-neck, you're asking for it. And Luke's Scooby Dooby Dooooo… '

And the door creaked open to Jo's gasp, Harry's 'Yah beauty' and Luke's quiet, intense and unsettling 'Yeeeesssss'.

CHAPTER
TEN

In her typically perverse way Jo was almost disappointed by what they found behind the secret Moviegoer door.

Instead of cramped stone passages with walls dripping subterranean slime this stretch resembled a deserted hospital, an abandoned school. Musty with a canteen-and-plimsoll smell to it, the lighting dim. Black-and-white checked lino, high walls painted institutional green to half-way then a light Seacrest yellow. The occasional filing cabinet or office-desk dotted about. Long curving corridors, dipping and rising, granting the place a woozy perspective, an Alice-in-Wonderland feel.

'Oh.' This is ridiculous, she thought. She should feel relieved she wasn't in the sort of place Indiana Jones got trapped in with a screaming female and several thousand insects for company. Instead she was left feeling a right idiot trying to put a bloody strappy head-light thing on.

Harry was about to vanish round a corner followed by Luke when he caught sight of her struggles with an elasticated headband. 'Jo, if you're going to be stop and stare every step of the way, pause to take notes in your fecking Moleskine or whatever, we're going to take forever. Stop faffing about and get a move on. We've a secret to find' and then he and Luke disappeared.

'Hey wait! And what's so very wrong with Moleskine notebooks, eh?'

Trotting after them, stuffing the redundant light back into her rucksack, Jo realised the only way she was going to get through the next few hours without killing Harry, thereby forcing her to kill Luke as the only witness, was if she treated the experience as a research mission. For *her* benefit rather than as one of Harry Lawson's trusty side-kicks. So come on girl. Focus.

This was the oldest part of the Tunnels, cut into the cliffs by robbers, brigands, smugglers and thieves back in the 1700s. Come the twentieth century and cinema owners had taken over, using them to store junk or run illicit drinking and gambling dens until they were commandeered, cleaned up and expanded by the Government during the Second World War. The odd atmospheric conditions and acoustics of Seacrest Bay had been of interest to the Powers That Be. Unusual acoustics had been experimented with by military communications experts, ministers keeping a close eye on the Studio's propaganda output. There were rumours George Orwell had paid a visit. Jo passed wooden, glass-panelled doors with name plates still attached, an intriguing mix of military and sinister show-biz. Lieutenant Harrison, Commander of Division Surveillance, Jack Kopple, Disguise Advisor (Make-up and Costumes), Professor Birtwhistle, 'Military Acoustic Research'…

The Tunnels pushed further in under cliffs and the town. Seacrest had been thought a prime target for German bombers but no bombs fell on the Fulmar or the lido. Then there had been the famous Nazi memo discovered twenty years ago proving Goebbels had been a fan of the Seacrest Follies, the Technicolour musicals produced here, the town to be his once the war was over. His 'Playground of film' he called it, sure it would be tempting enough for Dietrich and Fritz Lang to forget their morals. Jo couldn't help thinking of Callum in jackboots, imagining he would have fitted right in.

Old documents had been left lying on the floor and Jo didn't care if Harry shouted at her, she was having a look. 'Recent Experiments in Acoustic Transmission', 'Radical Listening and Visual Devices', 'The Use of Radio Puppetry in Child-targeted Propaganda.' She could include these in an appendix perhaps – oof!

'Harry! Could you watch where you're going?'

'Where *I'm* going? Think you'll find the eejit who did the walking into the back of another, nose stuck in a bunch of crumbly papers, was *you*.'

She was annoyed by Harry having the gall to shake his head as she gathered up scattered documents, Luke peering over his shoulder, tutting, like they were a cheap-rate, unfunny Laurel and Hardy tribute act. She could see the end of this little adventure perfectly, Luke scratching his head in tears while Harry harrumphed, 'Another fine mess you've… '

'Right, now you're *sorted,* we can get into the Tunnels proper. Gentlemen! Please adjust your headsets.' Both he and Luke pulled their headlamps on at a speed that suggested they'd been practicing. Jo managed to trap an ear that was rescued by some deft fiddling from Harry.

They were mid-way along a corridor next to a plain white door you'd expect to find detergents, brooms, buckets behind. When Harry opened it the contents were revealed as a long darkness and the same Seacrest scent Jo experienced on her trip with the Diaboliks. This time richer, more intense, redolent of old damp cinema seats, rotting admission tickets, clouds of candyfloss, the seaweedy stench of a bay at low tide. It made her want to gag and soak her lungs in it. The three of them were quiet, convinced that down there, underground, was *alive* in some way, the films and cinemas and people up top this creature's dreams. They switched on their lights simultaneously as if illuminated by the same bright idea.

Jo edged toward the threshold, peering in at the lack of linoleum and overhead lighting. This was more like it, the place living up to her nightmarish expectations. Stone walls damp and narrow enough to reflect the light from her head-torch, buzzing, flickering light-bulbs offering intermittent light. Even Harry hesitated and it was Luke who stepped forward, straight into the murk and when he turned to wave them in – 'Great, some proper exploring!' – his smile was as dazzling as the light on his forehead and Jo remembered something Shona had said about the Tunnels being Luke's ideal environment. Dark, obscure, cinema-cluttered.

'Well, you heard the boy', muttered Harry, following at the same brisk pace causing Jo to call after him, 'Thought *you* were leading this expedition?' She stayed where she was until the thought of having to navigate back to The Moviegoer alone forced her in.

Right. Stay calm, she told herself, imagining she was in *Star Trek* and these were ventilation shafts and any minute now she'd bump into Kirk or Spock crawling in the opposite direction. Yes. Concentrate on that, perfect, would help take her mind off the strange gurgling noises coming from dusty pipes, the growth of frayed electrical wiring set at elbow-brushing height every now and again and the... *Christ!* Was that a gorilla?

And it was. The beam of her torch flashed across the glaring yellow eyes of a gorilla caught in a head-lock by a cheerful Luke. Jo stared as her light raked the cinema storeroom, one of many that branched off from this section of the tunnel network. Practically all the cinemas had one, nicknamed by staff members as 'The Thirteenth Floor' or 'Norman Bates' Hidey-Hole'. The sort of cellar-like space nervous newbies were sent down to for a box of haggis-flavoured popcorn or Invisible Man face-masks only to find their supervisor in a Freddy Krueger outfit lurking in the shadows.

'Recognise it? The Scala, remember? The King Kong display?'

'Oh yeah! I *knew* that was too good for them to chuck. Thought for a second you'd grabbed Harry,' Jo laughed as Luke released his grip on the hairy beast, flicking one of the small toy planes encircling Kong's head held in place by fishing line. 'Where *is* Harry by the way? Shouldn't we… '

'Oh, he's up ahead somewhere, told him I'd only be a couple minutes. I mean, *look* at this place… whatever we're looking for is still going to be there after we've had a rummage here. Hey, excellent! 3-D glasses!'

It was too much of a temptation not to explore and, after a nervous glance further up the empty tunnel, Jo joined Luke, stepping gingerly over a pile of *Screen Star Monthly*, ankles brushing against and knocking over a cluster of Gizmo Gremlin soft-toys that began mewling eerily. A cardboard cut-out of a pink C3PO, a stack of plastic R2D2 rubbish bins, a box full of size triple-G bras courtesy of a Russ Meyer season and framed posters of long forgotten B-movies – *Werewolves From Venus*, *Devil Woman From Mars*, *Electroman Vs Fusion Girl – Their Love is Atomic!*

Harry loomed suddenly in the doorway. 'Hoi, you two! If we don't get to where we're going in an hour or two then we're *fucked* so come *on*. *Bloody hell*, it's like having a couple of eight-year-olds, numpties.'

'Numpties? Did it ever occur to you that some people might be grateful, might appreciate their friends following them on some wild goose chase? What d'you mean we have to be there by a certain time? What's going to happen if we're not?' Jo snapped back, realising too late she was punctuating each point with the fluffy banana she was holding. Looking to Luke for back-up was no good, absorbed as he was in studying a poster for *Amazonian Women of Uranus* in 3-D specs, breathing 'These *actually* work…'

'OK, so *he's* a numpty and I'm… putting the banana down. But an explanation would be nice.'

'Yes, OK, *fine*. In about ten, fifteen minutes we'll be at the Shooting Gallery. We'll take a break there and I'll explain. But can we get moving now, *please*, instead of fannying about?'

There was a desperate tone to his voice that shocked Jo, made her feel guilty about dawdling. She nodded and grabbed Luke by the shoulder, steering him away from Amazonian cleavages and back out to follow Harry's footsteps, his angry muttering.

Getting to the Shooting Gallery felt an awful lot longer than ten minutes to Jo, negotiating the detritus of The Old Queen Mary's basement. A cinema decked out in a nautical theme, up there visitors could sip on cocktails in the Starboard Bar, play a game of quoits or shuffleboard before going to watch *A Night To Remember*, *In Which We Serve* or *Titanic*. While the pipes above them vibrated to Celine Dion going on and on and on, Jo tripped over a coil of rope, nearly brained herself on a hefty brass bell, stubbed her toe on an anchor, narrowly avoided being impaled on a harpoon.

It was therefore a relief – a *harpoon* for Chrissake – to push through a plastic strip curtain still swinging in Harry's wake and enter the wide open space of the Shooting Gallery where strip-lights stuttered into life. The sweet pleasure of stretching her arms, lifting her head without fear of dunting it on some piece of junk and… wait. This place was… weird. *Seriously* weird.

It was made odder by the way Harry and Luke were treating it as the perfect place for a picnic. They'd cleared a square of the floor of spent cartridges, airgun pellets, the odd arrowhead before spreading out a tartan rug, Harry pulling from his rucksack tin-foil wrapped sandwiches, chicken legs, pork pies, scotch eggs, bottles of ginger beer. Ginger *beer*? It was like an Enid Blyton as directed by David Lynch. *Five Go Mad In Blue Velvet*.

'See, you think you know Seacrest,' she murmured, 'think you've searched every nook and cranny… and then you find a place like this. Anyway, I thought we were in a rush?'

'Yeah, but you should always make time for food. You never been before?' Harry asked, his voice muffled by chorizo. 'This place is legendary. Everyone who cares about this place should pop down here at least once. Gives you a whole new perspective.'

'Yeah… makes you realise what a whole bunch of psychos they are up top.' Instead of joining the boys she wandered around the perimeter with her notebook, taking in as much as she could. Because it was not the sort of place she would want to visit twice.

The top half of the walls was the same green as the military section of the Tunnels, which made sense. Here the army could get in some target practice without frightening the locals. But not even *they* could keep a secret in this town and soon the locals wanted in. All those hours spent listening to the general public complain about the price of popcorn, the quality of the toilet facilities, kids leaving bubblegum stuck to the red carpet, no wonder employees were attracted to a place where you could blast things to buggery.

Evidence of the strength of this desire covered the bottom half of the two longest walls. Thick cork replaced the plaster, decorated with round targets of various sizes. The three largest had the standard bands of yellow, red, blue, black and white but surrounding them were many others in brilliant colours; gold and silver, copper and bronze, psychedelic pinks and greens, acid oranges and lemons. Jo made a quick sketch of their layout then shifted her attention to the back wall where stood the widest, tallest, most eccentric amusement park shooting booth that Jo, the *world*, had ever seen.

'Harry, did you have a hand in this? It's got the Kinotech written all over it.'

Harry nearly choked on a cherry tomato. '*Me*? Oh, I'd love to take the credit but no. Some other mad genius is responsible. I have added bits and pieces to it over the years. Couldn't resist.'

Lord, Jo marvelled. It was like a shrine to show-time violence. Anything you could ever want to take a pot-shot at was there. Pots and pans, cowboy hats, tin ducks, geese, pigeons, Tweeties, dodos, chipmunks, badgers… *badgers*? And – surely not. 'What *sicko* put Bambi in?'

A spluttering noise from Harry, Luke chuckling.

'You boys… ' She turned away from the Gallery to face them, hands on hips as if about to give them a stern ticking off, stifling a laugh. Which faded when she saw the wall opposite.

'This…this is why it was shut down, wasn't it? The Rogues Gallery.' She approached it slowly, hesitantly. As if there was a risk of contamination by getting too close. 'I've read about it but to *see* it. There's something quite upsetting about it.'

'Jo, you're such a *girl* sometimes. Where's your sense of harmless brutality?' Ignoring Harry's teasing, she took notes on the crowd of painted figures in front of her. A way of keeping distant from what it represented, what it revealed about the dark heart of the town above.

It depicted generic types, cartoon-like. The middle-aged woman in her floral cardigan complaining about the cheap soap in the toilets, the spoilt brat flicking chocolates from the balconies, the sleazy Grandpa who could make a Confectionery Girl's shift a misery. There was just enough detail to suggest these were real people, copied from experience.

And that was the problem, wasn't it? Some idiot took photos, they found their way into the national papers and there you had it. Several lawsuits, a steep drop in visitor numbers and… Jo hesitated… was that…

The suit, the lavender handkerchief. It *was*. Shit… she knew he was hardly Mr Popular but *this*…

While most of the figures were lightly pock-marked with bullet holes Callum Boyd was recognisable only from his clothes, his head obliterated by a frenzy of pot-shots. What little paint remained resembled a half-finished Francis Bacon.

'God… OK, so it's Callum but this is… shocking. Vicious.' She ran her hand over the space where his face should be, tracing what remained of a cheekbone, the eyes. Who'd have thought it? Jo

Ashe feeling sorry for Callum Boyd.

'Och, he deserves it.' In Harry's brusqueness Jo heard the echo of all those Seacrest citizens who'd taken aim and fired. 'Come and have your picnic before it gets warm. You were the one nipping on about an explanation for why we're down here so take a seat. Got a treat for you.'

'What, cheesy coleslaw?' she asked sceptically, sitting cross-legged on the rug, accepting a cup of flask tea from Luke.

'No, Dr Smart-arse, *this*.' Harry pulled a brown cardboard cylinder from his bottomless rucksack. 'I believe you've been wanting to get your sweaty fingers on these for quite while.' He popped the plastic top off as if it were a champagne cork before easing out a roll of thin paper.

'Wait, *wait* till you see this,' Luke whispered and as Harry unrolled the sheet, holding the corners down with a few pork pies, ensuring paper napkins were underneath, Jo whispered too. 'The *Dominion*,' the stillness surrounding them becoming reverential.

'Christ, you two. Only time you'd see other folk getting as excited as you two is if they were looking at something normal like… porn. You can get your jollies for a minute and then we're having a geography lesson.'

'The *balconies*. And look at the decoration in Screen Three! It's insane! Insane but wonderful… ' For a short, blissful time Jo strolled the plush corridors of best cinema Seacrest had ever seen. The archways, the colonnades, the fountains at the top of every staircase, the projectionist booth…

The Projectionist Booth.

'Harry. Your dad. You said something in Bernies. We're down here because of him, is that right?'

He nodded. 'I did indeed, Dr Ashe', taking a final bite of a chicken leg, Henry VIII style. Chucking the bone aside he produced from an inside coat pocket a square of folded paper.

'You also said we were going to visit the Dominion... but how? There's nothing left of it. Callum had it demolished completely, didn't want any relics left, gave some guff about how it was too painful a memory for the town to – hey! Are those for the Phoenix? How did *you* get *those*? If Callum knew you'd... '

'Jo, Jo, Jo.' Harry lifted the tissue thin plans of the Dominion and placed those of the Phoenix underneath. 'Think of the target practice behind you. How difficult would it be to find someone willing to give evidence against Callum. Hmm? Couple that with my way with the ladies and... '

'Yeah right, someone with a grudge I am willing to believe. That or someone handing them over to stop being pestered by you and your beard.'

'Charming. This is where we're going,' Harry mock huffed as he pointed to a rectangle at the back of the Dominion labelled The Vault.

'What? Stop being so bloody cryptic and *tell* me what I'm supposed to see here, I'm... '

'Look closer,' Luke interrupted. 'See what's underneath. Proof that what Callum's said about there being nothing left of the Dominion is a lie.'

'The *bastard*' Jo said, quietly. 'He *swore* to me, told me when I asked when he gave me the tour, the Grand Tour of the Phoenix, there was nothing left. But I had a feeling... I *knew*. Knew he was keeping something hidden.' There, under The Vault, was the only section of the plans where the lines of the Phoenix matched those of the Dominion exactly. The one difference being its description, 'Storeroom'.

'Why would Callum want to keep that tiny bit? Right at the back, underground... doesn't make sense.'

She looked to Harry in appeal but he was frowning, staring at that small square of space. He wasn't angry with her, she didn't think, he was miles away, somewhere in the past... Jo, you idiot.

'Your Dad. Of course. That's where they found him. Trying to get into the Vault, his hands a mess because of the heat, that metal wheel he was trying to turn, trying to get to the safe, the money... '

Aw, *crap*. Harry's frown was most definitely directed at her now.

'No, wait, that's not what I meant. I mean, those were the stories but...'

'No, no, carry on. Always nice to hear just how well Callum *fucking* Boyd has managed to warp the minds of even supposedly intelligent types.'

'I'm sorry but... '

'But *what*? There is no 'but'. I know that's what most people in this town think but that's because they didn't know Dad. If folk took time to examine the *facts*' – Jo winced – 'researched things properly... '

'OK, I've said I'm sorry, now correct me. Tell me what really happened.'

Harry took a deep breath, his face fading from an angry puce. 'Right... well, as demonstrated there are some *idiots* who still think Alec was down there to sneak away the takings. And I suppose I can see why they think that. Why else would he be down there unless he was mad or greedy. But they forget the fire was on a Thursday night. Dad was found there at about 9.30pm. The takings for the week were taken away at 5.30pm every Thursday. Dad worked at the Dominion for twenty-five years, knew the runnings of the place as well his own projector.'

'So there was no money left to take. The safe was empty' Luke piped up causing Jo to roll her eyes at him being such a bloody teacher's pet.

'But that still doesn't make sense. All right, it does in the sense it means your Dad's not a thief, which we all knew anyway – don't give me that look Harry – but to risk all that, to ruin his hands, he must have been looking for *something* important, something valuable.'

Then she experienced the moment, that beautiful moment when revelation struck after hours of research. 'And Callum knows that too. That's why he kept that bit of the Dominion. He wants to find whatever it was Alec was after, what he'd risk his life for. And we're going to find it instead.'

'Fantastic! Give the girl a bloody big bunch of coconuts! Dad wasn't daft. I reckon he thought The Vault was the safest place in part because the safe was there. The perfect distraction. If anyone was going to nick anything they'd concentrate on that, not bother looking for anything else. So there you go, your explanation and why I was so keen to get a move on. At this rate it'll be morning by the time we get to the Phoenix, people starting to move about.' Harry motioned for the two others to shift off the rug, gathered up its four corners and in it, all the rubbish, and stuffed it into his rucksack.

'But' asked Jo, 'if it wasn't money, what was it? What exactly are we looking for?'

'Eh?' Harry kept himself busy with zips and getting his head-torch back in place, adding to his shiftiness.

'See, that's the exciting thing' grinned Luke 'we don't know. We're going to be the first to find out.'

'Luke, less chat, more action' growled Harry, pushing him along to a small hatchway that would take them to the Phoenix's basement.

'Wait a minute' said Jo, staying put. 'It's finally sinking in. You've not a clue what we're after, have you? Callum's been sitting on top of it for *years*, how do we know he's not already got it! That all we're going to find is a note in Callum's handwriting saying 'Too late suckers!' What was I *thinking*… trying to distract myself from the real problems of this town by burying my head in the Tunnels.' She clutched her stomach. 'I'm gonna to be sick. And cameras, he's bound to have cameras in there, will spot us straight away… '

Harry jogged back towards her, stopped a short distance away on seeing how green she was. 'Jo, listen. No cameras in the Phoenix, remember? That out of court settlement when they found the bugs in the staff toilet. But you're right, I won't deny it, we're chancing it. But I reckon, knowing what Callum's like, if he had found anything he wouldn't have kept the Vault intact. If he'd found whatever that place held he'd have knocked down walls, opened up more space for *his* cinema. To show he'd *won*, succeeded where Dad had failed. I admit I don't know what's down there but I do know my Dad. I know how his mind worked and I know one thing he would have risked everything for is a film. Stuff my Mum's said… I reckon someone, someone important, trusted him to keep a film safe and he was doing his best to make sure that happened. So are you with us Jo?'

The look on his face, eyes shining. Because of tears? Excitement? Jo sighed. How could she turn back? The thought of Alec running back into a burning building to save… what? Well… whatever they were going to find. But why was she suddenly wishing Shona was there? Here to hold her hand, pull her forward, be braver than she could ever be…

'OK. You've convinced me.' Jo heaved her bag on to her shoulder. 'Lay on Macduff.' She couldn't help smiling back at Harry beaming in response. Yes, he was a bugger, but a charming bugger and she'd follow him wherever he wanted to go. Who else was there to trail behind, with Shona away?

# CHAPTER ELEVEN

'You are *kidding* me. It's a human cat flap! The splinters we're going to get crawling through here…If I get a septic hand, Harry Lawson, I'm going to make you type for me. And spiders, you can bet there are going to be spiders, thousands of them, this is the sort of setting they have their *conventions* in. The only people skinny enough to get through there are Instagram influencers and…oh I dunno, Luke.'

Jo stood next to Harry, both holding open the heavy wooden hatchway door, contemplating the worn soles of Luke's shoes disappearing into the narrow tunnel. This entrance to the Phoenix reached the top of their knees and then only just.

'See, now Jo, if you could put all that energy you're using to moan into helping me keep this bloody thing open…What you looking for now?' asked Harry through gritted teeth. 'Come on, I'm getting a hernia here!'

'Checking to see we haven't missed a bottle with 'Drink Me' on the label. Keeping an eye out for white rabbit droppings and…hey! How'd'you do that? Great. Thanks,' the weight of the door having increased suddenly as Harry had ducked down and disappeared. Using her rucksack as a prop, she tried to ease herself into the crawlspace.

'So – *Jesus* – this thing is heavy… the last thing I see… God, really have to get to the gym more… trapped so many feet below ground… will be Harry Lawson's giant bum. Just… fantastic.'

The tunnel wasn't as narrow as the entrance suggested, enough room for Harry to turn his head and say, 'I'll have you know there are plenty of women who would be perfectly happy to have my arse as their last view on earth.'

'Ewww... You absolutely sure about that? I know Seacrest is home to some perverted types but *really*... It is *sooooo* dusty down here, either of you know what asbestos looks like? How much further is it? And where exactly does this lead to? Harry... *Harry*... right, *fine*.... you keep up the silent treatment, see if I care.'

Met with the indifferent swaying of Harry's bulk, Jo resolved to keep shtum, letting out only an 'Euch!' when she thought there was a spider in her mouth that turned out thankfully to be only a piece of fluff. She tried to work out where they would end up. They were heading towards the basement of the Phoenix and so... of course, the Memory Box!

How could she have forgotten her favourite place, Seacrest's centralised Lost Property store? Callum had puffed up the basement of the Phoenix as the safest place in Seacrest, fire and flood and nuclear war proof, the truth of it being it was another way of monitoring the town, even the stuff that slipped through the cracks. The detritus labelled and contained and catalogued with people having to come to *his* cinema to claim it back.

'Harry, how much further have we got?' she called out. 'Don't think my knees can take much more of this. Harry? Where's your arse gone?'

Harry was up and out, the torch-lit dark of the passage replaced by the square of grey light she was crawling towards. Once she was through, the surface under her hands changing from fluff-covered stone to smooth concrete, she could sense there was a high ceiling above her. It still took her a few seconds to trust the space, confused perhaps by the smell, a complex reek of old felt, wool, tweed and leather, shampoo, hair, Brylcreem, the sweat of a thousand foreheads. Eventually she raised her head, Luke and Harry hoisting her up by her elbows and the first thing she saw was – *HATS*!

A large metal sign, black letters on Seacrest yellow, hanging from the roof to their right. She burst out laughing until Harry shushed her. 'Keep it *down*!' he whispered. 'Old Smiler's patrolling. If he catches us we're stuffed.' He looked towards a group of unnervingly life-like mannequins, dressed as Seacrest tourists. 'Literally if that lot are anything to go by.'

'Sorry, it's just *that*,' Jo pointed to the sign, 'could be used as a dictionary definition of superfluous.' Harry, eyes flickering, keeping a look-out for the legendary night-watchman of Lost Property, couldn't help smile in agreement. Because they were standing in the middle of what appeared to be the store-room of the biggest, the *premier* hat-making factory in the world.

'Incredible… ' Jo knew they were supposed to be in a rush but not to stand and admire the display in front of them would be rude. To think of all the hundreds of people who had given up their headgear for *this*.

It felt like the lower-level of a multi-storey car-park where a car-boot sale had gone psychotic, obsessive. Rows and rows of metal shelves filled with mannequin heads – long-necked with a coolly appraising stare, red lips slightly parted – and hat boxes and stacks of clear plastic crates, their contents spilling out, perched on top of the boxes or stuffed into the space around then as if trying to return to their owners. Labelled alphabetically, 'BASEBALL', 'BERETS', 'BOATERS (STRAW)', 'BOBBLES', 'BONNETS', 'BOWLERS' 'CAPS (CLOTH), 'CLOCHES' through to 'PANAMAS' and 'PORK-PIES', 'SOMBREROS'. 'STETSONS', 'TRILBIES' and 'YARMULKES'.

Harry was gazing thoughtfully at one of those Peruvian woolly hats with assorted dangling pom-poms beloved of players of the penny whistle.

'Don't you dare,' warned Jo. 'Bet everything is recorded down here. Callum sees you wearing that about town he'll *know* you've been down here.'

'Christ, I wasn't going to *wear* it. I'm sure it's one I nicked off some dozy student a few years back. It was just after the Cinema Hat Ban had been, well, banned, remember? Some nonsense about human rights. Anyway, I go and see *Fargo* and this twat, instead of being outside playing hacky-sack with his hippie chums, sits in front of me wearing *this*… thing. Had it on the head of the Electrocuted Man in the Kinotech for a while after. Been wondering where it had got to.'

'See, under that jovial exterior you're actually a bit of a fascist,' Jo commented, disappearing into a small forest of hat-stands after admiring a row that resembled an exotic aviary, covered with flouncy, feathered affairs, then into a fur-lined darkness. It was like being transported into some Angela Carter story with benign wolves lurking. Running her hands over furry Russian hats – fox, mink, bear…and yes, it was awful and evil but so soft and sexy…

'Find any beaver?' Jo jumped – '*Christ*!' – Harry suddenly there, whispering hotly in her ear. He stepped back to grant her a full view of the ridiculously large, ridiculously camp peaked Russian Army General's hat he had on. 'Who you calling a fascist? I'm not the one wandering about getting all touchy feely with a bunch of dead animals.'

'Yes, thanks, for ruining the Narnia-like atmosphere with a dose of smut. Thought we were getting a move on.'

It was like a spell had been broken, Harry remembering why they were there, imagining Alec watching him now, disapproving. Jo, wandering past a tower of small pink cowboy hats and devils horns, saw him click into focus, snapping at Luke trying on a top-hat, his military bearing lending him authority.

'Hey! Peanut-head! Enough with the fancy dress, we're moving out. We stick close and we keep quiet. You're following me, no wandering off. Right? Comprende?'

Stifling an urge to salute, Jo and Luke nodded. 'And keep an eye out for Smiler. Remember the rumours. Killed a man with his bare hands during his SAS days.'

'Old Smiler?' responded Jo, incredulous, Harry having taken his hat off thereby losing all authority. 'He's not so tough, I've heard that scar he's got wasn't from a machete but an ex-girlfriend with a grudge and a sharpened nail-file. He was with us on the tour Callum gave me, making sure I was under strict supervision. Seemed nice enough. OK, the tattoos were off-putting and I made damn sure I didn't wander off but I thought that was more Callum's paranoia than… '

Wearily, Harry backtracked a few paces. 'Jo, can you *please* stop blethering on and remember that technically what we are doing is breaking and entering. So unless you want to add a police record to your CV shut up and walk softly. Now… aww for fucksake, where's Luke?'

Edging out of 'HATS', they peered down one of the passageways to see Luke waving back at them beneath a sign reading:

UMBRELLAS –
Section III: Ladies – clear and decorated
leading to
UMBRELLAS –
Section IV: Gentlemen's –Wooden handles/ automatic opening

'Looks as though Luke's taken on board all that advice about being discrete and not attracting attention,' Jo smirked as they trotted towards him.

In Seacrest the degree of truth in the tales that made up the legend of Smiler, Protector of Lost Property, could never be fully determined; that between army missions he would pay a visit to the pubs around Ibrox in a Celtic top, his drunken stand-off with a tram, the tram coming off substantially the worse-for-wear, although the story about him punching a Rottweiler was so odd Jo suspected it to be true. Here though, in the bizarre underworld of the Memory Box, with Harry making clear through the use of offensive mime how Luke's behaviour could put them at risk, she felt the stories having an effect. Old Smiler's presence was everywhere, turning her skittish, palms sweaty, breath short, wishing for the relative safety of the Tunnels. This was Smiler's labyrinth and they were caught up in it.

Twenty minutes later and it felt like a nightmare, Harry assuring them they were nearly there only to turn a corner and face a section featuring several hundred 'Purses and Wallets', 'Coats and Jackets' or 'Cardigans.' Cardigans, Jo tutted, I ask you. If ever there was an indication of the average age of a visitor to Seacrest. And it was proving difficult, having to squish her researcher's instinct. She could spend hours down there rummaging through boxes of lost diaries, pens, keys and jewellery. The melancholy of the place, stuffed to the gills with ephemera, some of the objects all that was left of their owners, what there was to remember them by. Bits of 'Medical Equipment and Supplies' …how on earth could someone forget a colostomy bag? Or *not* notice they'd left an artificial leg?

And where was that sound coming from? Like birdsong muffled and that *smell*… no, Jo thought, you have *got* to be joking. Surely the SSPCA would have something to say about *this*.

Jo paused, mouth agape, beneath a sign reading 'PETS – Section I: Exotic – Reptiles'. She noted where Harry and Luke were heading further up the walkway, taking a left into 'Pocket Handkerchiefs'. A couple of minutes couldn't hurt, could it? She remembered Smiler mentioning there had been some deal with Customs and Excise and the Seacrest Petting Zoo that had closed down a few years ago. Nowhere else to put them she supposed, peering into glass tanks where slow-moving snakes slid and coiled, lizards flickered across rocks and an iguana the size of a small cat gazed back at her with a supercilious 'Yes? Can I help you?' expression.

It was then, on reaching the end of the 'Reptiles' section leading into 'Exotic: Birds', Jo let out a scream worthy of any B-movie horror heroine.

What had given her such a shock was a huge scarlet macaw housed in a large brass cage. On sight of her it began flapping its wings, screeching out, 'Red Rum! Red Rum! Makes Jack a dull boy! Makes Jack a dull boy!' setting off a chain reaction of twittering budgies, yowling cats and barking dogs.

'Shit!' was Jo's response once she'd recovered, her panic not helped by the arrival of Luke and Harry, Harry as red-faced as Luke was pale. 'Jo! You all right? Fuck's sake, what've you done? Luke, go and find a fire alarm and set it off, eh? In case anyone within a five mile radius doesn't know we're here.'

'Could you maybe stop being so bloody sarky and give me a hand with this? *Please*? So I know this is my fault but at least I'm looking for a solution.' Jo was wrestling with a dark grey blanket left folded at the base of the cage, trying to heft it over the hysterical bird 'Makes Jack a dull boy! Makes Jack a dull boy!'

'That'll make two annoying birds on this trip then' muttered Harry as he took hold of two corners of the blanket. After a lot of huffing and puffing they covered the cage, the macaw's panicked cries slackening to a raspy croaking.

Standing silent, waiting, armpits itching, they listened for the heavy tread of Smiler's footsteps. But nothing. No heavy hand on the shoulder, no wailing of police sirens. Amazing. Harry and Jo were about to share a quietly triumphant 'High-five' when from beneath the blanket came a creaking and oddly gleeful

'Heeeeeeeerre's Johnny!'

The three looked at each other, then at the cage and then, slowly, delaying the terror for as long as possible, at the scarred, tattooed man behind them.

'Quiet there, Stanley,' Old Smiler said in his whisper of a voice, larynx damaged by a pub bet involving the eating of five light-bulbs and a bottle of Newcastle Brown Ale. The parrot started crooning gently to itself. 'Now... what do we have here?' Smiler let the long-handled torch he'd been holding upright fall from one hand into the palm of his left with a slap that sounded ominously like a fist making contact with flesh.

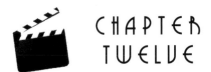 CHAPTER
TWELVE

Jo gulped, a sound that seemed so comically loud to her she expected to hear it ricochet back from the walls. She hadn't felt so terrified since school, when the headmistress called her into her office to find out *exactly* what she'd been doing with Ruth Parkington in the trees behind the playing field, and wondered if fainting might help.

She was discovering how weird the brain went under extreme stress. There they were, on the brink of arrest and Jo couldn't help thinking how impressive Old Smiler looked in his navy blue uniform. Like a scarier Robert Shaw with that scar extending from his right ear to the corner of his mouth, twisting the flesh, turning it into a perpetual sneer. There was definitely the air of a Bond villain side-kick about him with those pale blue eyes. She tried to remember, how old was he again? His sixties, *seventies* even? The material still straining at his shoulders to contain his bulk, well over six feet and she did find herself admiring his breast pocket badge, a lovely bit of embroidery, the Seacrest Seagull with wings outstretched over the Big Wheel. It was better to concentrate on that than the walkie-talkie clipped over the other pocket, fizzing and popping away and with Callum ready to listen at the other end no doubt. Christ… Jo realised she'd get chucked out of this town, stripped of her PhD, and started to hyperventilate.

Thank heavens for Harry. While the other two were proving useless, Luke trying to remember if there was some ancient Council by-law that disallowed a security guard from using excessive force,

Harry was letting his anger build, drawing on all those years in the Kinotech dealing with drunken idiots, pricks with attitude, neddy bastards and posh twats who'd start thumping a machine if it didn't pay out quick enough for them. It was like being a bloody bouncer at times. One good thing to come out of that hassle was he knew how to deal with a bully, a jobsworth who was going to try and stop him doing what he had come down here to do.

'Bugger… Harry's squaring up to Chuckles, isn't he? Shouldn't we be running away?' Luke whispered.

Jo was too horrified to reply, trying to dredge up memories of a first aid course she'd been on years ago as Harry was indeed taking up his battle-stance. Shoulders wide, back straight, feet firmly planted and there seemed to be *more* of him. Greater bulk, greater presence, Harry at his most *Harry* like.

Old Smiler's grin grew wider. He knew the signs, looked forward to their arrival at certain points during a night out. Someone brave or stupid enough to take him on. Happened less often these days but that meant he appreciated all the more the surge of adrenalin that came with seeing off a challenge. Just a crying shame it was Alec Lawson's son. No worries about the other two who were looking as though they'd be paying the 'Underwear' section a visit soon for some clean replacements. Harry could be awkward though. He had his father's stare.

Smiler addressed them all but held Harry's eye, his voice Corleone-quiet. 'What's the matter? Why so shy? Dr Ashe, these two,' Smiler waved his torch at Harry and Luke 'I would expect to find acting like idiots but you… you're an *academic*. I thought you were supposed to spend your time sitting at a computer being clever, not being led astray to take part in daft adventures. And you, Mr Howard. Considering the fuss in the *Gazette* about what's going to happen when Mr Fletcher gets here, I'd expect you to be keeping your head down.'

The tension in the air increased, Jo and Harry praying Luke wouldn't do something stupid, that he remembered as well as they did how useless he was in a fight. Thankfully Luke behaved. Grew even paler, his dark eyes darker, bony fists white at the knuckle but he kept still. Smiler kept smiling and shook his head slowly.

'You lot are bold enough to come breaking in here, giving poor Stanley here the fright of his life,' – the macaw piped up, 'Makes Jack a dull boy!' – 'stealing valuable property no doubt. But when you're caught you behave like a bunch of school-kids. *Pathetic*,' spat out with relish, his grin rising a notch on seeing the rage flare in Harry. Give the boy credit, he did a good job of keeping it under control, not doing anything silly. Smiler was almost disappointed. Nights could be hellish dull down there.

'Right,' he reached for his walkie-talkie. 'If I can't get you bunch talking then perhaps Mr Boyd can.' He pressed a button on its side, Jo and Luke stepping forward, shouting 'No!'

Harry said 'Duncan,' softly and Old Smiler released the button and froze.

'Duncan?' whispered Jo.

'His real name. Never heard of anyone say it to his face before,' Luke whispered back, eyes wide with awe. 'Harry's either being very, *very* brave or... when I give the word we make a break past the kittens'.

They tensed, getting ready to sprint when they saw a twist of annoyance tug at Smiler's scar. 'Eh? What was that?' his voice as cold as a November north-easterly.

'Stop playing silly beggars, Duncan Anderson. You heard me. You forgetting who my Dad was? That I remember you coming round the house every month to play poker? One of the few who kept turning up on our doorstep during the bad times?'

Something was happening to Duncan's face. It was losing its tension, becoming less that of a B-movie villain or an old lag in a Guy Ritchie film. It was turning into a guy in his later years remembering an old friend he still missed.

Harry moved forward until he was a torch's breadth away from Duncan's chest. Jo's mouth turned dry on seeing how he was dwarfed by the guard, held her breath as Harry's shoulders slumped, head falling forward, looking as tired as she felt. Then his head snapped back, looking Smiler in the eye, staring down the challenge.

'You know why I'm down here, Duncan. You *know* I wouldn't set foot in this place otherwise. I know what Callum would do to me if he found out. And *you* know the only reason I'd run this risk is because I'm doing something for my Dad. I'm doing this for Alec, Dunc. Trying to find out why he ran back into the Dominion, what he was looking for, what he wrecked his life for. Now. You can call Callum, bring him down here. I'm not going to stop you. Fuck knows,' Harry gave a short laugh, 'I wouldn't stand a chance. Like I say, I know you've had your problems with me, that Dad often felt I'd let him down but... I'm trying to make it up to him. If you help us, you'll be helping Alec.'

Once he'd finished the first thing that entered Harry's head was 'Shit. He's going to punch me and leave me for dead', as Duncan's eyes blazed with anger, a sight burned into the retina of others when they'd woken up hours later in hospital. Then there came a deep sigh as Smiler raised his eyes to the ceiling of the Memory Box.

He kept staring long enough for Harry to peer round at Jo and Luke, who mouthed at him, 'Round by the *kittens*. The *fire* exit' while pumping their arms up and down. The guard lowered his head, resting the end of his torch hard on Harry's chest, thumping it for emphasis.

'Harry Lawson, you are a chancer of the first order and if spending so many hours down here with only Stanley for company hadn't driven me mad, I'd be hauling you out of here and flinging you in front of Callum Boyd's desk. I want to make this very' – thud – 'very' – thud – '*very*' – *thud* – 'clear. I'm doing this *only* because your father was one of the best men I've ever met. To see that man at work, the way he treated that projector, the way he talked about films…' Duncan paused, looked away and for one horrible, sickening moment Harry thought he saw tears in his eyes. They were gone when he turned back, leaning in close enough for Harry to smell Murray Mints on his breath. 'But if I *ever* hear word of this slipping out, that I let you get on with whatever scheme you're up to, I'll give you three guesses where this torch is going to end up. And I *love* this torch.'

Harry nodded as Duncan backed off, pointing his torch at Luke and Jo, before disappearing off into 'Socks'. The three of them nearly collapsed with relief as Stanley started up with, 'Daisy, Daisy, give me your answer do… '

'Well then' said Harry as his two companions treated him to a brief round of applause. 'One good thing to come out of that is if I am ever unlucky enough to suffer constipation I'll just think back to the past few minutes and, there you go, cured. Now, let's vamoose our arses out of here before bumping into any more lions or tigers or bears.'

 CHAPTER
THIRTEEN

The encounter with Smiler having destroyed the urge to dawdle meant the rest of their journey was made in double-quick time. At the furthest end of Lost Property, they stopped at 'Ties and Scarves: Silk, Woollen, Cashmere.' In front of them was a back wall covered in rail upon rail of dangling ribbons of coloured material, a metal moveable ladder to their right, a long hooked pole leaning against it.

Jo shivered. It was like those shots on the news when some famous footballer had died and they showed the outside of a stadium, the ground in front of it covered with football scarves and shirts. Or those places in Tibet where travellers left a piece of themselves, a strip of material on a pole for good luck on a mountainside.

'Hey Jo, could you stop with the cultural analysis or whatever it is you're doing and help us out here,' came Harry's voice, muffled by a curtain of ridiculously long multi-coloured woollen scarves giving the impression a forgetful Tom Baker had visited the town regularly.

Luke called out from behind a revolving rack of bow-ties and cravats, 'See, this proves Callum doesn't want people poking their noses around what remains of the Dominion. Why else would he hide a storeroom behind this lot? We're looking for a metal door, Jo. A great big metal door like something you'd find in a bank vault with a combination lock in the middle of it and that's when we start hoping Shona gave Harry the right infor -'

'Hey, WOAH there, Mister! Back up!' cried Jo emerging angrily from a batch of ponchos – what the hell were ponchos doing there anyway! should be in overcoats or *somewhere* – as Luke buried himself amongst cravats, realising too late he'd revealed too much.

'*Shona*?' Jo shouted towards a section of moving scarves, indicating Harry's progress. 'God, I should have known she'd be involved somewhere but if she's coming over here to help out with the Festival, help her Dad out, being on his side, what's she doing telling *you* about bloody combination locks? On her Dad's property? How do we know this isn't some big wind-up? A trap, she *wants* someone to find us down here. Get us arrested, leaving the way clear for Callum and his plans! Harry. *Harry*. I know you can hear me, *answer* me.'

'Al-*RIGHT*!' bellowed Harry, breaking out from behind his woolly screen like some red-faced yeti. She jumped back, Luke leaping out too, his eyes fixed on Harry, knowing what could happen when one of his sudden rages took. Jo crossed her arms, stood her ground. She wasn't going to be intimidated by Harry Lawson even if he was doing his best Oliver Reed-as-Bill Sykes impersonation.

'Jo. Listen. I'm sorry.' The air around him vibrated with the furious energy he was holding back, an anger caused not only by flinging all those *bloody* scarves about but because Jo had managed to hit precisely on one of his own fears. That Shona was setting them up. 'I should have said right from the start Shona was involved but I was scared of... well, *this*. Your reaction. If you knew she had been helping, you wouldn't have come down here. Would you? And she only provided a *bit* of help. Not with the plans but with...information.'

Jo groaned, ran her hands through her hair, releasing a cloud of spider webs, the dust of old cinema tickets. 'Oh... I *suppose*.

Would've been nice to know that one of the people involved in this daft scheme is the *daughter* of the man we're trying to stop. Would have helped me make a more informed decision. Stopped me spending hours wondering when we were going to stumble across a toilet.'

'Why didn't you say?' asked Harry. 'I've got a plastic bottle in here that's got a top wide enough.' The look he got from Jo suggested she'd be able to hold on a while longer.

'And what's this about a *combination*. Are you *sure* Shona's given you the right set of numbers? Because she's got a pretty sick sense of humour. Probably had some spy camera installed so she could have a good laugh when that huge metal door stays shut and we're sat here crying.'

'Jo. I know your opinion of Shona is a little… skewed but believe me, I am willing to stake… I dunno, the Kinotech, my mum's life… no my *beard*,' – Jo and Luke gasped – 'that the numbers she gave me will get us in. Because who else would know, who else would Callum *tell*, they're the date his ex-wife first won the Miss Seacrest Beauty Contest and her stats for that year.'

Harry stroked his beard, assured he'd be keeping it for a while yet. Jo remained unconvinced, felt mildly sick at the thought of being confronted by his naked-face in the next few weeks. 'But Callum and Carol *hate* each other. She's always saying she became an alcoholic because of him, that she kept his name to remind everyone of the pain he caused. Why would Callum want to remind himself of the woman he calls Cruella de Vil, minus the fur coats and good looks?'

'Because,' Harry responded with heavy patience, 'each is as twisted as the other. These are the Boyds we're talking about. He'll get some sick kick out the fact that it's Carol, a woman who *loathes* him, who lets him into one of the places in this town he doesn't own completely, that hides something he wants.'

'Yeah, well, maybe.' Jo held up her hands, admitting defeat. 'We'll find out soon enough if... '

'Hey! Guys!'

A gap appeared in a soft pastel curtain of pashminas – 'I've found it!'

Luke shot out, triumphant. 'Behind here.' He started shoving the pashminas aside, Harry and Jo hefting them off in armfuls, until they stood breathless before a large red velvet curtain.

'Christ, he's even got the golden Phoenix crest shield thing at the top there,' Jo noticed.

Harry was too preoccupied with what lay behind it to comment. 'If you're bullshitting me, Miss Boyd... ' his heart pounding as he parted the red velvet to find a metal door that wouldn't have looked out of place on a submarine, in *Das Boot*.

Set into the wall about a foot above the ground, it was covered in flaking white paint, the raw metal exposed beneath a coppery shade of green. Damp had caused the edges and hinges to rust giving it an oddly organic appearance. This made the modern silver combination lock next to a hefty steel turnwheel look all the more incongruous but Jo's eyes were drawn to the paintwork at the bottom of the door. Bubbled and blistered, the Dominion bricks beneath were charred and blackened and to think what would have happened to a man's *hands*, turning that wheel, red-hot in the heat.

Instinctively, she put a hand on Harry's shoulder and when he faced her, and she saw his expression, pain mixed with determination, she knew he was thinking the same thing. His *Dad* down there, trying to shift that metal turnwheel, sparks flying, smoke choking...

'Right,' Harry snapped. 'Let's get on with it.'

He shook his shoulders, blew on the fingertips of his right hand. 'Is that actually going to help?' snorted Jo, 'Is that the first lesson they teach at safe-cracking school?' Harry continued his routine unperturbed, cracked his knuckles, rested his fingers delicately on the dial and his ear against the door while he kept up the mantra, 'Come on Carol, come on yah old alkie raving lunatic… '

It was only once he stopped with a 'There… ' Jo realised she hadn't been breathing. 'Here goes bugger all.' After spitting on his palms he grasped the wheel, trying to turn it and when it became apparent he was experiencing a horrible resistance, Luke and Jo joined him, squeezing in beside him, grabbing the wheel, using their combined force to get it turning, slowly at first, complaining then spinning freely to their combined cheers and Harry's 'Yah BEAUUUUUTY', before pulling the creaking, complaining door open.

There followed a short period of merriment before the smell of the Vault hit them. It smelt as tomb-like as it looked, just wide enough for the three of them, releasing the sort of draught that would have had Dracula sniffing with relish. 'Pewww!' said Jo, wafting her hand in front of her face. 'Like Zombie-breath that'.

'I think you'll find Zombie breath has a more meaty quality to it,' replied Luke, face unnervingly straight.

'Okaaaay,' said Harry. 'I *could* ask you how you came about that bit of knowledge… ' Instead he stepped through the doorway of the Vault, peering in as if waiting for some Mummy to lurch towards him, arms outstretched –

Jo yanked at his arm, causing him to shriek.

'Jesus *Christ*, Jo, what you trying to do? I'm a big lad who doesn't exercise, can't be doing with unexpected shocks!'

'Don't you think we're risking it here? How do we know Callum hasn't got it rigged up so there's an alarm flashing in the police station? Or as soon as we're in there the door slams shut and we're trapped until the next gang of intrepid muppets comes exploring?'

'Jo. If Callum had this place rigged up we'd be in jail by now. There'd be great big bloody cages crashing around us or the walls closing in or we'd be running away from a boulder. I know this probably isn't going to calm you down but I do believe Shona would have mentioned a thing like that. And as for the door slamming shut as soon as we're inside… ' He jerked his thumb through the open door at Luke who was already in, head-lamp attached, tugging at loose bits of brickwork.

'So… what is it we're looking for exactly?' asked Jo after a good few minutes looking for… what? An X marking the spot? An arrow pointing 'Here be treasure?' A wooden crate with 'Ark of the Covenant' on it?

'Ehmmm… ' was the best Harry could manage as he lifted up piles of old newspapers – how the hell did old newspapers always find their way into these sorts of places? Then Luke pulled him close, head-lamp shining in his face so he couldn't see where he was pointing.

'All right, calm down, what… holy fuck, Luke you are a genius! C'mere so I can kiss you! On the lips, tongues and everything!'

At this Luke broke away to the other side of the Vault, giving Harry a clear view of what he'd found.

'What? What is it? Where?' Jo crawled over with a face so like a Cockney chimney sweep Harry couldn't help whistling a burst of 'Chim-chiminee'.

'There. That's what we've found.' He traced an 'H' and a linked 'L' scratched so faintly across the bricks in the corner it had the effect of an optical illusion. Look too closely and it was gone. View it from the corner of your eye and it was there, obvious.

'Your initials,' Jo hunkered down next to him.

'Not *my* initials,' giving her a gentle shove with his knee, causing her to scratch her knuckles on the rough concrete floor as she steadied herself. 'Reckon Dad did this a few years before I was born. They're the initials of the man I was named after. Harry Lime. *The Third Man*. Dad's favourite film.'

Jo was about to hit him in retaliation for her scratches when she saw how distant he'd become and when he spoke it was to himself as he thought something through. *'The Third Man'*…and my mum… she said once, when he was drunk, he'd take off his gloves, be rubbing his hands, breaking the skin, making it worse, and he'd say 'This is Welles' fault. I loved the man and this is what I get for it… ' Harry stopped, the silence of the Vault thickening.

For an instant, so brief all three would later think they'd imagined it, there was a scent stronger than the Vault's trapped air; an uncannily homely smell of rolling tobacco, hair oil and celluloid. The scent of a gentleman of film. Harry twisted in shock to check a familiar outline wasn't standing in the doorway.

'You all right?' asked Jo hoarsely, knowing what they'd just experienced, not wanting Harry to confirm it but to get out of there as quickly as possible. While Harry calmed himself down she directed Luke to check the 'H' while she studied the area of the 'L'. Her head-lamp zig-zagged across the bricks until she saw a small circle of pitch-dark.

'Here! A hole!' She was shortly followed by Luke, 'Got one, no, two… four here!' Harry beside her, squeezing his thick fingers into two of the gaps, one at the end tip of the foot of the 'L', the other parallel with it at the top. Jo stuck her fingers into the two holes at the top and the bottom of the end of the 'H' and the body of the 'L', Luke concentrating on the holes topping and tailing the first line of the 'H'.

OK… in position?' checked Harry. 'Start heaving!'

All of them, romantic fools, expected the bricks to glide out on concealed tracks to unveil a treasure trove glowing in the golden shaft of mysterious light. Instead, a great deal of coughing and sweating ensued as blocks of bricks, stuck together in groups of three, four, five, were scraped at, pulled away to reveal…

'An old pile of *Gazettes*? You are *joking*. Should I laugh or cry hysterically?' Jo slumped against a wall, kicked disconsolately at a pile of bricks.

'Of course it's not a pile of old *Gazettes*.' Luke ducked into the gap they'd created, hauling out the package bound by a latticework of knotted string. Viewing it close-up even Harry looked as though tears of frustration were about to cut their way through the dust on his face. 'It's been years since I did knotwork in the Scouts, how the *hell* are we going to get through that without a carving knife?'

'Boys, boys' chided Jo, pulling a small Swiss Army pen-knife from her jeans pocket which she handed to Harry. 'Well, if any of us had any doubt about you being a lezzer beforehand. Though this is the girliest piece of kit... a nail file? A toothpick?'

'Give it here.' Jo snatched it off him, pulling out a blade with which she started slicing through the bunched knots and yellowing newsprint, catching a glimpse of dull silver underneath that caused Luke and Harry to join in, ripping the paper off like three hyperactive kids on Christmas morning until they were left with –

Three silver film canisters. Unlabelled, mysterious, perfect, the three of them sitting in a circle around them, silent, breathless.

'You know', murmured Jo eventually. 'It pains me to say this but *this* actually makes it all worth while. Like something out of a movie. In fact, probably *is* a movie,' as she tapped a canister with a toe.

'I think,' said Harry, magicking a hip flask from his coat pocket, 'this calls for a celebration,' taking a swig, passing it to Jo who took a shot, not caring about the greater strain it would place on her bladder. 'Three canisters... like someone was expecting us,' she said, handing the flask to Luke, Harry laughing in response, laughter that went on for longer than he could control, that carried on until his eyes were streaming and his throat was raw from whisky and relief.

'You know,' he gasped, 'I have absolutely *no* idea what these hold. All I know is they're important, important enough for my Dad… well. You know the rest. It could be dodgy stuff like film-star porn or some politician doing something they shouldn't or it could be… I dunno, some long lost Orson Welles classic. But what I *do* know, is that what we have here is most definitely, undoubtedly going to… '

'Fuck Callum Boyd right off', Luke finished, having gulped down the last of the whisky, raising the flask in a toast to his two friends. 'Let's get out of here and see if we're right.'

CHAPTER
FOURTEEN

Eventually, the three burst out of a rear fire exit door into an alleyway like deep sea pearl fishers breaking the surface of the ocean. Jo let out a 'Whoop!' before looking up, checking to make sure they weren't in view of Callum's rooftop office. Nope, no blinking red eyes of CCTV cameras pointing in their direction either. They had made it. They had entered the belly of the beast and come out unscathed.

There'd been just the one moment of terror when they'd emerged from the Vault. Exhausted but exhilarated the three had been chattering excitedly until stunned into silence by the sight of Old Smiler waiting for them, his smile ever sinister.

'Look at you lot. So scared you'd think you'd seen the ghost of the Headless Usherette. No need to worry, I'm here to help. And I'd appreciate it if you'd put whatever you're carrying into these. The less I see, the less I know.' He handed them each a black bin bag.

'Right. You done?' he asked after they'd wrapped a canister each. 'Let's get you bunch of aging juvenile delinquents out of here.'

'Dunc... listen, we do really appreciate... ' Smiler cut Harry short. 'Save it for my disciplinary hearing, Lawson. You start gabbing and I might realise what a mug I'm being and haul you up straight to the Manager.'

They trooped in silence through 'Pens' and 'Hardware', up several flights of stairs until they reached a rear fire exit door. Dunc stood in front of them, one hand pressing down on a metal bar that looked as sturdy as a twiglet in his massive grip. 'Don't let me catch you pesky kids down here again,' he warned them as the door swung open and they burst into fresh air and when they'd recovered enough to turn and thank him the door had already slammed shut.

'There,' said Harry, collapsing back onto the fire door for support. 'Didn't I tell you we were in for an adventure?'

'Not sure 'adventure' is *quite* the word I'd use to describe it', mused Jo. 'Trial' perhaps? 'Ordeal'? 'Nightmarish descent into hell'?' but she was smiling as she spoke. She'd done it. Faced something she was terrified of and got through it with a prize to show at the end of it. Treasure.

'Here,' she placed her black polythene parcel on top of Harry's. 'I believe this is yours.'

'Luke, go'an hold these a minute?' Once he was free of his burden, Harry opened his arms wide, gave Jo a bear-hug and although she protested – 'Jeez! You're choking me!' – she hugged him as tightly.

'I know it wasn't easy for you down there but I want you to know for definite, was great to have you there. Couldn't have done it by myself and would've ended up throttling the Boy Who Fell to Earth if there had only been the two of us.'

'It was a pleasure, honest. If I'd found out you'd gone and done this without me I'd have… well, moaned and whinged a lot. But honestly, if you need any help like this again… just ask Luke OK?' They broke their grip and laughed, noisy enough for Luke who was keeping a close eye on either end of the alley to shush them. 'Honestly', he whispered, looking over anxiously to a small group of cowboys who were firing off some cap-guns. 'I think we need to get these back to the Kinotech quick as we can. Get them safe. We don't know how the film in these is going to react to the change in atmosphere so… '

'Ok, don't panic, we'll get them sorted. Jo… '

'He's right, you'd best get on.' As Luke headed off, Jo moved towards Harry, laid her hands on his shoulders. 'You know how proud your Dad would be of you, don't you? What you've done for him, proving all those lies about him *were* lies. You should tell your Mum, let her know for definite he was protecting something.'

'It wasn't my Mum who needed convincing though, was it? It was me. She's never doubted. Always kept the faith. There were moments there when I was scared we'd get there and find…nothing. Imagine. His own son, doubting him like that…. ' Harry broke off. 'Anyway, I'll call you soon, OK? You get back and have a shower, a good night's sleep. Let you know what I find out about our booty.' He managed a piratical grin, following Luke down a passageway steering them clear of the main Seacrest streets.

Left alone, Jo, surrounded by overflowing waste-bins and the distant sounds of late-night fun, tilted her head back, stared up at the moon, full and bright in the gap between buildings, turned fingers and thumb into a pistol and took aim. 'Here's lookin' at you kid,' she said aloud and fired, for no particular reason. Feeling triumphant she considered celebrating alone in The Moviegoer… then dismissed the idea as ridiculous. She was shattered, looked like something that had emerged from a tomb, and decided to go home instead, have a nice bath having finally got to the toilet first.

She couldn't help smirking as she walked past the Phoenix. Looking up to see if Callum was there, knowing it would feel all the sweeter if their adventure had happened right under his nose. There he was, silhouetted against the office window. Lord of All He Surveyed or so he thought. Jo knew it was a bad idea, would raise his suspicions but she couldn't help wave at him, too tired, too bleary-eyed to check if he waved back.

Callum did, intrigued by the sight of Dr Ashe out late at night, alone. What did she have to be so cheery about? he wondered. Was it Gay Wimmens Disco night? His wave back at her was royally brief. He knew he was being mocked but up there in his eyrie, bang in the heart of Seacrest a fortnight before Festival time, a Manhattan in one hand, fine-blend cigarette in the other, it was difficult for him to care. He would let Dr Ashe have her fun. In a year the streets she would walk down would be *his* streets. Callum Boyd's plan, Callum Boyd's design. His town. Had he been more in the mood he'd have allowed himself a demonic laugh. The Manhattan hadn't kicked in fully yet and instead he took another long, lingering look over his model.

How his daughter Shona would have teased him if she'd been there to see him. He could be in a bar or restaurant with Bridget, a nice little usherette from the Queen Mary who proved so amenable to wearing her Sailor Girl suit after hours. Yet he was in his office, patrolling the circumference of a scale model of the Seacrest of the future. He'd have to relinquish it at some point, put it on public display during the Festival as part of the so-called consultation process. Until then it was his to tower over.

The white, uniform streets under Callum's gaze bore very little relation to the streets that currently surrounded the Phoenix. Instead of a maze of steep, winding lanes lined with shops selling cheap tat and flea-pit cinemas, there were wide avenues, boulevards, covered walkways, underground parking, multiplexes and malls. This was a complex where people could feel protected from uncertainty, the unpredictable. Where even the elements were controlled, shut out by retractable roofs. A showcase destination where the public knew what they were getting as soon as they stepped out of the car. No shocks, no unpleasant surprises. Everything managed and organised with the Phoenix at its centre.

He examined the redesigned pier, one that met the demands of the twenty-first century. The ramshackle collection of tawdry sideshows swept aside to make way for a gloriously sleek shopping development. Enough space left for a new Big Wheel, smaller and slower moving, far better than the current death-trap. He looked over to where the studios once stood, replaced by hotels to house visitors to the conference centre at its heart. Only one studio left for limited production. Callum smiled at the '45' painted in front of its door. No need for the Archive, no need for Luke Howard and his hoard of junk after *this* Festival. 'The truth will out, Lukey boy. The truth will out,' Callum murmured.

However, as his eyes swept across his own Bay, its smooth white curves, its crisp edges, he was suddenly overcome by a wave of melancholy at the thought of letting people in. The streets becoming grubby and scuffed, pavements sticky with bubblegum, littered with fast-food wrappers...

Depressed by the thought of what that bitch Reality would do to his dream of Seacrest, he turned his back on the model, stalked to a side door. The door to what he thought of as his office proper. Staff knew about it but weren't allowed to enter. We were privileged indeed to follow him in, to cross into hallowed ground. We had to remember not to breathe too heavily, no nervous coughing. Otherwise we'd be done for.

It was smaller than his main office and windowless, although this wasn't a difference we noticed immediately. This was because three of the walls were dominated by large plasma screens that bathed the room in a silvery light. Those screens were always on, always showing the same images. It brought Callum comfort when he lay in his bed at night to know that somewhere in Seacrest a little bit of Hollywood was always alive and moving.

What they showed were looped film-tests of Hollywood stars, legends of the forties and fifties, slowed down to the point it took a few moments to realise they were moving and weren't still images. Living, breathing photographs was how Callum liked to think of them. Before he took up his leather seat in front of the bank of small television screens that filled the fourth wall, he studied the face of Marilyn Monroe, her beautiful mouth frozen in an expression of delighted surprise, while James Dean and Greta Garbo looked on, taking an age to blink.

Seated, he raised his glass to each of them before facing the flickering bank of screens. This was where he was at his happiest, where he felt his safest. In front of his personal Panopticon, his birds' eye view of Seacrest. Cameras perched on window ledges, lamp-posts, telephone boxes, bus-shelters, cinema awnings, public toilets… you get the picture. Everywhere except his own cinema, a fact that had become a curious source of pride. He knew everything that went on there because people told him because they were afraid not to. (Or so he thought…) Callum had an eye peering, searching everywhere else and that night he wanted to drink it in, make a few notes. Check who was speaking to who, getting drunk, kissing someone they shouldn't.

There was poor Monsieur Reynard, his usually perky moustache all a-droop as he was thrown out drunk of the Bagatelle, no doubt for raving drunkenly about the 'merde' Callum was going to land them all in. Callum jotted a few things down in the black day-planner that always sat on the desk beneath the screens, pausing when he saw Kim stepping out of 'Eats With the Fishes', an Italian seafood restaurant. She was with a handsome young man Callum had recently promoted to assistant manager of Santoro's, a Boyd-run casino on the promenade. Foolish boy. He would have to have a chat with him.

Callum's sudden annoyance was compounded by reaching for his glass and finding it empty. As being irritated always reminded him of Harry Lawson he flicked a switch, moved a joystick, granting him a view of the front of the Kinotech. Although it was late Harry could usually be relied upon to provide some dumb entertainment and there he was, disappearing through the front door, Luke's lanky frame following. There was a speed to their movement that had Callum leaning forward in his chair. 'Up to no good eh?' as the silent stars surrounding him slowly shut their eyes.

Someone knew Callum Boyd was watching. As he leant in closer to the screen, Harry re-emerged and Callum flinched back when Harry pointed straight at him, glaring, out-staring the blinking red-eye of the camera before drawing his thumb slowly across his throat. He smiled gleefully, waved, disappeared back indoors leaving Callum to nervously check the unbroken skin of his neck.

'No good at all,' whispered Callum, not feeling quite so safe.

CHAPTER FIFTEEN

A fortnight had passed since Harry, Jo and Luke discovered the treasure buried deep in the heart of the Dominion. During that time only Harry had delved into the mystery of why Alec went to such lengths in his attempt to keep the canisters safe. Jo and Luke wanted to help but Harry made it clear this was a something he needed to do alone. The two of them weren't able to feel disappointed for long though. Like the rest of the town they were swept up into the whirlwind of the Festival preparation.

When residents referred to Festival Fever the phrase was entirely accurate. The lead-up to the Grand Opening had resulted in sufferers experiencing high temperatures, palpitations, strange visions, manic activity, racing speech followed by sudden exhaustion. A small price to pay for the satisfaction of seeing the town transformed into a location where visitors would pinch themselves to check they hadn't fallen asleep during a Douglas Sirk or Esther Williams movie and were dreaming that they had entered a Technicolour wonderland.

Let us return to where we began this story, our perch high up on the cliffs on the head of the seagull whose wings stretched out above a 'WELCOME TO SEACREST!' Lightly buffeted by the winds that always blew that high, we appreciated the changes that had taken place, the extra spring in Seacrest's step.

A beautiful clear blue day in late September, the water of the Bay shone aquamarine and turquoise. We lifted our faces to the sun, eyes closed, absorbed its warmth and took a deep breath before opening them, when we were momentarily blinded by white light reflected from the sign caused by its fresh coat of paint. The wobbly 'W' flapped no longer, the 'CREST' standing as securely and proudly as the 'SEA'. Painters in overalls were on the roof of the studios adding the finishing touches to the studio gull; its wing-tips defined, a sharper beak, an added glint to its oddly knowing eye returning our gaze.

We noticed the number on the tarmac behind it and realised its head decorated the roof of Lot 45. How curiously appropriate this was. Luckily we'd bought a pair of X-ray specs from one of the shops along the promenade, and so we could peer through that roof to find out what Luke was up to in that warren of his.

There he was, in the store-room amongst stacks of sealed cardboard boxes. Such was the amount of Archive material available, although the display area of Lot 45 was aircraft hanger-sized, the store-room was always full as more memorabilia found its way there. Luke worked hard to ensure every object, every press-cutting, scrap of film stock and scribbled-on script got its turn out in front of the audience. No matter how many times you visited, there was always something fresh to see, a new aspect of Fletcher revealed.

Luke had recovered more quickly than Jo from Harry's refusal to let them help but then he'd had his own major project to work on, the exhibition entitled 'Cameron Fletcher & Seacrest: The Special Relationship.' Luke's masterpiece. Not only *his* thank you to Cameron Fletcher, *Seacrest's* for all he'd done for the town; the articles that had kept interest in the town alive, providing justification for its devotion to film.

He was sifting through boxes, sitting on one, searching for finishing touches. He pulled out a pair of size 9 brown leather shoes kept sealed in a plastic bag, a white label stuck to the side. On it, in black felt tip was written 'A present from Jack, check out the sand!' Although Fletcher had never visited the first time he was alive, he often persuaded celebrity friends to take back a memento from their Festival trips. Luke laid the shoes aside and dug out a sheaf of press cuttings relating to Jack Nicholson's visit to the 1978 Festival. He quickly found the one he was after, featuring a photograph of a grinning Jack crouched on the sands of Seacrest Bay, hands in the shoes, pressing them into the sand. A near parody of the Hollywood Walk of Fame hand-print ceremony.

Luke read the text carefully, his finger following the words like a child's. 'Cameron's real sorry he couldn't make it this year. Chest infection, nasty. When I paid him a visit he got out of his bed, fetched these shoes, handed them over. Said, 'You make sure some shoe leather of mine touches that glorious beach. Bring some sand back between the toes.' When Cameron Fletcher asks you to do something there's not a lot you can do about it. Man's a genius and I feel privileged to help him out in any way.'

We watched Luke reading for a while. Got bored before we realised he was reading the same passage over and over again. As if committing it to memory. Although he appeared calm we looped the scene back, watched on repeat, and caught a flickering at his edges. The twitch of a cheek muscle, faint tremor in his fingers, the paper shaking lightly. Each time he read Jack's quote a new emotion appeared to take him over: admiration, pride, excitement… and fear.

Because what if Cameron Fletcher turned up and wanted his life back? Wanted it returned from the strange young man who stole it away from him, pronounced him dead and then put his remains on public display? The cutting trembled as if a breeze had brushed against it then stilled suddenly.

His jaw tightened, eyes darkened. Abruptly, he gathered up the shoes, strode towards his office where a ledger recording every exhibit in every display case lay on his desk. Beside it a glass of whisky and half-smoked cigar waited for him, a ritual he'd allowed himself every day for a fortnight. Less an indulgence than a means of invoking the spirit of Fletcher. Benign voodoo. But one of the older boxes caught his eye. A grubby white, it was one of the first, one of the foundation blocks of the Archive and he stopped, thrown back six years, reminded of the start of it all.

There had been a knocking at his bed-sit door. A knocking that became a hammering as he ignored it then a slow, dull thudding when he ignored it some more, as regular as a heart-beat. A sound that warned him it wouldn't leave until he'd answered.

He tried to remember when he'd last left the flat. A fortnight? A month of staying in bed with occasional trips to the toilet, to the kitchen for some cereal? How long since the funeral? Since he'd stood next to Mum's boyfriend knowing he should attempt to console him. Poor man in bits, sobbing by the grave-side and Luke too ashamed of his own lack of tears to offer any comfort. It had taken Mum years to find somewhere she felt settled, someone who made her feel safe and happy and when she'd found it all, there was the trip to the doctor, then the scans and the treatment refused because the look in the consultant's eyes had told her it was pointless.

All Luke had wanted to do was leave the other mourners and find a cinema. To sink into the warmth and dark and look up at the screen because that was what his Mum would have wanted. Instead of a handful of people crying in a graveyard she'd have wanted them watching *Singing in the Rain* or *South Pacific* or *The Wizard of Oz*. Laughing and enjoying themselves and thinking of her because that's what she deserved.

That pounding wasn't going anywhere. Even with two pillows clamped over his head he could still hear it. It was a need to stop it rather than find out who was causing it that forced him up to wrench the door open.

'Luke! *Fuck*ing hell… look at you! the state you're in! and a bloody *Fame* t-shirt, where'd'you get that tat! It *stinks* in here or is that your boxers?' Conrad Baxter had his foot in the door and, drawing on decades of edging into places he wasn't wanted, was in.

Opening curtains, picking up empty cereal packets, putting dishes in the sink, pouring water over them. In his mid-fifties but moving like a man half his age, charging around in his familiar brown suit and always immaculate white shirt, filling the bed-sit with life. Receding hairline, black hair slicked down with shoe polish above a sharp little face that made a rabid ferret look a picture of innocence.

Luke watched him and felt something wrench in his chest, an awful blend of relief and shame. How selfish he'd been, mouldering in his pit when he should have been out helping Conrad? Bidding in auction rooms, raking through skips, buying up house clearances, keeping a straight face while his boss charmed and cajoled an old dear out of some old piece of tat that would make them a fortune. Well, *Conrad* a fortune. But what was he doing here? It wasn't Conrad's style to get involved with personal stuff. He'd cut Luke off when he started telling him about his Mum, why he needed time off. He'd rather sell all the stuff off his stall for a tenner than discuss that sort of thing so he must be there on business.

'Now sunshine, why don't you stop standing there like a drying streak of piss and get yourself in the shower, sort yourself out. I've got a proposition for you. Don't look so worried, not that sort of proposition, 'specially not when you're smelling as sweet as Fat Larry's jockstrap. I've got a shipment coming in from that American friend of mine, what's his name again? The movie poster guy, the one you're forever chatting to about films and actors and Christ knows what else when you should be working… '

'Harlan. Harlan Montgomery.'

'Good Lord, it speaks! *That's* the one, knew it was some bloody stupid Yank name. He's got something coming over and thought I might be interested. Or rather, and I have to admit, felt quite put out about this, quite affronted, he thought *you* would be interested. It got me thinking. You've been following me around for a few years now and, don't get me wrong, you've been a good lad, but I reckon it's about time I gave you a job of your own to be getting on with.'

This was the closest Conrad had ever got to being sentimental and he did a good job of disguising it, busying himself with a teapot and the kettle. 'Fancy a brew son? Christ almighty, the state of this cupboard! I should get the Council down here, get it condemned 'cept I'd be embarrassed to admit I'm your boss,' and Luke smiled for the first time in weeks.

'Anyway, so yeah, where was I… that's right, Harlan keeps on going on about how Luke will love this and I'm telling Harlan, I don't know, never seen Luke get excited about anything much, plays his cards very close to his chest does Lukey boy and Harlan says, coming over all mysterious like, you go and see Luke and give him a name. You tell him what I'm shipping over is from Cameron Fletcher and see his reaction… '

'Fletcher? What, *Cameron*? Cameron Fletcher? *The* Cameron Fletcher? The critic?'

Luke recognised Conrad's expression from the auction showrooms. The look he got when he saw something underpriced, undervalued, like a fox catching sight of an injured rabbit. 'Yeah… that's exactly how Harlan said you'd react.' He rubbed his chin, Turkish-shaved that morning, thoughtfully, wondering what he might be missing out on. 'He was wittering on about setting up some archive. Sounds too poncey for the likes of me. More importantly, *most* importantly, doesn't sound as if there's any profit in it either. But I have to warn you son, there are conditions attached. This

Fletcher saying in his will that any archive – archive I ask you! - would have to be set up in some god-forsaken, fish-stinking town up North. Jockland way. What's it called… '

'Seacrest,' Luke's voice barely a whisper.

'Yeah, that's the place. How'd'you know that?' Conrad paused from stirring the six tea bags he'd put in the pot, his face acquiring several more angles than usual.

'It's famous. Famous for its cinemas. Fletcher wrote about it, said it was a place all cinema lovers should visit at least once.'

'Yeah?' Conrad raised his eyebrows in that way he had when a seller promised him he'd be buying a crock of gold when the crock in question reeked as badly as a sewage farm in August. 'Well, he sounds a right pretentious bastard, doesn't he? *Much* more your sort of thing. Glad I'm getting shot of it.'

After rinsing a couple mugs he poured out the tea adding eight heaped teaspoons of sugar to his own before handing one over to Luke. After gulping his down like a pint in a pub, he said briskly, 'So, might mean a parting of the ways between you and me, son. 'Cause there's no way I'm heading any further north than Carlisle, not after what happened between me and that antique dealer from Bishopbriggs. Those Glasgwegians, I tell you, faces like cage-fighters with manners to match.'

Seeing Luke's face return to the bleak mask he wore on opening the door, Conrad quickly changed tack, wanted to avoid things getting too soppy. 'We'll worry about what happens to us, to the *business* later. You get in that bathroom and get yourself sorted. We've terms to discuss.' Luke attempted a smile and Conrad Baxter softened, put it down to old age. 'And Luke… about your mum… I should have… '

'It's all right, Conrad. It's fine. I know.'

As Luke disappeared, scalp tingling with the knowledge that his life was about to change, we were privileged to see something he didn't. Conrad's face fell, every one of his years etched deep on it, knowing he was about to lose Luke. Muttered to himself, 'Well, Mr Harlan Montgomery – if that is your real name and I very much doubt it is – you'd better watch how you treat that boy. Any sign of a set-up and I'll swing for you.'

It was time to leave the past, that shabby, smelly bed-sit, Conrad facing the prospect of being alone again. We were back in the cool surroundings of the Archive, Luke shaking his head, marvelling at how far he'd come, wondering what Conrad was up to (actually on the run in the south of France having cheated the wrong Bethnal Green granny out of a piece by Lalique). Leaving him with his memories we tucked into a pocket those X-ray specs and returned to admiring the view.

 CHAPTER
SIXTEEN

And *what* a view! All the cinemas seemed brighter, scrubbed and polished, blown bulbs replaced, tattered awnings repaired and it felt as though we'd travelled back in time, to the Seacrest of its heyday.

Over at the lido the wire-fencing and graffiti were gone, the modernist white curves returned to their radiant glory. The skateboarders had also vanished, replaced by the Seacrest roller-derby team the Jezebels, racing the circuit in tight, bright costumes of neon-pink and emerald green, moving so quickly the colours seemed to streak behind them. They were practicing for the derby that would take place for the duration of the Festival, competing against other teams from all over the country and abroad. We could hear their whoops of excitement, thrilled by the prospect of some real competition.

Our eye moved along the elegant curve of the promenade, rainbow-coloured bunting fluttering between palm trees above the many visitors who paused to admire the sea-view or the street performers; acrobats, musicians, jugglers and mimes performing scenes from *Apocalypse Now*, *Psycho* or *Pulp Fiction.*

In two days the promenade would host the Annual Seacrest Festival Parade. In school gyms, the Town Hall, in squash courts and ballrooms, a spectrum of locals, from Primary Ones to OAPs were working on the costumes and choreography to appear on one of the twenty floats that would process along its length with fleets of Kazoo bands, pipe bands, miniature ponies, tiny motor cars, Chinese dragons and movie star look-a-likes.

They would make their way past the temporary pavilion set in the centre of the promenade where a throne, recently given a starring role in the Seacrest Players' production of *The King and I*, had been given pride of place. This would seat the Star Guest who, that very minute, was speeding towards us, carried in luxurious comfort by the Seacrest Special, the town's very own steam train, cutting through the countryside, racing to tell his magnificent lies...

We were getting ahead of ourselves. It was best to concentrate on the here-and-now, the pleasure of seeing every carriage of the Big Wheel full, the pier bustling, queues for the ice-cream and candyfloss vans stretching back to its entrance... then something odd caught our eye. The pier was the busiest it had been for years, practically creaking under the unexpected weight of visitors and yet the Kinotech was closed.

This needed further investigation and so we employed a dissolve to take us through those bolted doors, swooping past the 'Greatest Executions of Our Time' display, over the Harryhausen pinball machine and between the legs of 'Boris, the Bruiser from Bavaria', a Test Your Strength machine, until we were at the office door, left helpfully ajar.

Harry sat at his desk, laptop open, the three canisters next to him on his right, his elbow brushing against them. His expression was thoughtful but miles away, eyes unseeing as he listened intently to the voice emanating from the Apple Mac. He paused the recording to type up some notes and we took the opportunity to peer over his shoulder, saw the heading of the file playing: 'Kathy Bell – Assistant Projectionist'.

Of course, Harry could have gone straight ahead and opened the canisters up and, if any film was left, got it threaded through a projector, showing on a screen. But that was too great a risk, especially with old stock that had been near ravaged by fire and left underground for nigh on twenty years. Instead, he decided to approach them gently. To do some research first. Visit the older folks of Seacrest, the people who'd worked with his Dad and knew him well. Or, at least, as well as anyone could when it came to Alec Lawson.

And yes, although he wouldn't admit it to himself, there was part of him that was scared. Scared to discover by himself what his Dad had nearly died trying to rescue.

He'd felt a bit of a tube at first turning up on pensioners' doorsteps to ask them about a guy who'd been dead for years, worried they'd have forgotten him or have nothing much to say. Turned out the hard part once the digital recorder was on was getting them to stop. It was as if they'd been waiting for years for someone to come and listen to what they had to say about the glory days.

It could get weird for Harry, listening to them talk about this man, his Dad, a man he had difficulty recognising at times. Like with Kathy for instance. Lovely lady he'd only met briefly before but she'd laid out a real spread, sandwiches and home-baked cakes, his cup of tea never empty and he'd known it was as much for Alec's sake as for his. The way she talked about Alec, the intensity of it… Harry stopped listening at points. Such a gap between the man Kathy idolised and his own Dad.

Harry scratched his beard fiercely to get his concentration back. He tapped the touchpad and he was back there again in Kathy's sitting room, the walls decorated with framed movie posters, *Casablanca*, *The Man Who Would Be King*, *Dr No*, 'Oh yes, big Sean fan, me', Royal Doulton figurines on every surface, a coyly watching audience.

'So yes, his apprentice. Couldn't believe it! Unheard of then, a projectionist taking on a woman assistant. Didn't matter how good you were, what you knew about films, most of them were too feart to take the risk. Worried there'd be gossip, their wives down there every five minutes, ears pressed to the door. Not Alec. He was bigger than that. Knew how much it meant to me because of what it meant to *him*. Beaming down those wonderful pictures…

'Anyway, yes, so he took me on. Only for six weeks though I was lucky to get that, mind. Two of us in that wee room and Alec was a solitary soul, you know? Well, yes, 'course you will what with you being his son and everything… but yes, those six weeks… best time of my life! No kidding! The things I learnt from that man about films and audiences and cinemas… '

Harry tapped the pad, stopped her voice. That feeling he had when he was there with her but he recognised it this time. Jealousy. How come she got to learn all this stuff while he – ach. It was no use crying about it now. He gave his beard a quick rub, shook himself out of it, let Kathy speak.

'And, oh I don't know. All sorts! He'd seen me hanging about, waiting outside his door after a showing, wanting to ask him questions but not being brave enough because… well, he had a way about him, you know? Of carrying himself. I mean, he wasn't that big or anything… you just knew he was a man to respect.'

'This one night I plucked up the courage [laughter]. That was it, *Goldfinger* was on and I was on such a high I didn't care any more, I'd just stepped into the foyer and there was Alec down from the booth. Could tell he was distracted, still thinking over how it went. I went up anyway, tapped him on the shoulder. It took him a couple seconds to recognise me, like a sleepwalker, you know? When he did, the smile he gave… just nice and relaxed, not what I was expecting at all.'

'And I was standing like an idiot, trying to remember what I wanted to ask him when Mrs MacFarlane – God, that woman… in charge of Confectionery but nothing sweet about her, the auld bitch. 'scuse me language, she sees this and shouts 'Kathy! What you up to, where are your takings, everyone else has cashed in and you're late as usual!' She was a stuck-up cow that one, felt popcorn girls shouldn't be talking to any of the higher-ups.'

'Alec, cool as you like just turns and says to her 'It's all right Mrs MacFarlane, I promised to give Kathy – he knew my name! – a tour of the projection booth after the showing. It'll only take a couple of minutes. And the look on MacFarlane's face! I knew she'd be off gossiping but I didn't care. Didn't give two hoots because Alec Lawson was taking me up the stairs and into *his* den. I mean that… was like hallowed ground, y'know?'

'So I'm in there having a good look around, asking loads of questions and I could tell from the way he was answering they were good questions. And I think… I think he saw the way I looked at the machine and saw something of himself there… someone who really *got* it, y'know? And I'm about to leave for the next showing and I say, blush to think about it now, bold as you like, 'I'd love to be a projectionist Mr Lawson. I think it must be the best job in the world ever.' And he gives me this wee smile and says, 'It is, it is that Kathy. You tell Mrs MacFarlane when you're down those stairs that for the next six weeks you're working for me. I'll train you up and then we'll get you a job somewhere.'

'Tell you, I nearly fainted on the spot! I know some people might think there was something more to it, you know, him an older man, me a young pretty thing – honest! I was, though you wouldn't believe it now! [Harry's demurral] – but with Alec… you knew there'd be no funny business. Integrity. That was it. You knew just by looking at him he was a man of his word.'

As he paused Kathy Bell that was when Harry got the idea. How the unveiling of these films could be turned into something bigger than simple revenge against Callum Boyd. An event to remind this town what a great man Alec Lawson was, the type of man the Callums of this world would love to get rid of. It was about time his

Dad had a fitting send-off.

Harry started typing up his idea but then remembered something Kathy mentioned about the visitors Callum had. He frowned, tapped the top canister. 'What was it again?' he muttered, drawing the cursor along to a later point in Kathy's conversation. Here goes... bingo.

'Visitors. Loads of them. Because of this Lawson Luck nonsense. Y'know, that daft superstition that if you wanted a film to do well you had to shake the hand of Alec Lawson. 'Course, you know what showbiz types are like so whenever there was a premiere there'd be a queue right the way down from the projectionist booth and into the foyer. Can you imagine?'

'By the time I was working with him he'd stopped all that business. And actually... thinking about it now, that's probably why Mrs MacFarlane gave me such a hard time. Protecting him, y'know? His privacy... now, if I'd met all the stars he had I wouldn't stop gabbing about it. Burt Lancaster and Kirk Douglas and goodness knows who else but Alec only talked about it once.'

'Kathy,' he said, 'when I met those people it wasn't the way you'd imagine it. I always thought I'd be the one standing there gawping, nothing to say. But when you meet them you realise they're nothing special. No better than you or me. Limp grip or sweaty palms. And afterwards, when you see them up on the screen, something's changed. You've stopped believing them.' [A long pause]

'Listen to me, getting maudlin. Have another cake, son. No? Growing lad like you... but yes, the other thing Alec said that he really didn't like was they, the Big Star, would stand there *wanting* something from him. That blessed luck. Can you imagine that? The pressure? Them putting the success of their film on your shoulders?

'And... oh yes! The only time I ever saw Alec getting even close to angry was when I asked if it was true Orson Welles had visited.

I was gabbling on like a schoolgirl because Welles was one of my idols back then and I realised Alec had gone quiet. I mean, he was always quiet your Dad, but this was a different sort. And he broke in, mid-sentence and he says the strangest thing. 'That man, Kathy, is a very clever man. A *very* clever man. But there's something not right about him. You watch his films and you'll see it. Something devilish.' The exact word he used. Not kidding. 'Devilish'. Strange, isn't it? Gives me the shivers.'

Harry got them too but of a different sort, of realisation perhaps. Instead of typing up his thoughts he searched in his desk drawer for a notebook, wrote them down in a deliberately illegible scrawl. Because you never knew who might be watching.

CHAPTER
SEVENTEEN

We took the hint, the camera hesitating before tracking back, through the closed doors of the Kinotech, into the crowds of the pier. A shot of the Big Wheel which, we realised then, bore an uncanny resemblance to a certain famous Wheel in Vienna as seen in *The Third Man*... Thinking of cuckoo clocks we took off, up up and away, the people below us like ants and returned to the solitude of our cliff-top perch.

It was mid-day, the full sun shining on the brightly painted roofs of cinemas and our attention was drawn to the cinema dominating the sky-line, dwarving the likes of the Alhambra, the Black Cat, the Electric and the Regal. There was no doubting its grandeur, the modernist classicism, but there was a coldness emphasised by the quirky, ramshackle nature of the cinemas it towered over. As a commentator once remarked – and it may well have been Jo - the Phoenix gave us an idea of 'what Albert Speer would have come up with had he ever been asked to design the local Odeon.'

Still, when the sun struck its sides, turning them a glorious shade of amber, it was hard not to be impressed, not to feel the tiniest hint of admiration for the man determined enough to build such a landmark from the ashes of the Dominion. Shielding our eyes we could make Callum out, standing at the windows of his office. And we could *just* make out a second figure, shadowy in the background. We switched to close quarters, viewing the scene through one of the five hidden cameras Callum had dotted about the room.

This camera, disguised as a fake light-fitting and movement sensitive, was focused on Callum so we only caught a glimpse of his companion. It was enough though to promise us glamour to come; a high heel, the shimmer of a silk dress, long waved hair flicked over a pale shoulder. Although the image was in grainy black and white we sensed that dress, those shoes, were scarlet.

'You know, sometimes,' said Callum, tying his bow-tie, 'this old wreck of a town scrubs up quite nicely. I can almost see why people insist on making such a fuss about it.'

The woman's voice which answered was husky enough to have us dreaming of Lauren Bacall, Barbara Stanwyck. The sort of voice that had boyfriends and girlfriends phoning her mobile when they knew it was switched off so they could listen to it as they would a piece of music, without having to concentrate on what was being said; the lazy near-drawl of a woman sated, already wondering where her next cigarette was coming from.

'What's that, Dad? Getting sentimental in your old age? Dear, things *have* changed since I've been away. I'd phone the *Gazette*, 'Callum Boyd Has A Heart Shocker', only they'd never believe me. Here. Drink this. It'll bring you back to your senses.' The hidden figure came into view and we had to switch to Technicolour to do Shona Boyd justice.

Her hair as dazzling as her dress, a rich glossy copper, framing a face as sharply attractive as her father's; high cheekbones, infuriating half-smile and ice-blue eyes. The dress was low-cut, not so low that it would meet with Callum's disapproval but not so high it would disappoint others. This was old school beauty, a vision to make Cary Grant, Clark Gable, Robert Mitchum raise an eyebrow, turn them speechless.

She handed Callum a Manhattan and he glanced at the long, black gloves she was wearing.

'What? Too camp for you, Dad? Well, if a lady can't camp it up in Seacrest, where can she?'

'A *lady* is it now?'

'Watch it. I've been dossing around with film students the past couple of years, running about film sets making cups of coffee for ungrateful stars. Of course I'm going to take the opportunity to dress up. It is my home-coming after all. Two long years away. I want everyone who matters to know that I'm back. For good.'

'Daughter dear,' Callum sipped his drink, winced at its strength, 'for one I don't believe it was only coffee you were drinking on those film sets. And secondly I appreciate an homage to Rita Hayworth as much as anyone but please, try to remember that someone else is the guest of honour tonight. Not to disappoint, but not everyone is going to be focused on your cleavage.'

He took another sip, prepared for the kick of it and raised his glass to his daughter. If he'd been smiling at anyone else they would have believed he was genuinely happy to see them, that he wasn't suspicious at all about their timely return after such a long absence. But he was smiling at a fellow Boyd and Shona knew his eyes were a little too bright, a little too sharp to be entirely trusting.

They stood in silence, each trying to work the other out until it became easier to admire the view instead, to savour this time alone together before switching into their public personas. Incapable of letting things get too comfortable, however, Callum said, casually, 'Charming yes, but still, at heart, past its best. Talking of which… been to see your Mum yet?'

Shona shot him a look that would have had anyone else whimpering but he remained gazing out the window, only a twitch of the lips indicating he appreciated the effect the question might have. No arguments, not yet, Shona decided. There'd be time enough for that.

'Cheap shot. Nice to see you haven't changed *too* much. No, I haven't seen Carol yet. She knows I'm here though, that I want to see her.'

'Oh… so you've kept in contact with *someone* in this town.' Callum couldn't keep that undercurrent of jealousy out of his tone and Shona wondered at the pleasure that gave her. God, Jo was right, she thought and shivered. Like father like daughter.

The thought of Jo brought the usual guilt but also excitement, a tingle to her lips. She eased it by touching them gently with the silk tips of her fingers and walked to the other end of the office where she could best see the rows of painted cliff-top terraces. Her eyes were as keen as ours as she sought out Jo's flat, the white walls and blue roof, blue-framed windows and those thick, red velvet bedroom curtains… Her father called 'Shona?' and she wondered what Jo was doing now, how she'd behave when they met before turning to join him.

A seagull lifted from the roof of the Phoenix and we followed its flight as it glided towards the terraces Shona was studying. It passed one with white walls, blue roof, settled on the lamp-post opposite, stretched its wings and neck, a living example of the Seacrest crest.

We switched to its viewpoint, looking towards blue-framed windows, edging closer towards the window with the red curtains, drifting, dissolving through and then we were in.

There could be little doubt this was the bedroom of Dr Jo Ashe. Academic papers and books and magazines strewn about the floor but we ended up doing a double-take. Someone who certainly looked like Jo was standing in front of a full-length mirror on the back of an open wardrobe door. This woman though was in a dark trouser suit and cream coloured blouse of the sort Katherine Hepburn would wear when playing a tomboyish heiress or sophisticated newspaper editor. She looked… presentable! We gasped, as instead of her uniform of jeans and vintage t-shirts this version of Jo resembled a bona fide Seacrest resident! Her hair, not the usual short, thick mass of tangled curls but styled! It had a style!

Not only that but… surely not… *make up*? For all her new look Jo was unhappy. Instead of revelling in her sleek modishness, she looked like someone who'd just had a friend tell her they'd lost her imported deluxe Collector's Edition copy of *Le Samourai*.

Don't know what Kim's playing at, she was thinking, look like a bloody Edwardian male impersonator. She looked longingly towards the t-shirts hanging up in her wardrobe, picking out one of the few smarter items it contained. A red silk shirt bought for her by Shona, years ago – 'Here Dr Ashe. Something to brighten you up, put a bit of colour in your cheeks, your lips… ' She pulled out a sleeve, let the material whisper against her skin, felt a familiar ache in her chest.

There had been no confirmed sightings of Shona yet, Jo catching glimpses that had driven her half mad. A flash of copper hair in a cinema foyer, the echo of a familiar pair of heels clipping along the street outside her window late at night. She was *bound* to be at the Reception that night though. That gave Jo an opportunity to perfect those fantastically witty put-downs she'd been rehearsing for years like… um… bugger it. Maybe Kim would help her with the witticisms too.

She slumped onto her bed and gingerly prodded the make-up bag loaned to her by Kim who had made it abundantly clear three days before that it was Jo's *duty* to, 'Make that brazen… *hussy* realise what she's been missing all these years.'

This advice had been given in a disused tram station while they were helping out at a dress rehearsal for the Bugsy Malone-themed float of the Alhambra Matinee Juniors. Jo, flustered by the vehemence of Kim's declaration, laughed to disguise her embarrassment as she handed out splurge guns to the assorted ten year olds. It had felt as though she was being mobbed by a bunch of miniature Godfathers.

'I'm not sure if 'hussy' is entirely fair and anyway, she'll have moved on, I've moved on… '

The sharp laugh Kim gave in response had a number of kids fingering their gun triggers nervously.

'Oh believe me, Dr Ashe, 'hussy' is far too polite a word to use in relation to that woman. It's only because I'm surrounded by Primary Fours you're not getting a phrase *far* more appropriate. Right you lot! Everyone up on that trailer and we'll go through 'Bad Guys' one more time! And Ryan Moss, if I see you anywhere *near* those cream pies again I'll… '

As the petite Wise Guys bustled away, Kim granted her full attention to Jo. 'Listen, if you need a hand with make-up – no, wait, listen, hear me out. Just because you're an academic doesn't mean you have to go around looking like Aileen Wournos and I could *help* you, Jo. Give you lessons in mixing and matching, styling and highlighting. Stop laughing. Glamour is a *very* serious business, haven't you lived long enough in this place to *understand* that? Don't you, for once in your life, want to step out of the audience and be one of the people up *there*,' Kim waved out her arm as if introducing a stage floodlit and beckoning. Briefly, Jo could see it too. Thought yes, she's right! About time I found out what it feels like to be one of the admired instead of an admirer!

This new-found confidence had sustained itself through the following night round at Kim's flat when a transformation scene to rival any seen in *My Fair Lady* or *Pretty Woman* took place. Jo parading – well, slouching less than usual – in a range of outfits that would have had Dietrich and Garbo twitching with envy. An initiation into the mysterious ways of blusher, concealer and mascara had followed until Kim, witnessing Jo's delicate way with a lip gloss wand had finally declared 'By George, I think she's got it! We'll make a Seacrest soul of you yet, Dr Ashe. Now, let's see what we can do with that so-called hair 'style' of yours. Think it's about time you gave it back to the 14 year old boy you nicked it from.'

Sitting in the darkening light of her bedroom without the benefit of Kim's confident way with a pair of ceramic straighteners, Jo's confidence drained away through the soles of her shiny new shoes. Look at me, she fretted, not fit to be seen in public, hair ruined, running my hands through it every five minutes, nervous, thinking about Shona or Fletcher, the horrible dreams I've been having, those two locked in some icky embrace –

The clamour of her ringing house phone snapped her out of it and she was tripping over articles entitled 'The Ghost in the Machine: The Myth of Cameron Fletcher', 'Alan Smithee and Cameron Fletcher: Brothers in Arms', racing to the hallway.

Before the handset was to her ear, a voice huskier and sexier than a post-coital Kathleen Turner was purring, 'Well Cinderella? Are you ready for me to whisk you off to the ball? Thought you might want to catch a side-show before the main event. I'll be round in ten to pick you up.'

'Who – what? Is that you, Kim? God, you sound different. More... ah... '

'Alluring? That'll be the excitement, gin and fags, my dear. Come on, chop chop, get yourself ready, we're off to the train station, get a glimpse of Mr Fletcher before he's unveiled to the baying mob.'

'But... how... and... ' Jo stuttered. The time of Fletcher's arrival in the town had been a closely guarded secret, Callum wanting to save the glory for the Reception, the official unveiling of Fletcher.

'Oh, I have my ways, dear, I have my ways.' Kim's laugh was so wicked Jo wondered if she had Callum Boyd tied up somewhere, had just finished committing unspeakable acts on him. 'That wee hoodlum Ryan Moss' dad works at Seacrest Station. I made it very clear that either he let me in on the big secret or Ryan faced a life-time ban from the Alhambra All-stars. The thought of having to entertain that pint-sized psycho every Saturday meant he coughed the info up sharpish.'

A light tinkling came down the line, a noise suspiciously like a cocktail stick and olive coming to rest on the edge of a martini glass.

'Kim? How much have you had to drink?'

'My dear girl, it is far too early in the evening to be asking such ridiculous questions. The train will be arriving in half an hour and you and I are going to be part of the welcoming committee. I'll be round in the Aston in two ticks.'

'Kim… ' Jo took a deep breath. 'I was lucky to get invited to the Reception. Although, actually, luck had nothing to do with it, I'm being used as some kind of mascot, there to show how tame the opposition to Callum's plans is. Harry and Luke getting left off the guest list… I can't *stand* this, being used as some sort of pawn… in fact, I'm beginning to think I'm not going to bother. Boycott it in protest, make a stand, picket the whole… '

'*Jo.*' For a second the velvet silkiness of Kim's voice was replaced by more than a hint of iron fist. 'That hollow rattling noise isn't the sound of you bottling out, is it? Because if it is, you'll make me one very angry bunny, and you should know by now, dear, that my bite is always much. *Much.* Worse than my bark. So get your high-heeled skates on and fasten your seat-belt as we're in for a – oh, you know the rest,' followed by a throaty chuckle.

'But I'm… the mascara and it's only… ' Jo was left speaking to a thrumming dial tone. She stared at the handset, a grin starting. That woman. Possessed. Entranced by Kim's excitement, she wandered through to the living room, to the window and the view of the town that had led her to rent it.

Seacrest was looking wonderful, the sky darkening, autumn the perfect backdrop to the racing, chasing patterns of coloured light-bulbs flashing around the cinema signs, fireworks exploding here and there above the rooftops from back gardens. An official display had been arranged to mark the end of the Reception, but it was as if people down there couldn't keep their excitement to themselves, had to let it explode about them, add their own burst of light to the skies and – Jesus *Christ*!

An explosion above Jo's roof resulted in a downpour of cascading, whistling sparks and we shot up and away through the window, as far and as fast as a Chinese rocket. As we zoomed up we were caught in a pillar of light sent up by one of the huge spotlights dotted about the town that had sat dormant for years, waiting for perfect occasion to blaze into life.

The light swung off to the side and left us in darkness as we headed toward the Seacrest sign decorated with fairy lights. Switching on the spotlights signalled to the world this town was back in business and as we stared off into the dark countryside, searched the wooded hillsides, we could make out the reason for this change. A tiny glowworm snaking its way through the black, the slender chain of lights of the Seacrest Special. A train reserved for extraordinary journeys and carrying a very precious cargo.

CHAPTER EIGHTEEN

Although Arthur had spent weeks preparing his role it was only when he saw the effect he had on his two assistants that he realised what it actually meant to *be* Cameron Fletcher. The dangerous, delirious power of it.

Stepping out from his taxi, entering the shabby, back-of-beyond railway station, he reminded himself that, 'I am Cameron Fletcher, man of the world, friend to the stars, whose reputation had granted him the status of myth'. The sort of man who would take completely in his stride being greeted by a handsome young man and a delightful young woman whose eyes shone with hero worship. Both were so elegantly dressed in chic fifties clothing a Technicolour glow seemed to surround them. Not for one *moment* would Fletcher consider turning tail and sprinting back to a life of chocolate digestives and daytime telly. Oh no, that sort of behaviour would be reserved for the likes of Arthur Dott.

No, Fletcher would consider this his due. He'd retain his composure when confronted by the young lady's bosom, a proud display of the benefits of cantilevered underwear which caused Arthur's heart to twinge with nostalgia. Remember, you're a man of distinction, decorum! Not the sort who'd ever been referred to as the 'poor man's Sid James'. You're the sort of man who would stroke his beard in charismatic fashion, smile enigmatically at such breathless enthusiasm. And Arthur began to realise just how much fun being Fletcher could be. The wonderful possibilities.

The young man held out his hand and on feeling how slick it was Arthur – *Cameron* – grasped it reassuringly in both hands. He was aware of his responsibility as the star attraction, to keep everyone at ease, to let his confidence spread and relax those whose happiness depended upon his well-being. 'Mr Fletcher, it really is... I mean, *such* a great honour to meet you at last, sir.'

Cameron released his grip, a cigar appearing in his right hand courtesy of a concealed spring device, waved away any formality. 'Why, thank you, it's a delight to meet you too but I have a favour to ask. *Please* don't call me 'sir'. Yes, I admit I am old enough to be your great-grandfather but I'd rather not be reminded of the fact'. On seeing the panic on the young man's face Arthur told himself off. Chump. *Remember*, your opinion *matters*. Chuckle reassuringly. See, tension dissipating as he patted down his overcoat pockets, playing the bumbling old man, trying to find his matches.

He had to keep in mind that the best thing about this show was that there was no blasted script to memorise. Improv had always been one of his strong points. And give yourself a pat on the back, Dotty old son, accent wasn't too bad. Nice to hear it out in the open with an audience. Generic American, the baritone rich enough to keep listeners mesmerised...steady now. Best not get carried away before things had really begun.

'Let's start off on first name terms so call me Cameron, both of you,' he told them around a mouthful of cigar. 'Now, where did I put those... '

And there in front of him was the wondrous girl with her soft blonde curls and red, red lips, the very definition of pert, holding up a small silver lighter and offering him the flame. My. If all of Seacrest was as beautiful as this creature...

'Why, thank you, my dear. You really are a marvel, aren't you? I've indeed been an idiot for taking so long to visit.' Cameron took a few deep puffs, drawing the sweet smoke into his lungs, a luscious Cuban brand. Puffing out smoke-rings he thought, here I am. The genie released from the bottle, made flesh.

'Now, as you are my chaperones for the trip we're going to be spending quite a bit of time together so I suggest we start getting to know each other better. Shall we go and make ourselves comfortable?' Cameron strode to the door out onto the platform, crooking his arm towards the young lady as he went, a gesture Arthur wouldn't have made for fear of ridicule. But he was no longer Arthur, he was someone else entirely, and it filled him with delight when she smiled bashfully, took his arm and, with surprising confidence, led him eagerly, firmly forward.

The boy followed, looking put out by her close proximity to their guest of honour. 'I'm James Douglas, Mr Fletcher,' he called, 'Acting Assistant Manager's assistant at the Phoenix Cinema, the grandest in Seacrest, Mr Callum Boyd's. And this is Simone… ' And she interrupted, quick to steal back the spotlight.

Her voice was an intoxicating surprise, telling of late nights spent drinking cheap vodka in basement bars, endless filterless cigarettes. Not unlike Rita Mae from years back, Arthur reminisced… ah yes, dear Rita with her passion for gin, fake leopard skin and Italian men. Soon saw through his accent ('Arturo' indeed, what was he *thinking*) but there was that one glorious night during a nightclub lock-in in Soho… where was he now? Ah yes, Simone, looking up at him with that delightful smile. 'Beauvais, Mr Fletcher, sorry, *Cameron.* Simone Beauvais. Entertainment Co-ordinator at the Phoenix'. The way she smiled, coyly tipping her head, caused Arthur to stumble as he pondered just the sort of entertainment she could prove adept at co-ordinating. Steady Dott… remember, International Man of the World. Not elderly letch from Leeds.

She continued, 'Mr Boyd is very sorry he isn't here to greet you in person but he felt it best if he stayed in Seacrest to oversee the delegation that will meet you there at the station. He hoped you would enjoy a peaceful trip, time to prepare before your arrival. As you can imagine, we're all *thrilled* about your visit and Mr Boyd hopes that the Seacrest Special meets with your approval. It's only used for very, *very* special occasions.'

Trying to place her accent – soft undertow of Scottish West Coast but overlaid with an RP precision, as if she'd walked off screen after supporting Googie Withers, a good girl gone bad – Arthur took a few moment to notice the large steam train. They walked over the footbridge to the platform opposite and it chuntered beneath them like a nesting dragon, its gleaming green engine, long carriages of black and maroon decorated with the Seacrest crest, for him. Specially arranged for *him*.

Keep walking, keep concentrating on walking, don't let the fact your knees have turned to blancmange and your gut is trying to make a quick escape from the nearest orifice *too* obvious. That was it... one foot after the other... Why on *earth* had he thought it was a good idea to chuck that stash of beta blockers for first night nerves? OK, so he hadn't had a first night in years but this was turning into the mother of all first nights.

Making their way to the front carriage, James scurrying up ahead to open the door, Arthur saw the driver was waiting for them, wiping his hands clean on grubby rags. He became aware of a sliding, clunking noise following their progress. Windows sliding down as they passed, an audience growing, faces pressed against glass, people leaning out to get a better view, whispering, pointing, smiling. And the panic left him, changed into something else; a sense of entitlement, a sense of possession. This is what it felt like in the early days, walking out on stage and thinking of the people out there, 'Right. Got you. For the next few hours you're *mine*.'

'It really is an honour, Mr Fletcher' said the driver, introduced as Gordon Knox, giving him a hand-shake greasy with oil. Arthur didn't mind, didn't mind one bit. Gordon, ten years younger than me perhaps? Mid-fifties? But there was that look, clear in his eyes, like looking into a mirror. A man given a second chance, desperate to explain what this meant to him. 'I've driven – well, used to drive – the Seacrest Special for years, she's a lovely machine, a beauty, and it wasn't right her not running. I wanted to say, tell you face to face, I can't think of any better reason to start her up again.' He wiped his eyes with that oily rag. 'Smoke, sir, you know, from the engine.' Cameron nodded, sympathetic.

'And this is a great honour for me, Gordon, truly.' Aware of the audience at his back, some passengers even stepping out onto the platform, Cameron turned slightly, still addressing Gordon but granting others the opportunity to hear a man long silent. 'You know, one of the reasons it has taken me so long to get here, aside, of course, from the inconvenience of being pronounced dead, was I feared Seacrest couldn't live up to my expectations. I believe it is in my essay, 'The Lost Exposure', where I talk about the pleasures of unseen, unmade films. How lost films become perfect in our minds because we never have to face the disappointment of seeing them fall short of our expectations. And this is how I felt about Seacrest.'

Listen to that. The electric silence of people listening. Arthur paused, slipped a cigar into the front pocket of Gordon's blue dungarees. 'But I am beginning to realise what an old fool I've been. That reality might have more to offer than dreams in the dark. Now, Simone, James, if you'd be so kind as to show me to my carriage seat. We mustn't hold up these fine people any longer. Gordon, it's been a pleasure.' Before walking up the steps to his carriage he turned to acknowledge the applause greeting the first proper public performance of Mr Cameron Fletcher.

On entering the private carriage Arthur was almost disappointed to find it empty. More people would have meant more practice, an opportunity to fine-tune the fooling. But hey, comfy-looking brown leather couch, a couple of green leather armchairs, mahogany bar, James already pouring him a whisky… he couldn't complain.

Easing into an armchair perfectly moulded to his contours, Cameron sighed contentedly as James brought him his drink and Miles Davis played from hidden speakers. Arthur stretched out, took a long sip and wondered if Fletcher would be rogue enough to peer admiringly through the bottom of the crystal glass at Simone's legs pulled up beneath her on the couch opposite. Probably not but hey, a man should take the opportunity to appreciate such sights when he could… bugger, what was this? Young James in the chair next to him flourishing a clip board. Rarely a sign fun was about to commence.

James coughed nervously. 'I know you must be tired from your flights Mr Fletcher' – and did Arthur see Simone smirk at this? Did she know it took a train journey and two buses and a taxi to get here? – 'I thought we might be able to quickly go over your Festival itinerary. And give you a quick briefing on the people you'll be introduced to at the station. A select few before the Reception later in the evening.'

'A select few eh?' Fletcher responded distractedly, his interest taken by a stack of defunct movie magazines sitting on the round wooden table next to his chair. He selected a copy of *Flicker*, leafed through it idly. 'I don't suppose these were provided by the keeper of my Archive, Mr Luke Howard, were they? Will he be one of that select few? That *will* be interesting. I've been – ahem – *dying* to meet him.'

Simone and James glanced at each other in shock, Fletcher laughing, a deep rumble to reassure them. 'Oh, don't look so concerned. I don't mean any malice to the boy. If it weren't for him it's doubtful I would even be here. But I would like to meet him at some point, I've an *awful* lot to talk to him about, as you can imagine.' And to fool *him*, to convince Luke, Cameron Fletcher was there in the flesh… that would be achievement indeed, one Arthur could retire on.

'Ehmm… I'm not sure Mr Boyd would… ' Flustered, James flipped through the pages of his clipboard as if actually expecting to find Callum had pencilled in a meeting between Fletcher and his arch rival until Simone came to his rescue. 'I'm sure there'll be plenty of time for you to meet Luke, Cameron'. She unfurled those lovely long legs of hers to sashay towards the bar to mix a gin and tonic. 'Perhaps, instead of talking about timetables and dignitaries, Mr Fletcher would like us to tell him more about Seacrest from a personal perspective. We don't want to bore him before we even get there.'

Cameron leant over the gap between the chairs, gave James's arm a reassuring pat then whipped the clipboard from his grasp, flinging it to the furthest corner of the carriage. Simone giggled while James looked even younger, pale and aghast, lost without his security blanket.

'Simone's right, James. I would much, *much* rather hear about all Seacrest has to offer from two such bright young things than board members and council staff and dignitaries,' Fletcher purred.

The train shuddered as if in assent and the platform began to slip away as Simone returned from the bar with her drink and a bowl of green olives, placing them on the magazines beside Fletcher. 'Stuffed with anchovy and lemon. Just as you like them. Miss Shona Boyd made sure of that'. Curling back onto the couch her expression may have been flirtatious but also with the hint of a warning. Careful old chap. Exercise a little caution. Don't want to get carried away and piss off your employers before you've even started properly.

He chose the plumpest olive on offer, flicked it into the air, catching it in his mouth, chewed thoughtfully. 'Ah yes. Miss Shona Boyd. I've yet to have the pleasure of meeting that intriguing young woman. Already I feel that she knows me better than I know myself... so, we're off and that gives us, what, an hour? Plenty of time for you to tell me the places I *have* to visit.'

As the train sped through towns and villages where children stood along railway bridges screaming with happiness when caught in the sudden cloud of the Special, Arthur was able to compile his own private itinerary for Mr Cameron Fletcher; the sort of things *he* would like to see between special screenings and seminars.

James was quiet at first, constrained by nerves. But as Simone held forth with tales of fantastic club nights, the fancy dress cabarets, the late-night Tunnel showings, he gained confidence in her pride in Seacrest, saw how diligently Cameron Fletcher noted down this information in a battered black notebook. The same sort of notebook he'd no doubt used to draft those film reviews that had stunned James when he'd first been introduced to them at Seacrest High School, that he re-read at least once every month. So when Simone paused, trying to recall if the Thin Man Cocktail Championships took place before or after The Blue Dahlia All-Nite Dance Marathon, he blurted out, 'The Kinotech! My favourite place in all of Seacrest, full of old magic lanterns and slot machines and 'What the Butler Saw' reels. If you only go to one place, go there, run by Harry Lawson, the son of, you know, Alec Lawson, the projection – hey!' He stopped, rubbing the red spot on his forehead where an olive had ricocheted having been thrown with some force by Simone.

This was missed by Cameron who had been jotting down notes but when Arthur looked up he caught the look passing between the two. What was all that about? Simone creasing that alabaster forehead into a frown, James looking ashamed. What were they talking about then...he checked his notes. Ah-hah, there it was.

'Alec Lawson? I know that name. A projectionist, wasn't he? Yes...coming back to me. 'The Man With the Golden Handshake.'

Friends of mine spoke very highly of him, you know what a superstitious bunch film folk are. I don't believe I knew he had a son. This Kinotech sounds exactly my sort of place, strange that Miss Boyd didn't tell me about it. Tell me James, will Harry Lawson be on the guest list of this shindig tonight?'

'Ummm… ' was the less than helpful response. Hmm. Curious and curiouser… All *sorts* of people Callum Boyd wanted to protect Cameron from.

'Look!' Simone shouted, leaping up with a splendid athleticism that distracted away from her co-assistant's discomfort. 'You can see the bay from here!' Cameron was only too happy to join her as Arthur realised that, yes, the excitement he felt was genuine. Like being a child again, getting the first glimpse of the sea from the coach sat between old Mum and Dad on day trips to Scarborough.

Do it well enough and this acting lark, getting into character, could feel as good as pulling on a tailor-made suit, cut to make you look fantastic. Cameron Fletcher was proving to be a comfortable fit, a second skin, and experiencing an exhilarating rush of adrenaline, Arthur headed for the carriage door, pulled down the window, ignoring Simone and James' cries of 'Be careful Mr Fletcher!'

Sticking his head outside, feeling cinders scorch his beard, he blinked away soot-induced tears and could see the spot-lights raking the sky, the flicker and dazzle of fireworks, a neon-coloured tinge hovering about the town, a spectacle for his benefit and he let out a 'Wooooo-HOOOOOOO!', matching the sudden wail of the Seacrest Special, letting its destination know that it was speeding towards them, that Arthur Dott, that *Cameron Fletcher* was coming home.

# CHAPTER NINETEEN

'Bloody *hell!*' Jo exclaimed as Kim's Aston Martin jerked to a halt in the one remaining parking space of Seacrest Station. 'So much for this being low-key. Looks like all of Seacrest is here.'

She hoped Kim didn't pick up on her relief at seeing so many people thronging the entrances, pressed against crash barriers. The fan-boy hordes meant there was less of a chance of Callum Boyd spotting her and wondering what she was doing there without an invite. If she kept her head down she should be OK unless – 'Wait, Kim, no, hey!'

Unfortunately Kim demonstrated absolutely no desire to fade quietly into the background and was hauling Jo towards the central entrance where the crowd was most tightly packed. Past Fletcher devotees who'd travelled from around the world, the screens of mobile phones and digital cameras glowing as they were checked to ensure they'd be able to capture the moment when their hero touched Seacrest soil.

Kim really was an amazing woman, Jo appreciated. Those surrounding them had no idea who she was and yet she was able to carve her way through, the *authority* she gave off, resulting in a parting of the ways until they were right up to the station gates and... aww crap.

Two young policemen, trying their hardest not to look out of their depth, were stepping forward, lifting a hand to stop them passing through. When they realised who was approaching Jo understood they fully appreciated a bad night for them was about to get worse. Rampaging football hooligans, drugged up knife-wielding maniacs would have been a preferable option to Kim Taylor on a mission.

'Ah, Miss Taylor?' said the braver – or stupider – of the two. 'Sorry but, y'see, right, we know you're on the list here.' He pointed to the clipboard his visibly quaking colleague was holding, 'but we, ah, just need to check if Dr Ashe here is on it too. Under strict instructions see from… ah… ahem,' eyes flicking from side to side, checking there were plenty of reliable witnesses about should any act of violence be committed, 'Mr Callum Boyd.'

In a sweetly selfless attempt to draw the full blast of Kim's wrath from his colleague, the other officer coughed nervously. 'High security situation, Miss Taylor, no problem with you getting through like, it's just…' His voice trailed to silence after being stunned by a glare from Kim. Its effect was visibly breath-taking, the officers gulping.

It was an expression both of them knew and feared from their childhood, the Alhambra All-star days. Enjoying their discomfort, Kim was quite prepared to draw out their suffering, keeping them fixed with her stare as she slowly opened her handbag, reaching inside to draw out – please God, not the revolver lighter! Jo panicked – her silver cigarette case. She opened it with a click that seemed to quell the noise of the crowd behind them, drew out a black, gold-banded cigarette, held it to her lips, the other hand resting on her hip. 'Well boys… ' she drawled, 'isn't one of you going to match me?'

The two officers began obediently checking their pockets, the younger of the two triumphantly producing a packet of Moviegoer matches. The flame shook in his grip and Kim tilted back her head to send up a plume of smoke. When she faced them her smile was as welcoming as a shark's to a seal.

'Now, Angus,' a brief nod to the elder and taller of the two,

'Derek' – the younger one nodded back, 'I know you two are only following orders and, this town having been so *very* dull in recent years, I can't really blame you for behaving like glorified bouncers. But if you were to actually consult that list of yours properly,' – a flick of ash in the direction of the clip-board – 'instead of throwing your weight around like a pair of pre-pubescent Dirty Harrys you'll notice those invited are allowed to bring a guest. And Dr Ashe is mine. So if you'll excuse us. Come on Jo, stop hovering. People will think you're not supposed to be here.'

'Right, yes, I'll, ah… ' Jo dithered until Kim grabbed her by the wrist and headed towards the slight gap between Angus and Derek. Their police training kicked in, they instinctively drew together and Angus hardly felt afraid at all when he held his hand up and said, 'I'm sorry, Miss Taylor, but I will have to stop you there and… '

'Angus Leslie,' and he was instantly transformed into a 12-year-old caught smoking at the back of the Alhambra during a break in rehearsals for *Lost Boys: The Musical*. 'Are you *honestly* going to make me remind you of the help I provided after the unfortunate *accident* you had during that screening of *Jaws*? And you, Derek Connor, I'm *especially* disappointed in you… a full box of tissues and a tub of Neapolitan ice-cream was what it took to restore some sense into you after I had to take you out of *Bambi*. Never seen a young lad so hysterical, your mother was horrifie… '

And as it was with Charlton Heston before the Red Sea, the barrier to Kim and Jo's progress melted away.

'Thank you gentlemen, most kind. If you'll excuse us, Dr Ashe and I have a train to catch.

Jo let herself be pushed and jostled to the far end of the platform, content to be swept along, carried by the growing excitement. A few faces from the Consortium swept by, giving her a 'And what are *you* doing here?' look but she scarcely noticed, lost to her memories.

She'd been *positive* she'd taken a trip on the Seacrest Special once on a family holiday but after some research accepted it must have been a false memory. She'd checked those old Seacrest Special timetables, asked her Mum and Dad, getting them to dig out old diaries and accepted the sinking realisation the train ride was impossible. That she *couldn't* have sat on those creaking seats, rough tartan material scratching her through her jeans, crying out in delight at the first whoop of the steam engine…That was when she'd had confirmation of what Seacrest could do to a person. Mess with their head, blend dreams and memories…

Sighing, Jo decided to pay closer attention to the people surrounding her, struck by how different the atmosphere was to other events when celebrities had visited. There could be a nasty edge whenever a red carpet appeared, a taint of cynicism in the air but tonight… their *faces*. It was like Santa was coming to town. Even journalists were trying to get as close to the platform edge as security would allow, craning their necks, desperate to be the first ones blinded by the lights of the engine.

She noticed a group playing it cool. Five of them looking slick and corporate and definitely not from around these parts, they must have been Callum's business chums, smirking at the local yokels, the quaint provincials. She spotted their ring-leader, Callum, appearing behind them, leaning in to share a joke with the sleekest. Probably spent his time before being hired by Callum advising the Tory Party or Satan on PR.

Callum drew back from the Canary Wharf posse, taking up position between them and the official Seacrest Welcoming Party, a random mix of cinema owners, primary school teachers, councillors and cabaret entertainers wearing more clothes than usual and on best behaviour. Kim was chatting away to Harriet Kidd who looked as if she was about to faint, leaning against one of the barriers. Typical Kim. Tough talking broad but always sure to seek out the person who needed her support most, buoying Harriet up.

Jo smiled, felt a rush of affection for her friend but her eye was drawn back to Callum. Even Kim was glancing over at him with a blend of contempt, admiration and something else and Jo resolved to ask at some point, probably when Kim was safely drunk, if anything had ever happened between those two. There was always a certain frisson and the way Callum looked, it was perfectly understandable. He was like an old school Hollywood film star, suit immaculate, hair magnificent, bearing confident. His smile that of the perfect host who knew he was throwing the sort of party that would be talked about for years.

Wait though. While it might be smooth on the surface... Jo saw it. The same tic as Shona, the clenching and unclenching of the right fist, sure sign he was feeling the pressure and – shit! He was looking over, he'd see her, she'd be chucked out and then – Oh.

The beam of Boyd's gaze passed over her without stopping and such was his brilliance that night she felt disappointed. Those eyes of his. *So* like Shona's. She *must* be here. Surely. She couldn't have changed so much she'd want her Dad to take the glory.

Jo was distracted from scanning the crowd for that long red hair, those sharp blue eyes by three hoots from a train whistle and a hot rush, a blast of steam like a great shining green metal dragon coming into land. The crowd surged forward, drawn irresistibly to greet the cheers from the carriages, all windows open, people leaning out and waving ribbons, flags, newspaper, confetti, *ticker tape* even. Jo tried to concentrate on breathing, crushed between two large male Fletcher enthusiasts who were dementedly waving their phones aloft.

As the hissing of the engine quietened to a whisper, there was a shift in the atmosphere, a quietening. The crowd stopped moving forward, the pressure around Jo lessening, allowing her to take in the exquisite tension of waiting that held the hundreds still.

A door in the front carriage opened and there he was, waving wildly, taking in the crowd, the joy of being there, laughing in such an unrestrained way, his wide torso shaking, straining against that waistcoat. Impossible not to join in, to share his sheer delight and the applause began.

It was only when her palms started to sting that Jo paused. What was she *doing*? He was a fake and she was working to expose him and yet... she was still applauding. Even those business city types couldn't resist, clapping and whooping like a bunch of over-excited teenagers at a boy-band concert. Jo couldn't deny he had learnt his part to perfection. Remember, this was Arthur Dott, she told herself, that's who he was, Arthur Dott, last seen in one of those adverts they show during daytime, a frame-device for getting up after you've been gardening. But *look* at him... It was impossible *not* to think of him as Cameron Fletcher.

Tall, broad, old tweed suit, black waistcoat with a gold watch chain strung across it. The type of man who could wear a cape or a cravat and no one would laugh, it would be accepted as entirely appropriate. Grey hair swept back, a few strands falling loose, that pointed beard, grown to be stroked as though conjuring up some diabolical plan to hold the world to ransom. A right old rogue.

The sort you instantly wanted to spend more time with. Watching him made you happy, made everyone happy. Look at him, shaking hands with people behind the barriers, leaving a trail of happiness, standing on tip-toe to greet the people at the back, even producing silk-scarves from his sleeves with a nice touch of self-mockery, flinging them above the audience's head. He was enjoying himself in an absolutely honest way and that pleasure was contagious.

Jo noticed the way he brought forward his assistants, Jo recognising James and Simone from previous sightings of Callum's entourage. They looked a bit bewildered, James especially, but Cameron was taking care of them, asking the crowd to applaud them too. Simone was lapping it up and Jo couldn't believe she was actually feeling jealous. She shook her head, annoyed, as if bothered by a wasp. This whole exposé thing, might be *slightly* tougher than she thought. What hope was there when even *she* didn't want to believe this wasn't Cameron Fletcher?

But then... was this what Callum wanted? Surely it was going to be tricky to get rid of the Archive even if Cameron was exposed as a chimera if *this* was the response he got.

It looked as though Callum was realising that, his frown sharply at odds with the faces around him. His concern - what have I unleashed? - quickly passed, his smile reappeared and he was striding forward to take Fletcher's hand, greeting him warmly, introducing him to the rest of the welcoming committee.

Even then Fletcher didn't disappoint, his handshakes with the corporate suits polite but brief, those with Seacrest residents warmer, sharing a joke with the cabaret stars, pausing to kiss Kim's hand – and... what? Good *God...* it was actually still possible to cause Kim Taylor to *blush*?

Eventually Callum persuaded Fletcher towards a small raised platform with a microphone stand in front of the station's waiting room. Jo worked her way forward, wanting to get closer, to check for any glitches, any hesitation revealing the man beneath the disguise.

'Ladies and gentlemen,' boomed Callum, 'visitors and residents of Seacrest, I would like to take this opportunity to thank all of you for such a warm and memorable welcome to our honoured guest this evening. And I'm sure the gentleman I'm about to introduce' – cheers and whoops – 'will agree that tonight, feels less like a visit and more like a homecoming. So, after all these years I'd best not prolong the wait any further. Ladies and gentlemen, I give you... Mr Cameron Fletcher!'

The crowd surged once again and Jo found herself right up

against the barriers in front of Fletcher as he took Callum's place at the microphone. As he did so Jo was sure he caught her eye and there was definite recognition there. A cheeky nod, a quick wink as if to say, 'What d'you make of the show so far?' It lasted only seconds but was enough to turn Jo pale, to feel faint. He knew she knew... *God*, that was weird. Like a character in a film turning to face her as she was sitting in the cinema, stopping the action, pointing her out and saying 'Yes, yes, *you*, Dr Ashe. How do you think things are going? Enjoying the show?'

The really odd thing was she wanted him to look again, to have another moment of connection. But he was back in public mode again. The voice... perfect. Urbane, urban America, the voice she'd always heard in her head whenever reading any Fletcher criticism. Impressive.

'People of Seacrest!' – wild cheering – 'I have lived a life that has offered plenty of opportunities for regret but to that list I am forced to add the biggest regret of all. That I was foolish enough to leave it until I am an old, old man before finally making it to this wonderful town of yours! I know there are some here tonight who doubt my very existence, who have suggested I am a charlatan, a figment of the collective imagination,' – low boos and as Jo began to wonder if it might be an idea to sidle slowly towards the exit, there it was again. Unmistakable this time, Fletcher looking straight at her, his charming smile meant for Jo and Jo alone.

Part of her was desperate for him to look away and another part hated the thought of that. 'And to those I say, in the next few weeks I hope to prove to you just how real I am! A man of enthusiasm, with a heart-felt belief in the beautiful truths films can reveal!'

The applause rose, broke to a crescendo while Jo stood, clutching the metal barrier, trying to keep herself anchored against the energy and movement behind her, bracing herself against the seductive smiles of Fletcher and Boyd, as triumphant as Oscar winners.

After a while of sitting in the sealed quiet of Kim's Aston, staring at the station entrance as if not quite believing what they'd just seen, it was Jo who broke the silence, a lone seagull squawking on top of a dustbin having pulled her out of her trance.

The crowd had long since dispersed, the car park around them empty, the other cars having followed the limousine carrying Fletcher and Boyd to the Grand Reception at the Fulmar Hotel. Only the scattered streamers and banners fluttering in the wind, the glittering patches of confetti indicated that something extraordinary had happened.

'Well... that was... different. Quite a grand reception already. Didn't realise Seacrest still had it in it, eh Kim. Kim?'

Jo looked at her friend, suddenly worried. She'd never known Kim to be quiet for so long. Never known Kim to be *quiet* full stop. Jo could practically feel the energy fizzing off her like before a thunderstorm when your skin started prickling. Her eyes were fixed on the middle distance as if she could see Seacrest's future and the sight blinded her. Corners of her mouth twitching, lipstick brighter red somehow, hands in leather driving gloves holding the steering wheel tight.

'Kim are... you all right? D'you want to get a drink somewhere before we head on to the Fulmar?'

'What?'

'The Reception. The Fulmar. Do you want to go somewhere else beforehand, fix our make-up, straighten our seams, whatever. I mean, that was all pretty intense... one thing I'll give that Cameron Fletcher or whoever he is, he knows how to make an entrance.'

'He certainly does that,' came the murmured response. Kim was returning to her senses, refocusing and Jo realised with a sinking heart that one of her friends, a friend in a position of Seacrest power had fallen for Fletcher hook, line and sinker. If Kim, one of the most cynical, sceptical people she knew could be taken in by a hand-kiss and a bout of twinkly-eyed charm… what hope did the rest of them have?

'You know,' said Kim, still staring off towards the station, 'during my time in Seacrest I've met some pretty big stars. Legends even. OK, some of them were a little decrepit but the greatest still had that glow about them, that… aura. I'm talking Dietrich and Garbo, Jimmy Stewart, Cary Grant, that type. The sort who were a little bit *more* than human. Better than the rest of us, the *best* of us. They carried themselves differently. Not arrogantly, they just knew it was a privilege for ordinary folk to meet them and so they acted accordingly. With dignity, respecting their own talent, their own beauty. The only word to describe it is… grace. I know that sounds soppy and romantic and airy-fairy but you know what? That's what it was.'

'And all that? Gone.' She looked at Jo directly who nearly gasped, her green eyes were so bright with anger. 'You meet the stars of today and the most you can say about them is they're nice. That's it. *Nice* or worse, *normal*. We're left impressed because they didn't behave like the jumped-up prick or the obnoxious diva we expected. One of the *many* things that made it difficult living here is that I'd given up hope of ever coming into contact with anything approaching that level of glamour again. The sort of people we remember with awe. But *today*… that Cameron Fletcher. I tell you, girl… ' She smiled the ecstatic smile of the recently converted, 'I don't know if that man's a fake or not and quite frankly, after a performance like that I couldn't care less. That man is a *star*. He has '*It*' and he's *here* and he's *ours*.'

They sat together a few seconds longer, enjoying the giddy, light-headed rush of being star-struck. Then Kim turned the key in the ignition, revved the engine loud enough to send that seagull screeching. 'Let's go see what he does for an encore.'

 # CHAPTER TWENTY

Usually it would only have taken a five minute swoop along the Seacrest bypass to make it to the Fulmar. That night, however, the road was thronged, policemen directing traffic off to temporary car-parks set-up to deal with the influx of visitors. By the time they'd made it along the promenade, tooting at ditsy pedestrians, edged into and circled the Fulmar car-park at the back of hotel at *least* six times before parking and leaving the car, the earlier excitement had subsided somewhat.

Just as Kim was contemplating driving her ebony cigarette holder *hard* through one of Jo's lenses if she complained once more about the shoes Kim had bought her, they turned a corner, caught full sight of the Fulmar frontage and the bickering stopped.

'Scarcely recognise the old dear', murmured Kim and Jo nodded in amazed agreement. Magnificent. If Cameron Fletcher could do *this* to the Fulmar, what was he going to do to the rest of the town?

The twin staircases, sweeping up to the entrance, covered in red carpet, and *finally*, those old globe gas lights along the side of them were lit rather than dead and dull. Every window ablaze even, yes, up there, the penthouse, the Babylon Suite. A couple up on the balcony, admiring the view. 'Must be terrific,' Jo murmured, 'lucky sods.'

The lightest touch on the brass rail of the revolving doors and they glided in, Kim remarking, '*Someone's* been out with the oil can,' to a charming young man who offered her a glass of champagne from a silver tray.

Jo couldn't recall the last time she'd seen all the young members of the hotel staff wearing full Fulmar uniform. She couldn't blame them, at their age even *she* wouldn't have been seen dead in that navy and dark green tartan, the bow-*ties* even, looking like the air stewards for a soon-to-collapse Scottish airline. Tonight though the staff looked pretty snazzy, golden buttons given an extra polish, white shirts and blouses crisp and clean and so exceptionally cheerful Jo wondered how many sips of champagne they'd had themselves. And yes, she *would* have a glass, Jo accepted although she was unsure if it would lessen the sensation they were all about to start back-flipping and cart-wheeling like some mad 60s musical.

She stopped, shocked, at the ballroom doors. In the years she'd been here, every time she'd walked past previously there had been some forlorn looking tea-dance going on, a handful of pensioners shuffling about but that night it was packed, *heaving*.

Under the heat of giant chandeliers, reflected in the mirrors covering high-ceilinged walls, a jazz band on stage was swinging joyfully through a Cole Porter. The perfect accompaniment to the bubbles racing their way up to mess with Jo's head, the sight of a buffet table laden with every possible combination of canapé reminding her that she'd skipped dinner. Was it bad manners to attempt to fit two of those into her mouth at once, she wondered whilst doing so. And if she made a base in the palm of her hand of about five, then stacked another three or so, made a pyramid of food and…

'Hoy, Oliver Twist. Here,' said Kim, appearing at her elbow with a paper plate. 'Can't have you ruining any semblance of chic by resembling a starving urchin, can we now? I have a reputation as make-over queen to protect and if you end up doing a Mr Creosote you're going to lower the tone.'

'Mmph… yeff… sorry, tah.' After transferring her mini-food

mountain, Jo was able to better take in her surroundings in the company of Seacrest's finest. Breath-taking. A town full of show-offs had waited *years* for this, an opportunity to show-off as much as possible.

Jo felt distinctly underdressed although she wouldn't be telling Kim that of course. Everyone looked as fascinating, as fantastic as possible. Sally Bowles, Shanghai Lil, Louise Brooks in her Lulu bob, could waltz in there and feel right at home. It didn't matter if you were a man dressed as a woman or vice versa or somewhere in between, the only thing that mattered was looking as glorious, as *filmic* as possible.

There was someone dolled up as Carmen Miranda with a banana hat tottering at least six feet tall, Karl the barman as Greta Garbo's Red Empress blowing Jo a kiss, a handful of Marilyns, a blaze of Scarletts, even a splash of Esther Williams and – a Diabolik?

That couldn't be right... Jo hesitated, a mini fish supper half way to her mouth. OK, so Callum might have wanted to show how magnanimous he could be but a black-hooded, black-clad figure *here*? Surely he'd think that too great a risk, that one of those nut-cases would take the opportunity to tell the wrong suit exactly what some in the town thought of his plans?

Handing a bemused Kim her plate, Jo started to edge her way towards the figure lurking to the left of a set of swing-doors. They led to one of the hotel's kitchens and each time a waiter or waitress pushed through, Jo's view of the lone Diabolik was obscured. There was enough of a view of him – and she was sure it was a he – his skinniness, his twitchiness, to be familiar. It couldn't be... surely he wouldn't be that daft?

'Luke?' she called, but got tangled up by a group from *The Wizard of Oz*, a tuft of straw from the Scarecrow getting in her face, tripping over the Cowardly Lion's tail while Dorothy looked ready to give one of her ankles a kick with a ruby red slipper. Jo was sure her quarry glanced over at the commotion, saw her, backed away and went... where?

For God's sake, Luke, she thought, if that *is* you, hope you're not up to anything stupid... To steady her nerves, Jo whipped a glass away from a passing auburn haired waitress whose cheeky half-smile reminded her of Shona, filled her with hope that she'd be there followed by the panic about what would happen if she was.

After half an hour spent anxiously searching without success for a glimpse of either the Diabolik or Shona, wallflower Jo was doing her best *Carrie* impersonation, scowling at a band of Callum's corporate buddies. A merry Kim, having availed herself freely of several bottles of bubbly, danced over.

'Bloody hell, Jo, cheer up! Stop looking like a character who's just realised they're in a Michael Haenke film. This is the sort of do that would give Ken Russell in his heyday a run for his money. Come and have a boogie!' as the band segued neatly from 'It's Too Darn Hot' to 'Night Fever.'

'A *boogie*? Kim, don't you see what's happening here? This is the first major stage in Callum's battle for the heart and mind of Seacrest and it's proving to be a walk-over. Look at them,' she tipped her glass in the direction of Callum's cronies. 'See how they're changing? how they're letting Seacrest enter their bloodstream? You can tell they're realising the potential here. And everyone else is happy to go along with it, to live up to the Seacrest stereotype. Like zoo animals putting on a show for the visitors.'

'Oh, for God's sake, will you lighten up!' Kim's irritation was as eye-watering as champagne bubbles hitting the sinuses. 'For once in your life let yourself go and *enjoy* yourself. All this analysing and critiquing, it's *exhausting*. Stop sitting on the sidelines and *live a little*.' With that she was off, jiving away to 'Staying Alive' with the owner of The Dude's Milkshake and Steakhouse who was wearing an obscenely tight flared purple jumpsuit.

She was right, Jo sighed. It was just so *depressing*. Because she *knew* Callum Boyd had won, that Seacrest was doomed and the reason she knew that was because someone like Jo, who should be battling for its soul, understood deep down the fight was useless. She had already accepted it as inevitable, the town finally falling in line with the rest of the country, its high street looking the same as everywhere else. And, selfish cow she thought herself to be, she was less miserable about that than Shona not being there.

Surrounded by people having a good time, partying on the edge of a precipice and she was still waiting for that tap on the shoulder. The kiss on the cheek hello, the Kathleen Turner whisper… 'Pleased to see me?' The most attractive woman in a room full of film-stars in front of her, wanting to spend time with dull Dr Ashe.

'Idiot', she whispered. *So* not going to happen and Jo accepted Shona had been right when she'd pointed out champagne always made her maudlin. She would have to face up to it, Shona wasn't going to ride to the rescue, save her from herself. She'd just have to get used to her heart jumping every time she saw a familiar bare shoulder, a flash of red hair before realising it was a Ginger Rodgers, a Rita Hayworth instead…

As we started to wish we'd followed Kim's progress instead of staying with this suicidal wallflower downing another flute, the chandelier lights dimmed, the jazz band fell silent, the crowd noise lessened to an excited, whispered buzz in anticipation of the man they were here to see.

CHAPTER TWENTY-ONE

Let us rewind an hour, images zipping past, to share intimate moments behind the scenes with the great Cameron Fletcher, to find out what a legend gets up to when he has time alone to relax, away from his adoring fans.

We watched him bid goodbye to his mini-retinue at the door of the Babylon Suite, courteous to all, bestowing charm even on the besuited business types he'd taken an instant dislike to. Even *they* had become more likable in his presence because that was what Cameron Fletcher *did*; found something interesting in everyone he met, allowed them to feel more attractive, more intelligent than they thought themselves.

They lingered outside once he'd shut the door, bereft although feeling better for having met him, counting down the minutes to when they would see him again. We, back in the hotel room, held our breath and waited for the transformation to take place; the return to base matter from gold, as Fletcher slipped off his coat, loosened the top two buttons of his shirt and sat down heavily on the Emperor-sized bed.

We waited for the return of Arthur in vain though. Cameron retained his presence, his charismatic force-field, that wry look about the eyes suggesting he knew he was always being watched and how much he loved that sensation. He eased back onto pillows filled with goose-down, rested against rich Egyptian cotton sheets, closed his eyes and started to snore lightly.

When he awoke we almost cheered with relief because there he was, Arthur back amongst us, although confused, discombobulated. Good God, he'd had the weirdest dream. He was some kind of magician travelling about in a flaming *steam* train, two assistants hanging on his every word and *bloody* hell…Arthur looked around, shocked. What was all this then? Had he fallen asleep on set again? Some kind of Cleopatra remake? Liberace biopic?

The last time he remembered seeing *this* much gold lamé was that birthday bash Cilla Black threw for Chris Biggins. Arthur was never allowed to darken LWT's doors again after what happened that night. Wherever this place was it had a decent set of curtains though even if they did look as though they'd been stitched together from the contents of Shirley Bassey's wardrobe. Bloody massive windows those…

As Arthur heaved himself up and wandered over to his very own balcony we saw the transformation was complete. Strangely, we felt comforted by this as there was something *unnatural* about Cameron Fletcher, his ability to leave a room monochrome once he'd left it, whereas Arthur had a shabbiness that immediately put us at ease.

We knew he was back because of the rounded shoulders, a curious lack of bulk, of presence, the eyes less eager to absorb every available snippet of information. He was there in the lack of Fletcher cool. This was a man battling a slow war of attrition against his body; a finger rummaging furiously in his right ear, the irritable scratching of his beard, the remarkable trumpeting when he blew into a green silk handkerchief that had previously sat as a perfect triangle poking from a waistcoat pocket, now stuffed up a sleeve.

He reminded us of a friendly, eccentric friend of our Dad's we called an 'Uncle' even though he wasn't, and who'd visit on rare, memorable occasions when we were young. He'd bring inappropriate presents – a flick knife, a hamster, a grass snake – take advantage of the drinks cabinet, cause Mum to tut and whisper to our Dad who was secretly revelling in the freedom his visits brought about.

Arthur sneezed at a volume that set the bulbs of the chandelier tinkling. He should have brought some anti-histamines but then who the hell had hanging baskets on the *inside* of a place? He wouldn't want to be the poor sod who had to water them every morning. Still, least the flowers distracted from all those blooming *mosaics*... great beardy king things with lions bodies... not exactly Ikea now, was it? Wait... hanging baskets... the Babylon Suite.

Something chimed faintly in Arthur's head and he made his way to the bedside table where a sheet of paper intended to resemble papyrus lay beneath his room key. In letters so curlicued they were almost unreadable he made out, 'Welcome to the Eighth Wonder of the World! The Fulmar Hotel's deliciously decadent Babylon Suite! For mini-bar costings, room service options and available breakfast options please see Guest Information and Welcome Pack located inside the snake casket.'

Of course! You old fool Dotty, Arthur chastised himself, this was Seacrest and he was Cameron Fletcher! A man told by his host, silver-tongued Callum there, that any expenses should be charged to his account! How the heck could Arthur have forgotten a thing like *that*? When was the last time he'd been allowed gratis access to a mini-bar? Oh yes. That was right, never in his puff, so he decided to take full advantage.

Five minutes later, Arthur was reclining on a chaise-lounge with a crystal tumbler near filled to the brim with four miniatures of brandy, picturing himself as Richard Burton lacking only Elizabeth Taylor to make his happiness complete. '*Finally*', he sighed contentedly, he could have a relax, the tension in his shoulders vanishing, a relief to not be under surveillance. Very enjoyable most of the day had been but there were times when keeping up the Fletcher front had felt like being on constant alert as to whether his flies were undone. Talking of which…

Realising how quickly his drink had travelled through his system, after a brief tussle with gravity, Arthur made it upright and to the bathroom, pausing in amazement before bodily necessity took over. Flaming *Nora,* there was a touch of the catacombs about the bath, that amount of white marble must have weighed a *ton*. Lions-head taps and all, bit on the Vegas side but hey, Arthur wasn't complaining. It certainly beat a B&B, peeing into a toilet designed like a chariot. Positively majestic.

It was when washing his hands Arthur got his first shock of the evening. Looking into the mirror above the basin he started back. Flaming heck! Who the hell was *that* – oh. Himself, very definitely Arthur Dott and not Cameron Fletcher nearly giving himself a heart attack. If anyone ever got round to asking him why he decided to take such a daft job as this on, all he'd need to do was point to this mug. It looked as though he was permanently auditioning for the *Casualty* role of 'Dementia Patient.' Who *wouldn't* want to take a break from themselves if they looked like *this* on a regular basis?

Threatening to tip into a slough of self-loathing, Arthur suffered his second shock. A woman's voice in the bedroom, soft at first – 'Arthur?' – then louder, almost stern – '*Arthur*', sharply followed by Arthur knocking his glass over, sending it clattering into the wash basin. It came to rest in the plug-hole with the inevitability of a roulette ball falling on black when you'd bet your life savings on red.

'What the bleeding hell's *this*?' he whispered to his reflection that looked even more haggard. No one was supposed to know he was *him*, especially not some woman who'd strolled in without even bothering to *knock*. There was no use him trying to stay in there after that racket. Although…philosophically speaking, he wasn't there, was he? Not *really*.

He fixed himself in the mirror with a stare as tough and cold as Sheffield steel, ran the cold water tap, splashed his wrists, a ritual picked up in Rep for calming his nerves. Began one of his internal mantras to exact his transformation, call into being Fletcher's Jekyll to his Hyde, Buddy Love to his Nutty Professor.

'I am Cameron Fletcher. I am movies, New York skyscrapers, Underwood typewriters, cigar boxes, magic tricks, picture puzzles, single malts, cracked leather armchairs, blood rare steaks and mysterious dames with danger in their eyes.'

When he stepped out of the bathroom our breath left us. Arthur Dott had vanished and there, with a spring in his step and a glint in his eye, was Cameron Fletcher, met by an impressed Shona Boyd. 'My, Arthur... you do scrub up well, don't you?' She granted him a patter of applause and her sly half-smile as reward.

'Dear Shona, as always a pleasure, but don't you think you could give poor Arthur some warning the next time? His heart isn't up to surprises, even one as pleasant as this.'

'Very impressive but the accent, Arthur, remember the accent. At the moment it's hovering around New Jersey with a stop-over in Accrington.'

'It's Leeds *actually*.' Cheeky mare. Shona always put Arthur on edge. It felt like the audition all over again, then the secret meetings in cafes and pubs, Shona checking him out, sizing him up. Look at her, Lady Muck, giving him and the place the once-over.

'Where's the mini-bar then, Arthur?' – he *really* wished she'd stop calling him that – 'Could murder a G&T.' He nodded in the direction of a knee-high ziggurat in the corner. Crouching down to open it she revealed a length of calf that had Arthur wishing he'd brought along his beta blockers. She laughed. 'Good to see you're making the most of Dad's hospitality. Keep it up, he can afford it.'

Whatever he's paying, he should double it. That performance

you gave earlier on was quite something. Everyone in the palm of your hand.'

Arthur had met plenty of operators like Callum in his line of work and knew how to deal with his type. The sort who was too busy admiring himself to see what was really going on but this one he was going to have to watch. As sharp as a fox that's learnt how to use a bowie knife. Same eyes as her Dad's, but a cooler blue, giving off little flashes like those shards of glass you miss when something's broken and tread on later.

The way she talked about Callum, there was certainly no love lost there. She was making clear she was employee rather than a loving daughter, working for her boss rather than her Dad. Or at least *appearing* to... Cameron stroked his beard thoughtfully while Arthur considered his position working for a woman who resembled Goneril as played by a psychotic Katherine Hepburn and concealed a shudder.

Joining her on the balcony, with each step he allowed the armour of Cameron Fletcher to fall more snugly about his shoulders. Because it was definitely Fletcher who should deal with Shona Boyd. A man who dreamt about women like this, the sort who always have an insurance investigator dogging their heels, ready to question them on the curious circumstances surrounding their husbands' deaths.

She certainly knew how to carry herself. Arthur admired the sight of her standing there with the curtains billowing like something out of *Gatsby*, sipping at her hi-ball glass. When she looked at him properly, like just then, it was like being hit by the heat from an oven and the chill of a freezer combined. A not unpleasant sensation, both refreshing and... exciting. Arthur knew for definite Cameron was well and truly back because the look she was giving him was not the sort anyone would give to Arthur Dott but one reserved for the likes of Cameron Fletcher.

'Ohhh,' she breathed out and smiled. A full smile this time, not the coy half-sort she shared with Callum. 'That's better. You're back to walk amongst us, Mr Fletcher. No offence to Arthur, but… '

'I understand *completely*. Arthur does try his best, poor lad, but he lacks a certain dash, a certain *flair*.' The hypnotic Fletcher tone was back and Shona's eyes shone with pleasure.

'Quite. Now join me, take a proper look at your kingdom. You're going to save Seacrest from itself, be its knight in shining armour.' A less sensitive man than Cameron might not have heard the words she murmured into her glass, 'And mine too, with any luck.'

Arthur, on being properly introduced to Seacrest, felt his chest swell at the sight and thought, 'I'm *home,*' then 'Why in the name of Jesus, Mary and Joseph didn't I come when I was younger?'

He faced a skyline dotted with the flashing, buzzing energy of cinema signs reading like some fractured form of modern poetry and he wanted to visit each and every one: the RIALTO, ELECTRIC, ALHAMBRA, MODERN EASTERN and the GRAND WESTERN. The lights covered the hillside, up to the cliffs topped off with the Seacrest sign that sparkled with hundreds of tiny electric stars, then down and out to the pier, blazing with light and night-life.

That was the place he wanted to visit most. Even there on the balcony with the softest of winds blowing, you could hear the screams of excitement, that Big Wheel turning like some kind of generator, filling the air with an electricity Arthur felt tickling the back of his neck. Wasn't that where he'd been told the projectionist's son lived? Owned some kind of shop. No, *arcade*, that was it.

'That's where we're going tomorrow,' he said, pointing to the Pier. 'After the introductions and the presentations and the talks, we're going *there*. On the train James suggested I visit some place called… what was it now… the Cinematech? The Kinema?'

'Oh, *did* he? Dad *will* be interested to hear that.' Oh bloody hell,

Arthur cursed. Well done, probably got those two young souls into trouble but Shona was laughing and he knew their jobs were safe for a while. She had that expression, the one he'd noticed appearing on Callum's face. Ever so slightly patronising, yet appreciative. As if he were exceeding expectations.

'It's called the Kinotech. Harry's place, Harry Lawson. Can't say Dad will be *too* pleased that's top of your list of places to visit but we'll see what we can do.'

'See what we can do?' It was Shona's turn to feel unsettled, a sensation so rare it felt almost pleasurable. Because the tone of the man next to her was that of someone used to having his wishes fulfilled.

'Miss Boyd, I appreciate I'm here as a guest and so will pay due attention to the wishes of my host. But I am most certainly *not* here to be kept on a lead. As long as it doesn't conflict with my agreed commitments, if I want to visit a place while I am here, I will visit it.'

At this Shona giggled and Arthur wondered briefly how Cameron Fletcher would do in a court of law defending himself on the charge of having thrown Miss Boyd to her doom. Despite his conclusion, Shona remained next to him, blissfully unaware of how close she'd come to being murdered by a legend.

'Oh, this is *wonderful*. If only Dad knew what he'd let himself in for! Of *course* we'll go to the pier, Mr Fletcher, I'll take you there myself. And as we tour the attractions, including the Kinotech, I'll tell you all about my Dad's plans, how he's going to turn it from *this*' – she held her arms out wide, drawing them slowly together – 'into something with all the pizzazz and charm of a newly built Tesco. Because, unlike Callum, I think it's only fair that the man who is being touted as the mascot for the brave new Seacrest, should know *exactly* what it is he's been called upon to promote.'

Hearing the barely controlled anger in her voice Arthur wondered, not for the first time, what *had* he got himself into? Then something caught Shona's attention, people below them on the Fulmar steps and her ice-queen hauteur faltered as she slipped an arm round his waist, pulling him back into the suite.

What was *that* about? He'd caught a glimpse of a small blonde woman in an emerald green dress, someone he recognised. Kim Taylor, that was her, he'd been introduced to her at the station, all too briefly… lovely green eyes. That other woman, the one in the trouser suit was Dr Ashe, wasn't it? Excellent, Arthur almost purred. He looked forward to having a chat with her, proving to her how real Cameron Fletcher was.

Arthur felt his confidence return. Yes, tonight could be very enjoyable indeed as long as he managed to escape the Boyds for long enough. Those two seemed to have family problems enough to make characters in your average Ancient Greek tragedy weep.

'Why the rush indoors? Scared we'll catch a chill?' he asked, wondering which one of those two she was so eager to avoid, putting his money on Dr Ashe.

'No rush, *Arthur,*' Shona snapped, then composed herself, her public face setting. 'I think it's about time we made our grand entrance, don't you? You've left your adoring fans waiting long enough.'

'You're quite right, Miss Boyd. Some thought this day would never come and are no doubt very alarmed that it has.' A flicker of a smile there from Shona. Yes. Dr Ashe it was then. Arthur sensed there was something going on there, a weak point and congratulated himself. Such knowledge could be useful for later and he crooked his arm, winked. 'Ready for your close-up? Let's go give them hell.'

CHAPTER
TWENTY-TWO

Jo was clutching her warm champagne, eyes fixed, along with everyone else, on Callum who had climbed half-way up the ballroom staircase opposite the stage. There was something eerie about a ballroom packed to capacity she thought, close-dancing space only and yet silent, a few nervous giggles breaking the silence. Everyone's faces, looking like kids desperate for their first ever fireworks display.

Callum was milking every minute of it, like some super-villain gaining strength from the suspense. 'Just bloody well get on with it,' Jo muttered, drawing a bug-eyed stare from a Klaus Kinski look-a-like. 'And you can get back to your raft with your mini-monkeys,' she whispered once his back was safely turned, appreciating she was perhaps rather more drunk than she'd previously thought.

Finally Callum began his role as audience conductor, becoming a focus for the charged atmosphere. He didn't need a microphone this time, the natural acoustics causing his voice to reverberate around them.

'Ladies and gentlemen and all those in-between! Earlier this evening some of you were privileged enough to attend one of the most extraordinary events in Seacrest history. The arrival of Cameron Fletcher was an experience I will treasure many years to come and I'm sure, as he'll be with us for another fortnight, there will be many more fantastic memories. A controversial figure, I'm sure you'll all be thankful that rumours of his death have been greatly exaggerated!'

Laughter, a round of applause and Jo scanned the room, hoping she'd be able to remember through the fug of alcohol who cheered this cheap jibe against Luke. And thinking of Luke…

There was that Diabolik again. Skulking – and in that outfit it would be difficult to do *anything* but skulk – to the right of the staircase. His arms crossed, his thin, lanky body tense. 'Lanky'… And Jo knew. For God's sake, of *course* it was Luke, *why* couldn't she have realised that when she was sober enough to do something useful about it? The legend he'd devoted most of his adult life to turned up and what did she *think* he was going to do but try and meet him? Stay at home and shuffle his index cards?

Jo tried to move closer to him, squeezing through the crowd bunching together to guarantee a decent viewpoint for the arrival of the Big Man. *Surely*, she hoped, he wouldn't try and do anything daft in front of all these witnesses then realised, shit, of course he would. This was Luke she was thinking about and he had been in a pretty weird way lately, even by his standards. What was he doing? Reaching behind himself for something propped up against the wall, something long and shiny and black, looked like a cane, a walking stick but could it be… surely the only guns in the Archive would be stage props?

Jo's rising panic meant she only caught the tail-end of Callum's announcement. 'So, without any further delay would you please give a very warm welcome to my daughter Shona accompanied by… Mr Cameron Fletcher!' – before she yelled out, 'Luke! No!' as people erupted around her, moving forward, pulling her away from Luke but she was sure he turned, stared at her as she realised what Callum had said… Shona.

All thoughts of Luke and his possible shotgun, a potential assassination attempt vanished as, suddenly sober, Jo focused on the woman on the arm of Cameron Fletcher, walking down the stairs as waves of applause rose to greet them.

Jo clutched her glass so tightly it squeaked. Two years since she'd seen her last, two *years*. Shona had vanished one morning, a scribbled note on Jo's bedside table, 'Off to see the world, don't wait up'. She'd kept it folded up, pressed between the pages of a notebook far too long, like a love-sick teenager. Waited weeks for a following letter, 'Here's a plane ticket, come and join me,' but none came. Shona, out there, exploring new horizons while she was stuck in Seacrest like some gay version of Greyfriars Bobby, waiting for her to come back. Unable to leave because everything about the town reminded her of Shona. The kitsch, the excitement. Being kept at a distance.

But could you blame me, Jo thought as her heart filled, breath shortening. Look at her, just *look* at her, reason enough for God giving us eyes. Red silk dress, auburn hair piled high and tumbling, ridiculous and wonderful long black gloves. Gilda resurrected in glorious Technicolour.

It wasn't only Jo, the effect Shona was having so apparent on others, there should have been a license against it. Half of them wouldn't have had a clue who she was but they could tell she was some kind of star. Taking their cue from the way Fletcher looked at her, letting them know this was a woman to be respected and admired.

Jo raised her glass and found it empty, wished she'd another dose of champagne to damp down a quick stab of jealousy. Daft, the thought of Fletcher and Shona... but what *was* going on between those two? Surely it was too much of a coincidence, the grand old man of cinematic letters back from the dead just as the prodigal daughter returned?

They were taking ages getting to Callum and Jo knew that would be Shona's doing, revelling in the applause, stealing attention away from her Dad. When they reached him, Callum gave her a peck on the cheek, whispered in her ear and she gave him that cool half-smile. The one Jo had finally realised, after months of trial and error, was meant as a warning sign. Oh yes, Jo knew Shona Boyd. Could read her like a book, pull her apart like a film.

Shona spoke first, even more confident, more assured than Jo remembered her with a slight American twang.

'For those of you wondering who in God's name I am and what I'm doing dangling off the arm of Mr Cameron Fletcher, let me introduce myself. My name is Shona Boyd and yes, as my father will be happy to confirm, nepotism *can* get you anywhere.' Cheeky, a risk but on seeing Fletcher chuckling behind her the crowd laughed warmly. 'Over the past few years I've travelled across the States, been involved in various small film festivals over there. Nothing to match the size and scale of Seacrest of course, but still, good places to be'.

'It was while I was travelling, speaking to other lovers of film, that I really became fascinated by the myth of Cameron Fletcher. Of course, I'd been aware of him while growing up here, had read a few bits and pieces. And, I have to admit, I had my doubts.' An audible, if amused, murmur of disbelief from the ballroom floor. 'I know, I know, this is exactly the wrong place to admit to such a thing, particularly with the man himself standing behind me' – she turned to give him a grin and Jo felt another stab in her chest – 'but yeah, I thought it was an interesting story but nothing more. A fairy tale dreamt up to send film-obsessed kids to sleep.'

'All that changed when I was over in the States. Meeting people who had met Fletcher, worked with him, collaborated. Discovered how much he'd done to further the careers of talented young film-makers, be they directors, scriptwriters, production designers, sound recordists, helping them refine their ideas. As I spoke to more and more of these people that's when it became my obsession to seek him out and bring him to the town that could understand him like no other. It is with a truly heart-felt delight that I ask you to show your appreciation for Mr Cameron *Fletcher*!'

Bloody hell... Jo looked around her in wonder at the raucous applause that set the chandeliers shuddering. It was a sight wilder than it was at the station, nearly aggressive. As if directed not so much at Fletcher but the London meeja types hanging at the edges, clapping politely looking ever-so-slightly intimidated. They'd come expecting some bog-standard press junket and found themselves at a demented cult gathering.

This was why Fletcher was dangerous, Jo worried, buffeted and crushed by the giddy crowd of acolytes. It was like the town sensed revenge on all those who had mocked Seacrest, calling the place past it. Now the Messiah had arrived to save it with all this energy released and it wouldn't take much for it to turn nasty.

To give him credit, Jo could see Fletcher – no, *Arthur* – knew it. No triumphalism from him, no punching the air, the conquering hero. Instead he raised his hand, accepting the welcome but asking for silence. When he started to speak he was quieter than at the station and it worked. The audience quietened down too, listened carefully to his conversational tone. Like Kim said, he did have that magic touch and it felt as if he was talking to everyone individually.

'I have no doubt over the next few days there will be plenty of opportunities for speeches. I apologise that all of you here will find it difficult to escape my presence – though, if you find that prospect tiresome, think how I feel, I have to *live* with me! Strange though this may sound, disingenuous, *naïve* perhaps, believe me when I say I don't wish my presence to overshadow this Festival.'

From anyone else this would be false modesty but Jo knew he was being... well. *Genuine*.

'One of the many reasons I agreed to come here was the impressive range of Festival programming, the number of as yet undiscovered gems tucked away for you to discover over the next fortnight. And, of course, the number of wonderfully friendly and knowledgeable people there are to meet and become good, good friends. That's what I want to start doing tonight. Shift the focus away from me and put it back on *you*, get to know you all better. You know, I have heard it said by some poor souls that there's even more to life than films.' He shrugged his shoulders in a 'Whaddya know?' kind of way as cries of disbelief followed. 'So, in the admittedly unlikely event you see me standing without a drink in my hand, feel free to come over with a glass and we'll do our best to keep each other entertained. Now, Maestro, if you please!' Flanked by Callum and Shona, Cameron Fletcher descended to the bottom of the stairs, disappearing amidst a mob of admirers while the band struck up a wild 'Let's Do It!'

Should push forward, join them, Jo resolved. Call his bluff, hold her hand out, say, 'Hello, pleased to meet you, I'm Dr Joanna Ashe and I'm here to prove you don't exist, Cameron Fletcher, or should I say… *Arthur Dott*.' Her resolution faltered on seeing who was approaching. Oh Christ. Here she was.

Sashaying a path through the crowd and heading for *Jo*. None of that pathetic tapping on shoulders, having to repeat 'Ex*cuse* me' countless times for Shona Boyd. It was one of the many skills she had that Jo could only dream about, like the ability to complain effectively in restaurants, catch the bartender's eye.

She hadn't yet looked at Jo directly, pausing to say hello to people, old Seacrest friends but Jo was where she was heading. She could feel it, that link, that bond that was *always* there. Even when Shona was thousands of miles away, Jo could feel it, knew she would come back to her one day.

So why was Jo so keen to bolt for the door even though she was rooted to the spot, until…

Shona was in front of her and it was almost painful to look. The hair, the cheekbones, those eyes, a little bashful, *nervous* even? Shona Boyd? Nervous? It was daft and corny, Jo knew, but her vision had gone blurry and she was convinced the lights had dimmed, a hush encircling, a spotlight swivelling to land on them both and one of them should really be saying something. It would be Shona, Jo would leave it to her, she never could stand a silence. When Shona looked up and smiled, the pain of two years of waiting vanished, the anger and bitterness melting away to nothing, like the ice in a dry martini on a hot summer's night.

'So... finally did something with your hair then. Who made you do it? No, wait, I know. Kim wasn't it? Did she do it herself or drag you down to the hairdressers and lock the door till they'd finished with you?'

Charming, Jo almost tutted. Where was the heart-felt apology, the explanation, the tearful reconciliation? God, she was glad Shona was back.

'And it's lovely to see you too. Sure you can spend some time away from your new best buddy, Mr Fletcher?' Oh, well done Jo, she cursed herself. No better way of welcoming back an old flame than with some petty sniping. 'He'll be pining without you and looks like your Dad's keen on you rejoining the party. I know you wouldn't want to spoil *his* evening.'

Jo nodded over to Callum who was looking in their direction, his expression flashing from one of charming bonhomie to a frown at seeing his daughter in conversation with a cohort of Luke's. Jo wondered how much he knew about the two of them. She couldn't imagine Shona sharing too much info with him on her love-life. Although Callum would have his own ways of finding out about that sort of thing.

Shona responded to Callum's head-flick telling her to return to the fold by taking Jo by the hand, leading her off towards the main ballroom doors.

'Too hot and stuffy in here, too big an audience. Let's get some fresh air, find somewhere quiet. Because you and I have a lot of catching up to do.'

Jo knew she should resist, have a bit more pride and put up a fight. Kim knew it too, breaking off from laughing with a group of fellow owners to give Jo a look that conveyed both disapproval and a weary, 'I *knew* it. Shona Boyd clicks her fingers and you go running back.'

It almost worked, almost had Jo pulling away from following silently, biddable, in Shona's slipstream. Instead she shrugged and grinned and Kim looked away, not wanting to watch her rush into getting hurt again. Surely she couldn't begrudge me this though, Jo thought. That wave of old happiness, the dizzy mix of love and lust, a feeling she'd ached for, only caught in dreams since Shona had been away. It felt as strong as the first time she'd seen her.

CHAPTER TWENTY-THREE

They spun out through the revolving doors and into the air chilly after the heat of the Fulmar. Jo expected them to head for the promenade, find a wooden viewing booth free of fish supper-eating tourists and snogging teenagers. After they'd got down the stairs though, past small groups of smokers and autograph hunters looking hopefully at Shona, trying to give a name to that movie-star, they headed off to the left of the main entrance, on to a winding gravel path, running next to a high stone wall. Jo had to concentrate to get her bearings, so caught up in the heat of Shona's hand, the softness of it. The border of the Fulmar Pleasure Gardens, she realised. For use of guests of the Fulmar only, the general public most definitely not permitted, although normal rules didn't apply if you were a Boyd.

Shona stopped in front of a locked wrought iron gate, abrupt enough for Jo to nearly bump into her. She was close enough to catch that scent of lavender and Jo breathed in deeply then stopped thinking altogether because Shona's breath was hot against her ear as she whispered wickedly, 'I have a key'. She released Jo's hand, leaving it suddenly cold, bereft, but her eyes still fixed on Jo's as she took a few steps back, easing off one of those long black gloves. 'Jeez, Shona... if the whole film legend chaperoning business doesn't work out you could always go into burlesque.'

'You see, Jo, the whole trick with accessories, where their real power lies, is in the promise of their removal', as Jo thought, two years, two *years* without *this*… how did she cope? Shona opened a small black handbag Jo hadn't noticed hanging at her side, producing the sort of spindly-looking key only ever seen in movies on the key-chain of a cat-burglar.

'How did you… ' Jo asked as Shona rattled the key in the lock before the gate opened with a great creak of protest at riff-raff breaking in. 'I've given up putting in requests to get entry to this place, always being fobbed off with stories about there not being a grounds-man available to take me round. One time I booked a room there, cost me a fortune and I was given some guff about new plants and bedding having been introduced… D'you know the maze in there is supposed to be the one Stanley Kubrick… ' Shona came back through the entrance, gently pressed a finger against Jo's lips.

'Jo… for once shut up and enjoy yourself OK? Promise? I've had this key for years. Was one of the things I meant to show you before… ' She looked away, drifted off, disappeared.

' …you left,' murmured Jo. Well. Here we go again, up the garden path. She'd waited years to get into the Gardens, to see the Chinese lanterns hanging in the branches of trees and shrubs, watch their light catch and glimmer on Shona's figure up ahead. So why did she feel disappointed? Was it because things were already following the same pattern as before, Jo being distracted from asking the right questions by being shown some new Seacrest secret? If she tried to get too close to Shona she used to make sure the town got in the way. Protect her from intimacy. 'Shona! Wait! Leaving me again…and how come you're so close to Cameron Fletcher, eh? What have you been doing all these years? Shona!'

Nothing. Jo stood, kicked some gravel against the verge, waited for a response, wasn't surprised one wasn't forthcoming. She heard only murmured conversation, quiet laughter from hotel guests nearby enjoying the secrecy with no sign of Shona up ahead. She sighed, resolved to enjoy the experience of the Gardens without expecting too much from her mostly absent girlfriend. Go on Jo, breathe in deeply, appreciate the scent of blooming autumn roses in a garden close to midnight, where you turn a corner to find your path blocked by a small but perfectly to scale, fully functioning Trevi fountain or a large, half-buried head of the Statue of Liberty. And then there were the neon signs.

Jo's mood lifted, smiling at the treat of finding the neon as beautiful as the photographs, the stories she'd been told. Designed and built by Anthony Venturi, the Italian self-styled Artist of Light, who had moved to Seacrest in the early 1950s. His creations had once graced every cinema foyer in Seacrest but, in the aftermath of his terrible early death following a botched experiment with a neon suit, became rather less popular. It hadn't put off the canny owners of the Fulmar who'd installed them in the gardens. Everywhere Jo looked she saw glowing fragments, the names of forgotten cinemas and bars, lit up branches, were reflected in ponds, buzzed softly in tree tops, their curling script suggestive of some minor, camp god signing off on their creation: 'Andromeda' , 'The Lost Hours', 'Island Dreamers' 'The Cat and the Blue'. The colours, Venturi's true genius. So much more subtle, more varied than you'd ever expect of neon.

But Jo was undecided how she felt about the Gardens as a whole. They were so well planned, well organised, easier to admire than love. Like those Zen gardens where nothing was left to chance, so the visitor saw what the designer *wanted* them to see. It was like being on a film-set...no, more than that. Like being in an animated cartoon where every last detail showed the hand of the director.

This was a prime example of that fakery, Jo thought, examining an out-of-season cherry tree. It looked amazing at first, petals falling at a slight gust of wind before she realised most of the flowers were satin, with some pink confetti added to give that blossom-fall effect. The perfect place for a rendezvous with a Boyd. A family that had this pathological need to organise the environment around them. Jo pushed her way through a curtain of plastic flowers, lost in thought, until… she gasped, 'You're *kidding*. That's not… it *is*.'

Jo had been greeted by the sight of Shona standing at the entrance to the summerhouse from *The Sound of Music*, the only difference from the film being the neon sign arching over the doorway, bathing the surrounding area in blue light, causing the air to hum about them. *Electric Moonlit Waves*. Shona smiled at her, appreciating her reaction and Jo noticed she was pulling paper cherry-blossom flowers from a twig she must have broken from the tree. She loves me, she loves me not, she loves me… and Jo's mouth went dry at the realisation they were both as nervous as each other and a rush of tenderness caused her eyes to sting briefly.

'Shona'. It was so quiet there Jo wondered if her voice was somehow muffled. The kind of silence you got in a packed cinema when a declaration of love was about to be made. Jo coughed, recovered.

'Tell me. I think I'm due it. Why did you leave like that, without telling me, without giving me the chance to try and talk you out of it? And what made you come back, was it Harry, your Dad, was it Camer… ' Shit, Jo panicked. What was Shona doing, coming towards her so quickly and – what? Was that a flare? From the hotel? Yes, fireworks but what does she –

Too late, Shona's lips, her mouth on Jo's stopping the words, stopping her breath and it would be so easy to give in, to stop talking, stop thinking, to kiss back –

But she felt a flash of anger as another flare went up and Jo pulled away, holding Shona at arm's length, tips of her fingers turning Shona's pale skin pink. 'Wait, no, honestly, is that all you think it takes to shut me up, make it all better. Kiss and make up. Godsake, you BoydS, you're so… un*believable*! Just expect everyone else to do your bidding and… '

Shona cast her head down, held the half-shorn twig to her lips. When she looked up her eyes were a colour Jo had never seen before, one that brought her up short. A blue as cold and hard as Shona's voice. 'Jo, will you *stop* playing the victim for two minutes at least, for *fuck's* sake.'

'What? But I… ' Jo stepped back, brushing against the branches of a weeping willow, Shona stalking towards her, the vehemence stunning.

'No, it's *your* turn to keep quiet, take in a few home truths. It's *always* been easier for you to blame me, hasn't it? Piling on the guilt when we were together about how I'm the reason you'd settled in Seacrest, how it wouldn't be the same without me. You probably spent all the time I was away thinking you couldn't *possibly* leave because what about when I came running back? Did you ever stop to think, did you *consider* the burden that put on me? Lugging around your weight of expectation, not wanting to disappoint?'

'For *years* I hated this place, hated and loved it, kept on trying to break free of it, Christ, leaving the Mafia would be a *breeze* compared to this. I looked around and saw good, talented folk like Harry, like *you*, who could have left and *done* things. Instead you were all happy to stay stuck here, wasting away in a freak show. Plus everywhere I went in this *Smallville* it was 'Oh, there's Callum Boyd's daughter, what's she been up to now, disgrace to the family, *she'll* be the reason her Mum's the way she is. Jo… *listen*. I *had* to get away and I *kept on telling you that*. You just didn't want to hear it.'

Shona paused, voice and eyes softening, looking away from Jo as she pulled her hand along the small branch, pink confetti scattering. 'The only reason I stayed for as long as I did was because of *you*. You were the only reason I came back after my shorter disappearances. You, Dr Ashe. You were the one thing keeping me in this loony bin. Because I loved you, love you still. I'm sorry I hurt you, you've no idea, but honestly… what choice did I have? If I'd stayed I'd have gone mad, ended up hating you for keeping me here.'

Jo tried to swallow, throat so tight her words came out as a croak. 'So… why come back? Why now? You, working with your Dad. Surely his plans, you can't agree… '

Shona laughed sharply, her expression giving no doubt of what she thought of Callum's plans. 'I *have* been away too long, haven't I, if you're starting to think that I could let Dad turn Seacrest into a sanitised theme park. You of all people should know I'm not naïve enough to think I could waltz in here and persuade him to change his mind like that… ' a click of her fingers. 'Of all the people here I'm probably the least qualified to attempt that. Well… next to Harry perhaps. Luke.'

'Have you seen Harry yet? That postcard you sent.' Jo almost bit her bottom lip hard, annoyed at her bitter tone, like a love-lorn teenager and of course Shona had picked up on it, enjoying it, knowing she'd still got the power to make all the girls and boys jealous.

'No, I haven't seen Harry. Here's me thinking you'd be above such things as the green-eyed monster.' She moved closer, hips swaying, although a near-parody of a femme fatale still sexy enough to be dangerous. Not quite touching yet, but close enough that Jo had to keep reminding herself to breathe, to not start panting like that randy Wolf in those cartoons. 'Quite sweet though. Nice to be fought over.'

Jo knew she should be asking questions, demanding to be told how much Shona knew about Arthur Dott, about what she was up to, what would happen to Luke, all the cinema owners desperate for change but Shona was getting too close, those eyes, scorching, her words brushing Jo's cheek.

'Cameron,' Jo managed, 'how did you find him?' Shona laughed, the first genuine laugh Jo had heard from her in years.

'So many questions. Same as always. The things I had to do to stop you asking them. I'll give the answers to any possible question you might have about Mr Cameron Fletcher. I'll know them all because I *made* him. Made him for you, Jo. You're the reason I brought him here. Yes, to save the town, stop my father's evil plans, yah-da-yadda, but mainly to save *you*. Make you realise there's more to life than the stuff you find in books or in the dark of a cinema. Thought I'd give you a present to remember after my years away. Better than a t-shirt, isn't it?'

Then the talking stopped and the kissing started, a kiss deep enough to make everything better, to set off detonations of pleasure as the fireworks exploded. Great bursts of red and silver and gold showering down from the cliffs of Seacrest, drawing out ooohs and aaaahhhs from everyone who saw them, everyone apart from the two caught up in each other, making up for lost time as the sky above them filled with falling stars, the neon dimming as the cliffs ran with blazing light.

CHAPTER TWENTY-FOUR

The best view of the fireworks had been reserved for Cameron Fletcher or so he'd been told by Callum. They were standing side-by-side on a balcony at the back of the Fulmar of the sort used by royalty or minor dictators to wave at adoring crowds. It had previously served as a pedestal for film stars, looking out upon a wide lawn where grand garden parties had been held in honour of fabulous guests. Such had been the decline, the parties long since departed, the once pristine greens from which ladies in high heels were banned had been tarmacked over years ago.

Arthur, therefore, had an added incentive to keep his tired eyes fixed on the skies, watching fireworks burst into pulsating hearts, soaring sea-gulls, spinning Big Wheels. Looking down meant staring at a staff car-park with three large metal wheelie bins stationed to the rear from between which came the sound of drunken retching. Beyond the wooden fence behind the bins the back ends of cafes and bars could be seen. This meant the brief silences between zooms, whizzes and bangs were often shattered by a cascade of broken glass as another crate of bottles was dumped.

Arthur knew he should look all appreciative and charmed, what with ephemeral wonder being exactly Fletcher's thing but this being stationed at the rear end of things made him feel oddly homesick. The grubbiness behind the glitz, that was more his level, his home from home, he thought. The number of times he'd been stood at the back of places like these, sneaking a fag before introducing the next act or plucking up courage to give it one more try with the leading lady. Such sweet seediness.

He sighed and when Callum caught his eye was quick to switch his look to one of wonder instead of wistfulness. Bugger, he was tired, unsure how much longer he'd be able to keep this up. What with being so interested in everybody and everything that was going on around him, being Cameron Fletcher was threatening to turn into a right pain in the arse and he could feel his tetchiness levels rising. If one more pretentious, snidey-eyed git sidled up to him and asked what exactly he meant by the fifth line in the third paragraph of that bloody critique of *Jaws* from 1979, he was bleeding well going to swing for them.

Plus Callum was starting to get on his tits. The way he kept looking over as if he owned him, Dr Frankenstein keeping an eye on his monster to make sure he wasn't stepping out of line. You'd think he didn't trust Arthur, that with all this champagne and flattery flowing the puppet might get ideas above his station. He was getting tired of being treated like a mascot.

Callum's right hand falling heavily on his shoulder caused Arthur to snap back into focus. 'Enjoying the show Cameron? Specially designed with you in mind of course, look!' Callum traced the 'C F' signing itself in great blue letters above them. Cameron applauded politely. 'It looks like the signature of some sort of god, Mr Boyd, and I can't argue with that. I'll leave it up to others to decide if it means I made Seacrest or Seacrest made me.'

Callum's laughter, too loud, too long as Arthur felt his own smile becoming strained. You'd think Callum had been drinking but he hadn't, Arthur had been watching. Not a drop. He'd take a glass off a passing tray then slip it back when he thought no one was watching. Never trust a man who doesn't drink at his own party, Arthur had decided. It had been interesting that the one time the perfect host mask had slipped was when his daughter was talking to Dr Ashe, the two of them wandering off hand in hand. Should have guessed from her hair-cut that academic was of the lavender persuasion but Shona Boyd... Arthur smiled ruefully. Then again, Shona was one of those types you came across often in this business, so beautiful and confident they'd long stopped worrying about the genitalia of whoever got to sleep with them. Arthur couldn't imagine Callum being too bothered about his daughter's proclivities which meant Dr Ashe must be a greater threat to Callum than he'd realised. Arthur resolved to meet up with her soon, to try and get Shona to arrange it. He knew he'd have to be careful. Working out what Shona Boyd was up to was like wrestling with eels dipped in baby oil.

As others around them started clapping, Arthur felt relieved as the light of the final firework died. At last! Peace and quiet! Sleep! But Callum's hand was still on his shoulder, steering him back into the room behind the balcony decorated with such Rococo abandon it would have made a Sun King weep. Right, here goes, Arthur thought, I'll give him a dose of the old Fletcher magic, the extra-crumpled variety.

'Well, it certainly has been a wonderful evening but if you'll excuse me I'm going to retire. There was a time when I would have felt the night was about to begin but I'm afraid those nights have long since passed. I'd best away and get my beauty sleep, it's quite a packed fortnight ahead.'

Callum gave a sly half-smile. 'Come now, Cameron, you're being too hard on yourself. Bet you could give these younger souls a run for their money.' A few members of Callum's corporate entourage, faces flushed, ties askew, cheered.

Arthur struggled to hide his irritation. Oh, very smart, them an audience, making it harder for him to escape, a cheeky sod shouting, 'Come on Cameron, show us a magic trick, go on, make us all disappear.'

Once the drunken laughter had died down Cameron responded in a dignified baritone, 'Would that I could turn you into pumpkins but I'm afraid I don't have a handkerchief big enough. I'll go one better and make myself disappear. If a glamorous assistant would be kind enough to assist me back to my room.'

A shuffling silence followed as Callum glared at the idiot who'd called out. No Festival bonus for you, sonny Jim. Arthur suppressed a smirk, Callum's voice so chilly you could hear the young lad's balls shrivelling. 'Certainly Mr Fletcher, I'm sure one of the hotel staff will be happy to take you back to your suite. Simone and James will visit you in the morning to take you to your first engagement. There should be a full itinerary in your hotel room that...'

Cameron, checking his fobwatch, glanced up to see why Callum had stopped so abruptly, puzzled to see his host's face red and ugly with anger, staring towards the room's open doorway, pointing at the black-clad, white-faced figure standing there, his finger shaking with rage. '*You* – how – *security*!' as the object of his hatred moved into the room, a skinny young lad carrying something long and black and rifle-like.

Instinctively Arthur, in a gesture that was both entirely him and entirely Fletcher, placed his hand on Callum's chest, pushed him to one side, setting himself in the line of potential fire. Everything seemed to slow and he had time enough to think yeah, OK, being assassinated for a gig was a pretty tough call but think of the publicity... JFK, John Lennon, Cameron Fletcher... immortality guaranteed. Excellent.

But there was no sudden flash of light, no loud report, and the room relaxed slightly when those assembled realised the young man wasn't holding a shotgun, instead a silver topped cane. In the stillness, charged and crackling, Arthur studied this streak of black, a crack of dark matter absorbing all attention.

He was in his late twenties or so, although could pass for a teenager. He had that sweaty teenage intensity about him, handsome in a TB victim sort of way. Like Anthony Perkins, something not quite right, so pale he was almost shining. Impressive though, him a strip of a thing and they were all stood watching and waiting for what he'd do next. He was familiar looking too, Arthur sure he'd seen him… wait… bloody hell, it was him! Cameron Fletcher's biggest fan! OK, so he'd turned out to be mental but still. It was only polite his hero show him some respect.

'Luke? Luke Howard?' The boy hesitated, less sure of himself, relaxing his grip on the cane, letting it drop to his side. 'Why son, I've been *dying* to meet you,' said Cameron in a tone both stern and amused, lifting his hand from Callum's chest and extending it to Luke, giving him the benefit of a wide Fletcher smile. 'You're the reason I'm here, Luke Howard, the reason Cameron Fletcher was *always* going to come to Seacrest. Truly, it's an honour. What's a little death notice between friends?' As they shook hands Luke's smile transformed him from the potential assassin of a few moments ago to a delighted fan-boy.

Holding Cameron's hand tightly as if afraid he'd disappear if he let go, Luke presented the silver-topped cane. 'And it's an honour to meet *you*, Mr Fletcher. Sorry to interrupt your evening but I wasn't sure if you'd want to see me so I decided to bring you a gift. Well, actually, it's yours anyway, thought you'd want it back as soon as possible.'

Arthur took the cane, panic flaring as he tried to remember his notes, his background, to dredge up the significance of what he was being given and then he had it. A photograph of Fletcher on a foggy day in Central Park, hat pulled down, face indistinct but smile intact, and the top of the cane catching what sunlight there was, glinting at the camera.

'My old walking companion! Why thank…' As soon as Cameron released Luke's hand and took the cane from him, the room erupted in movement, four security guards pouncing, bundling Luke to the ground.

'Hey! *Stop*, there's no need to be so violent, leave him alone, he was only-' but Callum was moving Arthur back towards the balcony with smooth and convincing force as Luke was lifted to his feet, carried in an arm-lock out into the corridor. 'Someone, *you*!' Callum barked to one of the suits whose look of terror had less to do with Luke's presence than being singled out by Callum. 'Phone the police and get them to remove that *maniac* from the premises. And then we're going to find out who's responsible for this mess. Everyone else, stay here. I want to make sure the police take witness statements, that they put that *idiot* away for a very long time.'

Back on the balcony, the glass doors swinging to behind them, the cold air seemed to restore Callum's professional calm. 'I can't apologise enough, Cameron. How that fanatic managed to get up here, to get that close...' His face darkened, the prospect of future functions taking place at the Fulmar looking bleak. Arthur fought the urge to grab him by his razor-sharp lapels and shout 'Arthur, my name is Arthur, you thug! Why don't we stop this nonsense before people get *hurt*!'

Instead he lifted his reacquired cane, placed its top at the dead centre of Callum's breast bone. 'While I appreciate your concern, Mr Boyd, I *sincerely* hope Luke Howard will be treated with due care and consideration. As I was attempting to explain to him, his work, the Archive, is one of the principal reasons I agreed to come here. What he did this evening was kind, returning a much-missed item of mine and I'd like to thank him properly, without the potential threat of violence being meted out by one of your *hooligans*. I'll ask Simone and James to check on his well-being tomorrow. I hope for your sake their enquiries will be positive. Because if I hear otherwise.' He pressed the top of the cane down hard, 'I'll make you and others aware of my displeasure.'

Releasing the pressure, he dropped the stick to his side, opened the balcony doors. 'I'll thank you for a pleasant evening, albeit with a disappointing if... *enlightening* close. I'll find my own way to my room,' striding off, swinging the cane as though it had never left his side, silver-top fitting the grip of his palm perfectly.

Callum remained out in the cold, watching his reflection in the panels of the door. He touched the tight knot of pain Cameron had left on his chest, fighting the urge to punch one of those panels out, run after Fletcher, snatch that bloody stick and beat that bit-part actor about the head with it. Instead he breathed deeply before muttering, 'You watch your step, Arthur Dott. It's a very long drop from where you're standing. And an old man like you won't survive the fall.'

Outside the Kinotech, unaware that the sound of a siren told of a police van hurtling up to the Fulmar to take his best friend into custody, Harry stood drinking next to Donald Peel, superintendent of the Big Wheel.

Squat, with a comb-over and Sid Little glasses, Donald resembled a benign serial killer. They were a few feet away from a group of Diaboliks and other film fans who styled themselves as the Seacrest Fringe, there to watch the firework display. These were the types who'd outwardly condemn such gaudy, pointless displays, arguing loudly in The Moviegoer that the money should be spent on encouraging new film-makers. And yet, here they were oooohing and ahhhhing with the rest of them although with an audible edge of irony, cheering as the bay swam with fire, reflecting the red torrent streaming down the cliffs until Seacrest resembled an attractively decadent circle of hell.

'Say what you like about Callum,' Donald mused, 'and believe you me I will, but the canny old bastard knows how to put on a show.' Swigging from his bottle of beer, his glasses flared red until the cliffs returned to their usual state as the town's black boundary. Harry put his arm round his shoulder and hugged him. 'Steady on,' Donald protested, 'not as young as I was, bones like Edinburgh rock. What you so cheery about? Callum gets his way and you and me both are up a certain creek without a paddle. Big Wheel sold for scrap, I'll probably end up cleaning the windows of the London Eye. Have you seen how slow that thing moves? I'll be dead of boredom within the year.'

'You old misery,' Harry grinned, looking over to the Fulmar, hoping the flashing blue light outside it meant trouble. 'This marks the beginning of the end of Callum, believe me. I'm happy for him to have his night of glory, will make it sweeter when his plans come to zip. Someone's going to burn his playhouse down, Donald, and I'll give you three guesses who's going to strike the match. Another drink?' Donald nodded although his bottle was half full, glad to be released from Harry's grip. He'd lived here long enough to know certain types of madness were catching and the look in Harry's eye, the tight conviction in his voice, set him on edge. 'Never thought I'd be thinking this, Callum Boyd,' he muttered as Harry walked to the end of the pier, 'but I feel sorry for you.'

Harry was hauling up a clinking net of bottles, tied and left in the water to cool, when someone came and stood close beside him, his hands joined on the rope by a smaller, softer pair. 'Hoi, stop, you'll ruin your prize assets doing that, leave off, I'll manage.' Jenny Stokes let go reluctantly, pushing back a long strand of dark brown hair that had come loose from her pony-tail, gave Harry a wry smile.

'So you think my *hands* are my best assets do you, Harry Lawson? I *have* got a lot of work to do on you, haven't I?' she murmured, Harry too busy wrestling with the knots at the top of the net to hear.

One of the quieter Diaboliks, Jenny was a film editor who'd come up to Seacrest Studios on a placement during her Film and Television degree. A month after she'd graduated she'd moved having got a job in a small production company based in the studios. Harry handed her a bottle so cold from the sea it stung his fingers as she passed him an opener from her jeans pocket. 'Great party, Harry, bet the Fulmar can't beat this, beer with a hint of sea-water. Don't get this sort of thing in Beaconsfield.' She gulped down half her beer, smiling up at him, not caring if she seemed less self-contained than usual. Edging her way towards saying something she hoped neither of them would later regret as they chinked bottles.

Lovely girl, admitted Harry. He'd been out drinking with her a few times, her and a bunch of other Diaboliks, always had an excellent laugh. Damn fine editor too, real feel for film. A few times though it had just been him and her sitting there and he'd been spouting some nonsense, trying to make her laugh so much she got the hic-cups and she gives him this look. Shaking her head as if she was waiting for him to say something, do something…and he doesn't. And why doesn't he now?

Because even though she was there in front of him and there was that bit of hair over her left eye and that look again, like she knew far more than she was ever going to let on, cute smile, nice lips and any other sane man would be attempting to stick his tongue down her throat, all Harry was thinking was she would be another reason to stay. Another chain tying him to this bloody town. That and what would she want with a waster like him?

Jenny could tell, her face changing, losing its happiness and he should give her a hug, cheer her up but instead he stood there as she turned her back to him, looked towards Seacrest. Poor kid, Harry realised, hooked already on the place. Fun and games for now but give her a few years and she'd wake up one morning and wonder where the best part of her life had gone. Harry tried to summon up a warning but when she said, 'It *is* fantastic, isn't it?' he didn't have the heart to disagree. There'd be time enough to put her right. 'Shame Luke couldn't be here', Jenny said. 'Did you hear that rumour he was going to go up to the Fulmar, personally introduce himself to Cameron Fletcher? He wouldn't be that daft, would he? Can't imagine Callum letting him stroll up and… '

'Why does everyone think I'm that boy's keeper?' snapped Harry, regretting it as soon as he saw her confusion. 'Sorry Jen, I didn't mean to…but Luke's big enough to fight his own battles. For one I doubt he'd get anywhere near Fletcher and two, I reckon they'd get on just fine. Once they'd got over that business about Luke saying he was dead and keeping all his stuff in a warehouse and everything.'

Oh well done, fantastic, Harry, that'll make her feel *much* better. They both stood in silence, far from reassured until Jen hiccupped. 'Best get back to the party. Don't want people getting the wrong idea.' She gave Harry the sort of melancholy smile that had him thinking she should try and find some French film director to give her a starring role, while Jen wondered why do I always fall for the idiots?

As they wandered towards the eerie green light in front of the Ghost Train where an improvised disco had established itself, 'Stuck in the Middle With You' playing on someone's portable stereo, Harry said confidently, 'Luke'll be fine. His hero's in town, what could *possibly* go wrong?'

In a way, he was right. Luke *was* doing fine. In fact, he was better than fine, he was *ecstatic*, his face a rictus of delight sitting on a bunk as soft as reinforced concrete as the door to his cell in Seacrest Police Station slammed shut and clunked. Because although he faced a night, possibly longer, locked up, Cameron Fletcher had shaken him by the hand and called him 'son'. After years of waiting, of feeling half-complete, Luke felt fulfilled and ready. Ready to take on anyone who doubted the word of Cameron Fletcher.

CHAPTER TWENTY-FIVE

'What on earth…?' Shona wondered, drowsy, coming to. A baby? Siamese cat? A strange mewling was coming from beyond the curtains, the open window and then she understood. A seagull and so she must be in Seacrest, warm in Jo's bed. She yawned, just like a cat, Jo would have said had she been awake to see it. She was fast asleep, spooning Shona, arm tight across her stomach as if determined to keep a hold of her, not let her go so easily.

Shona turned, hoping her movement would wake Jo up but no. She'd always envied Jo's ability to sleep, her real talent for it. She would watch her, trying to catch the trick of it. Five minutes of drifting off was all it took and Jo was dead to the world. What was it she'd said once? About how she enjoyed dreaming so much. Like watching films, another way of escaping reality. Poor dear Dr Ashe. In contrast Shona and sleep had never got on. It got in the way of life, of living.

Shona was getting bored. She tried a gentle kicking of the ankle… nothing. Other tactics would have to be employed. Kissing Jo's fluttering eyelids, dreaming again, her lips, that soft, soft part of her neck, under her earlobe, the line of her jaw. What was the response? A sleepy smile, a murmur of pleasure, then nothing. Typical. Jo would rather spend time alone with her subconscious than entertain the naked lady in her bed.

Shona stroked Jo's hair from her forehead, murmuring. 'What am I going to do with you, eh? How'm I going to get you out of here? Wake you up properly,' becoming aware of the blue light of dawn bleeding into the room. That sensation starting up again. A twitching under the skin, the need to get up and out, to explore.

She eased Jo's hand away from her hip, body goose-bumping after she'd escaped the duvet until she pulled on the red towelling dressing gown from the back of the bedroom door. It was strange being back there and feeling like a stranger, an interloper. It used to be like a second home. Although it had been a while, it was nice that it still felt so familiar. Safe… and what was that?

Picking her way over to the window through the discarded clothing her foot brushed against her black lace bra revealing a photograph underneath. Black and white, a familiar face and she crouched down to study it, picking it up towards the light of the window. Pulled the curtain back a little and there he was.

'Oh Arthur,' she whispered and as we peeked over her shoulder we almost gasped. We had become so used to seeing Arthur as Cameron Fletcher – suave, handsome, urbane Cameron Fletcher – that to see him revealed as his true self, in all his ignoble glory, was a shock.

A publicity still taken three years ago, before things had turned from bad to worse, when there had still been the hope that he might land a big television part as a grumpy, hard-drinking, hard-smoking yet compassionate and maverick police detective say. This was a face that told of evenings spent swearing at the television, shaking his glass of blended scotch at John Thaw or David Jason – 'Bastard! I could do that! nicking my parts… *bastard*! Come round why don't you, steal the money right out of my pockets!'

Beardless, jowly, eyes charming but a hint of desperation about his smile. The printed summary underneath: 'ARTHUR DOTT: suitable for landlords, janitors, school teachers (retired), head-teacher, alcoholics, farmers, provincial police constables (grumpy). Can do accents/tap dance/magic tricks. Also available as background artiste (pub drinking speciality).

Shona's half-smile was sadder than usual as she kissed him lightly on the forehead, leaving a smear of what little lipstick remained after the night before. Dear Arthur, what would have happened if she hadn't been there to rescue him from a half-life spent in a booth at the Rovers Return? She might have guessed Dr Ashe would find them both out. She looked over to the sleeping Jo, half-smile near vanished, expression difficult to read in the half-light. 'We'll have to keep her quiet, won't we?' she whispered. 'And between you and me, Arthur, I know *lots* of ways to do that... well, perhaps not *quiet*.' The smile returned, remembering the catching up they'd done. 'But enough to keep her on side. Don't worry, Cameron, I'll keep our girl sweet.' She let Arthur glide to the floor as she parted the curtains, gave her full attention to Seacrest. A vista that brought back her first visit to Jo's flat.

A few weeks after Jo had moved to Seacrest and Shona had been trying to work out if their being together was a good thing or not. She'd been happy keeping it long distance, had suited her fine. Jo far enough away from all her dirty little secrets. And the way Jo loved her... it was like the way she slept. Deeply, completely, a trust that was terrifying. Left a person with so much to live up to. Shona had been swithering, sure it could get very messy, very quickly and had shown up at the flat with every intention of, if not ending it, certainly cooling things down. Then Jo had opened the door, the happiest Shona had seen her, happier than when they first got together. 'Wait till you see the view!'

She'd taken Shona by the hand, led her to the window and there was a moment of vertigo. Not because they were so high up and could see so far, every cinema in the town, the bay holding everything tight, every roof-top of this beautiful, maddening town shining after a brief shower, as if Jo had timed it for maximum effect. That sensation of teetering on the brink, standing there, Jo behind her, pulling her close, the bottom of her stomach plunged away because she knew it there and then. She was in love with not a clue what to do about it. Terrified.

She was fine this morning though. No dizziness, no telescoping drops. Instead she had a longing to be out there. Mist creeping, lingering about the streets, blurring the lights that had dazzled last night. Soft focus. She checked the time on the alarm clock by Jo's head (that Psycho thing... she *kept* it?) 5:06am. Perfect. Her favourite time ever since she was a kid, setting her alarm far too early and still late for school because of hours spent wandering. Enjoying the sensation of the place being all hers. No parents to keep her in check.

She gathered up her clothes and handbag, headed for the bathroom. Struggled into her red dress and took her time applying her make-up. When the final touch of lipstick had been added, she smiled appreciatively at her reflection. Back to the glamorous woman of last night with an added rosy glow. Just what the Doctor ordered.

Winked and her smile froze, faded. Because that look, the blend of the seductive and the self-mocking, wasn't entirely her own. It was one captured years ago by photographers and film crews back when it belonged to Carol Lancaster, Shona's Mum; bathing lovely, beauty queen, reigning Miss Seacrest from '63 to '67, years when she threatened to storm Hollywood after a handful of successful Britsploitation films. The years before marrying Callum, having Shona and the slow fade from view, declining to a faint camp memory. Shona knew Carol would be one of the few awake at this unearthly hour, waiting for her to show up. Greeting the return of the prodigal daughter.

She turned sharply away from the mirror, snapping out the bathroom light, comfortable in the muted shade of the hallway. Briefly contemplated switching it back on, attacking the mirror with lipstick, scrawling a time, a date and place where Jo could find her. But she remembered the last time, the reaction to such a grand romantic gesture. '*Romantic*? Do you *know* how long it takes to scrub a load of lippy off a mirror? Used at least two-thirds of a bottle of Flash.' Ah Jo, Shona sighed, tip-toeing back into the bedroom to retrieve her high heels. Always content to sit in the dark and watch but when the movies pay you a home visit you complain about the extra housework.

Jo was on her back, arms flung up above her head as if for a corny special effect, plunging from a great height. Instead of her usually peaceful, beatific expression, she was frowning, muttering, the only word distinguishable 'Luke'. Shona hesitated. She should stay, hold her, kiss that frown away. Then Jo shifted over onto her side, the muttering stopped and Shona felt relieved. Realised that her heels wouldn't do for the long walk across town to Carol's cliff-top bungalow, began to search for alternatives.

She stood shaking her head in front of Jo's open wardrobe at the messy bundles of sweaters and jeans, un-ironed t-shirts. 'Good God,' she muttered, 'when's that woman going to realise she's not a student any more?', kneeling to rake through piles of old trainers: Gola, Converse, Puma, before finding what she was looking for. An ancient pair of green flash Dunlops, as snug as a pair of old slippers. Jo would never miss them, she slipped them on – a perfect fit – padded over to give Jo a kiss on the forehead goodbye, jogging down the hall, eager to be on her way.

(Two hours later found Jo by the window nursing a strong cup of coffee to rid herself of an awful hangover, both physical and emotional. Cursing herself for getting involved again, for thinking Shona would be there when she woke up. She wondered where Shona was, what she was doing, who she was doing it with, hoping to catch a flash of auburn out there when she noticed the door of her wardrobe was ajar. Within minutes she groaned aloud, 'You *cow*,

Shona Boyd. Steal my heart fine, but not the *Dunlops*.')

Shona, blissfully ignorant of any upset her actions might cause, was enjoying her time alone. The sea mist retreating as the sky brightened, still enough to curl around her ankles. The town was never fully asleep during Festival time, its state as fitful as Shona's at night. This was as close as it got to feeling things had been put on hold, the streets filled with the same latent excitement held by an empty cinema.

A few drunken revellers were stumbling home and they waved blearily as she walked past, admiring her crumpled glamour. Café and shop owners were also about and they nodded and smiled at her, some even managing a 'Morning!' Occasionally she sensed a wariness there. Still Daddy's girl... she would have to work on that. Couldn't be dragging the Boyd reputation around if her plans for the future were to work...

Life had been so much easier when she was away from the place, not fixed in a supporting role as Callum Boyd's daughter. She'd been Shona Lancaster in the States, and the freedom that had given her had been wonderful. The satisfaction in knowing the contacts she'd made, the deals arranged, even the Festival she'd organised (OK, so it had been in Anchorage but they *loved* their films up there) had been successful because of *her* hard work, not because of Callum's name. Back here and what did that count for? Nothing. She'd been typecast again as the rebellious teenager, spoilt fourteen-year-old.

She stuck to the alleyways and closes where she'd spent her teenage years. Passed the seedy offices of talent scouts, photographic agencies, 'exotic film' companies... The things she learnt skiving. A proper education, far better than school as all you *really* needed to know to prepare you for life was here, behind signs for 'Blue Moon Studios', 'Black Jack Penny Arcade', 'Fantasy Island Pictures'...

There had come a point when her Mum and Dad had become

distracted enough from their arguing and drinking to notice the steady stream of letters from school. They'd responded by packing her off to boarding school, away from the gamblers, drunks, unsuitable boys and dubious women. Within a week she'd gone AWOL, jumped the school walls, hitch-hiked back to the places and activities that could turn a blue-eyed girl jaded. She realised leaving the murk of the back-streets to climb the steep white Powell Steps running parallel to the track of the cliff lift carriages, all that youthful debauchery was why the sight of Jo had come as a revelation.

Sixteen years old and with more in common with one of the Sex Pistols than one of her classmates, Shona had been getting bored of hanging about with dead-eyed veterans of the Seacrest underbelly. Calling her an amateur, Daddy a phone-call away from trouble and she'd push herself harder and faster, desperate to find out how she'd react if she went too far…she thought she was happy, pushing the limits and then there was Jo. Discovering how happy she *could* be.

The Festival of 2005, Shona dressed as Salome on the back of the *Piccadilly* float trying to act decadent, feeling bored and ridiculous instead, the seven veils a nuisance, twisting in the breeze. A fortnight to go to the end of the holidays, back at Colditz, already plotting her escape, how to smuggle in vodka, persuade the other girls to do things they shouldn't when one of her veils flew off. She watched it fly over the crowd, wondering if it would reach the height of the Big Wheel, looked down to see if anyone had noticed and there Jo was. Waiting for her.

Perhaps a couple years younger, short dark hair, geeky glasses – already thinking, 'We'll need to do something about *those*,' – a few feet away from her parents. Nice enough couple with their suburban jackets and polite hair, smiling and waving in the way of the sort who'd turn to each other on the drive home to say, 'Yes it's a lovely place to visit but you wouldn't want to *live* there'. Yet the look in their daughter's eyes…she was already too far gone to save. Another Seacrest sucker, someone who was looking for a place where they didn't feel different, where it was guaranteed the next person round the corner would be stranger, weirder than you, and knew they'd finally found it.

She stared at Shona with something close to awe, a little scared, suddenly realising life wasn't going to be as straight (hah!) forward as she thought and Shona licked her lips and winked. Seeing her blush, it was all she could do to hold herself back from leaping off that float and rescuing her there and then. Finally Shona had discovered what she'd been searching for those lost years, the perfect audience of one.

Having climbed to the top of the Powell Steps she paused to catch her breath, bent over, straightened up to take in the sight of the bay streaked with gold, the sky such a delicate shade of blue it broke your heart. The memory of how it was at the start with Jo and the certain knowledge that in a few weeks' time Seacrest would be hers again, hers completely, caused a surge of exultation. She threw out her bare arms, red dress rippling like blood, shouted loud enough to hurt her throat, 'Top of the world Ma!' her only audience a bemused seagull on top of a dark green cable car that stopped its preening to stare at her.

She rounded the cable car station, passed the Pressburger Steps and entered one of the shabbier parts of Seacrest, as suburban as the place was allowed to get. She'd forgotten how depressing it was there, the buildings slumped, boutiques with window displays protected by a sheet of yellow cellophane staining everything behind it – the polystyrene heads wearing bunnets and bobble hats, tartan rugs and leather ladies gloves – a gloomy shade of nicotine yellow. The sort of place no one choose to live in, they just ended up, too tired and resigned to move anywhere else.

The people were much less friendly. The sort who preferred how things had been before the old street signs were replaced to show the town's devotion to cinema. As she strode down the High Street, she gathered disapproving glares from the butcher, the baker, the fishmonger, out in their doorways to fold their arms at this haughty besom, this Queen of bloody Sheba and Shona loved every minute of it. Soaking it up, blowing them kisses, enjoying the notoriety that was so difficult to attract in the centre of Seacrest. They were loving it too, deep down. Everyone needed a bit of scandal once in a while to get the blood pumping.

Too soon and she'd arrived, turning into her Mum's cul-de-sac. She didn't have to worry about the time, about waking Carol up. When she was travelling, it didn't matter what time zone she found herself in, she always knew that if she rang Mum she'd only have to wait two rings before she answered, eager for any distraction. Always that slight disappointment, the 'Oh… it's you,' greeting, expecting one of her gentlemen callers. Shona had inherited Carol's attitude to sleep although in Carol's case it was because it ate into valuable drinking time. And Shona knew that was exactly the sort of thing Callum would say.

Angry at that thought, Shona caught her thumb under the lever of the metal gate leading to the garden of the bungalow named 'Shangri-La'. The resultant 'Fuck!' caused an old woman passing by with her Scottie dog to stagger against a privet hedge. Sucking the blood away, Shona stomped up the garden path, managed to be impressed by the neatly trimmed lawn, the trickling water features, late-blooming flowers. Every time she came back she expected to find it transformed into a creepy, overgrown place the local kids made up stories about. Carol must have been getting regular visits from one of the Fulmar gardeners, devoted to the memory of Carol Lancaster in her prime enough to dead-head her roses, trim her borders.

She'd scarcely touched the doorbell and set the first bars of

'Hello Dolly' chiming when the door opened and there was Mum in a brilliantly white dressing gown trimmed with gold thread, looking like the central character in a Tennessee Williams play, one cynical enough to know the kindness of strangers depended on how drunk they were.

'Oh... it's *you*. Well, come in, dear, nice of you to *finally* make it. Thumb-sucking, is that what the youth of today are getting up to? Good *God*, it's enough to make you weep with joy for being old and feeble. Come in then, making an exhibition of yourself on my doorstep. Breakfast is in the kitchen waiting to be poured. There's some fresh celery in the salad box. Pour one for me while you're at it. Only my third of the day. On a diet.'

It was always far too warm in 'Shangri-La', a damp heat that brought to mind hothouses and orchids. It was a surprise to walk its length and find a kitchen instead of a glasshouse. Callum said it was due to the ice running through Carol's veins but Shona had a different theory, that Carol craved the heat of the studio, of the photographer or the film set. Longed to bask again in a fake sunshine of lights, in a swim suit against a tropical backdrop, half-listening to some man giving her direction, closing her eyes to the snap of a shutter, the whirr of the camera. Relishing being watched.

After noting the fridge contained, aside from the celery, nothing more than a half empty bottle of vodka, a carton of tomato juice and a box of eggs, Shona poured the Bloody Marys, gulping down half of hers, topping it up before she pushed through the door to the living room. A room to make Norma Desmond weep.

She hoped her hands were steady enough not to spill any red onto the white carpet or either of the two huge white sofas. Carol, lounging on the one with its back to the window, watched her walk the length of the room. Always watching, always judging. Strawberry-blonde hair piled up in an artfully dishevelled manner and she would rip your eyes out before admitting she dyed it, like a depraved yet regal Lucille Ball. 'Thank you dear.' As she took the glass she grabbed Shona's left hand, turned it, making a show of examining the bare ring finger. 'Checking you haven't paid a visit to some Las Vegas chapel without telling me.'

Shona sank into the other sofa, closed her eyes but the room remained horribly bright and clear in her head. It maintained the white and gold theme of Carol's dressing gown, the wall facing Carol's sofa filled with a huge plasma screen that usually showed one of her own films. It was dark today, reflecting the room back at them in a way that felt faintly disapproving. To the left of the TV was a table where a combined telephone and fax machine hummed and buzzed, disgorging sheets of paper every so often. Shona had tried to introduce Carol to the joys of email but she always tutted in response. 'I prefer to see a person's handwriting, dear. Makes it easier to tell if they're lying or not.' For all her apparent splendid isolation, Carol kept in contact with many people all over the globe; fans, business associates, old flames. Many's the time Shona would phone her with some juicy piece of gossip to be told, 'What, you've only just heard? Dear, I knew about that *weeks* ago. Ryan told me.'

Those contacts were vital to her business empire. Carol had always been canny enough to make sure that if people were exploiting her she'd exploit them right back. Shares in cinemas, casinos, bars, the profits of the films she starred in. What did most of that money go on? Shona stifled a groan on opening her eyes. Tat. The gold fireplace, the angel statuettes, the glass swans, clowns and elephants, various objects covered in shells, the ceramic *whippet* for Christ sake... kitsch as an act of aggression.

Spread on the carpet in front of the fireplace, the fake coals of which were always aglow no matter the temperature outside, was the fake skin of a black panther. Its snarling head rose from the rest of the body at perfect tripping height, its violet-blue eyes with the uncanny ability to follow you about the room. When Shona had asked why she'd bought something so hideous she'd smiled sweetly. 'Because it reminds me so perfectly of your father. I take care to walk all over it at least once a day.'

At least if she kept her eyes on the panther Shona could avoid the wall opposite, the Wall of Glory. Covered in photos, posters and newspaper cuttings of Carol in her prime; winning that first beauty contest when she was 17, greeting stars and royalty at premiers when she was awarded the title of the Face of Seacrest, coyly squeezing the bicep of a Mr Universe entrant, sharing a joke with Kenneth Williams and Barbara Windsor, clinging to the arm of Sean Connery, smiling broadly as they strolled along the pier. The centrepiece, a thing of such fantastic, unrepentant vanity Shona couldn't help her gaze being drawn to it, was a large mirror decorated with the famous photograph of Carol in a one piece pale blue, white polka-dotted swimsuit. Long legs tucked beneath her on the sands of Seacrest Bay, arms stretched out above her head, teeth gleaming, blonde hair streaming, the banner above her head, 'Seacrest! A Town Fit For Stars!'

On either side of the fireplace were two glass topped coffee tables covered with framed photographs. Shona pointed her half-eaten stick of celery at one. 'Mum… always meant to ask. If you hate Dad so much, how come you've got so many photos of you two together? Look at you… the golden couple, riding on the Big Wheel, out on a pedalo… like Elizabeth Taylor and Richard Burton spotted on a holiday in Skegness.'

Carol stirred her drink slowly before sinking her perfectly white teeth into her celery with a snap. 'Dear, I'd have thought the answer was obvious. Hating someone is as tough a job as loving them. You have to keep topping that emotion up every so often, refuel it. And to be reminded of what we had, what we could have *become* … well, some days it's only the anger that keeps me going, gives my life more zing than any of those drugs the doctor insists on prescribing. That and knowing you're out in the world, dear, making enough mischief for the two of us.'

She smiled indulgently at the other table, the one Shona refused to look at, the one covered in images from her past charting her progress from a young girl dressed as Dorothy in the back garden, beaming with happiness or screaming with excitement with Carol on the Big Wheel, to a sullen teenager dressed as Alex from *Fatal Attraction*, holding up a toy bunny for a Hallowe'en party, scowling at the camera, at her Dad. The last photo she could remember him taking before they announced their divorce to the *Seacrest Gazette*. It would have been nice to have been told about it from them in person, instead of reading about it. And... God. Shona sat up, peered at a photo of her as Salome. She'd laid it on thick with the black mascara, hair and veils flying, and that smile... poor Jo. She really hadn't stood a chance.

'What are you looking so smug about? Oh, Salome!' Dammit. Her mum and her knack of knowing exactly what anyone in the room was looking at, as Dad had found out to his cost. 'Have you any idea what we had to put up with from the Press after that little escapade?' Whereas a few years ago the tone would have been scolding that morning it was soft with affection then sly. 'And that reminds me... How is the lovely Dr Ashe? Haven't seen her in years.'

Shona nearly choked on her Tabasco, such was her Mum's unsettling knowledge of her private life. But then Carol had always had a soft spot for Jo and her geek knowledge of her back catalogue. There had been a run of phone conversations when Carol would always insist on asking when they were getting back together again until Shona had snapped. 'This is because she's your biggest fan, Mum, isn't it? Someone there to stoke your ego,' and been shocked by the hurt in Carol's voice when she replied, 'No, it's not that dear, not like that at *all*. People like us *need* people like Jo. We need an audience, someone to pay attention. Otherwise what would be the point? What would be the bloody point?'

'Dr Ashe is doing fine, Mum, least she was when I saw her this morning. Recognise the trainers?'

Carol raised a weary eyebrow, the corners of her mouth curling ever so slightly, suggesting a hint of envy at her daughter out there, enjoying herself. 'And how much did you divulge of our little plan? Does she know that Cameron Fletcher isn't quite who he says he is?'

'Oh' Shona sighed, her head dropping back to examine the faux crystal chandelier far too big for the room. Suddenly very tired, desperate to fall asleep, get into the bed in the room Carol always kept clean and tidy for her, pull the cover over her head and not get up for a week. What with the plans and the people who weren't who they were supposed to be... exhausting. 'Jo doesn't need me to tell her anything. That's why we love her so. She figures things out. Digs until she knows the answers. She doesn't know everything as yet but she'll have fun trying to figure it out.'

'Just as long as she doesn't get over excited and spoil everything. The thought of the surprise your father's going to get... '

'Mum, remind me, if they ever need a female version of Hannibal Lecter, that I should pass on your phone number. And...,' this heat, the alcohol... ' Tell me. Why do you hate Dad so? You split up years ago and you weren't exactly Doris Day. There was that Mr Universe for a start.'

'Shona, you never cease to amaze me,' Carol retorted but quietly, watching her daughter close her eyes again, face settling into the same expression in her sleep as she'd worn as a new-born, frowning at the interruption. 'Perhaps one day you'll find out, and I pray you never will, the degree to which you end up hating someone relates directly to the love you had for them. I gave your father everything, adored him and yet…it was never enough. *I* was never enough. Towards the end he'd look straight through me, as if there was nothing there. Nothing left to see.' And despite the stifling heat of the room, Carol shivered.

CHAPTER TWENTY-SIX

We speed forward a week, past scenes of Cameron being adored, of Callum at his bank of television screens, keeping an eye on the town, Jo sitting at her computer, carrying on with her research interrupted by bouts of staring out the window wondering where Shona was, when she'd get her Dunlops back.

But we travelled too far, too fast, paused then played at the sight of Arthur – most definitely Arthur, not Cameron – alone in a pub looking through a pile of newspaper and magazine clippings, old documents and notebooks. We feared for him a little, wondered why he was looking so white, so shaken, the paper trembling as he turned another page. But how would you expect a man to react when he found out he hadn't been playing a character, a figment of someone's imagination but a ghost? Living the afterlife of someone real, someone who had died alone and anonymous before having his identity, all he possessed, stolen away from him?

We were getting ahead of ourselves. Rewound slowly until we reached a darkened cinema, the credits of *Orpheé* fading from the screen, showing as part of the Festival. Cameron Fletcher sat in a chair at the side of the screen and would shortly take part in a 'Q&A' session. This was a film he'd written about extensively, his essay on Cocteau's vision of the Underworld one of the first to bring him critical attention. In the dark, the shimmering light of the screen, Cameron himself looked like a character from a Cocteau film, *Beauty and the Beast* perhaps, so enchanted by what was happening around him he had decided to step out of the screen and enjoy what everyone else was watching.

But while he looked calm and content, Arthur, after the balm of the film, was beginning to fume quietly, a familiar sensation of the past week. He should be focusing, concentrating on his delivery of some witty remarks about Barthes but instead he was thinking, God, I'm fed up with this. Not so much Cameron, he *loved* Cameron, could play him forever. It was those security goons brought in after Luke had made his dramatic entrance that were driving him nuts.

Cameron couldn't do a bloody *thing* on his own, hadn't had a chance to find out what this place was like when people weren't acting on best behaviour. He was always being rushed from some screening to a prize presentation to some ball-crushingly dull judging panel meeting and when he complained, when he pointed out it might be good PR to have Cameron go for a stroll without the possibility of fans being wrestled to the ground, he'd get short shrift. 'You saw how close that lunatic Luke Howard got, do you have any idea what it would do to the reputation of Seacrest if anything happened to you?' Oh yeah, thanks Callum, Cameron would snort, nice to see where his priorities lay. Never mind *Cameron's* feelings about being assassinated, the big worry was visitor numbers being down next year. 'Your arrival here has stirred up a lot of strong emotion and I know you're finding it difficult but believe me, these extra measures have been put into place for your own protection. You're our prize asset, Cameron, and we mean to look after you,' followed by that smile, the kind usually seen wrapping itself about a gazelle.

Anyway, Arthur had to *concentrate* on what the young chap who'd been handed the microphone was saying, something about the Underworld and the Seacrest Tunnels, how he was a member of the Diaboliks and it would be an honour to have Fletcher visit them and…

What happened next was a perfect example of what Arthur had been concerned about. Two security guards were moving in, snatched the microphone away, tried to drag the lad out and he was shouting, asking what Cameron made of Callum's plans to convert the Tunnels into an underground car-park and Cameron Fletcher, honoured and respected guest, shouted out –

'STOP!'

Now why, wondered Arthur, couldn't *he* manage a voice like that, deep and sonorous and *commanding*, when he needed it? Like the time that bunch of Asbo-ridden kids were playing up during *Death of a Salesman* and he had a little outburst. What was it that arse of a director had said? 'Yes, Willy speaks for the common man, Arthur, but not *that* common.'

'Gentlemen… wait.' And they do, they freeze along with the rest of the audience and oh it was fantastic, reminded Arthur why he'd got into this acting lark in the first place. Even *he* was looking forward to what Cameron had to say next.

'Before carting that boy off I would like to make very clear to him and to all present that while I am a guest of Callum Boyd I am not his mouthpiece.' The collective gasp that followed was magic. As if the ventriloquist's dummy had got up from his operator's lap, walked to the footlights and started chatting to the front row.

Arthur kept going, focused on the faces glowing in the dark in front of him, agog, knowing they were watching something unscripted, not fixed into the timetable. He kept his eyes on them instead of the glare of the security guard holding the young man in the denim jacket, the terrified faces of Simone and James in the wing, the nagging thought that this was suicide, not just in a career sort of way but in a 'Callum Boyd could have you *shot*' sort of way. He concentrated on Shona Boyd, there at the end of the second row, nodding appreciatively, a sight so infuriating, so suggestive of the fact he might simply have switched from following the plans of one Boyd to another, that his anger forced him to continue.

'While I appreciate the tremendous hospitality Mr Boyd has extended to me, my presence should not be regarded as condoning all or indeed *any* of his plans. And yes, as I wish to take full advantage of my short time here I am more than happy to take up this young gentleman's offer and take a trip to the Tunnels.' The gentleman in question grinned, tugged his sleeve away from the grip of the guard, waved his thanks to Cameron, cheekily glancing at his former captor while pointing at the stage as if to say, 'Sorry mate, he's on *my* side.'

'James,' Cameron called to the wings, gesturing for his assistant to join him, a shove from Simone sending him blinking out into the stage lights. 'Go down and get some details from that young man. Find out when it would be most convenient to pay a visit to Seacrest's own Underworld. It sounds exactly the sort of place I could enjoy a few hours lurking.'

As James made his way down the stage steps he did so to applause, applause that started slowly, hesitantly, the audience unsure of the reaction of the security guards stationed around the fringes of the auditorium, then building in confidence as no one was dragged from their seats.

There, thought Arthur, satisfied. He'd given them permission to show what they *really* thought, to make clear their opposition to Callum's plans. Bet he was the only one there to have noticed the first person clapping was Shona Boyd. Slow and deliberate, like she was marking out the beat to a tune only she could hear. What *had* her Dad done to make her hate him so?

It was a question Arthur asked her the next afternoon in his room at the Fulmar, Shona with her back to him, standing on the balcony, while he tucked into his lunch at a small dining table nearby. A 'Deer Hunter Quarterpounder' with extra fries, the venison cooked to perfection, rare and bloody, a vanilla shake on the side and maybe it was that, the diner-like food that caused him to keep his American accent, to stay in character. Or maybe it was because he was braver as Cameron, the one who'd have the guts to ask a personal question of Shona.

She didn't turn to face him, her voice almost a sigh. 'I don't *hate* him, Arthur' and it annoyed him, the habit she had of always reminding him who he *really* was, her refusal to play along. 'But I do hate what he's done to other people.' Her gaze switched then, from the lido and studios over to the east side of the bay, beyond the Big Wheel to where there was nothing very much, only dull suburbia, bungalows and cul-de-sacs. Arthur remembered the day after he'd got here when she turned up at that evening screening, looking stunning but tired and he said something cheeky, 'Been helping Dr Ashe with her research?' A nudge and a wink, more Arthur than Cameron, expecting her to join in with the teasing and instead the curt response was, 'No. Visiting my mother,' translation, 'Back off you old fart.' This family. It made the Borgias look like the Waltons. The Addams like the Brady Bunch.

She turned, hands stretched along the balcony railings, wind blowing her hair, autumn sun turning it into a blazing copper, and Arthur felt a little envious of Dr Ashe. 'This may shock you but I think in lots of ways he's right. Seacrest does need to shake itself up, face the future, change and adapt. But I think he's going about it the wrong way and he'll do more damage than good. He always does.'

She left the balcony, walked over to him although 'walked' didn't quite do it justice. Hint of a prowl about it. She rested one hand on his table and leaned in close, granting Arthur as impressive a display of cleavage as he'd seen in years. Keep it together Arthur, keep it together… you're Fletcher remember? Cool and calm, not concerned about the stirring of bits that haven't shown any signs of

THE PROJECTIONIST

life since Joanna Lumley was last on the telly.

Shona raised a wicked eyebrow, 'Mind if I nick a chip?' As Fletcher shook his head she straightened up, dipping a fry into some tomato sauce, biting it with teeth as sharp as her Dad's. 'Delicious. Now, Arthur, what you did yesterday at the screening was very brave, very admirable but teetering on the brink of very stupid. Dangerous. You can be sure every word was reported back to Callum. I think at this stage he'll let you off. He might even see it as to his advantage. If Fletcher can win the backing of his opponents he might use you to try and convince them otherwise, see things his way. But,' she stole another chip, 'remember,' coming in close again, smoothing down the lapels of his black velvet jacket, picking off small pieces of fluff while Arthur tried to remember where he'd put his inhaler. 'Callum is not the most patient of men and if you keep pushing there will come a time when he pushes back. You're here because Callum *wants* you here and if you want to see that big fat pay-cheque you were promised at the start of this, keep him sweet. There you are. All set.'

And for one terrifying moment it looked as though she might kiss him... instead she straightened up briskly, picked up her coat left lying on the bed, leaving us to witness Cameron's shoulders slump in... relief? Disappointment?

'I've got to head out now, people to see, meetings to attend. You stay here and enjoy yourself. You've got the afternoon off so relax. Best to stay here, mind. Don't want you getting mobbed or into any other sort of trouble. I'll be in the foyer to pick you up at seven, there's that thing at eight remember? The Icelandic film, the woman with the horse travelling to the grotto. Wouldn't want to miss *that* now would you. Oh, and Arthur, try to go easy on the mini-bar will you? The way you've been going that's nearly half the Festival budget away.'

Arthur waited until the door slammed behind her before muttering

'Cheeky mare,'rubbing his chest. Bloody hell...he hoped that was indigestion rather than a heart attack. Because he was stuffed if anything *did* happen. Who would he tell the doctor he was?

He would have a Scotch and soda, a lie down and watch some mindless daytime TV, that would sort him out. Once settled on his Emperor-sized bed, drink in hand, Arthur flicked the switch on his bedside cabinet that caused the wooden screen opposite, decorated by two winged lion curly bearded blokes, to slide open revealing a large flat-screen TV. Lovely. Just the sort of décor Arthur would have installed at home if his plan of becoming a Bond super-villain had ever taken off. The perfect way to unwind after a day spent chasing pesky, wise-cracking British agents.

This, however, proved to be the high point of the next hour as Arthur proceeded to flick through all available 479 channels twice in a desperate attempt to find something to watch. Finding only mild satisfaction in shouting at some hammy psychics, his attention wandered back to the mini-bar but the thought of the telling off he'd get from Shona if he turned up at the foyer reeking of booze gave him pause and he put on some shopping channel. Growled at the poor woman trying to flog him 'Precision cut Diamantrix jewellery! An *incredible* £79.99! Only 16 left!', 'Think it'll help you get your Equity card any faster, love? Not a chance, best stick to Butlins,' and hit the 'Off' button.

He browsed through the 'Welcome' booklet for guests, pausing at the listing of 'Red Hot' channels... perhaps unwise. He could imagine the headlines in the *Seacrest Gazette*, 'World Renowned Critic in Hotel Porn Scandal'. Flaming hell, this was dull though. Worse than being in digs when he didn't have any money to go out. Least then he would have a script to keep himself busy whilst wondering if he could get any more tea out of a bag used seven times already.

With some difficulty he got up off the bed and wandered to the balcony, the phrase 'cabined, cribbed, confined' replaying in his head. Grasping the balcony rail he leant forward as far as he dared to get a better view of the pier, the slow-turning Big Wheel. The perfect place to be on a holiday and he was stuck indoors. It was like winning an all-expenses paid trip to Las Vegas and spending it in the hotel bar. And God knew, Arthur needed a holiday. He hadn't been able to afford a trip away in *years*. He could hardly count all those afternoons spent wandering dreary shopping centres in market-towns until the matinee as a break.

'Arthur Dott,' he said aloud, 'I do believe you deserve what the Americans call a little 'me' time. As if to confirm this yet another film geek called up from the top of the Fulmar steps, 'Hey! Mr Fletcher! My God, I can't… you're like my *hero*, could I… ' But Fletcher had already given him a regal wave then retreated into his room, closing the balcony doors firmly behind him. 'Yes', Arthur said determinedly. 'Let's stick Fletcher in a cupboard for a couple of hours. Do us both some good.'

Half an hour later that same fan ignored the scruffy, bearded old man who glanced warily about him after leaving the revolving doors of the hotel. In a pair of mustard cords that an eccentric university lecturer in English Lit would hesitate to wear, topped by a dark brown fleecy jumper bought from one of those catalogues that fall out of magazine supplements, he appeared remarkably unremarkable. Difficult to imagine any kind of connection between him and the darkly handsome, devilishly charismatic Cameron Fletcher.

Arthur noted with satisfaction the fan didn't give him a first, never mind a second glance as he ambled down the Fulmar steps but he was a good distance along the promenade before he stopped checking over his shoulder, making sure he wasn't being followed. He was a bit disappointed, had thought maybe Shona or Callum would have stuck some heavies outside, made sure he didn't get up to any mischief. Obviously thought he was too tame to try. Fools.

There might have been some in the crowds thronging the streets of Seacrest who looked twice at Arthur, who thought they'd seen him somewhere before. They probably *had*, especially if they were elderly, infirm or unemployed as he'd provided so much background colour over the years in ads and TV shows shown during weekday afternoons or early Sunday evenings. But if you'd pointed at the cheerily red-faced bloke who, judging by the way his paunch strained against the belt of his cords, really shouldn't be enjoying that triple-scoop cone quite so much, and said 'Look! There he is! Cameron Fletcher!' they'd have thought you mad. Even Callum Boyd, taking a break from Festival business to relax in his camera room, tilting a pier-side camera until it took in the sight of Arthur putting a 50p into one of the telescopes, kept the camera moving, failing to notice anything amiss.

It wasn't as if he'd done anything radical to alter his appearance, although he had removed the temporary dye that had granted him Fletcher's saturnine appearance instead of his natural mousiness. It came down to bearing, the different way each man presented himself to the world. While Cameron's bulk seemed entirely in keeping with the gravitas he brought to any room, Arthur's paunchiness didn't speak of authority but too many afternoons spent on a couch with a packet of digestive biscuits watching *Pointless*. As Gordon, Arthur's first proper drama teacher, a mad old queen he'd met in Rep, had said. 'It's all in the shoulders, love. Shoulders and a straight back is what an audience wants and needs. They love to see that confidence, to know they can trust you completely. Means they can relax and enjoy themselves.'

Arthur was so *ordinary* he could fade away entirely from view in a crowd and it was this that made his acting so skilled. Arthur was an actor who only felt truly alive, fully *there*, when pretending to be someone else. Otherwise his greatest pleasure was to stay in the background, to watch others, gather information, pick up tics and gestures, intonations and accents, absorbed for later use.

Here at Seacrest there were riches for such a chameleon in the variety of the crowds. Even the street performers, a form of life Arthur usually regarded with ill-disguised contempt, were entertaining. The town was like a great big dressing-up box, Arthur's idea of heaven. All these lessons on how to become someone else…

Busy studying the people around him he didn't notice the Kinotech until he nearly walked into 'Laughing Sal', the mechanised buxom woman standing guard at the front entrance whose rocking torso and wide gap-toothed grin would feature in the nightmares of many young visitors in the nights to come. The Kinotech… yes, Harry Lawson, Alec Lawson's son. Arthur tugged his beard thoughtfully. He should go in, have a chat, find out more about the history of the place… hang on though. A family were rattling the Kinotech's door, turning away in disappointment. Arthur read the sign propped up between Sal's hands behind the protective glass. 'Sorry to announce that the Kinotech will be open mornings 9-12:30pm only. Please ring to arrange out of hours visits,' but no phone number provided. Strange. Busiest time of the year, pier mobbed and he was choosing to cut down on his business. Arthur suspected there was something funny going on…

…and something funny *was* going on. Harry locked in the back room of the Kinotech, wearing headphones the better to prevent him being distracted by the noise of potential customers outside, lost in a sound world devoted to his Dad, memories and anecdote, laughter and tears being looped and layered, creating their own rhythm, their own music…

But Arthur knew nothing of this. While he was disappointed at not being able to see the exhibits part of him was also relieved. It would have been too much hassle, having to remember not to let anything slip, let one of Boyd's arch rivals know who he really was…well, not *really* was but who he was *mostly*… see! He was wrapping himself in knots thinking about it. Best to have a proper break from this Fletcher business altogether. So he walked away, back along the pier, up into the heart of the town and it was there Arthur's liking for Seacrest blossomed into full-blown love.

It was as if some mad professor had managed to grab hold of part of his brain, found a fever dream he'd had when he was a kid and turned it into… this. A journey back to the days when every town had at least three or four cinemas that were proper picture palaces, with murals on the walls and flashing lights on the front, red flock wallpaper, bouquets of plastic flowers in the toilets, an assistant manageress spraying insect repellent over the audience instead of bland, barn-sized multiplexes with their comfy seating and air-conditioned nonsense.

Then there were the people, the locals, dressed up in their outfits from the forties, the fifties, the thirties. It was like being in one of those films they made during the war to distract audiences from the threat of being bombed to bits. The musicals he'd stopped renting years ago because they were so relentlessly cheerful they'd started giving him migraines. The ones with Betty Grable and Carmen Miranda appearing in cameos…

After a couple of hours being as dazed as a child on its first visit to Hamleys, his face hurting from smiling so much after years of dolefulness, Arthur decided what he needed was a nice sit down and a cup of tea. He chose one of the quieter side streets largely devoid of neon apart from one green flashing sign pointing the way to the Emerald Lotus Bar and Teashop, a red-eyed green serpent coiling its way through the lettering.

He pushed through a pair of green doors decorated with paintings of grimacing Chinese dragons, an entranceway fit for Fu Manchu. They led to a narrow staircase at the top of which was a sparsely populated bar and... *bleeding* Nora, chap who ran this place liked his green. If Arthur had ever wanted to find out what life was like inside a giant lime, here was his chance.

Green bamboo screens, green dragons, a green water feature next to the bar, green tables, green chairs. He decided to sit by the window to keep his brain from panicking, thinking it had been struck down by a particularly specific form of colour-blindness, behind a screen so he didn't have to worry about any fan boys or girls taking too close an interest.

In response to a blank-eyed stare from a bored waitress in a green kimono he ordered a pot of lapsang souchong and a scone as it seemed to be a Seacrest law that no establishment could offer tea without guaranteeing access to a scone within thirty seconds. That was the Scots for you, unhealthy buggers, thank God. He was about to enjoy the second half, spread thickly with butter and jam, when he sensed he was being watched.

A young man with a floppy fringe sitting on the opposite side of the room, just visible behind the bamboo screen and who, Arthur was suddenly aware, had slowly been edging his chair round into his sight-line. That denim jacket... he'd seen it before... Christ. That was it, *Orpheé*. The chap who invited him down into the Tunnels. What was he doing here? Pure coincidence?

Wait, no, remembered Arthur, it wasn't *him* he'd invited but Cameron Fletcher. He had nothing to do with that business, he was just an old man, looking out the window, picking up a sultana, trying not to notice his hand bloody well shaking when he lifted his tea-cup... which returned to the saucer with a clatter when the chair opposite him was pulled out and occupied by the floppy-haired hipster who placed a brown paper package tied up with string on the table between them, holding out his hand in greeting. Probably a good sign that, meant he was going to be polite before stabbing Arthur who decided to keep holding his butter knife in a mildly threatening way.

'Mr Arthur Dott?' – *Shitting* hell, Arthur panicked, he knew his name? how the – 'My name is… well, that's not really important at the moment, let's say it's… ' He stared out the window, gave it some thought until a smile spread across his face and he said, delighted – 'Charles. Yes. That'll do perfectly. My name is Charles and I am a great admirer of your work. A *great* admirer of your work, Mr Dott.'

Right, Arthur thought, this would be flattering if it wasn't so bleeding scary. His accent, American, New York…Fletcher's. The intonation. Not an impersonation though, more a… whadyamacallit… an *homage* to Cameron Fletcher. Or to Arthur doing Fletcher. Whichever way you looked at it, it was pretty bloody odd considering he had most definitely been a Scot when he was shouting his mouth off at the screening.

Fine, Arthur decided, he'd play him at his own game, bluff him out, they'd see who was the best faker here. 'Why thank you… Charles.' And if the worst came to the worst at least he looked as skinny as any of the other film geeks, could probably take him if he hit him hard and fast with the teapot. 'May I ask the appearance that so aroused your admiration? My acclaimed performance as Forgetful Pensioner in the 'Get a Will Before You Pop Your Clogs' ad? Second shepherd on the right during the controversial sheep rustling episode of *Heartbeat*?'

Charles laughed, pushing his fringe away from his forehead in a young Hugh Grant manner Arthur found eminently punchable. 'No, Arthur, although, I have to admit, from the way you describe them I'll be sure to seek them out. No. I'm talking about your current role. The one you're excelling in.' He looked over his shoulder to check no one was listening in, hiding behind the screen then leant across the table, whispering, 'As Mr Cameron Fletcher.'

There was nothing amusing about him now, his expression

serious, even his hair less... floppy somehow. Arthur, not for the first time, began to wish he'd never heard of Shona Bloody Boyd or Seacrest or Cameron Fecking Fletcher.

Bluster, that was it, do some blustering, that Dickens director had said his bluster was fantastic, best blusterer he'd seen since Dennis Quilley. 'I'm sorry to disappoint you, Charles, but I've no idea what you're talking about. You've got my name right and that's about it. I'm here on holiday, trying to relax and haven't a clue who this Fletcher chap is, this seems to be a case of mistaken identity, you... '

'Arthur, Arthur stop, OK? Listen, don't panic, I'm on *your* side. I'm not here to expose you, to go running to the police or the papers. I'm not working for Callum Boyd or Luke Howard or Joanna Ashe or anyone else with an interest in telling people you're not who you say you are. Or rather, Cameron Fletcher isn't who everyone thinks he is. Because we know who you are. You're the amazing Arthur Dott!'

Yes, it was vanity, yes it was the desire all actors have for a grateful audience, yet seeing Charles smile, sensing his sincerity, Arthur couldn't help but trust him. A *fan*? Of *course* he was going to believe him, he thought he was great. What's not to like? Obviously a man of taste and that smile... squinty teeth an American orthodontist would faint at, made him like him even more. Someone else not exactly who they said they were.

That smile disappeared as Charles told him, 'I do know Shona Boyd though,' and Arthur turned cold as Charles continued. 'I, no, *we,* my colleagues and I, have worked closely with Shona over the past few months. We were responsible for passing on everything she needed to know about how to construct... well, *you.* Mr Cameron Fletcher, in the flesh... in fact, it was only because of my contact with her that I knew who you really were, Arthur, when I passed you by on the street just there. Because, believe me, if I hadn't seen the pictures there is no *way* I'd have connected Cameron Fletcher with you, here now, looking so… well…. Arthur-like. It really is *incredible*.'

Charles stopped as the waitress had decided to join them, realising her boredom could be relieved by a little light flirting with a young American. This granted Arthur time to decide whether to punch him or graciously accept the back-handed compliment. Cheeky arse. Surely some of the Fletcher charisma remained, he carried a smidgen of his aura? Arthur glanced at his reflection in the window, half hoping, half dreading seeing Fletcher winking back at him. But no, the bags under the eyes, the scruffy beard, there was Arthur Dott present and correct. Why did he find that *quite* so depressing?

'No, here for just a couple days longer. And yes, I will have a pot of green tea but no scone thanks. Arthur? Arthur, is there anything you'd like?'

Dragging his gaze away, Arthur waved a no, waiting until the waitress was back behind her counter before whispering, 'You said 'we'. Who is this 'we' exactly and does Shona know you're here? Is she behind this, why couldn't she speak to me herself? Or will you speaking to me get me into trouble… Christ, if Callum finds out… '

That bloody waitress was back again! Sensed a bit of gossip and was back there with a teapot in double-quick time. 'Anything else sir?' smiling away all of a sudden. 'No,' snapped Arthur, 'we're fine,' and she sloped off with a scowl.

Charles kept smiling after she'd slunk out of earshot, Arthur tempted to say, 'If you'd rather I leave you two alone together…' then Charles was back, his look intense. 'No, Shona doesn't know I'm here and I doubt she would be too happy if she did. 'We' are Cameron Fletcher. The *real* Cameron Fletcher.'

CHAPTER TWENTY-SEVEN

OK Arthur, breathing, remember breathing? He used to be good at it, back in the day, had directors commending him on the whole breathing thing. So he should keep calm and keep doing breathing, try and stop shaking his head as if he'd got Parkinson's as Charles sipped his tea, calm as you like, while he was feeling as though the Hulk had parked on his chest.

'The *real* Cameron Fletcher? But that's nonsense! You and I both know that's ridiculous, Fletcher's a myth, Shona said, she *told* me, I'm the closest there's ever been, ever *will* be to the real Cameron Fletcher. He doesn't, he didn't exist.' Arthur was aware he was practically spluttering, should have had a monocle popping out his right eye.

Charles pushed his fringe back from his face, shook his head slowly, his expression close to pity but kinder. 'That's where you're wrong. This proves it and that's why I'm entrusting it to you.' He tapped the package, slid it over to Arthur. 'I was going to wait until you visited the Tunnels but perhaps this is safer. No onlookers. Wait until you are somewhere quiet, somewhere safe before opening this. After you've read it, keep it secure, where no one can find it 'accidentally'. I'm part of a group of people who've dedicated themselves to keeping the memory – yes, the *memory*, not the myth – of Fletcher alive. We've been helped by Luke Howard but even he doesn't know the truth. You will, Arthur. Because you deserve to, more so than anyone else in this town.'

'But I don't… I mean, why? I'm jus… '

'You're not *just* anything, Arthur.' In that flash of anger Arthur realised what a risk Charles had been taking, how well he'd disguised his nerves. 'You are Cameron Fletcher to an extent none of us could imagine. When Shona approached us we were happy to help, thought she was doing so as a genuine memorial, a *celebration* of Fletcher's life and work. Having been here and seen how closely she's working with Callum, it's clear that isn't her aim at all. It's politics, Arthur. Business plans and redevelopment. We think that she and Callum are building Cameron up to bring him down. To expose him as a fake and show the success of Seacrest is built on shaky foundations so the town comes crumbling down. While we were taking this in we began to notice *you* weren't playing by the script. That you were willing to… improvise a little. Let the true spirit of Fletcher have some fun.'

'So that scene last night, when you invited me to the Tunnels…. that was a test. To see which side I was on.'

'Exactly.' That grin of Charles' reminded Arthur of someone. Almost… possessive. Callum at the Reception. 'We knew how *our* Fletcher would behave in that sort of situation and by that stage we'd a pretty good idea you'd respond in exactly the same way. We'd seen how you reacted when Luke was thrown about by Callum's heavies – oh yes, we were there, we're *everywhere* – and you passed the Fletcher Test with flying colours. We feel you deserve a reward for what you're doing, a reward that can act as protection. Stop you ending up the fall guy.'

'Protection? The *fall guy?* What – you mean… you seriously think Shona and Callum are setting me up? That I'm going to take the flak when this goes tits up?'

Charles shrugged in a way that made Arthur consider chucking the remains of his scone at him. 'I'm sorry, I hope I'm wrong but knowing what we do about Callum and his plans… believe me, there are people out there who don't want that to happen to you, Arthur, who believe you're a true artist and a gentleman. That's why we're leaving this in your custody. The holy grail.'

They both stared at the ordinary brown box until Arthur started to feel daft and Charles stood up abruptly. 'Right, sorry this had to be so brief, I'm afraid I'll have to love you and leave you.'

'What? That's *it*? You turn up all mysterious, hand me some package that could be a bomb or… I dunno, full of sarin gas or something and then you bugger off without telling me what I'm supposed to do next?'

'Arthur.' Charles leant forward, placing a hand on his shoulder. 'We have every faith that whatever you decide to do will be the *right* thing. The *Fletcher* thing to do. This is a man's *life* we're talking about, his legacy, and truly it's an honour someone of your talent is carrying that memory forward.' He pulled a crumpled £10 from his jeans' pocket, dropped it on the table top. As he pulled on his denim jacket Arthur noticed the initials 'CF' embroidered on the top right hand pocket. Sparkling red thread in a perfect match to Fletcher's curling script. 'I suggest you contact Dr Ashe. I know, might seem an odd choice, she's been a thorn in the side of the Fletcher movement, but that's been good for us. Something to work against. She's a good person, Arthur. The time may come when you need allies like her. Give her a call. She'll see you right.'

Then he was off down the stairs, pausing to give a small salute to the waitress, a quick wave to Arthur.

'I haven't even *met* her properly,' moaned Arthur, 'how am I supposed to know her *number*?' He briefly considered lurching down the stairs after Charles, grabbing him by the arm, demanding further information. Instead he sat, stunned, until gathering enough sense to wave the waitress over, ordering as much saké as the change from the £10 could buy.

Which turned out to be not very much, enough though to get

his heart settled. Half an hour later the panic had largely subsided while there lingered the expectation of a squad of Callum's goons leaping out from behind some bamboo. Could you be arrested for impersonating an imaginary character? Although not so imaginary according to Charles... Arthur gently laid the fingertips of his right hand on the package. Was that a... thrumming? He snatched them away.

Oh come on! Brace up! Get a hold of yourself! Count yourself lucky, Arthur told himself. There he was, presented with a trump card, a joker in the pack, a way of getting back at those who saw him as some kind of puppet. Yet it would be so easy, so tempting to stay, drink some more rice wine, let the alcohol run its course...

Arthur sighed, caught the eye of his reflection. Whatever he saw there was enough to have him stand up so quickly his chair nearly tipped over backwards. Right, Dotty old son, and he hugged the package close to his chest. Enough with the sightseeing. Time to discover the truth.

That was easier said than done and he found himself dithering on the busy Seacrest streets. He could head back to the Fulmar he supposed but ran the risk of Shona walking in any time, asking 'What's in the box? What's in the box?' He needed to get away, outside the centre of town. He'd stopped feeling safe there, as if his cover had been blown.

Arthur stared into the window of a camera shop, his tiny image caught in the lenses of dozens of cameras. Bloody saké, he had to think properly, clearly. What was it Shona had said? Something about the suburbs, the Dead Zone. She'd shown him a tourist map of the place, what there was along the east side, out by the caravan park, beyond the cliff lift. Asked her about the area where the dots showing cinemas thinned to nothing, where the only site of interest was a water fountain Lassie might have cocked a leg against. 'What's here exactly?' 'Oh nothing. Just a lot of angry and depressed people.' Perfect. Arthur's kinda place.

It took a while to get there, up the long, curving slope as Arthur couldn't face the crush of the cliff lift and the thought of the Powell and Pressburger Steps caused his chest to tighten. Once he reached the suburbs he felt calmer, at home. Bland homes housing bland people in bland clothes. No one making the effort to pretend that life was anything other than dull and relentless with nothing to show at the end of it.

After a few wrong turns down cul-de-sacs and around roundabouts he found the perfect hiding place, a pub called *The Griffin and Dun*. A box of a building with long, dark windows running along the top of its walls, whether to stop people looking in or the clientele looking out and scaring passersby wasn't clear. When Arthur pushed his way though the door it groaned in a way that sounded a warning, and he was suddenly aware of how bright his mustard cords were even in the dim light. Pints caught mid-way to the mouths of hardened drinkers, a dart suspended in mid-flight.

But bugger, it was still a darn sight nicer than some of the pubs he'd ended up in, less vomit and sawdust on the floor for a start and as he slouched towards the bar, the slump of his shoulders making clear he would be no bother to anyone, the low chat started again. It was difficult to make out how many people were in, such was the grubby nature of the light. The ideal location for a thorough examination of a suspect package. After taking his Guinness to the darkest corner Arthur relaxed knowing he would be able to do so undisturbed.

Two hours later he stumbled out into the twilight, pale and shaking, a different man altogether from the man he thought he was.

# CHAPTER TWENTY-EIGHT

It was unpleasant seeing Arthur in that state – discombobulated, unmoored – so we left him, sped along the seafront, the wild sea battering against the walls of the promenade, salt-water whipping our faces, in search of Jo and found her buffeted by the crowds in the heart of Lot 45.

She should've known it would be packed out, the wannabe Pauline Kaels who hadn't booked their Fletcher event tickets fast enough and couldn't afford the eBay prices, going there instead to get a whiff of the Big Man. Even so, she thought, this was just… daft and she scowled at every queue to peer into another tat-filled vitrine, to stare at the rumoured first cinema ticket Fletcher ever bought, his collection of movie star cigarette cards, the Homburg he was wearing in that fuzzy photo of him talking to Marlon Brando in Central Park. Marlon Brando, Jo snorted…more like Les Dawson if you asked her.

Though of course no one *would* ask her. Not here, because she was one of the heathen. A non-believer, an *academic*. No, the only person whose answers these acolytes believed in was Luke Howard. He was the only reason she was there, checking to see he was all right, not too shaken up after being *imprisoned* by Callum that… *twat*. She had been so angry on Luke's behalf, couldn't believe it when Harry told her, and there Luke was, perfectly happy, being followed about by a mini fan club.

The ring-master, with a weird manic edge to him Jo hadn't

seen before. A different kind of Luke. A showman. In control on the surface with an undercurrent of something wilder. Circling the displays, never stopping, pausing briefly to take questions otherwise keeping up a stream of little-known Fletcher anecdotes, regaling his followers. That same flush to his face Jo had noticed in Consortium meetings when he was caught up arguing a point, when no one, not even Callum could stop him.

She managed to grab him eventually as he was heading towards the toilet, asked him how he got on at the police station, if he was OK, if he needed a good lawyer and he looked at her as though she was the one needing sympathy.

'Listen, Jo, it was nothing. Don't worry, I can handle it. I can handle anything they throw at me.' That gleam in his eye... did he *know* how Norman Bates-like it made him look? 'They can lock me up, put me away, but it isn't going to change things. Not now. Because I *met* him. I *spoke* to Cameron Fletcher and he knew who I was and he was kind. And that's when I knew everything was going to be all right.'

Jo seriously considered yelling out the truth, had to dig her fingernails into her palms to stop herself shouting, 'He isn't real! Cameron Fletcher isn't real! He's Arthur *Dott* you idiot! This is all in your head, in the head of everyone here! You're all as sick as each other!'

Then Luke smiled at her and it was the old Luke, the Luke she loved and couldn't hurt, even though it would be for the best, would set him free. 'Now Jo, I'm sorry but hang around and we'll catch up properly but I really... ah, have to go.'

Jo didn't hang around, desperate for some fresh air, the bracing cold of the promenade. She knew she was a coward, should have risked a lynching and *told* him. But then, who needed protecting more, Luke or the population of Seacrest? Because if Luke *was* told the truth, if he did find out his god was false, impersonated by some washed-up old character actor, what was to stop him going all Travis Bickle? Taking everyone he could out before ending it all?

Jo was distracted from gloomier thoughts by the sight of the Devil himself. She had made it half way along the prom when she spotted him on the opposite side of the road. He was standing by the railing, looking out to sea, hands braced on the cold, cold metal, not caring about the spray soaking the sleeves of his jumper, his beard. She stopped by one of the empty wooden shelters sure it was him, Arthur Dott. Then something happened. He straightened his shoulders, stuck out his chin and there was an odd sort of flickering, a blurring of the edges and Dott had disappeared, replaced by Fletcher. Definitely Cameron Fletcher looking not the least likely, as Arthur had done a few seconds ago, to tip himself over into the waves. Instead it appeared as though Fletcher had simply paused mid-stroll to admire the view.

Jo took off her glasses, wiped them free of spray and when they were back on… For Pete's sake! She couldn't be sure it was Arthur or Cameron or someone else entirely. Although she didn't recognise the man she was staring at there was something oddly familiar about him. As if she had known him for years, had been wondering why he hadn't got in touch and it was a pleasant surprise to see him without warning. She blinked, the sensation vanished and she was looking at poor Arthur Dott committing suicide by hypothermia.

Sensible thing, she told herself, would be to carry on walking and leave the old fraudster to it. Then again, when had she ever gone for the *sensible* option? It hadn't been very sensible moving to Seacrest, falling for Shona and bloody *hell*, there was another blast of cold water going up his cords and he looked so lonely and lost. Less malevolent impostor than doddery grandpa. Oh well, if he tipped her over the railing at least she could claim death by fictional character.

When she touched him lightly on his arm, asking doubtfully, 'Arthur… are you all right? It is Arthur isn't it? Arthur Dott?' he turned to her with a look of such confusion, as though shaken from a deep sleep, Jo wondered if she'd got the wrong man entirely. Then the confusion vanished, replaced by a smile of pure relief. Like she was the one person in the world he'd been standing there waiting for.

'My dear Dr Ashe, at the moment I'm not entirely sure *who* I am but I do know that I'm very pleased to see *you*', his accent strange, fluctuating between Leeds and New York. He frowned, remembering something, glanced briefly out to sea before turning his attention back to Jo. 'You wouldn't happen to have the time on you?'

'It's ah… ' Jo angled her watch into the light cast from a promenade lamp – 'just gone 8:30. Wait… you're supposed to be presenting a film at eight, aren't you? The Icelandic one, with the donkey. Well, not *you*… Cameron Fletcher.'

'Ah yes… I knew there was *someone* I was supposed to be,' he chuckled and Jo couldn't help smiling too despite a jet of water shooting up her jeans' leg. The Fletcher effect, old rogue.

'I wonder if I could ask a favour of you, Dr Ashe. Or Jo, may I call you Jo? Would you mind escorting me back to my hotel room? For one I think your girlfriend Shona – oh, no need to look quite so shocked, the way you looked at her in that ballroom only a blind idiot wouldn't guess that – is back there waiting for me and is no doubt, oooh, *furious*. Your presence might help quieten her down. And for another I have something about my person I think you would find very interesting.'

Good God, Jo worried. She'd been right in the first place, should have carried on walking. The prospect of facing Shona in a rage then taking a dodgy old man up on a suspect offer… lovely. Still, he was doing that twinkly-eyed thing and there was something genuine about him, something… serious. What was the worst that could happen? Her mind flickered with possibilities.

Despite this she replied, 'I'll say this for you, certainly know how to sweet-talk a girl. How could I resist? Shona in a bad mood… great. Mind you, I do need to see her about a pair of shoes… come on, let's get you out of the cold.' She took him by the arm and those who passed assumed they were father and daughter out for an evening stroll, enjoying the fresh sea air.

They stopped at the Fulmar steps, keeping an anxious eye on the doors, expecting Shona to storm out at any moment. 'Right, there's no way we can risk the foyer,' said Jo, 'so follow me.'

She pulled Arthur down a narrow path leading to the car-park at the rear of the hotel. 'We can get in through the staff entrance, they know me here.' Arthur was impressed with the way they breezed through the kitchens without anyone questioning their presence, instead greeted with the occasional nod and a 'Hello Dr Ashe'. No one seemed to think it odd her down there on the arm of a man at least twice her age.

When they'd made it to the safety of the service lift for cleaners and room service, Jo caught Arthur grinning at her and blushed. 'What?'

'You. Coming over all masterful. James Bond-like, access all areas. Very impressive.'

'I wouldn't put it *quite* like that. Cheek… ' she replied with a smile. Should she be enjoying this so much? They were supposed to be arch-rivals but this was… nice. Teasing. 'There have to be *some* privileges to being historian of this town. People get used to seeing me where I shouldn't be, know I'm not any kind of threat. Interested more in the wallpaper than nicking anything from the pantry. People know they can trust me.' The look he gave her then, the hope in it, forced her to look away.

'Right. Here we are, top floor, penthouse suite. Give me your key, I'll go and check. Make sure no one's lying in wait for you.'

It was only after she'd put the key in the lock it hit her she'd no idea how she was going to react if Shona *was* standing there, impatiently tapping a red high-heeled shoe. They'd hardly spent any time together since the Reception, Shona proving suspiciously elusive. There had been that one meal in Pacino's but that had only been an hour, Jo with an event to chair at the Alhambra. She'd tried to talk to Shona about their night together on the walk up to the cinema, what it meant and then Shona had pulled her into that alleyway and used some very effective means of distraction, leaving Jo breathless as she wandered off, calling over her shoulder that they'd see each other whenever…

When Jo eased the door open and found the room empty it took some effort to convince herself she was more relieved than disappointed. Sighing she turned, jumped at finding Arthur peering round the door behind her.

'Thought I told you to stay in the lift!' she hissed. 'What if she's in the toilet?'

'But she isn't, is she?' Arthur replied at normal volume, shutting the door behind him. 'You can sense it. Things in here feel…calm. Believe me, in my line of work you get to know the type of woman who can charge a room by entering it.' Jo was about to argue back but didn't, stymied by the fact he was absolutely right.

'Drink?' he asked, flipping open the mini-bar while she examined the décor. No wonder they'd banned her from paying a research visit up here, saying it was restricted to paying guests only, they were obviously worried she'd call in the police for crimes against taste. It made Graceland look a picture of minimalist refinement.

'Umm… no thanks. Best keep my wits about me.' Jo had to keep reminding herself that for all his current chumminess this was the guy she was planning to expose as a fraud and – hey, thinking about it, was it such a good idea to be up there alone with no one knowing she was here? Jo's mouth ran dry. And what *was* that bulge under his jumper? Just pleased to see her or…

Arthur broke into her fretting with an accent entirely his own, broad and Northern without a trace of Manhattan. 'Dr Ashe. I know you have every reason to suspect I'm up to no good but honestly, I truly believe a gin and tonic will do you the world of good. Please. You've already been very kind to me for no reason whatsoever and I'd like to repay that. Offering free alcohol is the least I can do. I'll even throw in a tiny packet of dry roasted peanuts.'

Jo relented, sitting on one of the embroidered throne-like monstrosities on either side of the high windows leading out to the balcony, distracting herself with the view. 'Jo… here,' he said. She turned, expecting to be handed a glass, instead he was wrestling with something caught in the inside of his jumper. She tried to calculate how quickly she could make it to the door, panicked, did he lock it?

'Gotcha!' She flinched but instead of a gun pointing at her head, Arthur was holding a loosely tied bundle of brown paper which he placed carefully on the table next to her. He stared at it for a few beats, nodding thoughtfully and when Jo reached for it he pulled it away a short distance. 'Not just yet. Wait until I'm through there,' and he pointed to the bathroom. 'I'll make up your drink, get changed and then I thought we could get out of here. Go for another walk, find somewhere we can have a drink and talk about… well… about what's in here.' He tapped the package lightly, as if scared any further pressure might cause it to explode.

'Get changed… into Fletcher you mean?' Jo asked as he headed to the mini-bar. She felt oddly nervous at the prospect. Being here with Arthur, that was fine, surprisingly comfortable but Fletcher… the man whose existence she'd been working to disprove? She knew it was ridiculous yet was nevertheless thankful for the drink he handed her.

'Yup, me and Clark Kent, we're like that.' He held up two tightly crossed fingers. 'A Dott special, just the merest hint of tonic,' when she spluttered at the first sip. 'Believe me, you'll be thankful of it when you read what's in there... anyway, I think it's about time Cameron is given the opportunity to get out and enjoy the nightlife unshackled. I've a feeling, Dr Ashe, that you'll prove the perfect guide. I met a young man today who spoke very highly of you and from what I've seen of you so far I've a feeling he got that exactly right.'

He chuckled – and Jo realised she'd never seen anyone 'chuckle' more effectively than Arthur – when he saw her look of polite confusion. 'Happy reading. Say cheerio to Arthur now, he deserves a bit of a break. About time Cameron Fletcher took over, did the talking for a while'.

She waited until the lock of the bathroom door clicked into place, took a large gulp of gin, drew the package towards her. Untied the string to reveal a plain brown, unremarkable cardboard box, lifted the lid and it was the smell that warned her.

She breathed in deeply. That mustiness, so familiar from days and nights in archives, sifting through evidence, looking for clues. The unmistakable scent of the Truth. It felt wrong touching the papers inside without a pair of white cotton gloves to protect them. Like relics. She wasn't entirely sure what she was looking at, yet they had that feel to them. Important. The hair prickling at the back of her neck.

It took a few minutes for her to work out what she'd been given, how to piece together the jigsaw puzzle of newspaper cuttings, articles ripped from magazines, photocopies of diary pages, the typewritten transcript of an interview, crumpled black and white photographs of a man she thought at first was Arthur dressed as Fletcher. Looking closer, she realised it wasn't Arthur, this man was too old and thin and tramp-like to be Arthur's glorious incarnation of Fletcher and yet… and yet, there was a definite Fletcher quality to him. Those eyes, that beard…

By the time she'd found the two documents lying folded at the bottom of the box – one a photocopy, the other on thick, yellowing paper, edges soft with age – she'd worked it out and her heart was pounding. Her trembling fingers made them difficult to unfold and part of her didn't want to open them up at all. Part of her wanted to stuff everything back into that box, carry it down to the promenade and chuck it into the sea. Ever the good researcher, she carried on, laid both sheets of paper flat, smoothed them out, not reading them until she had drained the last of her gin, numbing her lips with the ice. She read the name at the top of the copied birth certificate and then on the original certificate and felt the blood drain away from her face.

'No,' she whispered, tears in her eyes, blurring the evidence. This was the *actual* Cameron Fletcher Archive. For *years* she'd been investigating this, building up a case, tracking down the individuals responsible, convincing others with the truth of Cameron Fletcher. That he didn't exist, he was a fiction, and there in front of her was proof those years were a complete waste of time. A bloody pointless waste of time. Luke had been right all along.

Because what lay before her was proof that Cameron Fletcher had been *real*, had lived and breathed and died, his continued life not the fantasy of a few obsessed film fans but an evolving, heart-felt memorial. How could she have got it so *wrong*?

She allowed herself a flicker of hope. It *could* be another part of the hoax… a double-bluff to put her off the scent, Arthur using his acting skill to convince her to reject the theory she'd been building for years. There was no reason to believe *anything* he told her, in fact there was every reason to *suspect* everything.

Chewing on an ice-cube, pain lancing through a molar, that hope guttered and died. She'd had enough experience with archive material, of studying the art of lying – because wasn't that all film-making was when it came down to it? One big, fat glorious lie? To know what was real and what was fake. She could feel it in the pit of her stomach. This… this was the real McCoy.

Accepting that, the instinct of a dedicated researcher took over and it was excitement causing her hands to shake as she picked up the interview transcript, whispering 'I *knew* it! Knew there was a link!'

CHAPTER TWENTY-NINE

When she saw the name of the interviewee, the wide-screen version of Seacrest stuttered and faded, the film stock changing to grainy, washed out black-and-white Super 8.

We were in extreme close-up, a blur of a face, the camera pulling back to catch glimpses of a young man. He looked like a young Bob Dylan, the same mass of curly hair, the lips fuller, the sort of face Caravaggio, Derek Jarman would have loved. He was wearing black jeans and t-shirt and was bobbing about as if to avoid the camera's gaze, joking with the cameraman who pulled back to show he was sitting on a metal chair next to the window of a disused warehouse. There were skyscrapers in the background. We could hear sirens, dogs barking and we know this is New York, the seventies, when to be a young film-maker walking those streets was to be on the cutting, burning edge of everything.

This was Avi Fleischer, director of *The Magician's Daughter* who died far too young and there was something almost unbearable about seeing him so vibrant, confident, riding the success of his short film, waking up to the fact the film world needed and loved him as much as he needed and loved it. Bright, sharp eyes, good at watching. The best. But he wasn't there to talk about himself and when the off-screen interviewer asked her first question the joshing stopped and he was keen to pay full attention to the story he needed to tell. To give credit where it was due.

'So, first off, Avi, tell us all about how you met Cameron. Was when you were making *Magician's Daughter*, that right?'

'Yeah, that's it, I'd noticed this old guy hanging about on the edges of the set and to be completely honest with you, the reason why I and most of the crew had noticed him was because he was a right royal pain in the ass! We'd be setting scenes up, working quick because we weren't bothering with permits and he'd ruin a take by shouting out directions, complaining about the lighting – the lighting for Chrissake! We were shooting down alleys, hoping the sun was in the right place at the right time! Yelling the director knew nothing, that he was letting his leading lady down. That if we gave him ten minutes he could tell us how to light May so she looked like a goddess, like Marlene Dietrich in *Shanghai Express*. Kidding us, right? On our budget?'

'So we're complaining about putting up with yet *another* crank, as if we didn't have enough of those to worry about, filming on the streets of New York in high summer but then I decide to do this crazy thing. Just for the helluvit, I think, OK, wiseguy, gonna take you at your word and for a day – because this guy, I tell yah, he was *persistent*, he was a nut but a dedicated nut – I'm gonna take the time to listen to what you're saying, take it on board, rather than ignore it. Because I figure this will be the best way to get him to shut up, prove what he's suggesting is so much bullshit.'

'And that's how I discovered, the advice he was giving? Shit, it was right! Every suggestion, made the picture better. Getting May to tilt her head down this way when she was looking in the mirror when she realises she's not going to work with her dad any more? It *did* make her look sad and wise and innocent. Doing one scene with the camera static, a distance away, looking through the window at the couple in the room, speaking but everything silent, the audience working everything out through gesture, that worked too. And I was going to do it handheld, getting right in their faces! *That's* when I realised, this guy may be crazy but he was a crazy guy who knew what he was talking about.'

'So I take it that's when you decided to get to know him better? Find out about his biography?'

'That's it. Decided if you can't beat them, you might as well let them join you. Especially when they care as much about the film you're making as you do. So yeah, after a long night shoot I go up to him, hold out my hand and he doesn't ask me *my* name, oh no, just takes my hand and shakes it, says 'Cameron, Cameron Fletcher,' [at this point Jo felt dizzy, almost *levitated*] 'like *I'm* the one who's privileged here. And I say 'OK, Cameron, now we've got the formalities over with, let's go get a drink.' Rest of the crew leave me to it, think I'm mad but I'm curious, need to know where he's got all this… *knowledge* from.'

'So you take him to Murphy's and… '

'Yeah, we go to Murphy's, into a booth and over a few bottles of Jim Beam I find out all about him, who this guy Cameron is. His secret history. How right at the start of the century he'd travelled from Inverness to Glasgow, got a cheap ticket on a boat out to New York, headed west, kept heading west 'til he hit Hollywood. And he was a jack-of-all-trades was Cameron, could turn his hand to anything. Carpentry, electrics, mechanics, you show him a machine and he'd get the best out of it within minutes. So he makes his way into the movie industry. Helped build some sets, with lighting and props, even some editing. Folks saw he had a talent and that he was willing to *use* that talent and it was such a joy to watch him work they'd give him free lessons.

'And he worked with some of the *greats* and I mean the *Greats*… you know, Lang, Sternberg, von Stroheim. OK, so they might not have been doing their very best work at that point but they were still great and they were willing to talk to a young guy who showed enthusiasm and skill. Eventually he scrapes enough money together, calls in a few favours and starts making his own short films. He'd show them to friends, people on the set of the movie he was working on, at the wrap party, and people liked them, said they were great but way too weird to make it out to a bigger audience. Like someone had filmed a fever dream they'd say. But Orson Welles – can you believe it? [incredulous laughter from Avi and the interviewer] I mean, I nearly fell off of my *seat* when he told me that – Orson *Welles* loved them, fascinated by them. Asked for copies, if he could show them during the interludes of his magic shows.

'I think we were on to our third bottle of Scotch and he starts to tell me where it all went wrong. How he got too caught up in the partying, the night life, making fewer films, chasing too many married actresses, that sort of thing. What did he say...oh yeah, 'If Stroheim couldn't find work what hope did a dumb fuck like me have?' he said.' Avi paused. No laughter this time. His gaze flicked away from the interviewer, out to the view of rooftops, and he was there in that bar, drunk, trying to think of something to say that would make it better. Make Fletcher happy again. [He ran a hand through that mass of curls, tugged at his scalp, then he was back, switched on again].

'So he drifted back east, back to New York, picked up work wherever he could, whoever'd take him. Working as a cinema usher, projectionist, popcorn vendor, ticket seller. He'd brought copies of his films with him but somewhere along the line they got lost, probably sold them for booze, and he was too far gone by then to care.

'And then... then he starts telling me about when he started to notice he was going mad. And I tellya, it was weird... it was the, the sanest, the *soberest* he'd been that night and what he was telling me was horrible, nightmarish...Shit, I don't know how he coped with it at *all*. But it... it was almost as if he was talking about someone else, someone he'd been, like, *observing* almost.

'He told me how things he thought he'd dreamt or seen in a movie turned out to be real, to have happened to him and vice versa. He'd be sitting in a bar with friends, telling them about some weird thing he'd seen happen in the street the other day and they'd be laughing until one of them would say, 'Wait a minute, hey, wasn't that in that Sam Fuller movie we saw last week?' And he'd laugh with them, turn it into some kind of joke, but then he'd go quiet. Because no matter how hard he tried, he couldn't *remember* going to see that movie. What he'd seen had been *real*. Happened in front of him.

'Got to the point he avoided films altogether. Couldn't run the risk of what it would do to his head. Knowing he could end up living that story, actually believing he was a *character* in that film. A fictional character.

'Can you *imagine* that? I mean really *imagine* that?' Avi didn't look at the interviewer but straight into the camera, dark eyes shining in the dim light of the warehouse, pinning our gaze. 'A man who loved cinema, who travelled thousands of miles across the Atlantic, away from his family, away from his *homeland*, to be closer to the people who made pictures and he ends up not being able to set foot inside a *movie* theatre? Can you imagine what that would *do* to a man like that?' He held our eye and it was a disappointment when he looked away, focused back on the interviewer.

'What was he doing when you met him? To get by?'

'It was, well… it was terrible. Really. Terrible. The way he was just… scraping by.' Avi hesitated, the anger, the loss throwing him briefly. 'He was living off the streets, sometimes getting a job flipping burgers, selling newspapers but then he'd get another attack of his… condition, and that would be it. He'd lose whatever crappy job he'd held on to for a coupla weeks. By the time I was talking to him he felt he was getting better. Holding it together. Had even made it as far as the foyer of a cinema the week before I introduced myself. Nearly bought a ticket but wasn't quite there yet. It was progress though and you know the reason he gave for how that had come about? Why he was getting better? Me.

'Yeah, he said it was all down to me,' – laughter – 'and he raised his glass to me. Said 'Reckon it was through watching you make that film of yours. Got me thinking again. Thinking outside myself, reminding me there *is* an outside.''

He stopped, looked out the window again, stuck in the daze of remembering that moment until the interviewer prompted him. 'And how long after that was it before he took you to his flat? Showed you his collection?'

'A few days after we'd finished filming. I was worried about him, y'know? Worried that because we'd stopped shooting he'd lose himself again, start getting sick. I met him outside Murphy's and we walked to this old brownstone down in Greenwich Village, right up into this tiny loft, this tiny, *tiny* flat. This old actress friend paid the rent on it, after she'd stumbled over him, *literally*, stumbled over him in the street. She remembered him from parties they'd been to back in Hollywood and I guess that's why she thought she'd see him right. Anyway, we go in and I tell you, I'm *amazed*. I mean, just... *overwhelmed*. Because every wall, every surface was covered, *covered* in pictures, photographs, movie stills, sheets, pages, ripped out of magazines, newspapers, books.

'At first it looked kinda pathetic, y'know, this crazy collection of stuff, no rhyme or reason to it. Then you looked more closely and you realised there were *strands* there. Connections, links and that's when it hit me. These were *movies*. On the walls you could see like, like a *narrative*. Stories, stories everywhere you looked made out of nothing, out of *scraps*. His versions of storyboards. I mean, OK, they were rough and ready but this was a guy who had *nothing*, absolute zip and yet here he was, making stories out of pictures. Doing what he'd always done. Making films in his head, trying to share them with the world.

'Then he showed me his collection of short pieces of film he'd found dumped all over the city, film cans salvaged from garbage bins at the back of cinemas, lying on the street, whatever. 'Haven't looked at them properly yet' he said, 'but I want you to have them, Avi. Reckon you could bring some life back to them.' He looked at me and it was like…like he was the sanest man in the world. A man who knew he didn't have much time left. 'I want you to look after all this when I'm gone,' – and I tell you, a chill went up my spine then – 'I know it's a responsibility to land on you but the thought of this being dumped after I'm gone… I can hardly sleep at night with the thought of it.' And I…I hardly knew what to say. I mean, what *can* you say? A guy handing over his life's work to you? Yes is all, and the smile he gave me…' Avi's smile, wide and amazed, gave us a glimpse of it. 'It was *beautiful*. The kind of smile you can't refuse.'

Our film version of the text Jo was reading froze then, faded, dimmed to black and we were back in the hotel room. Jo at the table, clutching the pages of the transcript, her eyes red-rimmed, starting at the sound of the bathroom door snapping open. She felt a prickling at the back of her neck. As if a ghost had walked in.

God, this is weird, she thought. I know who it is, know he's Arthur but… and when she looked up to see him transformed she couldn't help but wish Avi were alive to see him. Tears in her eyes, but it couldn't be helped because before her was the Cameron Fletcher who would have lived had everything worked out for him, if everything had gone according to plan. If someone of wealth and importance had recognised in those short films the true talent they displayed, talent that would blossom and create fantastic, unforgettable dreams if only someone would let it. Here was Cameron Fletcher as he *should* have been; healthy, sane, successful, admired.

'A second chance,' she murmured and Cameron smiled

and nodded. 'Worked out how it ends yet?' he asked, the voice Cameron's baritone and she couldn't work out if the sadness in his eyes was Arthur's or Cameron's or both.

He settled in the chair opposite, gave her time to compose herself and told her, 'Sadly, naturally enough. Couldn't really have ended any other way.' He leant over, teased out a cutting from the *Village Voice*, headlined 'Village Eccentric Killed By Taxi', passed it to her. 'I suspect it happened shortly after Avi had been granted a tour of his flat. He wandered out of a bar straight into the path of an oncoming cab. The details fit, the anecdotes from locals about how he'd been seen raking around trash cans, hanging about movie sets. There's even a picture.' Jo almost laughed in shock at the photo of an old man accompanying the obituary. Like it had been beamed from some parallel universe. The likeness to the Cameron Fletcher in front of her uncanny, this one at least ten years older, ruined, the damage done by drink obvious.

'Spooky, isn't it?' Cameron acknowledged. 'But they got the name wrong. Typical journalists. Called him Connor Fleischer. So no one picked up the connection.'

'Fleischer?' Jo lifted her glass, forgetting it was empty. '*Fleischer...* Avi must have had some involvement in writing that. I *knew* there was a connection, I'd been getting closer, a few more months and...'

'And what?' snorted Fletcher. 'You'd have had an even harder time convincing people this was the truth behind Fletcher after the man *himself* had spent the Seacrest Festival charming the doubters, securing the faith of the believers. And from the brief meeting I, or rather, Arthur, had with Charles who handed this over, I reckon the followers of the one true Fletcher would have made it very difficult for anyone else to find out about it. If people had discovered the truth, that the myth of Cameron Fletcher was built on the life of a tramp, it might have ruined his chance to live on in their, in *Avi's*, invention.'

'But Avi died, what… ' Jo checked the date at the top of the *Voice* clipping, 'only a year or so after Fletcher? That's hardly enough time to set up something on this scale, on *your* scale. But then… Avi's death… it might have been the shock the project needed. Like Frankenstein's monster. A bolt from the blue, the power to get it up and walking. Fleischer's set to be the next Big Thing, a group of talented people about him, who loved him… '

'Exactly,' the monster agreed. 'If Fleischer had stayed alive perhaps his enthusiasm for Fletcher would have petered out. He'd have made bigger films, lost sight of keeping the memory of Cameron, of *me*, alive. By dying he gave his friends and colleagues extra incentive to see it through, a memorial for both of them. His death resurrected Fletcher. Then Luke Howard comes along and it gets so much more *real*. Somehow he stumbles on a doctored, forged, version of Fletcher's death certificate,' he pointed to the photocopy, 'with the wrong dates, the cause of death 'heart attack' rather than 'death by cabbie', believes he's stumbled on the truth and his conviction is *so* great he's able to convince anyone he comes into contact with. Luke is a true believer, the perfect mouthpiece for the group. They feed him information, give him the props he needs. Turn him into Fletcher's life support.'

Jo groaned, rubbed her eyes, her forehead, hoping to ease the tension headache threatening to wrap itself around her skull. 'This is all too… So what you're saying, what this boils down to, is that for the past few years Luke has been… God, it hurts to admit this… OK, right, so what you're saying is that Luke has been… '

'*Right*. Yes. But then… ' Fletcher stretched out a hand and, before she could think properly, Jo took it, glad for the reassurance, his palm surprisingly soft. Tender. 'So are you, Dr Ashe. Both of you got close to the Cameron Fletcher in this box. Got it right in your own very particular ways. He was always somewhere in between the fiction and the truth.'

Jo pulled her hand away slowly, stood up, dizziness overtaking her briefly. 'Do you mind if I... ' She gestured towards the mini-bar.

'No, no, go ahead, it's Callum Boyd who's paying' She halted, panic surging.

'Wait – Callum. Does he know about this? Or... no, *Shona*. She *must* know about it, the New York connection, setting you up, how could she *not*. Keeping it from me, smirking behind my back... '

'Jo, calm down. Yes, she does know about this – no, wait, hear me out – but what she's going to *do* with that knowledge, only she knows. Some way of getting back at Callum they suspect. That's why they told Arthur, to give him a heads up... poor Arthur.' Jo wrenched the lid off a miniature Famous Grouse, downing it in one and it occurred to her it didn't seem in the least bit strange, Arthur referring to himself in the third person.

He was completely Cameron then, the way he moved, the way he looked at her, the way she felt tempted to tell him her deepest darkest secrets, favourite stories, the ones she knew would keep his attention. Arthur had vanished.

'Poor *Arthur*?' she gasped, the Grouse scorching her throat. 'How d'you mean?'

'Think about it. He'd taken this role on the understanding he was playing a character, following instruction, yes, but largely his own creation. His plaything with the freedom to do, say, anything he wants as long as it's in keeping with the Fletcher ethos. At the end of it he'd get paid and have an amusing anecdote to tell his friends down the pub. But to discover *this'*, he waved his hand over the papers strewn over the table as if attempting to magic them away, 'that it was someone's life and death he was fooling around with, that this was someone's *legacy*... that makes it different. Makes it -'

'Real,' Jo finished. 'That's why this is so strange. Cameron,

Arthur… You're both here and yet… not.'

'A second chance, Dr Ashe.' Cameron Fletcher's eyes burned. 'We've both been given a second chance and we mean to take full advantage.'

Did he mean 'we' as in Arthur or Cameron or… bloody hell, Jo's head hurt. She scooped up an ice-cube from the ice bucket, rubbed it over her wrists while Fletcher picked up the evidence on the table, bundled it back into the box then carried it to the safe installed inside the bedside cabinet.

After twirling the combination lock, checking the handle was secure he picked up the silver-topped black cane resting against it, dropped it sharply on the polished wooden floor, snatching it up on the rebound. He studied its handle closely as if communing with the decoration, a bearded head of a man with a look caught somewhere between Falstaff and the Devil. 'I don't know about you, Dr Ashe, but I feel the urge to get out of this place and get right royally *wasted*, an act I feel the original and best Cameron Fletcher would heartily approve of. Care to join me?'

For once in her life Jo answered such a proposition without a moment's hesitation. 'Yes, yes I would,' but she paused walking towards the hotel door. Where to take the most famous man in Seacrest? Where was the best night to be had here? Her frown turned into a slow grin as it came to her.

'Mr Fletcher, I think it's about time you were introduced to The Moviegoer.' And the sight of him, eyes shining in pure, joyful expectation, all trace of sadness gone… who'd want to be anywhere else with anyone else, resurrected dead man or not?

 # CHAPTER THIRTY

It would have been quicker to take the tram but instead they walked, taking their time to Scarlet Street, enjoying the night-time buzz. At first Jo was worried about taking Fletcher through the heart of Seacrest, that they ran the risk of being mobbed but she'd forgotten what once made this place so attractive to visiting film stars: they could walk the streets without fear of being pestered. Seacrest made film-stars of *everyone,* resulting in such a degree of self-absorption that everyone was too busy concentrating on giving themselves a good time to disrupt the fun of others. Plus film and reality blurred so frequently that leaving a cinema to see someone you'd just seen up on screen as a contract killer or vampire in front of you eating a stick of rock, choosing a postcard, seemed perfectly natural.

As they walked Jo provided Arthur with a richer sense of Seacrest than had been afforded by the glimpses he'd had between Festival appearances. Might as well give him the personalised tour, she thought, and he did seem genuinely interested, not once rolling his eyes in the way Harry or Shona or Luke would do. High on the thrill of a responsive audience Jo gave him the full spiel; potted histories of each of the cinemas they passed, who owned what, the forces that had brought them here from Budapest, Prague, Helsinki, Chicago, what experiences and quirks of taste accounted for the programme of films they showed. Which stars had eaten in which restaurants, who had been barred from that club, the star caught in a compromising position down that alleyway, all the gossip and rumour and myth that had built this town's reputation, that meant that visitors brushed past the ghosts of movie legends.

She'd been chattering ten to the dozen when she realised Fletcher had hardly said a thing. He was looking at her the way he had done back in the lift again, like, who was this strange creature? Jo stopped blethering, suddenly self-conscious. 'Sorry, I've been rabbitting on, haven't I? Information overload, Shona's always slagging me off about that, saying I could give trainspotters a run for their money in the geek stakes. But, have to say this, not really used to… '

'Being listened to. Properly. Wasn't bored in the least, Dr Ashe, this has been a real education. Just what I needed. And it's lovely seeing you enjoying yourself. Happy. But tell me, and I know I probably shouldn't be asking you this, that it's not part of my job remit.' He stopped in the middle of the pavement, brought up short by the contempt in his own voice, 'but I will ask anyway. If Callum were to get his way, where would all this *go*?'

He turned slowly, pointing out Garbo's Boutique, The Black Cat cinema whose frontage promised a late-night double bill of *The Invisible Man* and *I Walked With a Zombie*, The Silver Fox Cabaret, The Get-A-Head Hat Shop. 'Because I have a feeling, please correct me if I'm wrong, all this seems too… *messy* for a man like Callum Boyd. Difficult to control. Too much *soul*. I can't imagine any of these places make any kind of profit and for a man who appears to have a balance sheet where his heart should be I doubt he approves of any of it. Anathema in fact.'

It was Jo's turn to study Cameron closely. He'd changed, ever since finding out about the *real* Fletcher. Before you could tell he found it a laugh, another gig, one he was enjoying to the hilt but still, nothing too important. There wasn't the fervour he showed now, a sense of purpose. Knowing the real Fletcher meant he couldn't just make it up as he went along anymore. He had something to live up to.

'Well... playing Devil's advocate,' she replied, 'you could argue Callum has a point. That these places are bleeding Seacrest dry, that to have any chance of survival it needs to be dragged into the twenty-first century. But I have to say, on a night like tonight, people out on the streets having a good time, nostalgia feels pretty damn good.'

Cameron nodded thoughtfully as she took him by the arm and led him round the corner to Scarlet Street. 'A girl after my own heart,' he said. But it was Arthur who spoke and he stumbled, slumped against her for a few moments, enough for Jo to stop in alarm while he propped himself up next to The Moviegoer entrance. 'Arthur! You all right? D'you want to sit down somewhere, somewhere quiet? I'll see if I can get you some water or something or... '

'No, no, sorry I'm fine.' It was Arthur looking back at her, every inch his tired and aching sixty-six years. 'Give me a few seconds. This raising the dead is a serious business, isn't it? If I'm the one who's going to give that poor sod a second chance, I'm going to have to give it my very best shot. Least I can do.' He clutched the cane in both hands, took a deep breath, straightened up, filled out and Cameron Fletcher was there before her, looking as though the only thing they had to worry about was if the bar would have enough ice to see them through the night.

She went first, pushing the door open through a curtain of heat, turning to watch Fletcher's reaction. She was almost jealous, him seeing it for the first time. She was anxious she'd built it up too much, that it could only be a disappointment but seeing the broad grin spread across his face she knew she'd worried needlessly. Through the selection of John Barry's best Bond moments playing over the club's speakers she heard his contented sigh as he tucked his cane under his arm, rubbing his hands together in anticipation. '*Finally...* a place where I can relax *properly*.'

Although the club was packed with regulars and Festival visitors, respect for the great man meant the two of them were able to carve their way easily through the crowd, Cameron greeted warmly as he passed, patted on the back, thanked for a talk he'd given or for his presence at the premiere of a no-budget film.

Excellent, thought Jo seeing Karl on duty behind the bar, catching her eye. Even though he was pretty restrained tonight, tight black suit, white shirt, he still looked like someone who'd stepped off the set of *Cabaret*. Karl prided himself on never being star-struck but when he saw who Jo was standing next to, she saw that look and it felt *fantastic*, to be accompanying a star.

Karl did a very good job of maintaining his composure as Fletcher approached, the only tell-tale signs of his excitement being his widening eyes, a quick lick over those brilliantly red lips to give them an extra sheen. 'Jo! And Mr Cameron Fletcher!' he called causing three other bar staff to freeze and stare until Cameron said hello to each in turn, two barmaids famed for their cruel and vampish personas, shocked into curtseying.

It was amazing how he did it, admired Jo. How *did* he do it? Jo liked Arthur, *really* liked Arthur, felt more comfortable being with him than with Fletcher but when that switch took place... where did Fletcher come from? Chatting to people he made them feel the most interesting person in the room. It was supernatural almost and she told herself she would need to tell Arthur that. To let him know how *good* he was because she suspected he hadn't been told that often enough. If ever.

Then Karl was beside them, between them, an arm around each waist saying, 'Now, we can't have the likes of you two mingling with the riff-raff. VIPs only, that's where you're going. There are some people who will be very keen to spend time in your company.'

'Karl, really, we'd rather just... ' Jo's protests were futile as he whisked them towards the back of the club where a mezzanine area was cordoned off by an arrangement of waist-high metal poles, red cord and Andy 'The Bullet' Chan, a very polite but highly effective bouncer who'd emigrated to Hong Kong at the age of 16 and starred in 238 action films before retiring at 30, returning home to look after his arthritic Mum.

'I thought it would be nice if during the Festival there would be part of Seacrest that remained free of the influence of Callum Boyd,' Karl told them. 'No offence Mr Fletcher, but after Luke Howard's... ah... *encounter* with Callum's heavies the other night, things have been made difficult for folk who don't toe the Boyd party line. Here, with Andy keeping an eye out for them they know they can say whatever they want to without fear of one of Boyd's clique eavesdropping.'

Karl eased Andy, struck gawping and useless at the sight of Fletcher, to one side and, as Cameron moved forward, Jo saw them. A group of tables pushed close together and surrounded by various Diaboliks, Harry at the head, deep in conversation with a small, dark-haired woman with a pony-tail Jo recognised. She'd seen her at a few events sitting down the front looking keen and sharp, asking questions that were actually *decent*, didn't have the audience cringing with embarrassment. Jo might also have seen her down the studios too at some point, wondered if she worked there.

Before she could speculate further Karl shouted 'Harry! You have visitors! Visitors who deserve free champagne!' When Cameron raised a hand in a faint attempt to dissuade such extravagance Karl would have none of it. 'Mr Fletcher, you do us a great honour in visiting and it will be my pleasure to ensure you have as fine a night as possible. The business this will bring! I'll be dining out on it for weeks!' With that he was off to have the drinks brought over.

'Jo!' called Harry, getting up from the table to greet them and it was so *good* to see him, give him a hug not having seen him properly since they'd found the film reels, ages ago. Shit, she realised, that meant he wouldn't know about Shona and her. Or maybe he did, maybe he'd seen her but, hold on, shouldn't she really be worrying about turning up with the man most of the people there regarded as Callum's mascot?

Pulling away from Harry she was touched to see Cameron hanging back looking almost *shy*. He'd picked up from the silence greeting his arrival this section of the club was one of the few places in Seacrest where his presence would be greeted not with instant adulation but suspicion. 'Harry, this is Cameron Fletcher,' introduced Jo and when Harry gave her a 'What you playing at?' look, rubbing his beard, she moved in close, whispered, 'Trust me Harry. He's a good guy. Both of them. I mean, Arthur, Cameron, though it's Cameron now obviously but Arthur he's *lovely*, you'd really like him and… yes, well, anyway, be *nice*, OK? He deserves it. Shouldn't judge a man on the company he keeps.'

'What about on who's employing him?' came the muttered response. He made no move of greeting, just carried on scratching his beard, Jo tempted to hit him, *enjoying* making Fletcher sweat, knowing the other Diaboliks were looking to him to decide how they were going to play it.

Thank God for Cameron, a man brave enough to break any stalemate. He leant forward, held his hand out to Harry. 'It's a true honour to meet you, Harry Lawson. I have friends who knew your father, Alec. They speak very highly of him. They tell me what a fine man he was and I hope you'll do me the honour of telling me more about him. From what I've seen during my time here it looks as if we could do with a lot more people like him.'

Jo winced. Was that the right way to go about brokering a peace with Harry? Bringing up the topic of his Dad, whose reputation he'd lived in the shadow of for years? Maybe she was wrong about the Fletcher touch, she worried but… wait.

Harry gave one final tug of his beard, looking eerily like the figurehead on Cameron Fletcher's cane and grasped the outstretched hand, his smile as warm and friendly as the one that had welcomed Jo. 'Any friend of Jo's is a friend of mine, Mr Fletcher. Sit yourself down, meet some mates of mine. I warn you, you'll have chatted with some film geeks in your time – I mean, come on, you've been spending time with *Jo*' – a wink in her direction – 'but *these* guys...at last, champagne! Just stick it there Andy, tell Karl we'll have a few beers too, and sort yourself out with one. Oh, and some cocktails, get him to send some cocktails over. The pink and blue ones.'

After half an hour Jo accepted this was going to be one of those nights that led her to think the hundreds of hours she'd spent reading books, in darkened rooms watching films, trawling through archives, had been a monumental waste of time. Instead she should have been out in places like this, enjoying company, drinking, making instant friendships, admiring the likes of Harry and Cameron working the room, keeping everyone entertained, stories ricocheting, bringing out the best in the quieter members, giving them a chance to shine, laughter moving in waves about them. Films are a load of crap, she thought as Harry introduced her to Jenny and they started the sort of conversation that had her start loving films all over again.

Jenny told her about her editing work, how much she loved Seacrest, how she couldn't wait to live here after visiting years ago, the events she'd enjoyed at the Festival. After a safe enough amount had been drunk and she felt she could trust Jo or was too tipsy to care, she started talking about Harry in a way that had Jo asking, in a manner that would have embarrassed her sober, 'So... you and Harry, Jen. What's the score? Anything, ahem, *interesting* happening?'

Jenny gave a short laugh, shrugged her shoulders and Jo wasn't so far gone she didn't notice her blushing (aww, *blushing*! Sweet.

Too sweet for Harry perhaps? He'd better not mess her about, she was *lovely*). 'Honestly? With Harry, I've no idea. Sometimes I think I'm in with a chance and others – oh, I don't know. You know him better than I do. P'rhaps you could give me some tips?' Something in her tone, some mild insinuation had Jo stammering.

'What? What, me and Harry, you think we've… yeuch, *no*! I mean, no offence, he's a lovely guy and everything, could do with losing a few pounds maybe but me and Harry, we're not, we've never… I mean, we're close but not *that* close. Gay. Me, that's me who's gay, Harry no, not that way inclined.'

'Ohhh, riiiiiiiight,' laughed Jenny, pouring yet more champagne into Jo's glass, Jo picking up on her relief. 'You didn't honestly think that Harry and I… *God*. He is like a brother to me but even if I were *straight*… sorry, this is awful, listen to me, tact-free drunkard.'

'No, no,' Jenny reassured, 'don't worry about it, honestly. It's just, with all the mixed signals I've been getting from him I start to get paranoid, y'know? I suppose… I get the impression that yes, he knows everyone there is to know, everyone likes him, everyone has a good time when he's on form but… he keeps people at a distance, doesn't he? Can only get so far. It's like… he keeps people laughing because that's *safe*, keeps them from asking questions. And you, Jo, you're one of the few people, the very few people he knows and likes and trusts. Really trusts. You're important to him, y'know?'

'That's… ' Jo stopped, choked. God, she could feel herself tearing up. 'That's… lovely. Never had anyone tell me that before. Least of all Harry. It's… ' Jo was saved from having to think of anything profound to say by Cameron arriving with a tray of Tequila Sunrises, placing two on the table before them.

'Karl gave me permission to make them myself, chose these to ease myself into my extensive drinks repertoire. I have always believed that a man can't call himself a gentleman unless he knows at least five uses for Angostura bitters.'

Once he'd moved on, Jo sipped her drink, allowing the tequila to have its wicked way with her before saying, and it felt like a confession because it was, 'Harry *is* important to me. I love him. Not in *that* way obviously but if he wasn't here Seacrest would be a much harder place to live in. We've had our ups and downs.' She took another gulp of her drink. 'There was this woman, we both fell for her, and she's back in town and... ' She stopped, distracted by thoughts of Shona, wondering where she was, if she was searching for Fletcher, what she would do when she found him. But she still wanted her *there*... perhaps? Would she talk to her if she was? Wouldn't she be better off with someone like Jenny, sane and thoughtful, nice big brown eyes –

'Another woman?' Jenny asked and Jo wished she wasn't quite so quick on the uptake. 'Was this a recent thing, her coming back? Right... that makes sense. Because... ' Jo cursed herself, Jenny looking miserable now. 'I dunno, I sensed something wasn't right, that Harry was distracted. I thought it was to do with this thing he's working on for his Dad.'

'His Dad? A thing? He hasn't said anything but then, haven't seen very much of him these past few weeks.' A 'thing'? Jo fumed quietly. She bet it had to do with those reels he, *they*, found and he'd been keeping it to himself. After trailing through those Tunnels for him...

'Oh, but you know Harry,' Jenny reassured, sensing Jo's hurt at being left out of Harry's scheme. 'Once he's decided he's doing something and something personal, he's the only one who can get it done properly. He's not told me much, I've offered to help but he was having none of it. I do know he's been interviewing people, finding out more about his Dad, putting together some sort of memorial, I think. But you were saying... this woman. Is he, is he still hung up on her? Because I get the sense there *is* someone.

Someone he doesn't want to let go of.'

'*Really*? That's… interesting.' Jo looked over at Harry listening intently to Cameron. He'd seemed so blasé about Shona coming back but then… Christ, the *thought* of a flare-up of the mess that happened years back. Shona dangling them both on a string, taking her time about choosing… could Jo really be bothered with all that? Although, of course, she'd no way of knowing what was happening between Shona and her at the moment, not a bloody clue.

'Shona. Her name was, *is* Shona. It all got a bit messy, as you can imagine and, but Jenny, listen. This Shona she isn't the sort of person you end up having any kind of *relationship* with. You find her incredible at first, because she *is* incredible, and you're flattered she's taken an interest, have a fantastic time with… '

'Not *so* much competition then,' joked Jenny, failing to conceal her resignation.

'No, but, Jen, it's like… like she's *drugs*. A drug. Or drink. It's great being with her but there's always a hangover, always a time when you realise everything that's happening is being dictated by *her*. She messes you up, gets under your skin.'

'A cow then. A beautiful cow. The very worst kind.'

'Yes,' nodded Jo, solemnly. '*Exactly*. Because there's always part of you that wants to make them better, you think you've got the power to change them and – God no.' Jo's glass almost slipped from her hand at what she saw in one of the mirrored panels on the wall, the figure who had appeared at the top of The Moviegoer steps. 'Talk of the Devil,' she murmured and Jen followed the direction of her stare, took in the woman standing there and almost gave up any hope of claiming Harry's heart.

CHAPTER THIRTY-ONE

Recalling that night Jo couldn't be sure if Karl had deliberately killed the music to add to the drama of Shona's arrival. She'd probably imagined it although Shona did create that impression when she walked into a room. Everything else dimming, the volume lowered, as *she* became the focus, no mean feat in The Moviegoer.

Standing with hands on hips in a short black dress that Audrey Hepburn would have made demure and which she most definitely did not, Shona commanded the place. Not only because of her looks which caused ripples of envy and lust to course through onlookers, powerful enough to cause gay men and straight women alike to question their sexuality, but because, as Jo could tell, she was near incandescent with anger.

Her eyes, scorching, scanned the tables and floor and the place waited, her audience caught between dread and hope those eyes would rest on them. After an age Shona saw what she wanted. Cameron Fletcher, sitting a couple of tables away from Jo, chatting about the Icelandic film industry to two wonderstruck fans from Reykjavik, perfectly, wonderfully oblivious to the effect Shona was having on the rest of the club. Descending the steps she glanced over to the mirror, Jo instinctively ducking down, too late and the smile Shona gave when their eyes met was even more terrifying than the frown preceding it.

Heading towards her prey, people backed away, scared of brushing against her and she knew she'd one thing to thank her father for, the incredible power of the Boyd Rage. It had not been a good night, one involving a loss of control, something she and her father were never good at accepting. She'd even started to regret her decision to return to Seacrest during that awful wait in the hotel foyer with Cameron's two suddenly useless assistants. James jittery at the best of times, working himself up to such a pitch it looked as though he could faint at any second. The usually cool Simone had taken to snapping at him, until they were bickering like some old married couple.

'You definitely put 7pm on the daily itinerary, didn't you, James? You're sure?'

'Yes, you saw me do it, didn't you? I'm sure I, or maybe… yes, I remember typing it into Excel and… '

'I don't understand it, Miss Boyd,' Simone interrupted, 'Mr Fletcher is usually extremely prompt, turns up ten minutes before any pre-arranged time. He says it relaxes him, chatting to us.'

'Well, it looks as though he's changed his mind about your calming influence and who could blame him?' snapped Shona, checking her watch to confirm it was only 30 seconds since she'd last looked. '*Christ*!' she hissed and caught Simone's reaction, one that said 'If Miss Boyd is starting to panic then we really *are* in the shit.'

'I'm sorry, Simone, that was mean of me. It's not you, either of you. I'm angry with this old *coot* we're supposed to be looking after. You wait here, I'll go up to the room to check, see if he's left a note or *something* telling us where he is. He might already be there at the Phoenix.'

She forced a smile and although it felt horribly false it seemed to have the desired effect on Simone who smiled back weakly. 'If Callum phones Reception, tell him where I am, ask him to call the room.' Simone's smile wavered only for a second at the mention of Callum's name before she responded crisply, 'Yes, Miss Boyd.'

Could be very useful indeed that one, Shona pondered as she headed for the lift. Someone should find her the perfect post once all this business was over with…

After scouring Fletcher's room and finding nothing that gave the slightest hint of where he might be, Shona went to the balcony to cool off. Closing her eyes, she tried to concentrate on the feel of the sea breeze blowing through her hair, the chill against her skin, something she had missed during her time in places where the promise of summer every morning had started to become monotonous. When she opened her eyes, hoping ridiculously to see some clue pointing in the direction of Fletcher, she noticed on the promenade, next to one of the wooden shelters, a swirling column of discarded leaflets, tickets and chip wrappers lifted and spun by the wind. She couldn't help thinking it was some kind of sign. That, as it sank to the ground, it was trying to say something about Fletcher's disappearance. A man rustled up by a few newspaper articles and anecdotes, held together by the hopes and needs of his fans, suddenly vanishing.

'Dearie me,' she thought. 'This is what happens when you hang about with that Dr Ashe for too long. Start thinking all *sorts* of pretentious nonsense,' her laughter cut short by the ringing hotel phone. Briefly, she hoped it would be Cameron, although it rang with such insistence she knew it had to be her father.

'Daughter, I had hoped at your age, with your experience, you'd do a better job looking after things I entrust to your care.' His voice so cold she was instantly thrown back to his office, 14 years old, sent there for yet another telling-off. Every time resolving she wouldn't cry at the end of it, every time failing.

'And good evening to you too, Dad. I take it Fletcher isn't there at the Phoenix?'

Silence, then a sigh and she wished he would get it over with, start shouting so she could shout back.

'No. Mr Fletcher is *not* here. A lot of people who were very much looking forward to meeting him and who have a lot to offer Seacrest *are* and they are beginning to make clear their disappointment at his absence.'

'Well, I'm here in his room and it's *still* empty and there's nothing to…'

'Then it's just as well for you I *have* found him, isn't it?'

'What? How? And why are you phoning if you know where he is, why don't you contact…'

'It doesn't matter *how*' – but *we* know, we can picture Callum slipping away during a tense lull in the conversation, making it to his room full of video screens, searching, scanning, finding. 'He's been out, out for a stroll and guess who with? Guess his new best friend?'

Something new in his voice, something Shona hadn't heard in years caused her skin to prickle. Was it panic? 'I don't know, who? Hate it when you go mysterious, the All-Seeing Eye. A reporter from the *Gazette*? Not Luke is it? He hasn't been chatting to Luke?'

There was a noise on the other end of the line that could have been a laugh had it not been so bitter. 'No, I suppose I should be thankful it's not *quite* as bad as that. Near enough though. He was with your friend Dr Ashe. Looking quite the pair, walking along arm in arm, no doubt catching up on lots of juicy *gossip*.'

Shona hoped he couldn't hear her smiling. 'Jo? How did she…'

'I have no idea, Shona, that's for you to find out. They're at The Moviegoer and you're going there to find out just *how* friendly they've got. And after you've found that out you're going to keep Mr Fletcher on a *much* tighter leash. I will *not* have my plans ruined by some nosey dyke academic.'

As Shona's ear burned with the click and hum of the dial tone her anger started to build. Angry with Arthur for threatening to wreck everything by jaunting off on his own adventure, thinking he had a life of his own which was *not* part of the deal and angry with Jo for blithely wandering in and upsetting her plans. Most of all furious with herself for being the daughter of that awful, hateful man.

Her anger powered her up the hill to the club in a quarter of the time it had taken Jo and Cameron. When she saw them with Harry and the Diaboliks, laughing and drinking without any concern for the trouble they'd caused, it cooled to something like betrayal. Her eyes stayed fixed on Jo, locked, as she made her way towards them, until Andy blocked her path.

Andy, who had faced some of the best martial artists in the world, had thrown himself off buildings several storeys high and into the path of speeding lorries couldn't bring himself to stare down Shona Boyd. He stuttered 'Sorry, Miss but, ah, it's, it's ah, guests only.' As he braced himself for impact he hoped he didn't show too much relief at feeling Harry's hand on his shoulder.

'It's all right, mate, let her through. She's with us. Hello there, Shona. Long time no see. Thanks for the postcard.' He held out his hand for her to take, not for her reassurance but so the rest of the Diaboliks, those who loathed all her father stood for, wouldn't take it into their heads to attack.

'Harry. Good to see you too. See the diet didn't work out then.' She walked past him, ignoring his hand, focused on Jo, moving towards Fletcher who appeared completely unaware of the approaching danger until his companions started pointing behind him, staring with wide, frightened eyes.

'Is something wrong?' he asked with mild concern. 'A problem with our drinks?' knowing full well who was standing behind him as he turned slowly in his seat. 'Oh, Miss Boyd. So pleased you could finally join us. I hope the guests of the Phoenix aren't too disappointed. Dr Ashe here raved about this place and after all the *fascinating* things she's told me about this town, it would have been very rude of me to refuse.'

'How *kind* of Jo,' replied Shona with such scorn it brought gasps from the Icelandic visitors. 'I think you and I should have a chat in private, Cameron. You see, my father, your *employer* is somewhat put out you took it upon yourself to disappear for a few hours. You've caused a lot of people a lot of worry.'

'Oh, I am sorry to hear that,' Fletcher replied with gleeful insouciance. 'I didn't mean to cause any alarm. I felt it would do me good to get out and have some fun. But yes, of *course*, I'd be willing to go somewhere more peaceful with you. What man in his right mind wouldn't? Harry, does Karl have an office somewhere we can use? This won't take long.'

'Yeah, on you go and ask him,' said Harry, his disappointment at not being able to view any forthcoming confrontation remarkably well disguised. After the odd couple had disappeared it took a few minutes before the group resumed its chatter. Harry joined Jo and Jenny, shaking his head. 'Don't know who to worry about more, Cameron or Shona.'

'I've a feeling both will be able to take care of themselves,' said Jo. 'Harry, been meaning to say, about Shona, since she's got back we've, well… '

Harry laughed, 'Jo, there's no need, honestly. I saw the way she looked at you when she came in. Know a woman in love when I see it and I know that you should take full advantage of it when it happens. Congratulations and good luck! You'll need it with a psycho babe like that one. Though, it has to be said, a babe nonetheless, 'specially in that dress,' a remark that caused Jen to stand up abruptly, looking ill.

'Scuse me, I've got to head… get to the toilet.'

'You all right, Jen? Look a bit pale.'

'I'm fine Harry fine, just… fine.'

Jo and Harry sat in silence, watching her weave her way through the crowd until Jo thumped him on the arm. 'You're a right idiot sometimes. Spend so much time in darkened rooms you can't see what's staring you in the face.'

'What? What did *I* do?'

Karl's room was less an office than a large store cupboard with a green baize-covered desk and filing cabinet crammed in. Cameron went straight to the wooden swivel chair behind the desk, Shona perching on one corner, revealing enough leg to double Arthur's already pounding heart rate. But Arthur had Cameron along to keep him steady and when Shona opened her mouth he launched his first attack.

'When were you going to tell me I was real, Shona Boyd? That Cameron Fletcher had walked amongst us once and that mad Luke Howard was right all along?'

Ohh, that look of pure confusion crossing Shona's face. It was worth every ounce of hassle and heartache this job had caused Arthur.

'How, what... did one of them speak to you?' She stopped, knowing she'd already said too much while Cameron steepled his fingers, tapped them together.

'Tut, *Shona*. I was hoping you'd be able to keep the bluff going a *little* longer. What if that had been a lucky guess? A stab in the dark? I take from your reaction you've some idea of who contacted me this afternoon.'

Shona lowered her head, the fight visibly draining from her and until she looked up again with that familiar half-smile, Cameron almost felt pity.

'I knew they couldn't trust me,' she sighed, 'knew that when you turned up, Arthur, – you are in there, aren't you? Buried under the Cameron padding? – they'd see how good you are and want to use you for their own ends. Well done. You're one up on your boss. On me.'

She started a slow hand clap that stopped when Cameron said, 'Callum. He doesn't know the true history of Cameron Fletcher, that such a man actually existed. Does he? He thinks it's all a fabrication and that's where his power lies. That's what he plans to reveal. Discredit Luke, pull the entire Cameron Fletcher Archive down around his ears and clear the way for development. And his plan needed a fall guy. Someone to take the flak, to be revealed as the non-entity masquerading as a myth. And that mug' – Arthur's northern accent was coming through – 'is me.'

And I could have got it completely wrong, thought Arthur, sweating furiously while somehow maintaining Cameron's cool exterior but Shona's smile was fading. This strange combination of Arthur and Cameron too much to argue with, to try and distract with denial. She nodded and the feeling of triumph Arthur felt was quickly replaced by anger.

'Right. So Callum doesn't know his only child is on the side of his enemies, plotting against him, hoping to topple him by showing he's got it all wrong about Fletcher. I wasn't supposed to know, was I? Arthur Dott was so much collateral damage, someone to be paid off and swept aside once the fall-out started. Couldn't be trusted with the truth because he might go crying to Callum, tell him what his little girl was up to.'

For the first time in twenty years, something close to fear flickered in Shona's eyes.

They stared at each other like poker players, each trying to read the other's cards, searching for tells. Slowly, painfully, Arthur pushed back his chair, creaked to his feet. 'Look,' he said wearily. 'I may be a tired old goat of an actor but I'm no blackmailer. I don't want to cause you or anyone else any trouble. Jo knows too, it seemed only fair to tell her, put her right after all those years of theorising and you *know* she won't go blabbing. I've a *hope* what you're planning is for the good of Seacrest. I just wish you'd told me before, who I was *really* playing. Let me know I was giving a man a second chance. Now. If you'll excuse me, I've friends to rejoin.'

He hitched back his shoulders, stuck out his chest and was Fletcher again, his accent East Coast American. 'And I hope to see you out there soon. Karl has promised me full use of the bar after midnight and I wouldn't want you to miss out on some of the finest cocktails known to man.'

After he'd left, Shona sat until she realised the best way to deal with the situation was to go out there and drink until everything, this town, her Mum, her Dad, what she was doing with her life, fell away and didn't matter any more.

'Everything OK?' asked Harry when Cameron had rejoined them. 'Oh yes, everything's fine. Shona and I had a few business matters to discuss. In fact, here she is now,' resulting in Jo almost suffering whiplash she turned so quickly and yes, there she was, following behind Fletcher. Christ, what sort of mood was she going to be in *now*?

This was a different Shona though, one Jo had seen on the rarest of occasions, the Shona she loved the best. Subdued and thoughtful, content not to be the focus of attention and when she slipped in beside the rest of the group it was like the old times again, back when there was no sign of the trouble to come on the horizon.

Jo couldn't be sure what time it was when she realised The Moviegoer was empty apart from her, Jenny, Harry, Shona and Cameron and that Karl was stacking chairs around them. Cameron behind the bar, shaking up an endless supply of white Russians while 'Put the Blame on Mame' played on a loop over the speakers and she was dancing with Jenny, stumbling over each other's feet as they forgot which of them was the lead. '*You're* the man', 'No, remember, we agreed, *you're* the man.'

Recovering from another fit of the giggles, their attention was caught by Shona and Harry, dancing so closely and slowly it threatened to stop being dancing altogether.

'Just one kiss, Harry, for old times' sake… what's a kiss between friends,' murmured Shona, turning him so she could catch Jo's eye over his shoulder, her wicked grin obscured as Harry took her up on the offer.

'Huh,' said Jenny, followed quickly by, 'Well, if you can't beat them… ' Before Jo could protest one of her arms had slid around Jo's waist, a hand sliding up to her neck and it felt strange yet not unpleasant to be kissing someone other than Shona.

Cameron Fletcher looked over to Karl who smiled and shrugged as Cameron took a sip straight from the metal shaker in a toast. 'To Seacrest… where a man might think he'd died and gone to heaven.'

 CHAPTER
THIRTY-TWO

When Jo awoke hours later to find herself in bed and Shona there, standing by the window, she rubbed her eyes, looked again. Nope, she wasn't dreaming. That was most definitely Shona still there, in the morning. Must be something wrong and Christ, her *head*. Last night… dancing, kissing someone. Someone not Shona…

Her groan caused Shona to look over. '*Finally*, it awakes. Was thinking of getting people over for a séance if you hadn't shown signs of life in the next half hour.'

Right, let's think, try and work this out, Jo resolved as she fell back into her pillow. Shona didn't *seem* angry. She remembered walking back to the flat, waving goodbye to Harry, Cameron and Jenny as they'd headed to the Kinotech and she did like that Jenny, hoped Harry didn't mess it up, then back to here. Thought she was too drunk for sex but then Shona had her *ways* plus she made proper coffee beforehand. An argument? Did they have a row? No, she didn't *think* so but in bed it hadn't been rough exactly, more… fierce. As if instead of an argument. Then there'd been the weird role reversal of Shona fast asleep and Jo awake, trying to work out what was happening between the two of them. Knowing she'd have bruises in the morning. There had been something else niggling away at her… oh yes.

'You owe me a pair of Dunlops, Miss Boyd.'

Shona smiled briefly, turned her attention back to the view. It was as if she was keeping watch, looking out for someone she didn't want to see. Jo felt she should get up and give her a hug. She didn't though, in part because of the pain of her head and also because she could tell Shona was separating herself off, as if she was there on sufferance.

'Shona. You all right? Don't look so good. Worried. Not like you. Thought that was me in this relationship. The worrier.'

'I'm fine. Fine,' Shona replied eventually. 'Just tired and… thinking.' She sighed, looked back over to Jo who dreaded to think how bad *she* looked because Shona appeared thoroughly worn out. 'He told me. Cameron told me that you know, that Fletcher was real all along. Hope it didn't come as too much of a shock. Still, you could get another paper out of it.'

Jo's headache lessened as she sat up straighter in bed and tried to work out why she felt guilty, that she'd got Shona into trouble. Which, she supposed, by nicking off with Cameron Fletcher she had. 'I met Arthur on the seafront, we went back to the Fulmar and he told me. I think he had to share it with *someone* and I happened to be there. It came as a real shock to him. He said you must have known about it and you were keeping it quiet. Hidden from Callum. That's right, isn't it? You're going to use this against him somehow.' Oops. Jo knew when Shona's eyes went blue like that, it was best to head for cover and she pulled a pillow close to her in the faint hope of protection.

'For God's sake, this isn't *just* about my Dad. Why does everything I do have to come back to *him*. This is about *Seacrest* and I'm trying to help it, give it back its reputation. You know the main reason I brought him back? Raised Cameron Fletcher from the dead? For *you,* Jo. I brought him here for you. Risked everything, my reputation, to show you how things can't always fit some nice, neat theory, that you can't keep life contained in the pages of a book or up on a screen. I brought him here to *scare* you out of the rut you've got yourself into, to make you realise the longer you stayed here, the more you risked dreaming your life away.'

Jo's building anger caused her to forget her headache as she set the pillow aside. 'Right, so you're pinning the mess you've got yourself into on *me*? Should have known something like this was coming because it's always someone else's fault with you, isn't it, Shona? You never accept any responsibility for the damage you cause, and you didn't stop to think, did you, not for one second, how this could have backfired, messed up Luke's life, Arthur's, *especially* Arthur's. Because you *never* think about anyone else. It all comes down to the part they can play in whatever scheme you've dreamt up.'

Once she'd finished Jo felt sick, near blinded by the pain in her head though she could still see Shona staring at her as if she didn't quite recognise the woman she went to bed with last night.

'You see. You've proved my point. It's worked. Shook you out of yourself. Made you wake up to a few things.'

'It's made me wake up to *this*. To us. Shona, we need to sort this out. Work out what's happening. Where it's going, if anywhere.' The room filled with a silence dense with truths neither wanted to hear.

It was a silence only the crassest of interlopers would attempt to break and so we left them staring down the barrel of their future to find out where Cameron Fletcher had decided to lay his head. Found him in the office of the Kinotech, snoring on a camp bed that was doing sterling work supporting his weight. He'd stayed because it would have seemed churlish to turn down the opportunity to sample Harry's impressive collection of duty-free single malts, presents from international Diaboliks. They'd drunk so much they'd turned sober again.

Jenny had stayed with them for a while, enjoying being an audience, listening to them talk like old, long-lost friends reunited. Looking at her watch, seeing it was 3am, she decided to leave them to it, a gracious Fletcher shaking her hand goodbye at the Kinotech door. 'Was lovely to meet you, Jennifer.' When Harry headed to his office to find another bottle of Laphroaig, he whispered, 'Don't you worry about that Shona. I'll sort the boy out, make him realise what he's got in front of him,' before calling out, 'Harry! You oaf, aren't you going to say goodbye properly to this delightful girl?'

With the Big Wheel glowing above them like a huge full moon that had crashed to earth, Harry and Jen stood, suddenly shy with each other. 'Listen, Harry, that thing with Jo, it was nothing, you know? Childish, me getting my own back.'

'No, no, don't be daft, it's me who should be apologising. What happened with me and Shona… ' He looked so ashamed Jenny wanted to hold him, kiss that shame away. 'It was nothing, piece of nonsense, her up to her tricks again. There's nothing there you know. Nothing for you to worry about.'

Jen let her head fall back until she could see the very top carriage of the Wheel swaying gently even though she could feel no wind. 'Good, I'm glad to hear that. Because, thing is, I like you. Like you a *lot* and if I'm wasting my time, if nothing's going to happen, I'd like to know now. So I can get on with things. Waste my time on someone else.' She tipped her head forward and Harry, caught by her brown eyes trained to spot the perfect cut, the perfect point of action, kissed her until two seagulls started squabbling over a discarded fish and chip supper.

They broke apart, laughing, then Harry drew her in close again for a hug. 'I'm sorry for being such a tube, but what with the thing for my Dad and the Festival and everything… '

'It's all right, it's fine,' Jen replied, pulling away from him slowly. 'Now that things are good between us I'll wait until you're ready. Right, Harry Lawson, you've kept me from my bed long enough this evening. I've places to be, people to see in the morning. You take care of that old man in there, d'you hear?' That was her off along the pier, waving goodbye until her arm ached, her face sore from smiling.

Harry waved back, past the point of her disappearing into the town and felt calmer than he had done in years. Then Cameron's hand clamped down on his shoulder. 'Harry! It's the height of bad manners to leave a man alone with a bottle of single malt. Come on, come take a dram,' showing off his best Harry Lauder impersonation.

That morning Arthur was paying the price for Fletcher's overindulgence. He drifted up through a dream of Callum Boyd holding the head of Cameron Fletcher in the grip of a large vice, turning the handle with all his might, laughing manically, and Arthur awoke convinced that vice was still in place.

Christ *almighty*. He hadn't been that drunk since Peter O'Toole mistook him for Peter Ustinov in a bar in Soho. Great, fantastic, well done Arthur, he scolded himself, as he appeared to have fallen asleep in a junk shop. Bits of broken machinery everywhere, not entirely inappropriate the way he was feeling. Least he wasn't in that hotel room. The décor of that place combined with his hangover, he'd have ended up having some kind of psychotic episode.

He was about to doze off again when Harry shoved open the door with such force it thwacked into the side of a broken 'Mysteries of the Persian Boudoir!' peepshow. 'Oops, sorry,' he apologised in response to the noise that escaped Arthur, somewhere between a wail and a howl. 'Brought you some coffee, thought it might help perk you up.'

'Thanks for the thought,' croaked Arthur, 'but the last time I came close to 'perking up' was about eighteen years ago.' After a complicated bout of wrestling with the tartan blankets thrown over him, he got himself into a seated position, grasping the cup of steaming black coffee reverentially.

Harry sat behind his desk at the foot of Arthur's bed, smiling and sipping his coffee, waiting until Arthur had fully rejoined the land of the living before coughing, 'Ahem. Don't believe we've been introduced. Met a friend of yours last night. American. Name of Cameron Fletcher. Seemed to think very highly of you, great admirer of your work.' He stood up, held out his hand. 'Mr Arthur Dott I presume?'

'Bloody *hell*,' growled Arthur. 'Is there *anyone* in this flaming town who doesn't know who I am?' Grudgingly he slipped one hand free from his mug to shake Harry's. 'Arthur Dott, pleased to make your acquaintance. Nice to hear Fletcher had the decency to be kind about me. Reckon he's an A1 arse-licker myself.' He leant back against the wall, letting the caffeine flow through his system until he remembered something important, jerking back up, fixed his bloodshot eyes on Harry.

'Wait, there is one man who doesn't know who I am but got himself locked up on my behalf. That Luke Howard. Where was he last night? Is he all right? You're a friend of his, aren't you, his best friend Jo was saying.'

'Luke?' Harry felt guilt flare up. Luke…fuck. He hadn't thought about him for days. Some best friend he was. Harry had picked Luke up from the police cells, gave him a telling off for being such a nutcase. What with trying to work out where the canisters had come from, sorting stuff out for his Dad, he'd pretty much left Luke to it. But hey, Luke was a grown man, could take care of himself, Harry tried to convince himself.

'I think he's doing OK, staying out of trouble at least. Not a surprise he wasn't at The Moviegoer. Last time I saw him he kept on going on about how he wanted to be sure he was in the Archive when Cameron Fletcher paid a visit. I asked him how'd'you know when, *if*, Fletcher's going to turn up on your doorstep. He gave me his best Forrest Gump look. Went all mystic. Said Fletcher would know when the time was right. Freak… ' But Harry looked troubled, realising just what a crap friend he'd been.

It was Arthur's turn to look thoughtful before stretching and yawning noisily. 'I think the sooner I see Luke, meet him in circumstances more convivial than our last encounter, the better. He needs to be put right about a few things.'

Harry snorted. 'D'you think that's such a good idea? For one, Callum's not going to be too chuffed, his prize asset fraternising with the enemy.'

'Do I, Arthur Dott, whose Sweeney Todd was once described as possessing all the demonic menace of an old English sheepdog about to be put down, look as though I could pose any kind of threat to the mighty Callum Boyd? Honestly man, don't talk daft. Now, where are those toilets again?'

Harry handed him the keys to the public toilets round the corner and when Arthur returned to the Kinotech, familiar music greeted him. Zither music. And zither music equalled *The Third Man*. There was something different though. Words added, blending and merging, becoming part of the music.

He took his time reaching the office in part to get a better look at the machines but also to listen. Snatches of film dialogue, the music subsiding to make way for a woman's voice recalling, 'I'd never met a man with hands like his. You could tell by looking how sensitive they were, the care in them. He handled that machine like it was made of crystal. I tell you -' The voice changed, segueing smoothly into that of an old man, cracked and whispery with age and respect, 'You'd never think it was a great big lump of moving metal the way he cleaned it. It was like a pet to him. Something living and breathing he wanted to look after and love.'

Arthur, peering round the office door, discovered the source of the music, the chorus of voices, was the computer on Harry's desk. Harry watching the screen intently, absorbed completely in what he was doing. A labour of love. He rapped gently against the door's glass panel and Harry looked up, tapped the touch-pad and the music stopped.

'Sorry, didn't mean to interrupt. Carry on if you want, if you don't mind me hanging about. Sounded great whatever it was, not my cup of tea usually, that Radio 3 stuff, more a Radio 2 man. Your Dad was it? Who they were talking about?'

Harry didn't look *too* sheepish, acknowledging Arthur's praise with an off-hand shrug, watched his reaction closely when he asked, 'You liked it, sounded all right? Not too much like pretentious wank?'

Oh, I see, thought Arthur, nodding his appreciation, reassuring Harry it wasn't wanky at all. He'd *wanted* Arthur to hear it, test it out on an audience without putting pressure on either of them.

'And yeah, you were right. About it being about my Dad. I've been thinking a lot about him recently. This'll sound really cheesy I know but, well, you know about him dying and everything. Suicide. Was angry with him for years. This though, having people tell me about him…'

Arthur sat back down on his camp-bed as Harry told him about the Dominion fire, the broken man who'd taken his Dad's place at home and his death, the search for the canisters and his plan for the end of the Festival. Arthur let him speak with the skill of a practiced listener, understanding that Harry had to do this, to sort things out in his head. Explain himself.

'And the zither music?' he asked, following a pause. 'How does that link in?'

'Orson Welles. For some reason I think it all comes down to Welles. The canisters, him running back into the fire.' This chimed with Arthur, reminded him of something hidden by the fog of his hangover.

'Two or three folk on the recordings mention it, the night Welles visited Dad in his booth. He was there for a while and after that meeting Dad stopped doing the meet-and-greet at premieres. It even made the papers, a right fuss because of this nonsense about the Lawson Luck, how... '

'If you shook the hand of Alec Lawson your film would be guaranteed success. Yes, I remember hearing about it. Actors... tch. Superstitious bunch.'

'Yeah, that was why there was such an outcry. Anyway, people say they noticed a change in Dad after his chat with Orson. He didn't become arrogant or up himself or anything, the exact opposite. He'd always been a quiet man but he seemed to close in on himself after that. One of the women, Jessie, I've got her recorded somewhere, put her finger on it. Said it was a 'different kind of quiet'. Like he had a secret to keep.'

Then Arthur remembered what had been nagging away at him. The passing reference to Welles in the cuttings he'd been given by Charles, Welles borrowing copies of Fletcher's films. No mention of whether or not he'd ever given them back.

'Perhaps Welles had taken something that didn't belong to him. Something he wanted to keep a hold of and he asked your Dad to do that for him. Keep it safe several thousands of miles away.'

Harry was less impressed with his theory than Arthur. 'Possibly. I dunno, I've spent *ages* trawling through stuff about Welles since finding those things.' He jerked a thumb in the direction of the large safe in the corner. 'I've not found anything obvious. He was always leaving projects half finished, as if he got bored with them or was scared of finishing them because once they were, they were fixed. He couldn't play with them any more. Maybe he was experimenting with a film he felt was dangerous. Harmful, could cause a scandal if it was discovered. Perhaps he got frightened.'

At Arthur's snort Harry protested, if weakly, 'I know, I know, sounds daft, me havering on. It did turn out to be a bit of a curse for my Dad though. There was Callum's reaction to it for a start.'

'Callum?' Arthur leaned forward, 'Come on, spill.'

'Well, Callum had always been jealous of Dad, even though he was assistant manager of the Dominion. My Dad was always getting respect, getting the girls, my Mum who we think Callum had a soft spot for. From what people have said I reckon Alec meeting Welles tipped Callum over the edge. Made him do something stupid as revenge.'

They sat in silence until Arthur coughed, a racking, phlegmy cough. 'Curse those Cubans. Let me get this right. Are you suggesting, in a roundabout sort of way, that Callum started the Dominion fire to get back at your Dad? That's quite a claim, Harry. Much as I dislike Callum, you start putting that about you're going to have to back it up with evidence.'

'OK, I know, perhaps I'm going too far. It's just, the stuff in here,' he tapped the digital recorder at the side of the computer. 'Two witnesses saw Callum hanging about after hours, one of them saying he offered to lock up on that night which was unusual. Another saying they saw him heading for the projection booth when there was no good reason for him going that way. Fuck. I know I haven't got any CCTV footage, a smoking gun or anything but it *feels* right, you know? He got his revenge, didn't he? Killed my Dad in the end.'

Arthur saw tears start in Harry's eyes and said gently, picking up the bottle of Laphroaig from the floor, 'That's why you have to be careful, Harry. Because it feels *too* right to you. Skews your judgement, makes you see connections where none might exist. Only dumb bad luck. An accident.' The whisky glugged softly as he poured a shot into each of their mugs. 'You're not going to do anything daft are you? About Callum?'

Harry sighed. 'No, don't worry. You're right though. You have to be careful in Seacrest. A good story is always better than the truth. But yeah, I'm not going to go bursting into Callum's office with a gun shouting 'You're the son of a bitch who killed my father!' For one, couldn't afford a gun, and for two I've decided the best way to get back at him is to remind folk of my Dad again. Make them realise what a good man he was. I'm going to have an event, down in the Tunnels, last night of the Festival. And I would be very chuffed, Arthur, if you could persuade your pal Cameron Fletcher along. Guest of honour. Show Callum Boyd where the loyalties of a legend lie.'

Arthur lifted his coffee mug in acceptance. 'I'm sure Mr Fletcher will make it. Bloody hell. Washed up old actor like me being guest of honour at anything. What a messed-up place this is. You mentioned your Mum, she's still alive isn't she? What's she make of all this?' Harry suddenly became interested in a knot in the wood of his desktop.

'See, well, Mum and I haven't been getting on so well. That's why I'm living here. Had been staying with her but it didn't work out. She was always going on about Dad, about how great he was, how disappointed he'd have been to see how I was such a waster.'

'Harry, that's ridiculous, you *have* to tell her! What you're doing, a living memorial, it's great. You need to get her down here, get her involved. Imagine how *proud* she'd be, she's probably... '

'OK, OK, fucksake! Get your point,' Harry raised his hands, surrendering to Arthur's enthusiasm. 'I'll give her a call tomorrow. Oh, stop with those yellowing puppy dog eyes. Today, I'll call her this afternoon. Maybe. Jesus, you and Cameron Fletcher, you're like two peas in a pod. Both very persuasive.'

'That reminds me,' said Arthur, draining the rest of his mug and standing up, swaying. 'Talking of memorials, it's about time I got spruced up. There's someone Cameron Fletcher needs to meet. This Luke Howard... exactly how mad is he?'

Harry sat up, alarmed. 'You're thinking of seeing *Luke*? Arthur, I'm really not sure, I mean, I'm his best friend and even *I* think he's a right fruit loop sometimes. What are you going to do? Waltz in there and tell him there's no such thing as Cameron Fletcher? Why not take round the head of the Easter Bunny while you're at it?'

'Ah, you see, that's where you're wrong on the Fletcher front, the whole non-existence part. Luke's not as loopy as people think.'

'Eh? You still drunk?'

'Enough with the cheek, laddie. I'm off to the toilets again, get myself tarted up. You haven't got any black shoe polish have you? Need to give the beard and eyebrows a touch up. And where's that effing cane of mine?'

CHAPTER
THIRTY-THREE

After backing out of the Kinotech, leaving Arthur to his ablutions, we debate where to head for next. Jo's flat perhaps, to find out if the fight with Shona was resolved? Lot 45 to see how prepared Luke was for Cameron's imminent arrival? Then movement caught our eye. The camera posted outside the Kinotech on top of one of the pier lights, swivelling from side to side, back and forth, again and again, neurotically looking for someone who wasn't there. Interesting.

'Excuse me, sir? Mr Boyd?'

Neil, one of the security men who'd attempted to escort Charles out of the cinema at the screening of *Orpheé,* hovered in the doorway of Callum's observation room. His eyes flickered over the banks of screens, trying to identify which parts of the town they were focused on, his doubts about this job growing.

When assigned the work by the security firm, he'd assumed it would mainly involve bog-standard crowd control with some body-guarding, stalker-and-weirdo identification work thrown in. Things had gone smoothly enough and he'd even managed to catch up on a few of his favourite films, *Shane, High Noon, The Wild Bunch*, showing at one of the Western cinemas. There'd been that one incident that made the firm look pretty shoddy and which would *never* have happened had Neil been on duty. That kid, Luke Wotsisname getting too close for comfort to Cameron Fletcher.

Fair enough, a right balls-up but the way *this* guy reacts, shouting and screaming as if they were school-kids was bang out of order. Ever since Neil and his colleagues had got here Boyd had been throwing his weight around, giving them orders as if they were his own private army. And now this. A text sent from Boyd at 2:30am saying '9:30am. My office.' Arrogant arsehole. Then finding this room at the back, Boyd doing his Big Brother act. What the guys had been saying down the pub was right, he wasn't right in the head. Control freak. Creepy. Those screens with their bloody great close-ups of film stars. Think they're not moving and you look again and they are. What sort of weirdo chooses that for interior decoration?

'*Sir.*'

After a few seconds, during which Neil contemplated walking away and to hell with the pay cheque, Callum turned in his chair. He looked shattered and Neil bet he'd spent the whole night there, glued to the screens. He'd been watching the one to his right, showing the Kinotech sign.

'Neil, thanks for making it.' Here was a turn-up, Mr Boyd actually *thanking* someone. Neil could tell he wasn't feeling himself.

'I've some people to see today, business people. And I need time to get some sleep, make myself presentable.' He ran a hand down the lapel of his black suit, smiling in a way that acknowledged how crumpled he appeared. Neil had to hand it to him, he knew how to turn the charm on when it suited him.

'Unfortunately, not having mastered the art of being in two places at once, I need someone to stay here and keep an eye on things. From what I've seen of your work over the past few days, I can safely say you fit the bill. It would help if it was someone who knows as little as possible of this town's, well, 'politics' is too dignified a term for the squabbling that goes on. I remember you commenting in one of the briefings that you'd studied Seacrest's geography so you won't have any difficulty keeping track of him.'

There was a pause, as though Neil should know exactly who he was talking about. 'Him, sir?'

Callum answered in a tone that suggested anyone with half a brain would have known instantly who he was referring to and any sympathy Neil had for him evaporated. 'Cameron Fletcher. I want you to keep an eye on Cameron Fletcher. I know he's in there,' he jabbed a finger at the Kinotech screen, 'and I've no idea when he's coming out. It's Festival Sunday, no Fletcher events planned, but I want you to keep an eye on him. See where he goes, who he meets, who he talks to and I want it logged. All of it. There's a notebook here and I'll be checking it thoroughly when I get back in two hours.'

'Causing you some bother is he, this Fletcher?' Neil asked, enjoying the flash of exasperation in Callum's blue eyes.

'You *could* say that, yes. Some bother.' Callum stood up, straightened his tie, the triangle of lilac handkerchief showing from his jacket pocket. 'It's amazing these days how some people forget it's only common decency to show loyalty to the person who's paying your salary.' The sharp look he gave Neil left no doubt this comment didn't apply solely to Fletcher. 'Mr Fletcher seems to have forgotten this entirely and has left me, potentially, in a very difficult position. I want to make sure he doesn't make things much, *much* worse for himself.'

He brushed a hand over his hair and focused on the Kinotech display again. Neil could tell how difficult it was for him to delegate, hand control over his little empire to someone else. As if hearing his thoughts Callum turned abruptly, walking quickly out of his office, trailing a scent of lavender and the words, 'Two hours. I'll be back in two hours and I want a record of everything you've seen. *Everything*.'

After finding a kettle and a jar of instant coffee, Neil settled down with the Mars bar he'd brought for breakfast. Beats working he thought, although two hours of sheer, mind-numbing boredom didn't appeal. Seacrest was such an odd-looking place though, the cinema and shop fronts designed with entertainment in mind, the people dressed to impress, he soon started to find it quite enjoyable.

'Better than *Eastenders* at any rate,' he murmured, pretending he was a film director, selecting cameras, moving joysticks to track the flight of a seagull from screen to screen, right the way from the lido to the pier before diving down to attack some chips left outside the Kinotech. It was startled into flight by the appearance of a large suited gentleman at the door of the Kinotech. Neil started, scrabbled for the pen, turned to the first page of the notebook.

He was distracted from making his first note by the way Fletcher, after taking time to admire the view of the bay, turned his gaze directly on him. Well, not on *him*, Neil reassured himself, he was looking at the camera. That didn't rid him completely of the feeling that Fletcher knew exactly who was watching him and why.

Neil had had the opportunity to study Fletcher closely over the past few days, seen the way he could single out a person. In a good way, not the way Boyd did, to make an example of someone, an example that made you want to live up to the best he could expect from you. As Fletcher tipped his cane at the camera then strolled along the pier to the promenade, Neil found himself writing '10:32am'. Seagull resumes eating of chips,' starting a game of noughts and crosses with himself, comfortable in the knowledge he was backing the better man.

Bloody hell, it was difficult. This… *walking* business.
Although Cameron appeared relaxed and confident as he sauntered across Neil's screens, it was a very different story for Arthur Dott who felt tense. Exposed.

Last night in The Moviegoer, that had been fantastic, bloody marvellous. Everything clicking into place like those rare moments on stage when everything *flowed* and it was effortless, like flying. You were reading the audience, feeding off their energy, giving it back to them and you were both in perfect tune. The sort of feeling that had seen Arthur going back on stage during a wet Wednesday afternoon in Wigan to face a tiny audience smelling like an elderly damp Labrador because he knew there was a chance, a tiny chance he would hit a line just right and achieve perfection.

Now though, Arthur grimaced, he could feel himself slipping, Fletcher peeling away from him. Might have been the lack of preparation, he speculated, missing his daft actor's rituals. Not using his combs and brushes back in the hotel room that morning, having to rely on Harry to point out the patches of hair he'd missed with the boot polish. Or it could be his bloody nightmare of a hangover. That would have been how the *real* Cameron Fletcher had felt most mornings. Perhaps that was why Arthur felt so uneasy. Realising how big a gap there was between the original Cameron Fletcher and the one he'd created for him. Larger than life, assured, an ideal. A joke. A sham.

Now come on, Arthur. Get a grip. Sort yourself out. It was probably because there weren't enough people about yet, not enough of an audience, folk shouting out 'Hey Fletch! Give us a wave!' Too much time to think, that was his problem, about who he was going to see, how Luke was going to react.

Because, and Arthur shocked himself with his insight, it hadn't bothered him in the slightest, tricking the fans who'd gone to see the shows, hadn't concerned him one jot. He reckoned most of them were savvy enough to have heard the rumours, suspect there was some kind of scam going on but they *enjoyed* that. They treated coming along to see him as they would seeing a magician. They *knew* the guy on stage hadn't caused the table to levitate or pulled doves out of thin air, they were there for the thrill of being fooled. Being a kid again, allowing themselves to believe.

But Luke… Luke was different. Arthur reckoned he genuinely believed Fletcher had come back from the dead to see *him*. To visit the Archive. Christ…

All too soon Arthur was staring up at the gates of Seacrest Studios, a shabby actor with the power to wreck everything Luke had worked for. Shitting hell. He should have listened to Harry, stayed with him, finished off the last of the whisky…

'You all right Mr Fletcher? Looking a bit peaky there, need a sit-down?'

Good God, someone was talking to him. He'd met him at the Reception, he was pretty sure… Donald? Davie? No… Dougie! That was it.

And it *was* Dougie Thomson, remember? The sour-faced guard who, chapters ago, couldn't summon up a smile for Jo, never mind a 'Hello'? See him here in the presence of Cameron Fletcher, transformed! Looking ten years younger, smiling away while anxiously offering assistance to one of his heroes, the thought of having Fletcher share a cup of tea in his booth making him feel faint.

'Why thank you, Dougie, but honestly I'm fine. Now, I'm sure I have my pass somewhere about here… ' Cameron patted the pockets of his jacket and waistcoat while Arthur had a perfect vision of his 'Free Entrance to Seacrest Studios Pass' sitting on the top shelf of the hotel safe.

'Och, Mr Fletcher, you don't need to be bothering with *that*. Not a man of *your* status.' With a clank and a hum, the gates of the studios began to glide open. Dougie continued, 'This place is buzzing the way it was fifty years ago and you know who's responsible for that? Not your Boyd family, that's for sure, them wanting to knock it down, turn it into a multiplex… ' He was about to spit before remembering that might not be appropriate considering the company he was in. 'No, it's all down to you, Mr

Fletcher. It's an honour to have you here. Truly.'

Cameron modestly accepted Dougie's praise. 'Very kind and believe me, it's an honour to be here. Now, I wonder if you could do me a small favour. I need a map, a map to show me how to get to Lot 45?'

This was more like it, thought Arthur. He hadn't been in a studio complex for years, had forgotten how wonderful those places could be. All that nonsense Callum had been spouting about how dilapidated the studios were, how they hadn't been cost effective for years… rubbish. Look at the place, thriving!

Young trendy souls who should have been in bed nursing the kind of hangover Arthur was dealing with were standing outside editing suites, chatting, smoking under 'STRICTLY NO SMOKING!' signs, shouts and hammering coming from inside massive studio hangars, a trailer towing carts filled with saplings, grandfather clocks, white polystyrene limbs, heads and torsos shoggling past. Marvellous, the nuts and bolts of film-making, Arthur appreciated. He could always forget about Luke, carry on wandering. Get a walk-on part or two.

But, as if his subconscious had known exactly where to take him, Arthur found himself standing in front of an oddly familiar set of large green doors. He looked down and there it was, a huge white '45' painted onto the tarmac.

Gulping loudly, taking a big deep breath then praying to the souls of the real Cameron Fletcher, Avi Fleischer, his Mum, Gran and anyone else who might be listening, he stepped forward to press the button at the side of the doors then gave them a rap with what he hoped was Fletcher-like jauntiness.

Nothing. Arthur sweated but there was no sign of movement, no sound of footsteps, no creak of a door opening. Oh *dear*, what a shame, he wasn't in, oh well, best head back to the Fulmar and he'd turned to go when a 'click' sounded behind him, the small inner door swinging open. There he was, Luke hardly looking like a psycho at all, instead touchingly young and eager. Like a kid wanting to show you the den they'd built in their back garden.

'You're here. Actually *here*. People said I'd blown it, that you'd been scared off but I *knew*. Knew you'd know me better than that. Come in, come in! I'll show you around. It's all yours anyway, I was only keeping it safe until you turned up,' and he disappeared.

Cameron Fletcher paused before following and took a good long look at the sky, the passing seagulls, the buildings surrounding him, seeking reassurance that this solid, dependable world would still be there waiting for him when he re-emerged. Then stepped over the threshold into *his* world.

It took a few seconds for his eyes to adjust to the dim light and once they had the first thing he saw were the boards pinned up on either side of the entrance, covered in movie stills, posters, tickets, photographs of people outside their favourite cinemas, next to their favourite stars, scraps of material taken from the seats of demolished cinemas, napkins from concession stands. He stood before these offerings and felt his heart swell along with a sense of relief. So, it wasn't all about *him*, it was about everyone who visited the Archive. Everyone who still felt excited when they'd found their seat and the lights began to dim, the adverts finished and there was that special silence before the film started.

Cameron passed through the entrance and into the Exhibit and it was like walking into a museum but more than that, something close to sacred. There it was, spread out before him, carefully catalogued and displayed. His life set out for public viewing.

The wide, high space was filled with display cases, some tall, cabinet sized, filled with shelves, others glass-topped vitrines. They were arranged in chronological order initially, following the development of Fletcher's life, and then by topic: CHILDHOOD, TEENAGE YEARS, EARLY INFLUENCES, FIRST WORKS,

CRITICAL WRITINGS, THE FILMS, THE FANS, THE ARCHIVE. A biography in 3-D, one to walk through and browse as Fletcher did now, his initial panic replaced by amused fascination. A man haunting himself.

He thought he'd find it crueller. Full of nudges and winks, one big in-joke, taking the piss out of everyone from pretentious film critics to obsessives who pay thousands for tat picked up on eBay. There were things that sailed close to that, a bundle of typed pages said to be Fletcher's notes towards a book exploring the symbolism of facial hair in film entitled *Nicholson's Moustache*, but most of it was sincere. Heartfelt.

You didn't have to be a Fletcher nut to find things that would hold your interest. The early cinema tickets and cereal box gifts in the CHILDHOOD cabinet, the piles of dime novel pulp fiction books Fletcher cited as major influences, the diamond ring found at the bottom of a theme park water ride identified years later as belonging to Marlene Dietrich, a scrap of the curtain Errol Flynn's Robin Hood sliced his way down to escape attacking swordsmen.

Cameron found it wonderful until he was standing in front of the case displaying his death certificate. Surrounded by black bordered letters of condolence from the famous – Billy Wilder, Martin Scorsese, Russ Meyer and Katherine Hepburn – and the not-famous at all ('I am a middle-aged housewife who has never written a letter to the newspapers in her life but I felt the need to let people know how much Cameron Fletcher's writing meant to me. After reading one of his columns in the morning I knew I would find myself in the foyer of a cinema in the afternoon and to hell with the housework. He gave me the freedom to do that, to live my own life the way I wanted to.') There was Fletcher, his reflection staring back at him, lights glinting in his eyes, until he had to look away to find Luke standing beside him.

'Thought you'd like some time to look at it alone,' Luke said, holding out an espresso cup. 'Three shots, the way you like it.' As Fletcher took it from him, their fingertips touched and Arthur felt him trembling. Was that nerves, excitement, fear, that he'd be angry or underwhelmed? He downed the coffee, felt his heart pound and wondered, what could have happened to someone to make them want to disappear like that, give themselves over to living someone else's life... hey. Hang on. Who was Arthur thinking about then? Luke or himself?

'What you've done here, Luke, what you've brought together ,it's incredible. The only thing I can think to compare it to are those local attractions where someone has covered a house with shells, or thrown a shoe up into a tree where it's stuck and someone else decided to do the same, then someone else, until the tree is covered. A huge collaboration to make something new and strange and wonderful. The big difference with what you've done is the achievement of bringing a man to *life*.'

Arthur stopped, realising he'd put the coffee cup to one side and was gripping Luke by the shoulders, Luke's face a blend of joy, confusion and concern as Fletcher seemed to have difficulty breathing, tugging at his collar, gasping for breath. Knew he should have brought that bloody inhaler...

'Hold on, wait, I'll get a chair!' Luke pulled himself free, grabbed a fold-out chair resting next to the hat-stand that used to catch Bond's hat, and eased Fletcher down into it.

Once he'd returned with a glass of water, Fletcher was breathing normally but looking pale and exhausted. 'Thanks, being reminded of one's own death can do funny things to a man.' Gratefully he gulped down the drink which seemed to revive him, turned him from black and white to colour again. Handing the glass back he added, 'Suddenly became acutely aware of how lacking in windows this place is. Had an attack of... what? Claustrophobia? Vertigo? Not sure but whatever it was, it certainly wasn't pleasant.'

Oh Lord… it looked as though the poor lad was going to burst into tears.

'No, sorry, it's my fault, I didn't think. Should have realised, this would be overwhelming for you. And about your death… it was a mistake, honestly, I genuinely believed… '

Cameron waved a hand in protest. 'Oh, don't worry about that, being pronounced dead didn't bother me in the slightest. Did me a favour, in fact. Nothing like a faked death for freeing a person up, give him time to do all the things he didn't get round to when alive.'

The *relief* of the boy. His shoulders relaxing, terrified of causing offence to the man he was devoted to and Arthur found himself getting angry on Luke's behalf. That Charles and his mates should be ashamed of themselves. Taking advantage, taking over his life, leaving no room for one of his own.

Luke, having regained confidence, started up, 'There's more to see in the back. Your office, the green leather chair, the record player, set up the way you had, the way it was shown in the photograph. I've even poured you a whisky, we can… ' His voice trailed off as Cameron shook his head, lifted up his cane, offered it to him.

'Here. I brought this back for you to put in its display case.'

Luke regarded it with horror. 'But… no, it's *yours*. You wrote about it, said a soul should always carry a cane to measure his steps. You should keep it, it'll sit here useless otherwise.'

'Useless eh?' The old Fletcher glint returned to his eye. 'But what about the crowds who'll come and admire it?' Luke shook his head vigorously.

'No, it should be out there, being used by you. That's what it's *for*, that's its *purpose*. Otherwise it's like a dead thing, a relic.'

'Hmm… ' Cameron sat back, smiling at the cane's demonic silver head as though it had answered a question he'd asked a while back. 'There may be hope for you yet, Luke Howard. I'm glad you won't take it back, it was a relief to find it again, felt like being reunited with an old friend. As does meeting you.' Wait a minute, was he *blushing*? Dear me, this boy really needed to get out there and find himself a girlfriend or boyfriend or *someone*. Staying cooped up in here was doing him no good whatsoever.

Cameron stood up, wobbled, Luke's arm there to right him. Safely planted he said, 'Let's you and I get out of this place, stretch our legs, get to know one another better.'

'But the office… ' Luke looked disappointed, a little fearful. 'I've polished the desk and it's just through there, won't take a minute, then… '

'Luke,' Cameron scolded. 'Why would I travel thousands of miles to spend time somewhere that reminds me of home? There's one place here I've yet to visit that I've wanted to ever since I glimpsed it from the window of the Seacrest Special and you're going to take me there. The Big Wheel, that's where we're going and when we get there you and I are going to have fun, godammit!'

As Luke scurried to the office for his coat, Arthur murmured, 'I'll make you enjoy yourself. Even if it kills me. Which, when you find out the truth… '

When they emerged blinking into the sunlight, as disorientated as two cinema-goers who'd sat through a double matinee, Cameron was shocked to see how pale Luke was. Like some underground creature or those alien fish you see in documentaries about ocean trenches. The thought of Callum actually being *scared* of a guy like this. Then Luke smiled, broad and gleeful, and there was something in his eyes, a look of absolute justification, that gave a glimpse of how formidable an opponent he could be.

'I *knew* it, before you arrived I thought 'The Big Wheel, Fletcher's bound to love the Big Wheel'. I'm surprised you haven't been up it yet. Because it's exactly the sort of thing you write about in some of your essays, like that one about the circus and fairgrounds in cinema. Was there a particular place you had in mind when you were writing that? Coney Island? Or one of the fairs that visited your town when you were young or… '

Cameron stopped, swinging his cane in front of Luke's chest, forcing him to a halt. 'I understand, Luke, you'll have hundreds of questions to ask me and in time I'll be more than willing to answer them. But over the past fortnight all I seem to have done is answer questions. I'm an old man and tire easily, especially when I'm forced to listen to myself day in, day out. So, ' he pointed to the gates some distance away, 'once we're through those gates, up until we reach the Wheel, I want you to put those questions on hold while I ask some things of *you*. Because, let's face it, when it comes to Cameron Fletcher, *you're* the expert. You know more about me than I do myself! Do we have a deal?'

Luke appeared doubtful, glancing over his shoulder in the direction of the Archive as if wishing they'd stayed put in his place of safety. Then he looked towards the gates and Fletcher could see a change come over him; Cameron Fletcher, listening to me, interested in *me*.

'OK, it's a deal. I warn you, we'll probably have run out of things to talk about by the time we get half-way there. I'm not very interesting. The only interesting thing about me is… you. The Archive.'

'Oh, I doubt that, young man, I doubt that very much.' Cameron Fletcher put an arm around his shoulders, steering him away from the Archive towards something close to freedom.

It wasn't easy at first. Took a lot of coaxing and gentle persuasion. Luke was unused to talking about himself, initially unnerved by being the focus of Fletcher's attention. It was like watching a newborn deer learning to walk, his conversation full of stumblings, hesitations. But the combined skills of Fletcher and Arthur, knowing when to stay silent and when to ask more, picking up the points of enthusiasm, following the pauses, drew him out. Both of them oblivious to the curiosity of passers-by on the busy promenade, some gawping and stopping to take a picture on their cameraphones, realising the importance of what they were seeing. Luke Howard, Keeper of the Archive, and Cameron Fletcher together at last, deep in conversation.

Always the same, thought Arthur, the quiet ones with the most to say. A bit of prodding and before you knew it, it was *pouring* out of them. They'd been waiting all their lives to find an audience and when they found one, they were determined to make the most of it. Luke had been *desperate* for someone to listen to him but he didn't think he deserved it. So he created an audience for Fletcher instead.

It all came spilling out. His Mum moving from job to job, home to home, the lack of a dad but how that didn't matter because they always had the movies, the game they would play when they were there in the dark, when the most handsome actor would come on and Mum would nudge him, whisper loudly, 'There he is! There's your dad! What's he doing there, told me he was only nipping out for a pint of milk, gonna kill him when he gets home!' She would laugh, popcorn shaking, until tears would roll down her cheeks and Luke would laugh along too, not as loud, not for as long, part of him keeping quiet because that part wanted to *believe*. This time maybe, this time, she was telling the truth. About how he would spot a detail, the way the actor frowned or chewed his bottom lip and store it away, try it out back at home in his bedroom. See how natural it felt.

About how he'd found an old, battered copy of Cameron Fletcher's *Flicker and Shine: A Movie Nut's Diary* during a visit to a public library when he was about fourteen. Remembered starting to read it in a café and that *excitement*…Heart racing, palms sweating at finding someone who loved movies as much as he did, who spoke to him directly. He'd never taken that copy back, dreaded to think what the fine would be.

The years of drift, working in junk shops, auction houses. He'd thought about getting a job in a cinema but he'd wanted to keep that pleasure separate from work. Keep it special. Then meeting Conrad Baxter who took him under his filthy wing, kept an eye out for him, taught him how to spot a bargain, how to fleece an old dear without feeling too guilty about it. Yes, Conrad Baxter was a rogue and a chancer but he looked after his own, was loyal and happy to teach a bright young lad.

Then the cancer. Mum dying.

How he'd thought about dying too until Baxter saved him, put him in touch with Harlan Dexter who presented him with the Holy Grail. The thing he'd dreamt about for years, the job that would make life worth living again, give him a purpose. The Cameron Fletcher Archive.

They paused to buy two cups of tea, sat in one of the wooden shelters, admiring the view. Or rather Luke admired it while Arthur blew steam from his tea and fretted. Bleeding Nora, what had he been *thinking*, planning to tell him the *truth*? After this spiel, Fletcher some kind of father substitute, giving him a reason for going on after his dear old Mum pops her clogs... Harry had been right. The whole Cameron Fletcher thing was a lie but it was a lie that was holding Luke's *life* together. If that went, what was left?

But then – he sipped his tea, letting the heat burn his lips – surely that was up to Luke to decide. It might force him to find a life of his own rather than someone else's. Wait, there Luke went, off again. Arthur reminded himself to look like he was listening rather than planning an escape bid. He could maybe jump over the railing... Bleeding hell, Arthur, you get in difficulty in the shallow end of your local pool, never mind the North Sea.

'And that's how I ended up here. Part of the conditions of the will, *your* will or what we thought... anyway, Harlan had boxes of stuff given to him by a contact in New York, full of scripts and notes and paperbacks and mementoes and stuff jumbled together that needed to be properly catalogued. He had too much work on and there was the condition it had to be taken here, to Seacrest. Conrad had no interest in taking it on, especially when he found out he had to 'live amongst the Jocks.' I didn't have any ties down there. Well, apart from one girl but that… ' Bloody hell, Arthur nearly spluttered into his tea. He had a choice between a girl and Cameron Fletcher and he chose *Cameron*. Harry was spot on, right fruit loop indeed. 'That didn't work out. So I was ready for a new start and when I arrived here it was like coming home. Felt settled for the first time in years.'

'And once I was here, had the Archive out and organised, something incredible happened. It started to grow, people sending me stuff from all over. Some of it nothing to do with you but it always had something to do with films, with the movies. Because that seemed to be so much in line with what you were saying in your work I thought I'd include it too. You know, there are some people, like Jo, who always said you didn't exist. But I saw the effect you had on people. Saw how you touched them, how they believed in you and I knew… I knew you were out there. You had to be.'

Luke got up from the bench, took a few steps forward towards the sea rail as Arthur tried to control his panic (Christ! What was he going to do, jump overboard and expect Cameron to save him? Prove his divinity?) and turned his back to the sea to take in all of Seacrest. The expression on his face was one of pure happiness, a man who'd found nirvana in his own back garden.

Were you taking note, Arthur? Fully appreciating how revealing your true identity could rip that away from him? Turn him back into a poor, hopeless orphan boy, cast adrift in the big bad world filled with those only too pleased to point and laugh at his folly?

From the greenish tinge edging up Arthur's jowls we can assume that yes, he was taking that on board and wishing he'd never bloody well agreed to this job in the bloody first place.

'Enough of me chattering. We'd best get a move on if we want to get a carriage to ourselves. Been ages since I've been on the Big Wheel. See, you being here makes such a difference. Makes me *do* things'.

Best get up or he's going to start *skipping* Arthur thought glumly, staying seated for a few seconds longer, returning to the idea of heaving himself over the railing, swimming for freedom, away from Seacrest and the mental patients who lived there. Until Cameron gave him a talking to and he rose to his feet, smiling in twinkly-eyed fashion at a beaming Luke as the Big Wheel loomed ever closer.

CHAPTER THIRTY-FOUR

Mopping up the last of the baked bean sauce with a slice of soft white bread in Saturday Night, Sunday Morning, the caff at the foot of her road, Jo was pleased to note her hangover appeared to have called a truce. Eggs, bacon, chips and beans accompanied by a tall glass of Irn Bru had once again proved itself as the best hangover cure known to womankind. Her headache had reduced to a dull throbbing although there lingered an unpleasant sense of unease. That had less to do with alcohol and far more to do with the argument with Shona. It had left an atmosphere in the flat afterwards, one she had to escape from.

Nothing had been resolved of course. Shona had stormed out, saying she had a meeting to go to after refusing to say what she was going to do once the Festival was over. Stay here? Get on the first plane back to the US? Jo rubbed her temples, trying to work out what she was going to do if she went through with either of those options. More importantly, did she really care? Kissing Jenny last night – God how *embarrassing*, she needed to speak to Harry about that though only after he'd explained what was going on with him and Shona. Bad of her but the realisation that *yes*, there were other women out there. Ones who could make her happy without all this *drama*.

Leaving her last slice of toast uneaten, she headed down the hill to the Kinotech, in part to apologise but also to find out more about the 'project' Harry was working on that Jen had told her about.

It took a while to spot him in the crowded Kinotech, parents and children taking advantage of its return to normal opening hours. Just as her hangover was threatening a counterattack in revenge for being put in close proximity to squealing eight-year-olds, she found him showing off on the Harryhausen Pin-ball Machine. How did he *do* it? she wondered. He must have had quadruple what she'd had to drink and yet he was laughing away, building up another high score while she felt as though she was on the brink of an aneurysm.

She tapped him on the shoulder as the last metal ball disappeared into the Tunnel of Hydra, resulting in a groan from Harry and a cheer from the crowd who'd been waiting half an hour to have a go. 'Jo! Great, was just about to call you!' Right, she thought. Either he was so drunk last night he'd completely forgotten about The Incident, or he was lulling her into a false sense of security, building up to some twisted form of revenge. Jeez, Jo, listen to yourself. She really should stop watching so many films.

'Come through into the office, have some coffee, sure you could do with some after last night, want to ask you about something'.

As he pulled her along she attempted an apology. 'Harry, about last night, what happened with Jen was childish, stupid, me getting my own back after seeing you and Shona.' Annoyingly, he didn't seem the least bit bothered.

'Oh, don't worry about all that nonsense. When Shona did what she did I knew she was up to her usual shit-stirring, pushing folk's buttons. Being a big dumb bloke I did exactly what any big dumb bloke in that situation would do. Didn't exactly fight her off but let's forget about it, eh? Not give her the satisfaction. And Jen and me, we're sorted, hunky-dory. Now, quit your blethering and listen to this.'

The quiet of the office was a relief when Harry closed the door, shutting off the clamour of the arcade. He sat down at his desk, booting up his computer. 'I want you to tell me if you think this works. Cameron or Arthur or Whatever-His-Name is had a listen to it earlier and seemed to think it was all right. But getting your opinion would be very useful indeed.'

Jo, sitting in the seat opposite Harry, took in the unmade camp bed next to her with its large Arthur-shaped dent and felt oddly jealous. Harry and Arthur, best mates were they? Don't be petty now, she told herself, Arthur wasn't hers and hers alone, he was his own man. Sort of.

'Is this the thing for your Dad? Jen mentioned it last night, was wondering why you hadn't said anything about it.'

'Because I wasn't sure what the fuck I was doing. If it would sound any good or like something Radio 4 would broadcast at half eleven at night, call it 'Soundings' or some other crap. But I think it might actually be all right.'

He tapped the touch-pad, surrounding them with voices, fading in and out of each other like a well-rehearsed choir, catching and riding the underlying zither music at times, speaking over what sounded like silence at others, until Jo picked up the whirring of a projector or laughter over the noise of a popcorn machine, the hush descending as the curtain parted, the film about to start, the chatter of leaving a screening.

When Harry stopped it after far too short a time she was amazed he was looking at her anxiously. 'Well?' He genuinely didn't seem to know how good it was, how beautiful. Jo felt her throat constrict, praying she didn't start to cry, otherwise she'd never hear the end of it.

'It's… wonderful! Your Mum, she has to, has she *heard* this? Harry, you have to let her hear it, if you haven't you have to get her down here soon, honestly, she'd *love* it.'

'Yeah, yeah.' He screwed up his face. 'Cameron was going on about that too. Nagging me to get in touch with her.'

'We're not *nagging*. After what she's had to put up with through these past few years she *deserves* something like this. And your Dad, he'd want her to hear it too, wouldn't he?'

It took a few seconds before Harry nodded grudgingly.

'There. See, you know I'm right. Where is Cameron by the way? Bet Callum's keen to know too, he's not going to be too chuffed when he finds out he's been fraternising with the enemy. Harry?'

Harry was absorbed in staring at his computer screen as Jo's vague sense of unease grew increasingly definite. 'Haaarry… '

'What? Eh? Cameron? He *might,* ah, have mentioned something about going to see Luke to tell him…what was it again? That -' He was drowned out by a blast of Pearl and Dean from the computer.

'Tell him *what?* This is *important.*'

Harry sighed, cutting off the jingle. 'That he's not Cameron Fletcher. That Fletcher *did* exist before or something, couldn't work that bit out, thought it was the whisky talking, but that he's not. He's Arthur Dott.'

'What!' Jo stood up and when her head realised what she'd done, punished her for it. 'And you let him *go*? You *idiot*, you of all people should know that Luke will *flip*! Can you *imagine*, those years of work, gathering material, devoting himself to this man who appears out of the blue to tell him it's all one big joke and he's the punchline?'

'Now, wait, hang on there a minute, *Dr* Ashe. A few weeks ago you were all for Luke knowing the truth. Couldn't wait to tell him about it, bring him back to his senses. You thought it would do him good to know all about Arthur, remember?'

'Yes, yes, all right, don't need to go on about it.' Jo slumped back onto her seat. 'An academic's allowed to change her mind. After meeting Cameron, Arthur, *whoever*, it didn't seem such a bad thing, letting Luke believe what he wanted to believe. Sustain the lie for thousands. Don't you sit there looking smug. Even *you* haven't a clue how Luke's going to react. Can't imagine him being thrilled. And Arthur…the thought of anything happening to him…'

'Hey, don't worry, they seemed to be getting on fine when I saw them a wee while ago.'

'You've *seen* them?'

'Yeah, walking past here. Waved at me, on their way to the Big Wheel, chatting away.'

They both sat silent, processing that information. Luke and a man impersonating the critic he idolised and loved, alone together in close proximity in a confined space, hundreds of feet above the ground. As they contemplated this the perfect soundtrack to their fears started up outside, beyond the doors of the Kinotech. A commotion, impossible to tell if the crowd was reacting with excitement or distress and they jumped from their chairs to find out.

This was all that mad bloody queen Gordon's fault, cursed Arthur, with his oh-so-useful acting tips back in Rep. One of them being that if you're in any doubt about how to approach a line, always go for the option that scares you the most. You might fail horribly but if it works it's like flying and, even if the audience doesn't get a thrill, you will. Arthur had known they could easily spend the whole day traipsing around without Cameron saying a peep about his true identity. To put Luke right Arthur knew he had to get them both into a corner, a place of no escape and scare himself into it.

It had seemed such a good idea on the ground. Not *such* a fantastic plan in a tiny, swaying, creaking wooden carriage at the top of a Big Wheel – a *very* Big Wheel – so high people down below appeared as small as midgies. Add to that sitting opposite a young man, so close their knees were nearly brushing, who had devoted himself to the life of a man Arthur most definitely was not and it seemed far more like a bloody stupid ridiculous idea. Suicidal even. Oh well. He'd always hoped his death would make the papers.

A seagull swooped by, letting out a wild bout of squawling as if shouting at him for being such a wimp. He took a deep breath and when he spoke it was as Arthur entirely, more Arthur-like than he had been for weeks. His shoulders slumped, his American accent gone along with the presence, the Fletcher charisma, the change reflected in Luke's expression. Pure stunned confusion as Cameron Fletcher vanished before his eyes.

'Luke. You might not realise it now, it's going to be too much of a shock, but I reckon when you think about it later you'll realise you knew what I was going to tell you as soon as you met me. It's going to be difficult but it's for the best, believe me and I sincerely hope at the end of this we're both going to be friends. Because I like and respect you, Luke, though what you'll think about me... Anyway. Here goes... '

The rest came out in a rush, running over Luke's interjections, trying to stop the speech he would have tried to escape had they been earth-bound.

'I'm not Cameron Fletcher, never have been, never will be, more's the pity. My real name is Arthur Dott, I'm an actor, not a very good one, 57-year-old on my CV, 66 in real life. Born in Leeds, lived there most my life, apart from London for a while, and touring all over with Rep, ended up in Dundee for four years, not too sure how that happened but then, I'm not sure how anyone ends up in Dundee. What I'm saying is, I've never lived in America in my puff, been there on holiday twice and that was to Florida, nowhere near New York though I'd like to go and I got this job because Shona Boyd heard me on a repeat of a radio play about the Mercury Theatre company and she liked me, heard something in my voice, what I haven't the foggiest, but it convinced her I could pull this off and that's why I'm here. Been so long since I'd been offered a starring role, seemed daft to turn it down.'

Arthur stopped when he saw Luke's face. His natural pallor had disappeared, his cheeks flushed red, his expression unsettlingly similar to the same blend of anger and hurt and disbelief Arthur had seen on the faces of those few women he'd been lucky enough to dump before they dumped him.

After a horribly long minute filled only by the ominous groaning of the carriage, Arthur praying the bloody thing would start moving again and soon, Luke whispered, 'So Jo's right. All this time, a fake. Everyone laughing behind my back.' Arthur glanced nervously at the increasingly flimsy-looking door convinced it contravened Health and Safety Rules (was that *string* holding it shut?).

'*No,* Luke, it's not like that, not like that at all. No one's laughing at you and you were closer to the heart of Fletcher than Jo ever was. There *was* a Cameron Fletcher, a real, live Fletcher and when we get down from here I'll prove it to you. I have evidence.' Luke was shaking his head, refusing to be taken in by a man who had lied to him, to the *world*, for weeks and Arthur could hardly blame him. 'In the safe in my room in the Fulmar is the proof, proof that you can take away and put at the very centre of the Archive. Imagine how Callum would feel about *that*.'

He sensed a change in Luke, could see the slow dawning that this revelation could be to his benefit. What took him by surprise was this annoyed him, made him want to slap some sense into Luke, although the thought of causing the carriage to sway even more stopped him.

'Anyway, what does it matter if Fletcher existed or not? What you've done, what you've achieved here, whether it was founded on the 'truth' or not is remarkable. What you've done for this place, giving Seacrest a reason for existing, it's *magnificent. You're* the one responsible for the success of this Festival, for granting Fletcher a real presence in this place. You should be proud. All of *Seacrest* should be proud.'

Arthur watched the colour fade from Luke's cheeks, saw that he was listening to what he was saying, regaining his trust.

'But you have to be careful. What you've created is great but people have taken advantage of you. And it's burying you, Luke. Trapping you here. I've been Fletcher for a fortnight and it's *exhausting*. What it must be like living with him day and night, week after week, month after month…What you've made is big enough to sustain itself and there are people out there who'd be happy to help and give you a break. There's a world beyond those cliffs, son, and you deserve to see it.'

Lord, this boy should have been in the silent movies, Arthur appreciated. His face, his eyes, everything reflected in them. Taking the hump at the suggestion staying away in the Archive might not be that healthy, doubt then acceptance that there were people out there who could run the Archive as well as he could. Looking over Arthur's shoulder at the cliff boundary, weighing up what he was being told, knowing he was right. That he was as desperate to get out of this town as he was to stay. As much as the rest of them. Jo and Harry, Shona and Arthur.

Arthur spread his hands, feeling tired and heavy as the carriage jolted and they started their descent. That gravity was a right bastard sometimes.

'I know you probably hate me right now, not too keen on myself at the moment. But I'll tell you this for nothing. In the short time I've known you I've learnt that you deserve more than staying in the shadow of Cameron Fletcher. You deserve your *own* life. It won't be easy, believe me, it'll be bloody difficult, but you've some good friends down there, friends who'll be more than happy to help. And I hope, once this has blown over, that you'll see me as one of them.' Wearily, Arthur held out his hand with no idea if Luke would take it.

Luke stared, as if Arthur had produced a white dove from up his coat sleeve. Cameron Fletcher was dead. Definitely dead. Years of hoping it wasn't true, of wanting him to walk through the door of the Archive and for them to become friends, perhaps be mistaken for father and son... gone. In his chest he felt the same aching hollowness he'd always felt when he'd left the cinema with his Mum. They'd emerge sore-eyed into the daylight and he'd realise how daft the game of 'Spot My Dad' was. How it was only him and his Mum alone and that was that.

Then the disappointment would pass and he'd feel... relieved. Him and his Mum alone together and that was fine. It was real and it was good and his Mum was there and real, smiling down at him, kneeling to do up his jacket properly, to give him a hug and a kiss while he squirmed in mock horror before whispering in his ear, 'Fish and chips for tea?' That's what going to the movies could do. Bring you back to real life with a bump, a bump knocking some sense into you.

He looked hard at Arthur then, noticing the yellow stains on his fingers, the untrimmed beard, the wary look in his eye, and it was like seeing documentary footage of the making of a film; the actors in front of the cameras, acting out an intimate scene surrounded by camera men and sound-boom operators and runners, the director watching not them, instead the monitor. You'd expect that to ruin the magic of the film itself, showing you the workings, the snake-oil salesman behind the curtains pulling the levers. For Luke, seeing the mechanics had the opposite effect. It left him in awe of how the magic on the screen could be conjured up out of something as ordinary as people doing their job.

Arthur had brought about a transformation without lighting and props and a director telling him what to do. He'd turned himself from a failure, the old, worn-out man in front of him into something fantastic. He had turned himself into Cameron Fletcher. Luke's smile when it came, when he took Arthur's hand, was like the sun breaking through rain clouds over Seacrest bay, creating columns of light as though shot from a hundred projectors, turning grey water silver and sending rainbows soaring.

When they left the carriage they were greeted by the excited cries of a group of Japanese Fletcher enthusiasts enraptured at finding both Cameron Fletcher and Luke Howard there in front of them and only too happy – Cameron at least – to have their photographs taken and sign autograph books.

It was this excitement that Jo and Harry had overheard, causing them to rush outside and watch with delighted bemusement as Cameron and Luke made their way towards them. After the four of them had retreated to the peace of Harry's office, one of the fans, frowning at the autograph they'd been given, turned to his friend asking, 'Hey, does that look like 'Arthur' to you? And the surname is a mess. Just one big blot.'

The camera outside the Kinotech moved back and forth, back and forth like a restless sleeper attempting to escape a bad dream.

Callum sat staring at the screen a long time after they'd disappeared. When he'd returned to the viewing room after a nap and freshening up, he'd found Neil clapping and cheering what he was watching, 'Come on, Cameron, my son!' The security man had glanced at Callum but carried on clapping then got up, put on his jacket, saying, 'No need to sack me Mr Boyd, I quit about half an hour ago.' He left Callum contemplating the image of Luke and Cameron Fletcher sharing a joke in front of the tourists.

He was surprised by how calm he felt, how certain he was of what to do next. With a flick of a switch the screens turned black displaying Callum's reflection as still as a lizard as he planned and plotted while Rock Hudson, Montgomery Clift and Greta Garbo began hour-long smiles. Eventually he walked through to the main office, picked up the phone, pressed the first number on speed-dial.

'Kim, Callum. There have been some developments some…

unforeseen developments. I want you to get the word out quickly, I'm bringing the Consortium meeting forward. Yes, the final meeting for the vote... no. No Kim, it can't wait. It needs to happen and soon. Tomorrow. If anyone can't make it then tough, that's their vote lost. Phone me in an hour, tell me who you've rounded up.' He hung up, cutting off her tinny protests.

Looking out beyond the Phoenix sign above which seagulls hovered and spun 'Oh, you'll get your future, Seacrest, you see if you don't,' he muttered. 'One that's going to be on *my* terms. Clean and smooth and efficient,' as the film stars bared their teeth.

# CHAPTER
THIRTY-FIVE

In the hours that followed Callum's phonecall, the town reacted to it like a large hive-mind. From our bird's eye view high above the Big Wheel, we could see the news of his decision to bring forward the Extraordinary Consortium meeting spreading through the streets like the famous Seacrest haar. It entered the foyers, the auditoriums, cinema owners stopping each other in the street, ushers gossiping by fast-food stalls on their way to work, sellers of the *Gazette* telling customers who stopped at one of their booths, 'You won't find the *real* news in there, mind, not yet, I'll tell you for nothing right now'. No need for mobiles and emails in a town so closely packed, galvanised by the knowledge its future would be decided within 24 hours.

Jo sat in the packed Fulmar Conference Room, more seats having to be brought in by staff, cinema owners she thought were dead walking through the door, the air thick with chatter, excited and tense, and she tried to keep calm. It wasn't proving easy, she fretted, well-nigh impossible what with Callum's model vision right in front of her. It was about as calming and reassuring a presence as the black obelisk in *2001*.

Callum's hideous, shiny vision of a future Seacrest took up most of the conference room table with all the rackety cinemas, built from love and obsession, gone. Like smoothing down a Gothic cathedral until it resembled an Ikea warehouse. Bugger, Jo felt a tightness in her chest starting up, had to think of something else, how she'd heard about the meeting, about Luke being banned due to 'an impending criminal charge', 'breach of the peace' which was ridiculous. If they took run-ins with the police into account on deciding Consortium membership there'd only be about five of them there.

Her gaze drifted toward Shona's empty seat, one of the three at the top of the conference table, and her heart pounded to the point she felt faint, wondering if they'd find out about the plot against her Dad today? What her plans were for Arthur…

Enough of that. Jo thought back to ordering a mint choc chip cone at an ice-cream stand whilst walking Arthur back to the Fulmar. Instead of a flake, she'd got a full Callum update from the sixteen-year-old serving. She'd been outraged, had almost lost her second scoop of ice-cream she was waving her cone about so much, ranting at it being such a blatant attempt to get rid of the threat of Luke.

Arthur hadn't seemed that bothered, ridiculously calm in fact. He'd thought it was a good thing Luke not being there, would stop him becoming a focus for Callum's attack. When Jo had said, 'Yes, but that means he'll focus on you *instead*,' what was his response? A cheery shrug and the offer to buy her another cone. He was probably still blissed out at not being shoved from a Big Wheel carriage from a great height, him and Luke best pals now and she wondered what they'd talked about up there….

She turned her attention to the man sitting next to her with a combination of respect and bemusement, a man seemingly blithely unaware of the interest he was attracting, the nods in his direction, the whispering from Consortium members. Cameron Fletcher sat happily doodling a drunken tripod picking a fight with a disdainful looking projector on the writing pad provided to each member. Jo couldn't work out how he did it, coped with the pressure. By the time she'd left him at the Fulmar he'd been so Arthur-like, tired and dishevelled, pleased things had gone well with Luke, more concerned about having a decent bath than the Consortium meeting. A meeting that could see him held up to ridicule, run out of town, out of work.

Deep breaths and relaaaax, Jo told herself. A panic attack wasn't going to help anyone. But yes, at that point he had seemed as far away from Cameron Fletcher as it was possible to be, about as Cameron Fletcher-like as, well, Jo. Had she slept a wink last night, worrying about that, worrying if he could handle the pressure of today? No, she had not and she rubbed her tired eyes, stifled a yawn. When she turned up early, a good forty-five minutes before the meeting was supposed to start, there he was. In position as Cameron looking composed, charismatic and more *Fletcher*-like than ever before. Not as chatty as usual, understandably, distant, like a magician in the wings before a show was about to start. Getting in the zone, running through the tricks in his head, working out the smoke and mirrors. Jo felt a strong rush of warmth towards Cameron, towards Arthur. No matter what happened, the man was a legend. Both of them.

She put her hand on Cameron's right arm, gave it a squeeze and he stopped his cartooning to offer her a Fletcher smile of such brilliance that it caused Jo to think, to *believe*, that, actually, everything might just work out fine. Absolutely fine. Then he looked to her right and grimaced, his smile turning rueful. 'Hey, hey, the gang's all here,' he murmured and Jo's mouth went dry, her palms damp at the sight of Callum, Shona and Kim making their entrance.

The chatter died down, two guards taking up position on either side of the doors. To keep them in or others out? Jo wondered, checking the cinema and business owners surrounding her to see if anyone else had noticed, if any kind of protest would be offered. However, all eyes had switched from Cameron to following the progress of the trio making their way to the top of the table. Jo saw beneath the Consortium members' expressions of confident excitement brought about by the success of the Festival an underlying desperation. Make it stay, they'd soon be pleading. Don't let the glamour leave us again.

Kim, looking magnificent in a Savile Row-tailored lime green dress suit, caught Jo's eye and winked. The only sign of any possible tension on her part was a long strand of stray hair brushing her neck that had escaped from her otherwise immaculately sculpted hair-do. Jo noticed this and her anxiety built because if *Kim* had allowed herself to get into that state – and for Kim that *was* a state – what hope was there for the rest of them? Was she worried the plans would go through? That they wouldn't?

Switching her attention to Callum, she reckoned he for one believed success was guaranteed. No sign of the panic that must have caused him to reschedule, as suave and assured as ever in his soft grey suit, lilac triangle exact in his coat pocket, the Boyd smile smoothly bestowed upon his followers. Jo's attention was caught by the small black suitcase he'd brought in, set on the table in front of him. Hands resting on it as he nodded to his favourites but wasn't his grip that bit too tight? she speculated as his knuckles whitened. The lights from the model reflecting on the sheen on his forehead, a trickle of sweat down his right temple…

Of the three of them it was Shona who looked the coolest in a light, flowing dress that would look stylish in any decade, whether worn by Deborah Kerr, Rita Hayworth, Maureen O'Hara, the material as brilliant and shimmering a blue as Seacrest bay on a summer morning, that all-knowing half smile directed at Cameron. Jo knew that if only she didn't fancy Shona so much, *ached* for her, drank the sight of her in every time she was close to her, life would be *so* much easier.

Although the room was silent apart from nervous shufflings, a few coughs, Callum stuck to protocol, stood and struck the gavel three times. No need for the usual list of apologies as everyone who could be there was and instead of an official welcome, Callum slowly scanned his waiting audience, building the drama, until reaching down, snapping open the briefcase, pulling from it a large sheaf of paper. With a sickening feeling of dread, Jo knew what he was holding. God, no, please don't let it be... and she looked towards Cameron, didn't know whether to be puzzled or relieved by his expression, as patient and tolerant as that of a chess grandmaster about to face down a showy young upstart.

Callum split the paper into two bundles face down along either side of the table, saying as he did so, 'Please, no peeking *just* yet. If you could wait until I ask you to turn them over. Excuse the showmanship but I am a Boyd after all.' There was a nervous murmur of laughter. Cameron passed Jo a sheet – how could he be so *calm*? Her hand resting on it, sorely tempted to turn it over there and then, to face her fears. She resisted, her fingertips leaving sweat-marks.

Callum continued, 'For all the differing opinions held in this room, I'm sure we all agree this Festival has been a tremendous success. I'd like to congratulate each and every one of you for ensuring such a triumphant return to Seacrest form'. Although Cameron startled Jo by shouting, 'Hear, hear,' clapping vigorously, she quickly followed as did others until the room was filled with a cacophony of success, the sound of Seacrest releasing its joy at discovering it still held the power to bring the world to its doorstep.

Only Callum didn't join in the applause and Jo, seeing this, started to slow down. Him standing there, arms opened out as if in acceptance, making it look as if *he* was being cheered on, celebrated, the *bastard*. Others slowly seemed to realise this too and the clapping and cheering petered out as Callum raised one hand, asking for silence. The last man to stop was Fletcher, Jo amazed when she understood he was actually *enjoying* this.

She couldn't help but sneer at the slight quaver in Callum's voice when he said, 'That reaction tells us more about the past two weeks than anyone here could hope to put into words.' Then the tremor was gone, his tone cooler, businesslike. 'But I'm sure some of you think such success proves there's no need for change. Surely we can leave well alone if people are willing to come here in their thousands?'

'I want to make clear to you today that *because* of that success Seacrest *needs* to change. For every bit of praise – the quaint glamour, the quirky, old-fashioned ways – there was a negative. The limited parking, the crush of the narrow streets, the sprained ankles, and if visitors are going to come back these things will become increasingly important. The lack of raked seating, the poor ventilation, heating and toilet conditions, worn seating and carpets… eventually, the shabby charm will wear off completely and tourists will go elsewhere. Nostalgia isn't enough to keep them coming back.'

A mumbled protest started up but mainly from the older members and Jo felt a stab of self-disgust at admitting, dammit, he was *right*. He talked a lot of sense, did the cure have to be so brutal though? Would such a shock to the system bring the town back to life or kill it stone-cold?

'I know many of you don't want to hear this when we're riding high on success but when we come crashing back down to earth in a few months' time, we're going to find it harder than ever before to recover. Unless we want Seacrest to become an out-moded, out-dated curiosity, a relic from a by-gone age, it has to change. To adapt. Become the twenty-first century town you see here before you.' He swept his hand towards the model, pride bright in his eyes. 'For Seacrest to survive, it is imperative you vote for change today. It will be a difficult process, I'm more than willing to admit that, but if we don't, the results could be far harder to live with. Not only for us but for our successors. *If* they decide to stay and live with our mistakes.'

Jo felt a strange rumbling start up next to her, a vibration along her elbow resting on the table, developing into a loud cough from Cameron Fletcher, preparing to speak, the tension in the room prickling along her arms.

'Ahem. Mr Boyd.' Cameron's baritone was as rich and seductive as ever, lending his words weight and balance, while conjuring up an immediate intimacy. A voice you'd always want on the side of the good guys, Jo thought, hoping her sense of relief was justified.

'I appreciate I'm here as a guest but I wonder if I might interject. Indeed, as a visitor, you may find my views of interest.' Probably *not* from that look of pure fury from Callum. Jo admired his recovery, quickly appearing to look as if he gave a damn about Fletcher's opinion. 'While I understand the need for the improvements you suggest, the wholesale redevelopment you propose appears less for the genuine good of the town and more like,' he wafted a hand at the model, a gesture brilliant in its casual contempt, 'exchanging the delights of Coney Island for the wonder and vivacity of, oh, I don't know, a shopping mall?' Jo joined in the mildly hysterical laughter, delighted by the patches of red appearing on Callum's cheeks, the strain on his smile.

'As mentioned, I speak as *your* guest, Mr Boyd, and I have loved every moment of my time here. The cinemas, the people, the atmosphere but it strikes me that you're missing the main element that makes Seacrest great, once visited, never forgotten and *dreamed* about.' He paused, enjoying the concentrated silence of an attentive audience. Flaming hell, I'm going to miss this, thought Arthur.

'And that is its utter uniqueness, its refusal to be quite like anywhere else. And from what I can see in front of me, Mr Boyd, you plan to turn it into that: Anywhere. Into an experience that anyone can emulate by driving to a retail park, a shopping centre, a *mall*. If someone was plonked down in the middle of Seacrest, it would take seconds for them to know where they were. How many towns can that be said of today where high streets are filled with identical chain-stores, individual character wrung out of them? Do you think people stop to worry that things here are a bit battered, *lived-in*? Not in the least, that's exactly why they come here! To revel in idiosyncrasy. To visit a place that has developed not out of the chase for profit but out of *love*, crafted by the people who live here and displaying all their quirks and failings and eccentricities. A town that feels human and *humane*.'

The applause that followed was loud enough to cause another trickle of sweat to course down Callum's temple, his jaw tightening visibly and he was forced to resort to the gavel to restore silence.

'Why, thank you for that Cameron *Fletcher*', the surname spat out as he flipped over the paper in front of him, indicating everyone should follow his lead, and Jo experienced a sudden plunging sensation as if dropping too quickly in a Big Wheel carriage when he said, 'Or should I say... *Arthur Dott*.'

There was a collective gasp as they greeted the sight of the picture in front of them, the same publicity photo she had discovered weeks ago. A Fletcher lifetime ago.

Jo turned her copy over slowly and there he was. Arthur looking up at her with his hangdog expression, anxious eyes, the silent plea not to be cast as yet another barman/bus driver/kindly derelict and she couldn't bring herself to check on the man himself just then. Coward, she knew, outrage kicking off around them, Kim on her feet, appealing for order, turning to Callum, demanding an answer and Shona sitting there, a still, blue centre, calm as you like, that bloody half-smile as if everything was going to plan and how Jo would love to crawl the length of the desk, say or do something to wipe that smile right off her face.

She didn't. Instead, she turned to Arthur and… amazing. He was as serene as Shona, his small smile an uncanny echo of hers. He gave Jo a wink, ignored the near-riot around him and produced a small bottle of something from his jacket pocket. For a second Jo thought he was going to take a swig and instead he poured some of its contents into a handkerchief, started dabbing away at the dye in his beard to allow Arthur to emerge.

Callum raised his voice to shout over the hubbub. 'If the name of Arthur Dott doesn't mean anything to anyone, I'm not the least surprised. Why on earth would you know the name of a bit part character actor? I brought *a* Cameron Fletcher here to prove to you all there *is* no Cameron Fletcher and there never has been.'

A wake-like hush descended as the full import, the full *horror*, sank in.

'I hired this man, this *actor*, to show you the *truth*. That Luke Howard and his cronies have been fooling not just each and every one of you but the thousands of visitors who flock to his Archive. If you vote to reject my plans today, *this* is what your future is based on.' He stabbed his finger at Arthur's image, into one of his eyes. 'A fantasy dreamt up by a boy who should be sent to jail for fraud. I want all of you to think very hard about the consequences if this were to go public. What it would cost us if it was revealed to the world that for the past fortnight, instead of being in the presence of one of the geniuses of cinema they were being fed lines from a washed-up old soak!'

During this speech Callum's fringe had flopped down over his left eye, granting him a slightly deranged air, but his authority remained intact. Jo felt the fear of his audience brush against her skin and knew Callum felt it too, sweeping his hair back, his grin wide and triumphant.

Jesus. If she didn't hate him so much she'd almost admire him.

He understood the psychology of Seacrest perfectly, pin-pointed what it feared the most: reality. Luke's Archive *too* effective in its fortunes, the prospect of losing that prop with nothing substantial to replace it, terrifying. What hope did they have but to put their trust in Callum, the man who had built a success up from the ashes once before and who promised he could do it again?

A slow hand clap began, followed by one man's laughter, Arthur's chuckling getting louder and louder until he stood, shouting 'Bravo!'

'I have to say, Callum,' and there was no trace of Fletcher's accent, although Cameron remained present in the way Arthur commanded the room, 'you missed your calling. You should be up there on the stage, the silver screen. You've got the looks and the ego for it, believe me and the *conviction*… fantastic. You even had *me* believing you for a moment.' Abruptly he changed from jovial to caustic. 'Shame it was a load of old bollocks.'

Go on Arthur! Jo cheered inwardly as he continued, his tone light but deadly.

'As your delightful daughter will tell you, you're wrong to suggest Cameron Fletcher exists only as a fantasy of Luke Howard. In my hotel room I have proof that tells otherwise. There *was* a Cameron Fletcher, one whose life left such a strong impression on others, they wanted to build a fitting, *living* memorial in his name, and they succeeded. With Luke's help they created the tribute of the Archive.'

He stopped, drew attention to Callum standing silent, mouth agape, staring at Arthur, his face bright with sweat. He turned to glare at Shona, expecting an explanation but she paid him no attention, was focused entirely on Arthur in admiration. Like a proud teacher watching a star pupil destroy the opposition in a debating competition and Jo shivered. Christ, that family… the only thing that made them truly happy was causing each other pain.

'I take on board there will be many who'll feel let down because I'm not real that, as Luke told us, Cameron Fletcher died some time ago, was never in a position to make his big comeback. But from what I saw in the reaction of audiences, telling his fans that I'm a fake would be like taking people aside at the end *Hamlet* to tell them it wasn't a *real* Prince of Denmark up there. Yes, some will feel duped although I suspect more will feel proud to have been here. To have played a part in the con, shared the scam.'

'And if you doubt me, think that people will react to Callum's revelations with a vow never to make a return trip to see the lido, the promenade, the Big Wheel, then you fail to recognise the Seacrest I've grown to love in the short while I've visited. This is a place that can *easily* survive without Cameron Fletcher. If Luke hadn't turned up with his van something else would have come along. This town has a history of reinventing itself, you don't need to resort to ripping its heart out. Look at us, all of us here are putting on an act and what better stage set than Seacrest? Look at what it did for me, a 'background artiste.' It turned me into a myth. And if you let it, this town can do the same for anyone who visits. Walking these streets is like walking the red carpet, you turn people into stars and they will come here in their droves.'

No applause greeted Arthur this time as the Consortium contemplated whether they had the confidence to follow his hope or Callum's promise to save them from disaster. Kim took the gavel, loose in Callum's hand. She gave one sharp rap that caused Jo to flinch and said, 'Right. If no one else has anything to add? Let's proceed with the vote. All those in favour of Callum Boyd's proposal to renovate the centre of Seacrest, please raise your hands,' and Jo closed her eyes whilst Arthur gripped her hand and squeezed.

CHAPTER THIRTY-SIX

Luke and Harry spoke little as they ate chips in one of the wooden booths on the promenade outside the Fulmar. Instead both contemplated the sea view, attempting to take their minds off the decisions being made in the hotel behind them, from worrying too much about what the outcome might be. When Harry scrunched up his chip wrapping and walked to the bin, checking his watch at 3:45pm, the front of the Fulmar was still quiet, no sign of the meeting having finished. He plunked himself back down next to Luke and sighed.

'He's a good guy, that Arthur. Sound. Will be a shame him leaving when this blows over. Asked him if he'd thought about staying on but he said being here for a fortnight was quite enough at his age.'

'Don't believe him for a second. There's plenty of life left yet in old Arthur Dott,' replied Luke, scraping the last bits of batter from the bottom of his chip bag. 'Told me he was thinking of heading to London after this. Being Cameron Fletcher has given him his confidence back, reckons he'll have a better chance of getting work.' In a manner as casual as the way he then lobbed his balled-up chip wrapper at the wastebin, scoring a direct hit, he said, 'He offered me a place to stay if I wanted to visit. Make a go of it down there. Sounds good.'

Harry had to take a very long gulp of ice cream soda before responding. '*What*!? You? Leave Seacrest? The Archive? I thought you were here for good, that this was your home! You've given your life over to Lot 45, you can't just abandon it, that's like admitting Callum's won!'

'Harry, listen,' Luke was patient with him. 'What Arthur said to me up in the Big Wheel made a lot of sense. Made me realise no matter what happens in there,' he jerked a thumb towards the Fulmar, his eyes determined, 'the Fletcher Archive is strong enough to survive. Maybe not here but somewhere and it will be as strong as ever, whether I'm there to manage it or not. That and it's about time I started taking care of myself instead of living for others. It's time to find out what *I* really want to do. I'm not like you, Harry, I don't really feel at home *anywhere* and I should start to see that as a good thing. The way it frees me up. Seacrest is in your bones and blood. You could no more leave here than a fish could live on land.'

'Why you cheeky *bastard*,' Harry's furious reaction had Luke worrying what he'd intended as a compliment had sounded cruel. 'You sound *exactly* like Shona, saying I'm never going to leave, that I'm stuck here, built into the bricks and mortar.' As he spoke the rage left Harry, leaving him deflated. 'And you know what the really fucking annoying thing is? You're both right.'

Harry took in a deep breath, inhaled the perfume peculiar to his hometown: the candy floss, the salt and vinegar, the popcorn and the diesel fumes from the fairground attractions. A scent he'd lived with all his life, that he would be breathing in on his deathbed. He held it in his lungs before exhaling forcefully. 'I've been thinking for a while it would do you good to get out of this place. Only wish I could take my own advice but hey. This place needs me as much as I need it. Especially if Callum gets his wicked way. Somebody needs to stay and lead the fight, take the Diaboliks into battle. Even if he doesn't win, someone's got to keep an eye out so that Callum doesn't try anything on again.'

'But Luke, you're my mate, OK? My *best* mate and if you

leave I'm going to miss you. Honestly. You and your weird geeky ways. Up you get. Come on, man-hug! Quick, before I come to my senses.' Although Luke had to be practically dragged to his feet by Harry, they were smiling as they embraced, patting each other's backs too hard in a butch display of affection.

They broke apart quickly when Jo's voice called out, 'Aww, a touching homoerotic tableau! Is no one safe from the charms of Harry Lawson?', turning to see her and Arthur approaching, arm and arm, and they cheered at the sight because they knew there could only be one reason why they would both be smiling so ecstatically and Jo screamed out, 'We won! Callum's model is firewood!'

After their group hug, as they walked back along the promenade towards The Moviegoer to celebrate, Jo explained further. 'Was a close run thing, the majority was tiny and if it hadn't been for this man here… ' She patted Arthur's arm, 'I doubt we would have won at all. Callum had them terrified. It took Arthur to remind them they *all* had a responsibility towards Seacrest. That its future didn't belong to one man, be it Cameron or Callum.'

'Oh, all in a day's work', Arthur demurred in a mock pompous tone, giving his fingernails a quick polish on his jacket lapel. 'Though I doubt I should bother waiting for Callum's cheque in the post.'

'Don't you worry about that,' reassured Jo. 'After the show you put on today I'm sure there are plenty of people here who'll see you right.' For some reason she couldn't quite fathom, she thought of Shona. Not worrying about her exactly, but the way she and Callum and Kim had looked as the rest of the Consortium had filed out of the conference room doors. Lonely, the three of them. The talk in the foyer afterwards about a vote of no confidence in Callum, about the search for a new leader…

'*That's* why she did it,' Jo muttered, stopping in her tracks.

'Eh? What's up, love?' asked Arthur, brought to a halt alongside her.

'What? Oh, no, nothing, it's fine.'

They carried on walking, Jo keeping a slower pace than before. *That* was what she'd wanted, why Shona had come back and why she was going to stay. Nothing to do with Jo, she bet, but the prospect of being Festival President. The perfect candidate with her experience of festival organisation plus a sense of continuity, another Boyd to appeal to the more conservative Consortium members. 'Shona Boyd, back with a vengeance,' Jo whispered to herself. 'Seacrest in the palm of her hand.'

This was exactly what Callum had realised as he'd stayed seated between Kim and Shona while the other members left, many hardly able to glance in his direction, those that did wearing a horrible look of pity. When the last of them had gone he pushed back his chair, stood with as much dignity as he was capable of, but as he straightened his tie both women noticed how badly his hands were shaking. Staring straight ahead because if he looked at the model, its lights switched off, the beautiful buildings, their sleek lines obscured by shadow, he knew he might break down.

He was relieved to hear his own voice so strong when he said, 'Well, on their own heads be it. At least I *tried* to save the idiots. They've only themselves to blame.'

'Dad... ' started Shona and he couldn't bear to look at her. Instead he gazed out the window towards the eastern arm of the bay and had a sudden vision of that dreadful bungalow with that witch inside sitting next to the telephone, desperate for her daughter to ring, to start cackling when told of her ex-husband's downfall.

'Dad. I know you won't believe it now but what I did, letting Arthur know, was for the best. I know you love Seacrest but what you were going to do was too big a risk. The town's not brave enough yet, it needs time to get used to success again. That and new blood being brought in. I know if I get the chance I can change things but I'll need your help, your experience -'

Callum gave a short sharp laugh and Kim joined his side, taking his arm, leading him away from his daughter, her green eyes blazing, tears threatening to break. 'I think it best if you stop right there, young lady. You've done quite enough damage, both to your father *and* to this town. You two… unbelievable. It's like *All About Eve* crossed with *The Godfather*. Callum, you and I are going to drown ourselves in martinis and to hell with this place.'

When the two of them reached the door Callum broke free of Kim's grip, finally facing Shona. 'You know, I've always had my doubts about you. Whether you were truly a Boyd or a Lancaster at heart. And now I know the truth.'

The smile he gave her before he disappeared caused her to shiver, to stare at her reflection in the darkening mirror of the window, layered over the bright, glittering lights of Seacrest below as she counted to ten and waited for the urge to pick up a chair and send it crashing out into that view to pass.

Luke raced ahead towards The Moviegoer shouting 'My round!' to the amazement of the others. 'Truly, this is a day that will go down in Seacrest history!' laughed Harry. As they were about to push open the door to the club he remembered there was something he needed to do. Someone he had to see.

'Keep a seat for me,' he told Jo, 'I'll be back in an hour or so.'

'Eh? Where you going?' she asked. 'Didn't you hear him? Luke's going to buy a round, surely that's an event worth waiting for?'

Harry hesitated before admitting, 'My Mum's. I want to tell her the news, about the plans not going through. She's probably heard about it already, mind, knowing what this town is like but…there's other stuff too.'

'Wonders will never cease… we'll have a pint waiting for you,'

Jo promised. 'And, I know this sounds daft but I'm proud of you. What you're doing for your Dad and your Mum and… '

'Yeah, yeah, stop being so soft, Dr Ashe, or I'll change my mind.' After they'd hugged, he set off towards the home he'd left a year ago and not been back to since.

Standing at the front door, swithering to use the key he'd kept or ring the bell, he was shocked to find himself nervous. Him! Harry Lawson! He *never* got nervous! He wished he'd stayed in the bar though, got himself a drink before this… fucksake. Last time he'd left slamming the door so hard the windows shook. Daft idea, he should have phoned instead…

He was on the brink of turning back when it was too late, the door opened, his Mum standing there, shaking her head and smiling, and he knew he needn't have worried at all.

'I've been waiting for you, son. Saw you through the window there, knew I'd be waiting till midnight unless I came and got you. Heard all about what you've been doing, making the recordings and I think it's… well, come inside and I'll tell you exactly what I think. How proud I am.'

It was as if he'd never been away but better, the arguments gone and Dad, Alec, in the room with them, living in Mum's anecdotes, the details, her love for a man who'd left them both because he'd felt he had nothing left to give, who hadn't realised how lucky he was when the Lawson Luck left him.

Harry's seat in The Moviegoer stayed empty all night and the others raised glass after glass to it.

 CHAPTER
THIRTY-SEVEN

Another one of the things she disliked about underground screenings, thought Jo, standing in the queue for a specially convened Secret Cinema, was the cold. It didn't inspire enthusiasm seeing them handing tartan rugs out at the door yet what struck her within minutes of entering this particular event was the warmth she felt. So much so she handed her blanket over to one of the older attendees, a woman who remembered selling tickets to Alec Lawson when 'he was just a wee bairn, no higher than my knee.'

The Tunnel location of the Alec Lawson Memorial Event hadn't required a great deal of effort from the Diaboliks to transform it into a cinema. The members of the Second World War forces couldn't help but be influenced by their location and as a result the staff canteen doubled up as a cinema at night. One with the added benefit of tables where filmgoers could sit with friends and chat and eat and drink while films played in the background. Jo had thought it was a terrible idea when she'd first heard about it but then she could hear a noisy eater of popcorn from ten rows away. Tonight though… tonight it worked perfectly.

Candles flickered at the centre of red table lamps borrowed from The Moviegoer, the light intimate, while stereo speakers discreetly dotted about the room played the reminiscences of many of the guests. Their voices mingled with the recordings Harry had made, the sound of laughter rising as someone recognised a voice playing as their own.

The bar at the back was busy as people took full advantage of the free drinks along with the opportunity to catch up with people they hadn't spoken to properly in years, remarking how happy they were Callum's plans had been rejected before getting down to the important business of reminiscing about the old days. About what a good man Alec Lawson had been and how proud he would be of his son. During pauses they could watch film clips showing on the white tiled walls, Harry having spliced together a number of his Dad's favourite films, finding echoes and resonances in *Miller's Crossing*, *The Searchers*, *White Heat*, *The Wizard of Oz*, *Night of the Hunter* and, of course, *The Third Man*.

Jo walked back from the bar with a gin and tonic as Harry Lime caught her eye, smiling that half smile of his, so wistful and wicked and seductive, reminding her of someone. Who? Not Harry, he was too open in some ways, too honest. Arthur, Luke and Kim were waving her over but her attention was taken by Shona in animated discussion with a small group of Diaboliks. Shona saw her, broke off, smiling that half smile at her, those lilac blue eyes… Ah. Right. That'd be it. If Harry Lime had made it out of those sewers what would his granddaughter have looked like…

Shona was walking towards her and Jo would have *loved* to brush past her, to join the others, find out more about what Arthur's plans were for London, what Luke was going to do with the Archive, if Kim knew if Callum had a Plan B but… wait, the cheeky cow! She was wearing Jo's Dunlops! And looked different. Dressed down in jeans and a jumper, not like some unapproachable screen goddess. More like *Jo's* Shona. Comfortable in herself now she'd got what she came for.

'They're mine you know,' Jo challenged. 'The trainers. I want them back before I leave.'

Lovely to see you too, dear,' and she allowed Shona to kiss her on the cheek, enjoying the mild swooning sensation that followed being surrounded by her perfume. Might as well enjoy it while she was there.

'Cosying up to the enemy are we?' Jo asked, nodding towards the Diaboliks, who were obviously awestruck by being consulted by Shona Boyd, new creative director of the Seacrest Festival, on possible programme ideas. 'Your Dad would have a stroke if he saw you.'

'Dad's not in any position to decide who I can and can't talk to about Festival matters.' Shona's near gleeful tone meant Jo didn't know who to feel sorrier for: Callum or Shona or Seacrest. 'You're not still annoyed with me, are you?' Shona chided. 'Things have worked out for the best, even a doomsayer like you has to admit to that. The Archive's safe, Arthur's safe, I'll be able to shake up the Festival, nothing too drastic, bring in some new people. I know you don't approve of how I went about it, dragging Arthur into it and yes, it could have backfired but it didn't and – hold on, what… the trainers. What do you mean 'before I leave'?' Shona's smile disappeared, replaced by a look of such pure concern Jo's heart lurched. No, come on, she had to be strong, carry on nodding in a 'My mind's made up and nothing you can say or do will change it' sort of way.

'You're *leaving*. But Jo, you've become *part* of Seacrest, I *need* you here.' Those blue eyes fixed on Jo who hoped the gin would keep her resolve strong.

'Shona, you don't *need* anyone. You've made that clear over the past few weeks.' Ouch. That had come out stronger than she'd meant it to, Shona glancing away. 'No, sorry, listen… just hearing Luke's plans for a break from here, it's made me think. If *he* can do it… and anyway, you're the one who's been telling me for years that I need to get out and do some exploring. For my own good and for the good of my work. Staying here it's too easy to forget there's a whole other world out there. And one of the reasons I've lasted so long here is knowing you were out there, living a life big enough for two of us. Daft, I know, but now you're back... well. It's my turn.'

'To leave.' The brittle laugh Shona gave did little to conceal the hurt she felt.

'Yes. For both our sakes. If I stay here things will just stumble on in the way they have done for the past few weeks. What we've had between us, whatever it is, has survived this long only because we've spent most of the time on opposite sides of the globe. Stick us together for too long and we'd end up hating each other.'

'But the things we could do! I'll give you a film season, your choice, complete carte blanche.' Jo was shaking her head, wearing that rare determined look that Shona knew from experience was impossible to argue with.

'No... thanks but, no. I'm going back to Manchester, clear my head and then... who knows? New York maybe? Find out more about Avi Fleischer, the real history of Cameron Fletcher? Or maybe something completely different. Instead of writing about films, have a shot at making one. No idea to be honest but I'm determined to have some fun finding out.'

'Well... ' Shona shrugged, admitting defeat. 'You be sure and keep in touch, OK? Send me a postcard.' Before Jo could stop her, she leant in and kissed her. A kiss so fine, so tender and loving Jo's head burst with a succession of quick-fire love scenes, Bogart and Bacall, Grace Kelly and Jimmy Stewart, Hepburn and Tracy, Scarlett and Rhett. Until the magic was broken by Shona whispering, 'By the way, the Dunlops are *mine*. A leaving gift.'

'Need any rescuing, Dr Ashe? Or are you busy researching famous Seacrest ladies of the night?' It was almost a relief to Jo hearing Kim's voice, crackling with tobacco and sarcasm. Arthur on one side of her and Luke on the other, all three looking like the sort of odd, dysfunctional family Charles Addams would have been pleased to dream up.

Ignoring Kim's dig, Shona began, 'Good to see you Kim, was going to call, ask if you had some time free next week to meet up to discuss… ' Kim swivelled slowly to face her, bestowing a look that would have had Medusa quaking.

'Let's leave it a month, shall we, before we start being civil to one another. I know only too well your father is no saint but, God help me, I have a lot of respect for what he was trying to do. He genuinely thought he was doing it for the best, out of love for the place, rather than for his own benefit. So when I'm ready to talk *I'll* call *you.* Agreed?'

The others scarcely dared to breathe as they awaited Shona's reaction, a possible display of the Boyd temper threatened by the flush of red appearing on those sharpened cheekbones. But the colour faded and Shona's humble nod of acceptance appeared very nearly genuine. Will wonders never cease? marvelled Jo, breathing out slowly.

'Well, I think we can all agree Seacrest is in for a very interesting time of it,' laughed Arthur, releasing the tension, and with a pang Jo realised just how weird it was going to be without him around. It had been fantastic what happened, all that fretting about the exposure ruining him, making the front pages of the *Gazette* and a few of the nationals, offering to step down from the remaining Fletcher events and there had been an outcry! Couldn't believe it, there in his hotel room, sorting through the Fleischer material, when a delegation of Consortium members turned up asking him to stay. Kim giving that fantastic speech, 'I don't care who you say you are, when I first set eyes on Cameron Fletcher I knew you were someone special, that you have something we don't see often enough these days. Arthur Dott, you have *star quality* and if the Festival ends without you, Seacrest will forever regret it.'

How could Arthur refuse? Especially as Kim offered to

accompany him to most of the events and Jo speculated if there was something going on there she should know about. Maybe wait until Kim had a few more vodka and tonics to find out. Plus he had been inundated with acting offers. Couldn't happen to a more deserving chap.

'You've all got to promise,' Arthur said, tipping his whisky glass at each of them in turn, 'that you'll come to see me off tomorrow morning. Afraid it won't be *quite* as fancy an event as my arrival. No Seacrest Special for an old charlatan, it'll be a coach trip home for me.'

'Of *course* we'll be there to see you off,' Jo assured him, chinking her glass against his. 'All of us,' and she looked towards Shona who nodded and said, 'Place won't be the same without you, Arthur. Which is why I'll be booking you in as a keynote speaker for next year. If we can meet your extortionate fee by then.'

'Oh, I'll be back here soon enough, don't you worry about that. Kim here has offered to put me up – or should that be put up with me – for Christmas and New Year. And I know, because he's promised me, that once I get myself established in the Big Smoke Luke's going to visit. The offer of free bed and board goes for all of you. Will be most disappointed if you don't all come down and see me. Is that understood?' He was greeted with a chorus of 'Yes!'

Shona went off to catch up with some useful contacts and as Kim and Arthur entertained each other with showbiz anecdotes, Jo edged towards Luke. 'So are the rumours true? You're leaving the Archive? I mean, that's great, it's time you did something different but the Archive without you... It's a big change. Could take some getting used to.'

'A change is exactly what I need,' Luke replied happily and Jo noticed how un-Luke-like he appeared. Less of a pale wraith and more like a young man who believed in himself. He'd filled out a bit too, courtesy of the Dott effect, those long liquid lunches he'd insisted on taking each of them out on.

'I've been hiding behind the Archive for far too long, Jo. Talking to Arthur's made me realise that. Haven't much of a clue what I'm going to do next but that's good. Exciting. From all the offers of help I've had over the past few days I know the Archive's going to be well looked after. Didn't realise how much of a burden it had become until that responsibility was lifted. I can let go of it and that's for the best. It was *made* to be shared. That was the whole point of it.'

How relaxed he looked. Free and Jo knew exactly how he felt. Time to step away from the comfortable dark, out into the sunlight.

'Oi, you two, stop your gabbing about film theory or whatever and say hello to my Mum.' There was Harry, arm around his tiny Mum's shoulders, her looking as proud as it was possible for any Mum to look. This, out of everything that had happened, was the best thing to come out of the Festival, thought Jo. Harry and his Mum back on speaking terms. Not that he'd be moving back in any time soon, doubt either of them could stand that for too long, but at least he'd promised to move to somewhere more comfortable than the Kinotech. And his Mum didn't need to start nagging at him to get a nice girlfriend as that had been taken care of. Jenny came over with their drinks, giving Harry a kiss as she handed over his Guinness, Jo and Luke nudging each other like school kids.

'How are you finding all this, Mrs Lawson?' asked Jo. 'Is it not overwhelming hearing what everyone has to say about Alec? His favourite films playing?'

'I suppose it is a wee bit, dear, but after all these years of no one mentioning him at all, the whispers... ' she faltered and Harry squeezed her close. 'Sorry, silly of me, but yes, I think it's *fantastic*. Alec would have kicked up a fuss about it, made a show of being embarrassed, but secretly he'd have loved it, that people recognised what he was doing, the skill he had. He loved his job, you know?

You don't find that so much these days but when it was taken away from him he didn't know what to do with himself. Didn't feel life was worth living… ' She looked away, over to the films showing, Dorothy pulling aside the curtain to show the old man behind the wizardry.

'You know, I think he wanted to *live* in those films. That was his problem. Real life wasn't enough for him, he needed a daily escape from it. A place where you can forget yourself a while. We all need that, don't we?' The small group around her nodded, each of them recognising how true that was.

'Right,' said Harry, breaking the moment. 'On you go and sit yourselves down. Time for the special showing. Mum, you go off with Jenny, she'll see you right. You two', he pointed at Luke and Jo, 'down the front, I've reserved a couple of seats.'

'Is the film actually going to run?' asked Jo. 'I mean, they were down there an awfully long time and there was the heat from the fire, maybe damp… '

'For God's sake!' Harry replied, exasperated. 'Whatever you've had to drink tonight, it isn't enough. Luke, get this woman a whisky and slip a couple Valium in. No, Jo, to be perfectly honest, I haven't a clue if this is going to work. I've had a quick look and it does look pretty corroded but we'll just have to pray to the gods of cinema, won't we? If it all goes tits up I've got a few films in reserve. But considering what my Dad went through to guard those canisters, I reckon it's the least we can do to find out what he was protecting. To be honest, if they *do* go up in flames it'll be good riddance. Now. On you go and sit down.'

He stood and watched as Jo and Luke headed off meekly to a front table, Shona slipping into the seat next to Jo, offering her hand for Luke to shake who blushed as he took it.

'Watch yourself, my boy,' laughed Harry, moving towards the projector at the back of the canteen that pointed towards a temporary screen. He signalled for a Diabolik to dim the lights, and the canteen became a darkened auditorium.

At the projector, the film already loaded, he took a few seconds to wipe the machinery down with a shammy cloth. Making its black surfaces gleam, treating it with the love and respect it deserved. As he did so he could feel his gestures weren't his own. That they had been passed down to him, were bred in the blood and the bone. 'For a while you were the luckiest man alive, Dad,' he whispered, 'you were just too caught up in films to see it.' He flicked a switch and as the machinery cranked up and started to whirr it filled a deep hush as the countdown ticked down on the screen.

In the years that followed football stadiums could be filled by the number of people who claimed to have been in the Seacrest Tunnels that night and watched that much debated film. Even between audience members who'd had the good fortune to be present there would always be arguments about what had been shown.

Some say they caught a glimpse of a Don Quixote-like figure on a horse, tilting at a windmill, others a magician about to reveal the contents of his magic cabinet. Some, like Shona, say they saw nothing, a burning white filling the screen before the film fell apart, disintegrated, leaving only the dust caught in the projector beam. Harry didn't tell anyone, not even Jenny, what he really thought he saw, the silhouette of a man floating down underwater, while Jo was sure she saw a young girl standing in front of a mirror, lifting up a hand, pressing it against the surface until her fingers disappeared into the world beyond.

Only Arthur and Luke know what was shown on that screen. They knew they were witnessing the truth when they looked over at each other in shock during the charged silence that followed; a close-up of the demonic silver head topping Cameron Fletcher's cane being tipped against the rim of a black top hat, the face beneath the brim not visible. But neither could be sure whether what they witnessed was a greeting or goodbye.

It seemed a suitable time to leave them, sitting there in the dark, the white still bright in their retinas, blinking away their temporary blindness. We rose up from underground, passed through streets still busy with Festival visitors who wanted to linger, who had no desire to return to their ordinary, work-filled lives the following Monday. We lifted higher, flew as the seagull flies, not in a straight line, the very opposite, full of sudden elevations and swooping dips, and we turned to Seacrest stretching its arms out to us, wanting to hold us and never let us go. How tempting it would have been to give into the place, the studios, the lido, the pier and the Big Wheel, the bright, garish neon lights of the cinema and club signs that caused patches of colour to appear both against the clouds of a dark night sky and as shimmerings on the dark sea below us.

And because we had taken a trip to Seacrest, had stayed there long enough for it to enter our bloodstream, it came as no surprise we imagined two large red curtains sweeping in from either side of the bay, shutting off our view, hiding that impossible town whilst elegant gold letters shone in front of them, spelling out

Also by Kirsti Wishart
from Rymour Books

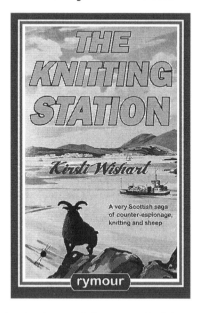

'*The Knitting Station* is one of those wonderful wee books that you might begin with a bit of wariness but ultimately end up loving.' SCOT LIT DAILY

'Delicious escapism and clever storytelling; ideal accompaniment for a dram by a winter fire. Just lay off the mushrooms and let the plot handle the hallucinations.' NORTHWORDS

'Just finished *The Knitting Station*. Brilliant Scottish island story set in the 60s with hunners of layers to it. Well worth a read.' JOHN GERARD FAGAN

'My books of the year... *The Knitting Station*... Sheepy shenanigans on a Scottish island. Wonderful debut.' DREW GUMMERSON

'If you're looking for something totally different, I recommend *The Knitting Station*. Wonderfully wacky and Scottish.' ELISSA SOAVE

RYMOUR BOOKS

poetry · history · debate